ADRIANA KOULIAS was born in Brazil and migrated to Australia with her family when she was nine years old. She studies Philosophy, History and Esoteric Science and lectures on these topics internationally.

TEMPLE
OF THE
GRAIL

ADRIANA
KOULIAS

ZURIEL PRESS

This edition published 2013 by Zuriel Press Pty Ltd
First published 2004 in Picador by Pan Macmillan Australia Pty Ltd
Copyright © Adriana Koulias 2004
National Library of Australia
Cataloguing-in-Publication data:
Koulias, Adriana. Temple of the Grail
ISBN 978-0-9874620-6-0

The Abbey

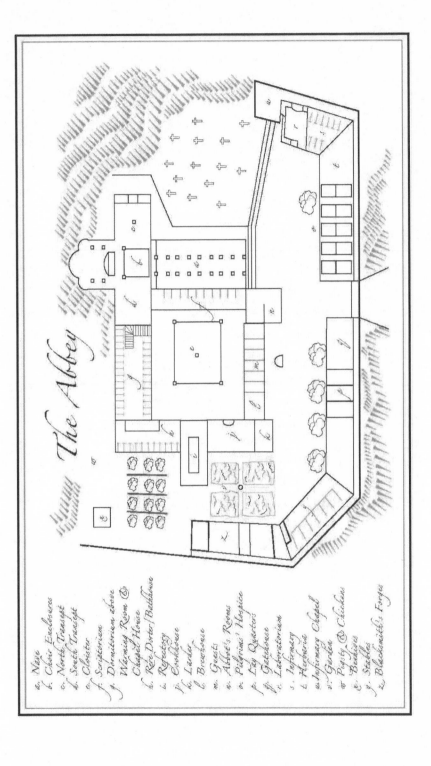

a. Nave
b. Choir Enclosures
c. North Transept
d. South Transept
e. Cloister
f. Scriptorium
g. Dormitorium above
   Warming Room &
   Chapel House
h. Rez Dorte/Bathhouse
i. Refectory
j. Cowhouse
k. Larder
l. Brewhouse
m. Guests
n. Abbot's Rooms
o. Pilgrims' Hospice
p. Lay Quarters
q. Gatehouse
r. Laboratorium
s. Infirmary
t. Herbaria
u. Infirmary Chapel
v. Garden
w. Pigsty & Chickens
x. Beehives
y. Stables
z. Blacksmith's Forges

Canonical Hours

Matins: *between midnight and 2 a.m.*

Lauds: *after matins at sunrise*

Prime: *6 a.m.*

Terce: *9 a.m.*

Sext: *noon*

Nones: *3 p.m.*

Vespers: *before the evening meal*

Compline: *at sunset*

Prologue

Jean de Joinville closed the manuscript. Outside the sky fell over the grounds of the palace in a torrent and the wind made the torches flicker, threatening to deliver him into darkness. An attendant entered the apartment and prepared to set down a tray of scented tea and honeyed cakes. Joinville shook his head and waved the servant away, searching for the cross beneath his garments.

He was afraid. He had not been afraid in a long time.

It took him some moments to lower himself to the floor. The stone was cold and his knees old and thin of skin. He knelt to pray for his soul and for God's guidance in the matter of the manuscript. For what must he do with it? How must he hide it and its secret from the Pope and King Philip, whose hospitality he enjoyed?

At the hour of Matins he called for a trusted servant and made arrangements for him to travel to Spain, telling him only where he must take the item wrapped in linen and nothing more regarding it.

He made his way to his pallet then and, overcome with fatigue, called for his confessor.

The Manuscript

ternal, unchangeable and infinite God, whose goodness knows no bounds and no limits, eternal virtue and perfection, embracing all qualities, from whom all things spring and without whom there is nothing, who art good without bounds, great without limit, eternal without time, omnipresent without space, grant this poor sinner, in thy infinite goodness, the soundness to impart a clear and concise account of this sacred and most holy wisdom which thou hast favoured to leave in my care.

Now in exile, this servant living on the threshold of death longs for the eternal and blissful rest that has been promised; to be lost in the silence of nothingness in which the spirit seeks the womb of the universe; where there is no time and space, or anything else, save the quiet perpetual union with the all-embracing divine light, in whose shadow the devout soul stands. But for now, I sit in silence, in contemplation of my eternal ascent towards that naught of naughts. My back torments me, my hands ache, and as I prepare to write on a parchment that is hairy, I tremble as though I were drenched with water, for I am never warm these days. Perhaps Brother Setubar had been right those many years ago at the monastery, that is, fear manifests itself as a paleness, a chill? As I prepare to recall the events of those times I feel my body weakened by the demons of deception that compel me to a dumb silence . . . and yet, obedience begs that I must tell this tale . . . even as mountains coil and fold in a world that has grown old and hardened in spirit, as you have perhaps already seen; even as humility becomes unknown, and man hides his face from the truth because, once it is revealed, its faithful signals cannot be denied.

Only a few days have passed since I received word of my old master's death, and since that moment I have been filled with a consummate grief. There were so many things left unspoken between us, for the nature of our parting was confused and hasty. Perhaps I should have told him that I loved him with a spiritual sweetness, that I admired him deeply? But words drift from this sinner's lips as an autumn breeze passes silently over a wheatfield, for what does the wheat care if the breeze is filled with sadness?

Now, as his form turns to dust, can his eyes see the rosy dawn, or the pale snowflake as it falls? What would be the point of saying that I still see him so clearly? Should I tell you, dear reader, that I remember his countenance as broad and frank, accentuated by an aquiline nose whose character was perhaps a little Roman? And that above his eyes – the colour of the north sea – hovered the thickest of brows that, in moments of concentration, became a mirror to his thinking? It may not interest you to know that I loved him, not because I thought him the wisest or perhaps the bravest man – though I now see that indeed he came closer to these attributes than anyone I have since known – but because he had a good sense of humour and an air of adventure about him, a liberal nature that was much the opposite of mine. Consequently, I confess to having many times mistaken his imperfections for virtues, and his virtues for so many imperfections. Now that I am older and wiser, I know that a good man has a measure of each.

All I have left of him is a letter sealed with his seal, a testament that will accompany this chronicle to its owner when I too have left this mortal carcass behind me.

Finally, I look out from my cell to the endless blue waters of Famagusta knowing that I will soon be reunited with the moon, and the sun, and the stars . . . and there, shimmering with the brightest of lights, will be my dearest friend and mentor, casting his ray of goodness over the path that I must tread to divinity, in the same way that he shone the light of knowledge over a young mind those many years ago.

And so if every instant of time is like a pinprick of eternity, as Marcus Aurelius tells us, let us then make haste . . . slowly.

In the year of our Lord 1254, the year that Frederick II, the excommunicate emperor died, ending 116 years of Hohenstaufen rule, I was a youth of no more than sixteen springs – though at the time I would have said that I was already a man. It was also the year in which my master's dearest friend, Jean de Joinville, was released from his incarceration in an infidel prison at the side of King Louis, and the year in which my life became inexorably changed by the events that will become, in the course of this tale, apparent.

I was six years old when I was placed in the care of a Templar knight of good repute (whose name I will only reveal as Andre), after the untimely death of my father during the battle of La Forbie. In the context of this manuscript, my master was nigh forty years of age, of robust body and strong complexion, an early riser, though he slept very little, and a lover of all things pertaining to nature.

He was a 'poulain', that is to say, he was a colonist and therefore born of mixed blood. He rarely spoke about his family, but youthful ears being what they are, I learnt much by overhearing a little here and a little there. I came to know that his father had fought beside Richard Coeur de Lion in the third Crusade, and that his mother had been the daughter of a Christian from Alexandria. This made comprehensible the darkness of his skin, his singular ways and his peculiar vital spirit. A spirit that in my opinion seemed always a little impious. However, the infidel in his blood made him an excellent physician, as we are told Alexandrians are exceedingly astute in the medicinal arts. From him, I not only learnt which herbs were best for treating wounds, and how to mend a broken limb, but also, and perhaps more importantly, to cherish knowledge, always remembering that a man is only truly honourable when he honours another. He also taught me the practicalities of holding a sword, and how to saddle a horse, and the best way to ride in battle, for he was accomplished in all knightly duties, though I suspect he did not wish that I should ever have use for such things.

It was thus, travelling in my master's train under the banner of the Red Cross, that I came to know the wonders of the Islamic world even if, at the same time, I was witness to the endless cruelty and brutality of battle.

My master encouraged me to read, for he was a fine scholar, having spent some time in Paris and in the esteemed school of Salerno before taking his vows. It was his belief that I should learn of other things besides war and so, with his guidance, I became adequate in Greek, and was therefore able to absorb the ideas of the Greek philosophers from folios he found in his travels. These revealed a world of thought previously unknown to me. But I am prideful, as my master often told me, for I linger too long on insignificant details, when instead I should tell how, not yet of fighting age, I was to become my master's squire, as was the custom in those days, not only in charge of his horses and armour but also his scribe and confidant, taking an oath of loyalty that I, to this day, solemnly uphold.

As fate would have it, we remained only a few short years in Outremer because, during the battle of Mansourah under the orders of William of Sonnac, Grand Master of the Temple, my master Andre was to become grievously wounded. His body never fully recovered and the battle seemed to plague him. I believed him to have been torn by loyalties. Perhaps his faith was not where it should have been? In any event, after a long convalescence we left the holy land for a Templar house in France, in the fateful area of Languedoc where my master would take up his position as preceptor. I must pause here for one moment to acquaint you with this area's peculiarities and the turbulent, political miasma in which we found ourselves.

Languedoc is a province in the south of France, separated from Aragon by a rugged and mostly impenetrable chain of mountains known as the Pyrenees. In those dark days it was a very rich province, held in cohesion by a succession of counts allied with the king of Aragon. It was a province of harsh contrasts of climate and of temper, and it enjoyed a close proximity to the East, to which it was tied by the umbilical cord of the Templar Order. Many have attributed the infiltration of unorthodox doctrine into this area to this peculiarity, however, for our purposes, suffice it to say that with the passing of years it became home to a number of heresies, the most infamous sects being those of Cathar and Waldensian origin.

For many years these sects flowered, relying on the liberal attitude of the secular ecclesiastics, the noble classes, and the Count of Toulouse. That is, until that horrible day when thousands of northern knights led by Simon de Montfort with the sanctity of the pope and king, descended like locusts on Languedoc, in a war of persecution that lasted more than forty years. Cities and towns were razed and brought to the sword. Women, children, and the elderly were killed indiscriminately. At Beziers alone twenty thousand were slaughtered while seeking sanctuary in the churches, as they knelt praying at the altars. My master condemned the Crusade against the Cathars, saying that it was nothing more than a political exercise, whose aim was the annexation of the region into the hands of the French king. Young man that I was, I did not fully understand the extent of this terrible crime, believing in the integrity of the mother church and its intentions with the full-hearted religious zeal of one who holds an uncompromising view of the world, though I had lived little in it.

The heretics argued; Christ had no place to rest his head, while the pope had a palace, Christ was property-less and penniless, the Christian prelates were rich and powerful, living off the fattened calf while others starved. In truth the church had been in a state of appalling corruption, and it was easy to see why it enjoyed no high esteem. Stories were told of churches in which no mass had been said for many years because priests busied themselves running their large estates. It was even rumoured that the Archbishop of Narbonne never once visited his diocese! These worldly priests and fat bishops were seen as the Pharisees reborn, the Holy Church was the whore of Babylon; the clergy the synagogue of Satan, the pope the antichrist. With no religious guidance and with hunger in their bellies the people took matters into their own hands, preaching without licence, giving the sacraments without having first been ordained into the priesthood. It was impossible to stem the tide of reform; Languedoc was like a tree with poisoned fruit. Even our blessed St Bernard, on his visit to the area half a century before, had been more appalled by the corruption of the clergy than by the heretics themselves. Later a young Dominic Guzman managed to convert some, though for every conversion, there were many more who fell by the wayside. Count Raymond of Toulouse, who had at first condoned the heresy, opposed the Crusade, but recanted when faced with overwhelming papal pressure, and led his own army of knights to slaughter those whom he had previously supported. Many noble families that had been his benefactors, some of them Cathar believers, were forced to take refuge in various Templar preceptories or face their fate on the pyre. In the end, however, the count had been deceived, for his lands and titles were passed to Alphonse, the brother of Louis IV, and therefore became the property of the French king. This Crusade not only destroyed the cohesion of the heretical groups, sending those who remained loyal to their beliefs underground, but also meant the ruination of a once-lucrative area of rich commerce.

This was the situation, then, when we arrived in Languedoc, almost ten years after the stronghold of Catharism, Montsegur, was taken. At a time when the ravaged province attempted to rebuild itself anew. So, dear reader, one cannot judge my master too harshly if he seemed less than pleased at the prospect of his forthcoming designation. But as I look back – with the clearer sight of one detached from the impatience of youth – I know it was a fortuitous one, for not only did his injuries make it impossible for him to serve his order with the required physical strength, but had we not been sent to Languedoc I would not now have occasion to narrate this remarkable story.

My master's appointment seemed to fill him with a terrible dissatisfaction. I suspect that he missed the hot country of his birth and the doctoring that he loved so well, and so he was seized (so it seemed to me) by a restless demon, filled with a desire for new experiences from which he would draw some vague comfort. At times I did not understand him, at least I did not try to. I followed him obediently though he seemed to be a man tormented by many ideas in need of resolution.

A year after our arrival in France he was called to Paris for an audience with the king who had, only months before, returned from the holy land. Present at this meeting my master was surprised to find Reginald Vichiers, Grand Master of the Temple, and the Paris Preceptor and his treasurer. What grave and serious Templar business had wrenched the grand master from his duties in Outremer? Grave matters indeed, for he had left the commander of the order, Guy of Basainville in his stead, to face an attack on our strongholds by the Mamluks.

After the customary formalities, we were informed that our preceptory held the titles to a tract of land in the mountains south of Carcassonne, the perpetual use of which had been granted to the Cistercian order by Gerard of Ridefort in 1186.

The grand master told us that a monastery had since been erected on this site and that it housed monks from the Cistercian rule. The abbot of Citeaux expressed concerns that the abbey had not been brought to his attention, and that for many years it had existed *incognitus* without the spiritual guidance of a mother house – without its abbot ever having attended a meeting of the general chapter! No matter how important these concerns may have been, they did not justify the presence of the grand master and the preceptor at the meeting. No, there were graver matters to be addressed, as we shall see.

There was to be a papal review of all the monasteries in the area of Languedoc. The monastery of St Lazarus had been singled out because it had conducted healings to which no physical cure could be ascribed. The significant aspect of this inquiry, the king informed us, was that it would be headed by one Rainiero Sacconi da Piacenza; a man who I later learnt was an Italian inquisitor of some renown. It became clearer now that both our order and the order of Cistercians were greatly concerned lest anything be found in the abbey's conduct which could be used by the Dominican inquisitor for his own purposes, namely, the advancement of his career. The king, on the other hand, was concerned that the inquiry provided the pontiff with an excuse to recoup monies directly from any monastery found guilty of heresy, in lieu of papal taxes, which Louis had promised, but had not delivered. He told us two pious orders would suffer the pope's wrath with the Dominicans of Italy being the victors and the Italian Bishop of Toulouse – a Benedictine with formidable family connections in Rome – taking possession of all the abbey's holdings with the *ratum facio* of the pope.

We were informed that a legation was soon to leave Paris and that our mission was to accompany it. My master was to oversee the inquiry in a medical capacity and to ensure its equitable resolution. To this end we were given a letter with the king's seal, and several archers were placed at our disposal, so that we might return with prisoners, if necessary.

The nature of our assignment, indeed our duty, became less clear to us, however, when the king drew my master aside and requested that we report to him before all others, even before our grand master, on our return from the monastery. Of course my master did not agree to this, for it would have been against the rule of our order. In his wisdom, however, he gave the impression that he would do as he was asked. Later, again, as we were leaving the palace, we were intercepted by the grand master, who appeared to be exceedingly anxious. He told us that it was most important that we not return to Paris at the conclusion of the hearings, but that we should await his orders . . .

What more can be said?

And so, I must confess that even this day I feel a flush of shame rise to my cheeks as I recall how I was taken by the Devil of curiosity. And as I sit here in my imposed exile, this shame is mingled also with another sentiment, that of longing. Longing for youth, excitement, and the smell of the mountains, and yes, a longing even for those feelings of uneasiness and foreboding.

So let us continue, patient reader, and digress no longer, for I must lend my unworthy faculties to angelic beings whose heavenly light illuminates the eons, and elucidates the dark annals of history. History is a temptress whose deception is food for the blind and comfort to the mercenary:

The story begins . . .

1

Capitulum

*'A scorner seeketh wisdom and findeth it not; but knowledge
is easy unto him that understandeth.'*
PROVERBS XIV 6

The journey from Paris to Languedoc was uneventful.
The roads, built largely by the Romans, were well
maintained because they were used by those merchants headed for the Provençal ports, and by the
pilgrims making their way to Santiago de Compostela in Spain.

Our party did not proceed directly, at times we diverged
eastwards and once or twice it was possible to catch a glimpse of
the sea. We reached Languedoc three weeks after our departure
from Paris, and it was not a cheering sight that greeted us. It was
a scarred and disfigured country and we travelled with watchful
eye, wary of our own shadows, for even after so many years, the
sword and the boot of the northern crusaders was evident.

Those not accustomed to these parts commented on
the black remnants of burned farms, broken fences, crumbling
bridges and deserted vineyards. They pointed at the weeds and
thistles that overtook churches and everything of value. What
people could be seen – miserable creatures, lean and scratching,
wild as forest animals – would scatter on our approach, for our

archers bore the flag of the inquisition. In their eyes I glimpsed the familiar terror, the sullen hopelessness, and dangerous desperation. They were truly men beyond hope, beyond heaven, and I prayed for their souls.

We travelled in a solemn, moody, silence, until we reached higher country, where there were fewer reminders of the devastation, and as we toiled through the landscape of steep gorges and narrow valleys, the retinue seemed to relax and my master began to ride a little ahead of me. His mount was a gallant Arabian horse Gilgamesh – named after the great Babylonian king. I travelled upon a mule whose name was Brutus because, as Plato tells us, names should show the nature of things as far as they can be shown – if they are to be real names.

Ahead, the prelates of the Papal Commission journeyed by carriage. I do not know which of us was more comfortable, for the awkward vehicle bounced on the stony road, throwing about its occupants. As we passed I dared to peer into its interior. Surrounded by cushions of satin and velvet sat firstly the inquisitor, hiding always behind his black cowl, suffering his discomfort in silence. Opposite him sat the Franciscan, with his head lolling from side to side and his thin lips emitting resonant snores. Bernard Fontaine, the Cistercian, sat next to him. As straight as the towers of Lebanon, his long face funereal, his unblinking eyes wide and staring, he seemed perfectly content in his misery. Only the Bishop of Toulouse, whose size made it exceedingly uncomfortable, attempted to relieve his distress by accompanying us upon his mule. I must confess to not being fond of him, for he was a man of volatile temper and boring conversation whose disposition was entirely dependent on the quantity of wine he consumed. Therefore, I cannot say that I was perturbed (God forgive me) when Brutus searched out the rump of his mule each time he neared us, going as far as giving it chase and consequently occasioning the bishop to topple off his saddle. I need not tell what commotion ensued, nor what terrible tempest of

articulation was unleashed on all and sundry, whose only consolation was that it was followed (alas!) by the bishop's return to the
carriage, once and for all.

The hours passed slowly. Indeed I longed for the company of my friend the venerable Eisik, whom the bishop had
authorised to accompany us by a special dispensation, now following behind the company because he was a Jew.

Observing him sitting atop his animal, stooping slightly
as was his custom, his long grey beard and thinning hair blowing
in the wind, one would have thought him of venerable age, but
if one looked closer, one saw a much younger man in his brown,
angled face, though it was indeed a face moulded by hardships
endured, and years of persecution. I waved to him, but he did
not see me, for between us numerous servants, notaries, scribes,
and archers made up the entourage. They tagged along, talking
among themselves in their vulgar tongues, laughing and jesting,
making sure to keep well away from the Jew, united in their hatred.

This particular day had dawned crisp and clear after a
bitterly cold night spent in a little priory at the foot of the mountains. The previous evening, after a sparse meal, the prior had
told us the monastery of St Lazarus was troublesome to find.
The road leading to it, he said in his dull slur, veered sharply
through a tangled forest, and was impenetrable in the depths of
winter due to the heavy falls of snow and subsequent avalanches. Similarly, in summer, the abundant rainfall, caused the access
to become perilous; mud slides and other horrors were regular
occurrences.

'Who knows,' whispered the drunken prior, 'what heresies abound in the womb of secrecy? One dare not contemplate
what abominations lurk behind its heinous walls.' He directed a
malevolent smile at me, pregnant with meaning, 'Heresy!'

I slept little that night.

Early the following morning the inquisitor had made an

announcement to the townspeople, seeking those with any information about the monastery and its practices to come forth on the date set for the inquiry. And so it was then, after all the arrangements had been made, that we set off for our long journey over the steep roads to the abbey.

We followed a lonely track, observing how ash, chestnut and beech trees were succeeded by oaks. Soon the strong scent of pines announced that we were approaching our destination. Above us, snow-covered peaks were lost in cloud, and not long before the sun had reached its highest point, a mist gathered around us, blocking out the thrilling blue of sky. Here and there patches of snow grew into a thick groundcover and presently we came to a junction dividing the road into four smaller roads that led in various directions.

The cavalcade came to a halt, with my master and others alighting from their horses for a better look around. Above and beyond, a milky haze obstructed our view. Of the four roads the middle road seemed the straightest, but what we could see looked thick with undergrowth covered by a deep layer of snow. To the right, another coursed its way perilously down the slope and disappeared below us. The left road was very steep and rocky. The last was no more than a track and headed directly up the incline.

There was terrible confusion among the various navigators (for there are always so many). The captain of the archers, a wise and usually sensible man, advised that we should take the lower road. The bishop, however, alighted from his carriage and demanded, since he was an Italian and therefore more versed in the ways of mountains, that we should under no circumstance travel any other save the higher road. Others joined in and soon one man raised his voice against the other until there ensued an intense disagreement, with each voicing his opinion in a heated and discourteous manner.

The mountain is a changeable beast and without warning generated a wind that parted the mist and played with the ecclesiastical vestments of the retinue. Nervous and suspicious, the archers looked about them, having been taught to notice and react to the slightest thing, but the churchmen and the captain of the guard continued in argument, raising their voices higher and higher so as to be heard over the rustling of the trees. That was when, of a sudden, a gust swept our little party, taking the bishop's skull cap from his head and sending it rolling forward into the middle road like a little wheel. Clutching at his exposed, tonsured head, the large man turned in dismay and took to running after the small black article, stumbling over the rocky ground, almost grasping the cap before another gust set it in motion.

From the corner of my eye I saw my master mount his Arabian. 'It seems the bishop has taken matters into his own hand', he said, signalling his animal forward in pursuit. Needless to say, in a general state of bewilderment, the retinue was forced to follow. Moments later the narrow path miraculously widened to a safe and level road, seemingly well kept despite a snow cover that, as it happened, turned out to be shallow.

'A most astute choice,' my master congratulated the bishop in his carriage.

The bishop's round face peeped through the aperture and creased into an uncertain, pale smile, *'Deus vult, deus vult,'* he nodded, 'God wills it my son, God wills it.'

Presently Andre joined me at the back, allowing the captain of the guard to resume his position, and we rode in silence, hugging our cloaks for warmth. I refrained from asking any questions. It was he who spoke first, without turning in my direction.

'Well . . . Have you learnt anything, Christian?' he said.

I deliberated a moment. 'That God works mysteriously, master?'

There was a long silence. The trees moved like living things around us and snow fell from the branches over our heads.

'So this is what you have learnt?' he said presently. 'Ten years at my side and this is what you have learnt?'

'Why?' I retorted with indignation. 'Is there more?'

He paused and his obedient animal paused also. He looked at me with mild irritation. 'Have I not told you more times than I can count, Christian, that a good physician and a fine philosopher have much in common?'

'But how does that . . .?'

'That they both endeavour,' he interrupted, 'to establish a standard of perfection in their minds to which they can turn, and this I have been trying to teach you, but I can see it will require some attention. Would you like me to enlighten you?'

I sighed, knowing there was nothing else I could say, 'I am ready, master.'

'Good . . .' He jiggled the reins and the horse obeyed. 'Now firstly, what you should have learnt is the difference between knowledge and opinion. Knowledge and opinion . . .'

'You infer that they are not always the same?'

'An intelligent observation,' he said smiling – though I suggest that he meant the opposite. 'Knowledge we know to be eternal and immutable, am I right?'

'And ignorance is the knowing of nothing,' I added.

'Precisely.'

'All the same,' I argued, 'where does one place opinion?'

'Opinion, Christian, fluctuates between the two states. Between what fully is and what absolutely is not, and so it is never reliable.'

'But what has this to do with the wind and the road, master?' I asked, exasperated, looking up at the strange clouds beyond the canopy of trees.

He popped some nuts into his mouth, chewed, and gazing upward shook his head, 'At the cross-roads did we hear any expressions of knowledge? No, only opinions, estimations. Am I right?'

'Yes, but I still do not understand what this has to do with –'

'None of our esteemed colleagues, Christian, knew anything about these roads, never having travelled through this region before. And yet, each had so many fine opinions based on this and that, that and this . . . all erroneous.'

'So it is lucky for us that the wind is wise, master,' I said, knowing that the elements are celestial letters, signs through which God bespeaks his wisdom to man.

He gave me a sharp look, 'And unfortunate for me that you are so stupid!' I was glad the wind caught it before the others could hear. 'You would try the patience of St Francis, boy! The wind had very little to do with it!'

'No? Not even as an instrument of God?'

'It was my own doing.'

'It could be that you are his instrument,' I answered.

'Do not speak nonsense that is better left to senile theologians. I swear you are an exasperating boy! No. This morning before we left, while taking my usual walk I came across a merchant, a travelling man, whose knowledge of these roads is born of necessity. After a little polite and instructive conversation I learnt a little about the route we were about to undertake. He told me, and as we have seen quite rightly, to be on the lookout for a junction with only one possible course, the middle one. As it happens he had once found himself lost along this road and was given safe harbour by the very same monks of the monastery, of whom he spoke highly. Now do you see that there is no mystery to it? A good knight is always well informed, remember that, it may one day save your life. Where one finds one's information is not important. What is important, however, is that one use the laws of observation, Christian, namely the God-given senses. Then one need never rely on opinion, or faith in miracles or any other such thing.'

'I see . . . but tell me then, how did you know the wind would throw the bishop's hat in the right path?' I asked, trying to trip him up.

'Christian . . .' he sighed with impatience, but he was smiling for I believe he always felt a great pleasure in proclaiming his knowledge, 'of course I did not know which way the hat would blow! Had it not been the wind I would have found some other pretext, that is all. That does not mean that we cannot thank the Lord for whatever aid he gives us.'

I must have had a look of amazement on my face because he laughed so loudly that others turned to look, but I eyed him suspiciously, 'Why did you not just say that you knew the way?'

'Ahh . . .' he smiled a broad, white smile that wrinkled his brown face all the way to his eyes. 'This is the lesson, the lesson is this! Prudence, dear boy, prudence! To be too confident of one's own aptitude,' he lowered his voice and I could hardly hear him, 'especially in the company of those whose tendencies are to bull-headed vanity, is dangerous. Prudence begs that those whom we cannot instruct we must . . . direct. In other words, it is essential for a man to be tranquil and obscure.'

I was suddenly filled with a great admiration. 'I see,' I said proudly. 'You had the knowledge while the others had only opinions, but they could not blame you for showing them up.'

'Mashallah! – what God can accomplish! Now you have it! Know much, but disclose little – that's a good axiom. Remember this in days to come, this too could save your life, for it is the usual case that those who hold opinions most strongly rarely know anything of the things they hold opinions about.'

So saying, we continued in silence, toiling for a long period in the worsening weather, and it was mid-afternoon and almost dark before we finally neared our destination.

Above our heads we encountered firstly the fortified battlements that ran along the exposed eastern side. In the gloom, they seemed imposing and ominous. Behind this rampart, a fortress of darkness was framed by a steep mountain whose gigantic snowy peaks were hidden under a blanket of cloud, and whose cold formation – thrust out of the earth perhaps by devils – loomed its stark, craggy walls over the surrounding landscape. It communicated a solemn, fearful respect, and I decided (thinking again of the untold symbols through which God speaks to us) that it was a warning, a sign that we should turn back.

The air was turbulent and hugged the walls of the abbey, rushing past us in whistles and whines. I felt small looking to the pines that arched upwards forming a moving vault that was cathedral-like, and I was glad when at last we neared the gatehouse.

To the right of the great gates, I noticed that someone had started a small fire, and had constructed a crude shelter of dead branches that had as its support the stone wall. Some moments later, I saw the shape of a man gathering kindling not far from the encampment. I asked my master why this pilgrim or beggar had not been received at the abbey, thinking also how brave he was to be alone in the unwelcome shadow of the battlements with the elements raging around him.

'I do not know, Christian,' he replied and the wind stole it. 'He does not seem to be a pilgrim, perhaps he is an aspirant novice who must, as is the custom, wait for some days outside the walls of the monastery before he is welcomed. The Apostle has said, 'one must try the spirits, whether they are of God.''

I shivered, it was indeed a harsh test.

We arrived at the monastery gates as the service of nones echoed from the chapel. The captain of the archers alighted, knocked hard on the doors of the great gates, and after some moments a pair of elderly eyes appeared from behind a small opening. The monk peered at us myopically and shouted, 'Welcome in the name of the Lord God.'

An instant later the doors' yielded, revealing the compound, indistinct beneath wind-stirred dust that made our animals irritable and nervous. And they were not the only ones, for as we crossed the stone flags of the threshold, a black raven perched on the arch let out three cries and I trembled, praying silently, trying to hide the fear that must surely have been evident on my face.

The abbot was at the gateway, the ascetic grey habit of his order flapping about him. He was a man of large proportions, and I am glad to say, possessed (for I was coming to expect the worst) of a pleasant face. He blessed each of us quickly in the customary fashion, said a short prayer to frustrate the wiles of the Devil and told us to follow him. 'Storm!' he shouted, pointing upwards at a blackened sky.

We headed with rapid steps for the main courtyard that led to the abbatial church. Here the compound was shaped in the form of a crescent, following the curve of the mountain. To the left of the church and facing south-east stood the cloister building, an imposing rectangular structure surmounted by a series of square battlements of austere stone. In it were housed the abbot's rooms, cloisters and other facilities with the dormitories above. Further along I surveyed the stables rounding the curve of the compound's perimeter, and a little ahead of this, nestled on the southerly side, sheltered from the northern squalls, was a patch of ground that I later learnt was the garden. To the north of the church, and spanning to the point where the mountain met the north-eastern wall, I observed the graveyard, appropriately in shadow for most of the year, and situated, wisely, near a building that could only be the infirmary.

The abbot led us through an aperture in the main building and we found ourselves in the cloisters where, away from the wind, he welcomed our party by quoting the words,

'We have received, O Lord, in the midst of your temple.'

He made the sign of the cross, smiled and embraced us, and each man kissed the other, albeit timidly, in peace, he then accepted the pontiff's letter, sealed with the papal seal, from Rainiero Sacconi.

He signalled his assistant to bring forth the jug and bowl and proceeded to wash the inquisitor's hands and dry them carefully. 'Your fame, my lord, has reached even as far our modest abbey, and we are honoured to have you as our guest.'

To which the inquisitor from the folds of his cowl replied, 'We come in peace, in search of truth, for it is great and it prevails — *Magna est veritas, et praevalet.*'

The abbot turned to my master and sprinkled water over his hands. With a warm smile, as though meeting an old friend, he said almost in a whisper, 'May the brotherhood dwell in you, preceptor,' and in a louder voice, 'I am always elated at seeing a member of the Templar Order, especially one whose skill in the medicinal arts precedes him. Our infirmarian will be delighted. No doubt many erudite conversations will ensue in the coming days. Also, I am bound to ask you if the king is well? I hear his health has been compromised by the infidel?'

'To the contrary,' my master answered jovially, 'he seems to be in good spirits and appears to be enjoying fine health, your grace.'

'Oh! How I am gladdened!' the abbot exclaimed with genuine warmth. 'He is a good man and a fine knight . . . Even in our seclusion we hear things of importance . . . You are welcome to remain with us as long as is your wish.'

Finally, the abbot also washed Eisik's hands, an action that impressed me a great deal, but caused the inquisitor and the bishop to bless themselves and exchange looks of disbelief, the Cistercian to glare with indignation, and the Franciscan to say a paternoster.

So it was that after the ritual the abbot entrusted us to the care of the hospitaller who was to take us to our quarters.

The hospitaller told us that our cells were situated in the pilgrims' hospice, connected to the infirmary by another building, all facing the main courtyard, and merging with the body of the eastern wall. The inquisitor and his colleagues would be housed in the main cloister building, closer to the abbot's own quarters, and thankfully some distance away from us.

My cell had a window overlooking the compound. My master's, on the other hand, faced east and had a wonderful view over the mountains and the valleys beyond. To my surprise he seemed unhappy with this arrangement, and asked to change cells with me. I agreed readily, but the hospitaller was a little concerned.

'I have been instructed,' he shook his head. 'This is most unusual –'

'My dear brother,' my master answered, a little irritated, 'it concerns me not if the cell is smaller and other such things, I merely wish to have my window face the compound and not the external world, which I find a distraction.'

The hospitaller nodded his approval. 'So it is, so it is . . . If one could only ignore external things, oh!' he sighed. 'What a blissful place the world would be then, preceptor,' adding hastily, 'but the wine?'

'The wine?' My master raised a brow.

'Yes . . . the honey wine, our specialty. Every room is graced with one flask, that is, with the exception of the novices, of course, though we only have two, and that is a good thing', he gave me a sideways glance, 'for the young have no control over their urges; they drink wine as if it were water, they eat too much, and they are filled with pride.'

'I see,' my master smiled with amusement. 'I do not partake of liquor, dear brother, so you may take it away.'

He stared at my master as if he had not understood him. 'No liquor?' he said with a vacuous mouth. 'None at all, preceptor?'

'Not a drop these days.' He patted his middle, the circumference of which had increased of late.

The man hesitated a moment longer and left us with a frown, returning again in a mood of agitation because he had omitted to advise us that after the service there would be a dinner in the refectory, in honour of the legate. Having said this, he rushed off into the cold night, talking to himself as old men do.

My room was sparse, but comfortable. My pallet was

constructed of wood, fashioned into a crude frame and filled with clean, fragrant straw. I had one sheepskin for warmth, and the only light came from a lantern attached to the wall by iron clasps, a luxury extended only to guests. The abbey monks would have no light in their cells.

In the centre of the small room a large vessel had been filled with warm water. This, too, was a rare pleasure, and I must admit that the thought of it made one instantly glad. I said a small prayer thanking the Lord that this abbey did not follow that aspect of the Benedictine rule which forbade regular bathing, for I had become very accustomed to it in the East.

I sat heavily on my pallet, feeling an overwhelming weariness. From my cell window I could see only a strange greyness. I stood and found that I could look down on the forest, now almost completely in shadow, to see directly below my window smoke coming from the fire at the encampment we had seen on our way to the abbey. I shuddered with cold, thinking of the poor pilgrim as I prepared for my bath. I said a short prayer that this night would not be too cold for him, shed my road-soiled clothes, and immersed my broken body into the grateful warmth. And, having resolved that I must be exceedingly tired, I set out to prove my hypothesis by falling into a deep and contented sleep.

2

Capitulum

Prior to Vespers

I awoke to the sound of a loud knock. Still in the bath, my head dull, I realised that I was very nearly frozen. I dressed in the habit provided me by the fine monks of the abbey, and in haste opened the door to reveal my master standing before me, his foot tapping the ground and his face contorted into a scowl.

'Come, boy,' he remonstrated. 'What have you been doing? You look like a plucked chicken. Have you been sleeping?' He searched my face, and I nodded, uncertain of his response.

'Well, good for you.' He smiled then, and slapped me on the back. 'There will be little sleep these coming nights, for we must be prepared to make our inquiries at the oddest hours, at the same time attempting to follow the customs of the abbey. Come, we must conduct our preliminary inspections before dark.'

'But where are we going, master?' I asked, following him outside, unaccustomed to the long habit that, because of the wind, became entangled around my legs with each step. 'Must I wear this . . .?'

'Is your head a sieve, boy?' he spoke as he so often did, loudly. 'What did I just say?'

'That we must follow the customs of the abbey,' I answered. Not mentioning, of course, that he, on the other hand, continued to wear the uniform of the order. Instead, I merely followed him, trying to keep up with his short, though exceedingly brisk strides, as we walked past the graveyard.

'Just one moment.' He paused, casting his gaze over the graves. Having satisfied some unspoken question he continued as before, and I followed him as we came upon the body of the cloisters. He said something, and I did not at first realise that he was speaking to me, for he was looking away, as though addressing an unseen person.

'The *rere dorter* . . .'

'Master?'

'In answer to your previous question, Christian, before anything else, I need to attend to the call of nature and so our first hunt will be for the rere dorter, the latrines . . .' He looked up at the building. 'The dormitories are likely to be situated on the second level, and following the Cistercian model, so too the lavatory. However, it will not surprise me if we find that there is another lavatory on the ground level, that is, somewhere just off the cloisters and close to the refectory, for old monks have weakened bladders . . . now where is the aperture? Here we are . . .'

We emerged from the same arched doorway through which we had earlier entered the cloisters with the abbot, situated on the left side of the church, just after a small architectural projection. In the dimly lit east walk, a monk with a taper was lighting the great torches that here and there provided some relief from gloom.

'*Benedicamus Domino,*' the brother intoned as we passed.

My master answered, '*Deo gratias.*'

The cloisters, usually a hive of activity, were deserted. With the exception of the brother – who we later learnt was the master of music – we seemed to be alone. We made our way around the central garth or courtyard whose low walls were surmounted by arches. It had snowed only a little these last days, and here and there one could see a patch of dead ground around the fountain which, as was customary, marked the garth's central point.

We walked hastily past the scriptorium and the numerous carrels housed in the northern cloister alley, and at the apex, where the west aisle met the south walk, we found the rere dorter, just where my master had said it would be. Here we entered into a long central passage with individual cabinets on one of its sides for privacy. The other side housed the baths. Both led to a great fire whose warmth was a comfort to my cold bones. And as he relieved himself my master told me that cleanliness was very important to Cistercians. They always built near a good source of water, he said, which they redirected to suit their purposes in much the same way as the Romans. As was the custom, the stream or body of water was diverted to run beneath the cookhouse or kitchen, and downstream it would flow beneath the rere dorter, carrying the refuse out of the monastery into the great unknown. I thought this an exceedingly wise plan, until my master also added. 'But you don't want to be a cook when the wind changes, my boy!'

My master also noted that in this abbey the monks must have made use of an underground stream fed by snows from the towering mountains. And as we re-entered the cloisters, he concluded in a whisper, 'Now we know there is a web of tunnels and channels running beneath the abbey, because if the rere dorter is situated here, in the south-west, and the kitchen . . .' he pointed in the direction of delicious smells, 'is situated there in the south-east and, of course, downstream . . . it stands to reason that there must be more than one channel with more than one exit out of the abbey. Otherwise you would have a stream running uphill.'

'And what significance do you apply to this?' I asked.

'Where there is smoke there is a pyre. Or more importantly, where there are channels there must also be tunnels . . .

naturally. Come . . . next we must inspect the church.'

Still trying to understand the relevance of his statement I found myself leaving the cloisters and entering the church through the south transept door. Immediately, the sweet pungent smell of incense assailed my nostrils and, God forgive me, I sneezed.

Inside a young acolyte was attending to the sacred vessels and church ornaments, in preparation for the forthcoming service. He turned, searching for the source of the disruption, and upon seeing us, returned to his work, but not before giving us a look of disdain. We were, after all, part of a legation sent here to condemn their community. I would no doubt feel the same if I were he.

We walked past the high altar, crossing ourselves devoutly, and paused for a moment before the rose window as a beautiful shaft of afternoon light pierced the gloom. It illuminated infinite indissoluble particles that, aroused by the daystar's caress, swirled around us in a dance of joy and gladness. For light we know not only chases away darkness but also death, and so I felt a little better than I had felt all week, following this light which even now waned slightly, directing us, it seemed, to the *pulpitum* – or screen, that sequestered the sanctuary from the eyes of the lay community. It was behind it, unseen, that monks took their places during the services, in the choir stalls that were made of carved wood on bases of stonework, with high ornamented canopied backs. Inside there were hinged seats, wisely constructed so as to enable a tired monk to sit, thankfully (though unofficially), through a long service. At the eastern end there was a lectern of brass in the shape of an eagle with spread wings on which music books were placed. Here there was also a seat for the master of music and beside it a more ornate seat for the officiating priest or abbot. To the west of the stalls were the presbytery and the high altar, and the shrine. There on the floor before the sacred space a monk, we realised, was speaking to us, but his voice was muffled for he was lying face down as though dead, his arms spread out so that his body formed the shape of a cross. We had not discerned his form when we had stood at the altar, for his habit was grey like the floor, and we had been taken by the daystar's blessing, and so I was startled.

'Is somebody there?' we heard his muffled inquiry. 'If you are the Devil, be on your way. If you are goodly men help this poor old monk up from this cursed floor!'

My master went to the man, and helped him easily to his feet. He seemed ancient, with a dry wrinkled face whose pale eyes would have been very frightening if they did not also exude a certain gentle warmth.

'Ohh! My bones ache!' He squinted, sniffing us. 'I am brother Ezekiel . . . who, in God's name, are you?' 'I am the Templar preceptor, venerable Ezekiel, and to your right is my young apprentice, Christian.'

He sought me with his hands and, finding my face, at once began to explore it with cold fingers. I tried not to recoil at his touch but was startled out of my wits when he gasped suddenly, feeling for his heart with one hand and reaching into his scapular with the other, retrieving something from it, which he placed in his toothless mouth. It must have had some beneficial effect, for he wiped the sticky residue from his lips, and continued a little calmer than before.

'A Templar preceptor . . . you say?' he blinked, peering at me. 'Your boy is remarkably like . . . Are we in the . . .? No . . . during . . .? Oh!' he cried exasperated. 'Where is Setubar?' Very slowly then, in a circumspect tone, 'I suppose you have come about the antichrist whose countenance lurks within these lamentable walls?'

My master smiled, 'No, venerable Ezekiel, we have come to advise the inquiry.'

'Oh! Inquiry?' He drew even closer, grabbing my master's vestments, his sweet breath making feathery phantoms in the cold air. 'Where is Setubar? Is he about?'

My master narrowed his eyes, 'Who is Setubar?'

'Is he about? ' the man pressed, wringing his hands.

'We are alone, brother,' my master answered.

'Then I can tell you. That is, if you are a Templar . . .' He felt for the cross stitched to my master's habit and brought his eyes very close to it. Immediately he smiled with satisfaction and his eyes filled with tears. 'It has been many years . . . There is little time, so listen to my words . . . in these sacred walls there are men who . . .' he paused, squeezing his eyes shut as though to say these words caused him pain. 'There are men who are wedded to error, men seduced by the Devil! Yes, impossible, you say? But it is true, the days of the antichrist are finally at hand, preceptor . . . *We have seen our first martyr.'*

'I saw the new grave,' my master remarked.

The old man winced and placed both hands over his eyes. 'The Devil will kill us all!'

At that moment, from out of the shadows of the south ambulatory, the figure of a cowled monk appeared whose bent form moved toward us in a peculiar fashion. After some moments he reached us, and taking the old man's hand in his he spoke, in a gruff German accent, 'Brother Ezekiel, you have graced the Lord with your prostrations long enough.'

'Setubar!' Ezekiel gasped. 'I was telling the preceptor about . . . about . . . the antichrist.'

'I see . . .' the man nodded his head, 'but he has existed, my friend, for thousands of years, and we have only moments to ready for the service, now come,' he said. Then, placing the man's hand on his arm and turning in our direction, so that we only caught sight of a wrinkled chin and toothless smile, he added, 'If we let him, dear guests, he would lie prostrate all day . . . so dedicated to our Lord is our dear brother.'

'Ahh!' the old man was suddenly irritated. 'The floor was colder than the crypts at Augustus. The Lord is not with us today. As you know, the antichrist roams the abbey.'

'The antichrist is everywhere, dear brother, that is precisely why he is so formidable an opponent . . . now come,' Setubar coaxed paternally.

'No . . . no . . . you must tell the preceptor about him . . . tell him!' He coughed then as though something had caught in his throat. 'He is a Templar, Setubar . . . they are here!' There was a desperation in his voice that the German brother tried to mask, by placing an arm over Ezekiel's shoulders and directing him away from us hastily. 'Come, you are tired. I shall take you to your cell.'

'The boy . . .' the monk said to the other, 'does he not look like?'

'He looks like an angel. Youth is angelic, brother, precisely because it is young . . .' Having delivered himself of this statement he directed the other man away from us and out of the church.

This strange encounter left me a little unsettled and I began to look about me in the shadows. My master, sensing my apprehension, diverted my mind with other considerations, showing me the church, and telling me about the architecture of the Cistercians, but this only soothed me a little.

'That man . . . do you believe that he speaks the truth?'

'Perhaps there was something to what he was saying,' Andre said.

'What? That the antichrist roams the abbey? That there are men here who have been seduced by the Devil?' I asked incredulously.

'No, of course not!' he snapped. 'I believe he is frightened, but then it is also known that the old live in constant fear. However, he mentioned a martyr and I did see the fresh grave. Something has happened here and I begin to find myself curious. Come, let us look about, let us see what we can see.'

So we left the sanctuary through a door in the pulpitum and, once through the rood screen, we found ourselves in the area reserved for the laity.

If the sanctuary was the head and heart of a church then this before us was the main body, the limbs. My master told me that this church, no doubt built before the times of master masons and artisans, had been – like so many scattered all over Europe – constructed by the monks themselves. It was a great achievement, though it was indeed a curious church because of its peculiar orientation. I queried my master on this point and he concluded that it may have been unavoidable, considering the aspect and the mountain. One other church he knew of in the area was built similarly, the monastery church at Arles-sur-Tech whose sarcophagus of its patron saints Abdon and Sennen is said to fill mysteriously with holy water. Even a tiny amount of this liquid, he told me, had been known to cure the most vile disease. I thought, and said as much, that no matter what vile disease I contracted, nothing could persuade me to drink the water from a sarcophagus. He pointed out to me that if I were willing to drink the blood of Christ to save my soul, why not the water of Abdon to save my body?

It was a good question.

So we stood, our eyes leading us down a central aisle or nave, whose flanking colonnades supported arches, curving to meet across the ceiling vault. The rood screen became its central point, and standing in front of it, I had the impression that numerous and converging arches were rushing towards me in fast succession. Like waves of water, they seemed to defy the earthly forces of attraction, rising with an unbridled momentum before collapsing upon the calm and quiet shores of a delicate crucifix.

I remembered fondly our visit to Reims where my master had shown me the marvellous carved reliefs on the capitals of the columns and I recalled being spellbound and I confess that I very nearly risked worshipping the creation more than the creator, having to remind myself of what St Bernard tells us about this very sin. For I could have spent a whole day gazing at such details in preference to meditating upon God's laws! St Bernard believed, as do many others, that the murals and statues, so often employed by the Benedictines in their churches, interfered with sound meditation and training in religious gravity. And yet here in this fine Cistercian model, my eyes sorely missed the statues, individual in their grace and pose, they missed the fantastic murals where artists, armed with powders and tinctures of unequalled perfection, added flesh to gods and saints. Where were the golden candlesticks? Nowhere did I see ornate tripods of silver, lovingly encrusted with gemstones of brilliant hues!

'A Cistercian monastery,' my master said, reading my thoughts, 'must adhere strictly to the ideal of poverty, to the ideal of the universal that shuns the individual. Even their habit, if you are attentive, Christian, will illustrate this point, for these monks can abandon differentiation from those things that surround them by the use of grey, which allows them to diffuse into the stone of the walls, into the dirt of the floor, indistinct even from the grey mist that descends downward from a grey sky whose milky blanket comes to rest on the greyness of the compound.'

I took a moment to reflect on my master's wisdom, seeing that indeed it was a world that shunned the particular for the homogeneously universal. It seemed to me a quiet peaceful world, if not a little dull. However, as we walked down the central nave, we became immediately aware of the windows that, in their nature, were the only departure from the strict rule.

The long windows illuminated the five bays on either side of the nave with brilliant light, casting resplendent reflections in a play of colour – more effective perhaps, because of the grey background onto which it fell. All ten windows, with their exquisite plate tracery, depicted in a glorious concordance of transparency the four temptations of Christ, the ascension, the twelve apostles, but it was the Madonna and child between four angels that especially caught my attention. High above the second bay the Virgin sat enthroned, her violet robes simply draped over her pubescent body, cradling the Jesus child to her plump bosom. I paused in reflection, for the Virgin, dear reader, was black! I thought that my eyes and the dim light had been the cause of this strange illusion. I turned, but my master was already near the east door.

I walked to him and waited. He did not like to be interrupted while deep in thought, this could unleash a tempestuous mood that many have innocently, though unequivocally, come to know, so I waited. Moments later he turned to me.

'To appreciate the art of architecture I am told that one must learn to see it with different eyes. You must first learn to follow the contours as they rise.' He traced the journey of a vault, following the curves, which flow to meet a column in holy communion. 'In doing so, you will be lifted high into the heavenly vaults!'

I remained silent, waiting impatiently.

'It is as important,' he continued, 'to appreciate art as it is to create it. Architecture raises us above all temporal things . . . It is also a fair shelter from the elements.' He then looked at me squarely. 'You wish to ask a question? Come . . . come . . .'

I asked him if he had noticed the Virgin, showing him where it was. He stood staring at it for long moments in silence, before remarking in an ambiguous way.

'Yes?'

'Do you not think it strange, master?' I asked, thinking that it was surely out of the ordinary.

'It is remarkable, but strange, no,' he said, and walked away.

'But what of the Virgin?'

'Ahhh! The Virgin. Yes . . . Let me show you something.'

He led me the short distance to the east door, through which a wind thrust its cold hands.

The entrance spanned approximately ten feet, and was

lit by two great torches whose flames licked and yawed and threatened to go out. They were attached to the stone wall on either side of a great oak door, left open throughout the day. Accompanying the proportions and bound to the very body of the two columns that flanked the entrance were two unnaturally tall figures. My fascinated eye fell firstly upon the image of the Archangel Michael who stood to the right of the door, and I was curious to find that he was dressed in knight's mail and armour. On the left side, as one would expect, stood Gabriel, gazing upward with a smile of perennial praise, almost kneeling, preparing for a prayer that would last for all time. Above the doorway, and surmounting the arch – the area called the tympanum – there was an intricate working of Christ on his throne, surrounded by his twelve apostles.

'What are you looking at?' Andre broke through my speculations. In my enthusiasm for the door's impressive sculptures, I had not noticed him pointing to a place above the Christ figure where there was a large cross intersected by a circlet of roses.

I felt my master's breath on my cheeks as he whispered excitedly into my ear. 'The Rose Cross! I saw it on our way to the cloisters.'

I frowned, 'Rose Cross?'

'Yes . . .' he trailed off pensively.

'But master . . . what of the black virgin?'

'The black Madonna is not so strange.' He shook his head. 'There is a black Mary at Notre-Dame in Dijon, and also at Chartres, on its stained glass windows. It is the combination of rose and cross, Christian, which makes this abbey's ornamentation interesting, it harks back to . . .'

I was about to risk a reprimand by asking more questions, when we were interrupted by a voice behind us.

It was the abbot, trying to keep his hood over his head in the inclement air, accompanied by another monk. *Domine dilexi decorem domus tuae, et locum habitationis gloriae tuae ...* Lord I have loved the habitation of thy house, and the place where thine honour dwelleth . . . You are admiring our door.'

My master smiled wryly. 'He found it wood and left it marble.'

'Poor abbot Odilo of Cluny . . .' the abbot continued with good humour. 'He built a beautiful fortress of gold-mounted reliquaries, more admired for its beauty than venerated for its sanctity . . . Here we only have a door.'

'A most beautiful door, your grace,' my master bowed.

'Perhaps a little indulgent . . . In any event, I would like you to meet our infirmarian, brother Asa.'

The other monk removed his cowl to reveal a very thin face, darkened by the sun. The bluster swung the thin, lank hair about his tonsure but his brown eyes showed a keenness, as though little fires burnt behind them. I liked him instantly.

'Our dear brother,' the abbot continued, shouting slightly, 'was very excited to learn that you have graced our abbey. And he is most anxious to discuss with you many things of a medicinal nature.'

Brother Asa nodded his head, a broad smile lighting up his features, but he seemed tongue-tied, and it was some moments before he spoke with timidity.

'I would be most grateful for any exchange of knowledge, preceptor. We are very removed from worldly things here, and I have not had occasion to hear of any advancement in the medicinal arts.'

'I am always happy to converse on this most holy of topics.'

'Thank you, preceptor. Perhaps tomorrow then?' he asked no one in particular, and drew his cowl leaving us with the abbot.

The abbot watched his monk walk away with paternal affection. 'He is a very fine physician,' he said with pride. 'I believe one of the best this abbey has known, though our brother Setubar taught him everything that he knows. He has never attended a university . . . all his learning comes from books.'

'Yes . . .' my master said in an offhand way that signalled his deep interest. 'We met Brother Setubar inside the church, with Brother Ezekiel. You say he learned everything from books?

Your abbey must have a very fine medical library then, your holiness?'

The abbot became serious, 'It is adequate, though not in the same league, perhaps, as others you've seen in your travels. Now then, you must let me know, preceptor, if you are in need of anything. Your accommodation is suitable?'

'In every aspect, your holiness.'

'Good! That is good. And so I must take my leave, and prepare for the holy service. You will, of course, join us in the choir?'

'Of course.'

As the abbot was about to enter the church, my master added, 'May I have your permission, your grace, to make some inquiries?'

The abbot turned, a wary smile dawning over his singular features. 'I thought this was the duty of the inquisitor, preceptor?'

'Yes, of course,' my master conceded very quickly. 'However, two men, your holiness, not working together, and bound by different natures, will inevitably see things differently as Augustine tells us. In other words,' my master continued, marking every word, 'one eye may see something that the other does not, or on the other hand, one eye may choose . . . *not* to see, by virtue of its faithful – or indeed unfaithful – service. And as this inquiry delves into the medical practices of your abbey, it may be in your favour to have a physician overseeing . . . matters . . .' he trailed off.

The abbot raised both eyebrows in an unspoken question. I too wondered at my master's meaning. As if to instruct us further then, which had been my master's intention all along, he proceeded. 'It is the king's wish that I observe the conduct of this inquiry with the utmost care, and this means that I must hear what the inquisitor hears, and I must also see what he sees, or perhaps even what he does not hear and see. In this capacity, I will need your permission to question the brothers.'

I felt the abbot's uncertainty.

'There has been so much disturbance. '

'I will remain mindful of the delicate nature of these matters, your holiness.'

'And what does the inquisitor say to this?'

'My authority comes directly from the king, and as we are these days on French soil . . .'

'Yes, but the inquisitor has his authority directly from the pope! And so, I believe, we are to be caught like a fish between two rocks. Between the pope and King Louis, as we have been in the past between the King of Aragon and the Count of Toulouse?'

'And yet it is indeed in such a spot that a fish can best elude the wiles of the fisherman, your holiness, as you perhaps already know.'

'Yes . . .' He smiled a little but it did not reach his eyes, 'but who, in this case, is the fisherman, preceptor?'

'Ahhh . . .' my master nodded his head, but said nothing more.

There was a long pause and I assumed the abbot was debating the wisdom of his forthcoming decision. 'You have my permission to ask what questions you deem necessary, preceptor. However, I cannot allow you to wander about the abbey at any hour of your choosing, especially at night. No one should, indeed, no one must.'

'But if you will forgive me, it is often at night, away from the distractions of everyday life, that one gains a true impression of . . . things, your grace.'

The abbot became annoyed. 'Your impressions can surely

wait for the appropriate hour. I would like you to conform to our simple rules. In this way we can best prevent this tiresome inquiry from trespassing unnecessarily on the life of the community.' He gave my master a pointed look. 'I trust a Templar's vows of obedience are as sacred as ours . . .?'

My master bowed. 'Without obedience, your holiness, there is precious little.'

'Having said this, obedience begs that I must leave, for the bell will soon toll the hour.'

'One last thing, your holiness?' my master added, once again demurely, but I could see how brightly his steely eyes were shining. 'May I ask who is the oldest member of your community?'

The other man hesitated, perhaps wondering what my master was up to. 'Why, the brother whom you met in the church, Brother Ezekiel of Padua. But I will not have him disturbed, do you understand? He is very frail, needing constant care. His mind is . . . shall we say detached. After all he is very old.'

'I see,' Andre answered, a frown darkening his brow.

'However, you must not tax him with unnecessary questions.'

'Of course, your holiness, we will only disturb him for the most important of reasons.'

The abbot hesitated, perhaps a little unsure of my master's sincerity, then he blessed us and disappeared into the grey void of the church.

'Very well,' my master whispered to me, in heightened spirits, 'now we know three things.'

'Do we?' I asked, amazed.

'Naturally, haven't you been listening? We know firstly that when this abbey was built, its architects used underground tunnels to divert running water. We also know that the abbot is most anxious that we do not inspect the abbey by night, and also that he is not comfortable with us asking the old brother questions. A man who may know with accuracy the abbey's history! I should think this is enough for one afternoon.'

'If you ask me, master, I say we still do not know anything at all!'

'Patience, patience! Knowledge does not consist of what one knows, but rather, knowing what one does not know, as Plato tells us.'

'What do we do next?'

'We disobey the abbot, and inspect the monastery by night.'

'Disobey? But, master –'

'Hush, Christian, in this case God will forgive us.'

I hesitated, observing how the shadow of dusk was settling over the compound. 'And what about the antichrist?'

'The only devil, Christian, exists in ignorance and folly, as I have told you, don't look for Satan behind every shadow, rather learn to distinguish his form in the eyes of a man. Now to vespers!'

It was only later, after the holy office, as I lay on my pallet that memories of Mansourah returned with vividness. I had no wish to cast my mind back to those days. I tried rather to forget (if only it were possible!) the crazed blood of battle, the anguished cries and tortured faces, the clatter and thunder of hoofs stirring up grit, the rattle of armoured bodies charging, pressing. Yet in my ears the groans still echo with such clarity that I almost feel the pain of wounds that gape and fester. I watch as though I am standing, once again wide-eyed, as the standards are raised and the banners unfurled. I hear the wild snorting of animals on the spur, the cries of the young captains. I observe the carnage, and note everything on parchments for future chroniclers. I see the bits of bodies flung about, discarded, and I watch as others lose their stomachs, or cry silently. Everywhere life-blood, sweet and metallic, and the suffocating smoke that settles to reveal the charred flesh of Greek fire. I witness my master's devotion as he stitches up flesh, stuffs bowels back into abdomens, cauterises or uses his fist in a vain attempt to stop the rush of blood . . . hours and hours, too many bloody days with his arms to the elbows, his white mantle stained with carmine, wading through the fields of bodies.

I remember now, old man that I am, how a cloud of scourge struck those of us who survived in waves of fever and dysentery, sending mucus spilling from the nostrils and spasms wrenching the gut. I see my master, so clearly, cutting out the lower parts of his drawers and continuing his work in a camp that is no longer filled with the stench of blood, but excrement and doom.

Andre had urged a retreat, the king had agreed, but it was too late for many. The Comte d'Artois, on whose command we had proceeded to Mansourah though we were short in numbers, who laughed at those who had advised caution, the same man who disobeyed the king's orders by pressing ahead to battle, had, in his ignorance and vainglory, led hundreds to their deaths at the hands of thousands.

All I recall of the night we left was that it was filled with cries. A confusion of arrows tipped with Greek fire, star-like, falling around us in conflagration as we escaped. My master was wounded by two Saracen arrows, one in the knee and the other in the chest, as he helped men onto our little boat overflowing with terror, sickness and dying. Damietta seemed a lifetime away.

Why did these recollections return at that moment to torment me? I can only say, now that I am far removed from those days, and so, able to see them all the more clearly, that in my heart I perceived an equivocal peril in the monastery. A peril whose dissimilar similitude may have appeared all too vague, because in my spiritual illiteracy I could only ascertain the letters and not the words (as yet unknown to me) whose nature reveals truths gradually. So that I saw only the signs, or sign of signs (alas!) illegible, and yet unmistakable; our capital tells us that a Templar must not walk according to his proper will, and to honour this rule is the duty of every faithful knight, but my master, like the Comte d'Artois, had a will of his own, and although devoted to his faith, I believed some part of him (perhaps the infidel part) sought to be as free as those eagles one sees soaring above all things, and I feared for him. I feared that his disregard for the rules of obedience, driven as I knew it was by his love of logic and freedom – so similar and yet dissimilar to that other, whose nature was driven by pride and ignorance – might lead us all into the pit.

At last, in the grip of such sensations I said a prayer, letting it rest in the bosom of those higher beings of whom it is said that they are wisdom personified. Deciding that all learning and reason is for naught, when one is bound by other laws, laws that bind a monk to his superior, and he to his conscience, and then finally to God . . .

The bell tolled the hour as we crossed the compound on our way to the refectory for the great dinner. With the relief afforded by prayer I found that I welcomed the idea of going to the table, even though in my heart I continued to feel a profound dread.

My master accompanied me to the cloister buildings, dressed in formal dress: the usual padded undercoat beneath the surcoat of the order, which was long and came to the ground at a severe angle. It was made of burel cloth, or coarse linen bleached white bearing the well-known red cross of the order. It had no lining of lambskin, or wool, so it did little to protect one from the cold. My master, not one to savour the vanities that others found essential, never complained, even on such a night, for although the storm had not come as predicted and the wind had died down, the cold air penetrated to the bone. When I asked my master if he was cold he reminded me that habits of coarse wool such as the one given me by the abbey, although warmer, also harboured fleas and lice. A lifetime of itching, he told me, was often responsible for turning away many an aspirant novice from the ideal of monastic life. I scratched, certain that my body was already food for some unseen, but no doubt hideous, vermin.

Thus we continued, seeing little beyond a few paces as the evening fog descended. Half way across the main courtyard, my master handed me a parchment. I held it to my face, and as we neared the lighted cloister door I could barely make out a message, written in Greek,

Those who inquire the light of knowledge, die in blind ignorance.

'But that does not make sense,' I remarked.

'I suspect that what he meant to say was . . .' my master instructed, 'those who seek the light of knowledge die in blind ignorance. An incautious translator such as yourself may very easily confuse the words seek and inquiry. The Greek vernacular, like Latin, Christian, is fraught with traps for the unsuspecting.' He proceeded to tell me that someone had left the parchment in his cell while we were out investigating the abbey.

I was about to ask many questions when I realised that we were almost upon Eisik whose figure stood just inside the east door. He looked like a man unable to decide his next movements, taking one step forward, and then shaking his head, taking two steps back. All the while he muttered lengthy lines of dialogue in Hebrew below his breath, which, in the cold, created billowy clouds around his form.

'Holy fathers!' he exclaimed, turning around and staring at us with his big eyes as though he were looking at the Devil himself. 'You startle me! Feel my heart, for the love of Abraham! It pounds like that of a hare!' then, 'You're late, late I tell you! And now what misery . . .! All eyes will be upon me. I think I shall return to the stables to eat in peace!' He turned to leave, but my master stopped him.

'Nonsense, old man! It will be a fine dinner, you are my guest and therefore welcome. Walk with us and tell us your thoughts. Come, what do you think of the abbey? Is it filled with the ghosts of dead monks, then?' my master said, laughing a little because he thought lightly about such things, but I shuddered as we entered the dark and solemn cloister.

'By the God of Israel you are impertinent!' Eisik scowled and pointed his finger at my master. 'We must not laugh before mysterious and holy things! We must have reverence!'

'I beg your pardon, Eisik,' my master said, 'but you have not answered my question. Tell me, what are your impressions of the abbey?'

'That you should ask me such a question is beyond my understanding!' He shrugged his shoulders, 'Have I not trained you to see the signs? They will have eyes to see but will not see, ears to hear but will not listen . . . It seems you have forgotten what I have told you, namely, that everything is an outward and visible suggestion of an inward and spiritual being.' He sighed. 'Well, well, it seems an old man must repeat himself *ad infinitum* or else leave men to their ignorance . . . There are signs! Signs that point to signs whose indications allude to other signs, some-times tangible, other times indiscernible, though always, to an initiate, very clear; that is to one who cares to listen. For one who is able to decipher the meaning of meaningful things, the voice of the spirit is crystalline.' He paused then, stopping us with his hands and cocking his head to one side. 'Ahh! You see! Every-thing speaks!' he affirmed with a shake of his head.

'Come, it is you who must speak, but not in riddles,' My master said.

'Bah! Knowledge lies not in the person who speaks but rather in the person who listens . . . or was that eloquence? I cannot remember now . . . In any event, this will be the first day that a Nazarene admits to needing Jewish knowledge! As I have said, the signs are all here. The abbey faces east, accessed through a forest, like the mystery temple at Ephesus where the image of the Goddess Artemisia also faced east. Behind it the mountains, ahead of it the valley, the sages tell us that the orientals consider this alignment quite favourable,' then he smiled. 'And also strategically it is very wisely constructed, my friend. To attack such a place would be difficult.'

'Then you are saying it reminds you of the Cathar strongholds?'

The old man nodded. 'I sense a Gnostic temple where the four ethers are concentrated and fused, linking the past with the present and future. Then too, one cannot discount the position of the planet Mercury at our arrival, nor the portal and the raven as a messenger that spoke three times indicating the three *Templa* or sacred places dedicated to God, and so it scarcely goes without saying, my friend, that there are Templars here. You know it as I do, I feel their presence . . . after all, the abbot greeted you with the *greeting* didn't he?' He slapped two hands together happily. 'Soon you will see that I am right!'

'I take your point,' my master conceded, 'and yet I must say that it is remarkable that a Jew should know the greeting, considering it is only used by those admitted into the order. Perhaps you would like to enlighten us?'

Eisik lowered his eyes cautiously, 'I know many things, Andre, and yet I know nothing! Nor do I wish to know anything as it happens for it is blissful to live in the divine numbness of ignorance . . .' then he graced me with a rare smile, 'but knowing nothing is also something.'

'Not according to Plato,' answered Andre. 'Tell me then, what does your knowing without knowing say to you about the inquisitor?'

'For one, his hair is frizzy, which means he has a choleric temper. Secondly he is balding . . .'

'But he is tonsured,' my master pointed out.

'Even so, he balds and we are told that such men are crafty, avaricious, hypocritical and make a pretence of religion. But his eyes . . . his pale eyes indicate to us that he is touched with madness . . .'

'You may call me an unbeliever, dear friend, but in this case I do believe you.'

At this point we arrived at the dimly-lit south walk that led to the great doors and I was struck by the devil of curiosity, no longer able to refrain from asking more about the note.

'Note?' Eisik's faculties were immediately aroused. 'What note?'

My master explained about the parchment with the strange Greek message, and Eisik shook his head before exclaiming.

'You see! Gnostic, as I have told you! And worse still, a warning . . . a peculiar thing, for one knows not if it warns against a possible tragedy or a probable one!'

'Perhaps both, as Aristotle tells us,' my master answered.

Eisik huffed, mumbling under his breath. 'You think too much of that Greek, perhaps it is your Alexandrian blood. Your race has always thought too much of Greeks and look where it has got you!'

'Maimonides, whom you revere as a great philosopher, used many Aristotelian laws . . .'

Eisik shook his head, waving a finger in the air, 'And it was philosophy, Andre, that led to his downfall . . .'

My master sighed. 'How can a man so erudite be so stubborn! Even Maimonides knew that logic illuminates the mind and strengthens the spirit, Eisik!'

'No, you are confused,' he shook his head, 'philosophy addles the mind, and confounds the soul...and moreover, it will not help you decipher the threat on your life which you have just received!' His face softened. 'Oh, my son, my son, when will you see the error in your thinking? When will you devote your life to the spirit? Don't feed your anima the errors of reason, for if you do, your soul will dry up as have the souls of so many in these days of wickedness. That is the bitter lesson that I have learnt, though I atone that one error until the day God calls me to answer for my sins . . . ah!' He waved a hand, closing his eyes and shaking his shoulders. 'An error too horrible to contemplate!'

My master looked grave, and perhaps as much for his sake as for his friend's he said, 'What happens in the past must be forgotten.'

'You are mistaken, Andre,' Eisik sighed. 'It must never be forgotten, we must remember that we were wrong! We allowed our zeal to transform us into instruments of execution . . . the lamb became the wolf, and the intimidated became the intimidators! May the God of our fathers forgive us for allowing the shining face of love and compassion to elude us . . .'

'That was a long time ago.'

'Not so long ago . . .!' There was a wide-eyed feverish quality to his face. 'You may say, because you love me as I hope you do, that I was only defending the memory of Maimonides, from whose lips I learnt so much . . . but to defend him, a man died . . . do you hear me? A man died! Oh! It is horrible! Horrible to cast one's mind back to those terrible days. You should listen to the mystics, who say that knowledge and faith should never be brought together, that the lust for such things is distinct from the beatific sacrifice that is innocence. Maimonides the great Spanish Jew tells us that happiness lies in the immortal existence of the human intellect contemplating God.'

'But, Eisik, the rabbi condemned Maimonides, he condemned the mystics, and . . . Cabbala.'

'It is true . . . it is true . . . he was blind to the light that emanates from the holy source through which our fathers have always spoken. In his ignorance he despised knowledge because he was tempted by the devil of envy. But learned men also succumb to temptation because even more than ignorant ones, they know the ways of sin . . . Perhaps the rabbi was right?'

'But I am certain you didn't desire the rabbi's death, and that is all I need to know . . .'

'But you are wrong!' Eisik exclaimed, horrified. 'I confess that for an instant I desired that very thing! For one terrible moment, a shadow, a mire, prevented me from seeing the divine precepts of the Holy Law. He was burning books! He was destroying knowledge and so he should be punished! But it was as I stood calling for his death, snarling like a rabid animal, that I realised that learning does not better man, it only makes him better at being clever. It does not lead a man to the path of brotherly love, but to that of self-love. It never leads to tolerance. It leads only to arrogance!'

'But you are an erudite and insightful man whose knowledge has been a blessing to many.'

'Ahh!' spat the Jew. 'It is a curse!' Then to me, 'One thinks in his youth – and you had better listen to this my young one lest you become like your master – one thinks that he learns in order to better understand the world and its laws. A holy pretext if it weren't also a foolish one because after a time of gazing into the vast distances, a man no longer sees what lies at his feet, he loses himself in the universe of ideas because he neglects to see the connections between entities that unite those ideas.'

'But my dear and wise friend,' broke in my master impatiently, 'surely the world would be paler and far less appealing without the wisdom of men, but we are not only speaking of the wisdom of master mathematicians, teachers, and rulers, but also the wisdom of farmers, herdsmen, blacksmiths!'

'Very well, but I fear that your pursuit of philosophy, as you call it, will lead you to your ruin and I will be forced to witness it, it is my destiny . . . Do you not know that there is little better than the simple soul that strives for nothing more than what is given him by the grace of God? I beg you, do not allow your pride to take you to hell, for I suspect this note of yours mirrors what we have been discussing.' In a softer voice he said, 'Throw away your reason, my son, and bask in the light of the one eternal wisdom that no man can know!'

'How am I to meditate on heavenly things that I can

never know, my good and loyal friend, when there are so many things here on earth that may instruct my ignorance!' my master said, patting his stomach.

Eisik smiled sadly, for I knew he loved my master. 'I should pray twice the number of prayers for you if I weren't so tired after our long journey which has left me too weary to speak . . . too weary indeed and in any event . . . we arrive at our destination, though my legs would lead me in another direction, preferably its opposite.'

Without my noticing, we had indeed come to be standing before the great doors to the refectory. And so, we washed our hands as was the custom, in the crisp cold waters of the little fountain, and my master declared, 'Something bothers me about the note . . .'

'Of course it bothers you,' answered his friend, 'it is an admonition . . . those who want to know too much die knowing very little . . . or perhaps it is that those who know very little die wanting to know a great deal? However, my senses tell me, and they are never wrong, never, that tonight someone will meet his death! It is written . . . of *that* I am certain.'

Andre must have seen my eyes widen with fear, for he said in a very jolly manner, 'Then let us enjoy life while we can, Eisik, for there is nothing to excite one's appetite better than the smell of a mystery!'

Only now do I know how right he truly was!

3

Capitulum

Rainiero Sacconi da Piacenza, as he was formally addressed, entered the refectory like a man conditioned to power. His thin frame, unusually tall, was moderated by square shoulders whose proportions carried the black and white habit of his order well. Moving with strength and agility, as I had seen him do during our travels, he showed little sign of fatigue. Indeed this night he appeared particularly tireless, having – as we heard during various conversations at the table – found suitable housing for prisoners, and another site for the questioning of suspects. In this he was not unlike my master whose own energy seemed to far surpass my own.

What I knew of the inquisitor I had heard through terrible stories whose accuracy I cannot attest to. Nevertheless, he was portrayed as a zealot, ambitious and ruthless, with both eyes focused keenly on the position of supreme inquisitor. Gruesome tales denoted a sadistic nature that delighted in the smell of burning flesh, and so no one can blame an impressionable youth for holding his breath just a little as the man reached the great table and prepared to draw his cowl for the first time. What can I say, dear reader? That I expected to see the face of a devil?

That is, pock-marked and creased, perhaps even biliously yellow? Instead, I was surprised to find that he was, after all, no hideous demon. He was a man whose countenance possessed a kind of comeliness appropriate to a man of his years, but when he lifted his eyes to look upon the congregation, making a long calculated sweep of the room, I saw within their paleness a cold cruelty, a mark of his strong and tested will. For a moment they fell upon me, telling me of devils subdued and men brought to judgement. They said, 'Come, I am ready to challenge any opposition to my wishes.' They revealed his indifference to the opinion of others and at the same time conveyed that guilt – which he knew to be inherent in all men – would be sought out, condemned, and punished, albeit with fraternal understanding . . . all in one brief glance.

The abbot showed the inquisitor to a place beside him at the great table, raised above the others on a dais at the end of the rectangular hall. The table was covered with a grey linen cloth and set with crude but practical implements for our use; wooden bowls replaced silver, and iron candlesticks, not golden ones, provided a soft and pleasant light.

The abbot occupied a central position proper to his station, to his right the inquisitor, my master, and I. To his left, the bishop and the Friar de Narbonne and the esteemed Cistercian brother, with the obidientiaries or more senior brothers of the order flanking us on both sides. Beside me, Brother Ezekiel of Padua made strange noises, perhaps preparing for his forthcoming mastication. He was standing alongside Setubar whose place was beside another brother named Daniel. The rest sat on tables below us, placed at right angles to the dais.

Rainiero noticed Eisik at once, for he was dressed in a plain russet cloak covering a tunic of forest green which contrasted in an explosion of colour amid the toneless grey. He had a place – because of the abbot's generosity – among the monks of lesser station on the tables below, and this made the inquisitor frown in a tempest of disdain. He fixed the Jew with a hard look, muttering some remonstration against the devil under his breath, and blessed himself with ceremonial hatred. Below, the monks stood in silence, cowls drawn, awaiting the intonation of the *'Edent paupers'* and after the benediction was granted, all withdrew their cowls and we gratefully sat down.

As soon as we were all seated, the inquisitor leant in the abbot's direction and pointed to an empty chair on the dais. I heard the abbot say that the infirmarian, because of the distant location of his infirmary, was generally a little late for meals.

'Indulgence,' said the inquisitor, 'leads to disobedience, stern discipline and obedience to the rule is the cornerstone of order, as you know dear abbot, to obey is better than a sacrifice,' he concluded.

Who would argue further?

It was then in silence that we listened to the weekly reading which continued devoutly, even as the refectorian and his assistants placed dishes of unsurpassed variety before us, whose qualities I have since contemplated on more than one occasion. With each dish – and indeed there were many – I was transported to distant lands; Italy, Spain, Portugal, perhaps even unknown places of which old travellers speak. And the guests, particularly those with good appetites, praised the cook and complimented the abbot on a fare that far surpassed the modest meals usually served in monasteries of those times – especially so close to Lent, when one ate almost nothing.

We ate roast pheasant stuffed with red peppers; terrines of pigeon; goose eggs in a sauce of goat's cheese and various delicious herbs. There were black olives stuffed with anchovies, and green olives in a garlic marinade, and on each table, little vases contained golden honey, so light and sweet that even the inquisitor could not help smothering everything he ate in it. All partook of the fare in quiet thankfulness, all except the friar, who behaved in a manner typically Franciscan – because they are of humble birth and so often poorly educated – letting out loud resonant belches.

Afterwards, there was fragrant bread, cooked with cinnamon and almonds, then honeyed dumplings – like those found in Florence. Finally, they brought in the wine, a small flask for each of us, and the abbot told us, because abbeys are known to take pride in their abilities, that it was a delicious mixture of balm leaves and the abbey's own honey. When he saw that my master was declining he told him that it was also said to have wonderful curative and calming properties, because bees were a virtuous insect, as was well known.

The inquisitor made a gesture of disapproval. 'Wine is a mocker, it induces even the wise to apostasy.'

'In that you are quite right!' added the Franciscan yawning.

The Cistercian agreed, casting his unblinking eye over us, 'Wine is not proper for monks.'

The bishop alone said nothing, but filled his glass and downed the lot without taking a breath. 'Ahh . . .' he said at last in his throaty voice. 'Our Lord found it agreeable and I, his simple servant, cannot find it otherwise.'

My master smiled and thanked the abbot graciously, conceding that it did indeed possess a fine colour and was no doubt delicious, but refused his portion.

On hearing this, Brother Ezekiel edged closer to me, and because of his poor vision reached out his hand, searching for the flask. 'Give it to me! By Mary and all her saints, I shall drink it!' he exclaimed loudly, and the server placed it in his hand.

The abbot motioned to stop Ezekiel when Asa, the infirmarian, entered the refectory looking flushed. Hastily finding his seat at the end of the table under the glare of many eyes, he begged his abbot's pardon in inaudible whispers.

The inquisitor muttered, 'I shall put a curb upon my mouth!' but no one else heard him, they were far too preoccupied with their meal, as yet another course of cheeses was brought before them.

When a man eats well, the world appears not only more pleasing to his eye, but he feels gladdened and cheered, and perhaps a little indolent. My master attributed this to the illusion of digestion. He said that the internal organs borrow from the heart and head the energy with which to accomplish this wonderful work and, as was his custom, indulged in eating as much as possible in order to rest his mind. Whatever the cause, however, it had a pleasant effect on all those seated at the table. Even the inquisitor's voice was gradually tempered, and soon he was forgetting his own admonition concerning the silence.

'I see you live contrary to the fifty-seventh capital of your rule, preceptor, namely, *Ut fratres non participent cum excommunicatis.* That is to say, that you are in communication with the excommunicated.'

My master remained surprisingly silent. The pause seemed to last too long, however, and the inquisitor, not about to miss his opportunity, glared in Eisik's direction and in a voice that carried well in the large hall, continued. 'He is a Jew and therefore diabolical. What is your order coming to, preceptor, when it allows into its ranks infidels, and condones communication with Jews?'

My master's face reddened, and I saw his fists clench in his lap.

'The order shall soon stink of dog.'

'Then it shall smell like a most learned dog,' Andre remarked, 'for that dog speaks not only Latin, Rainiero, but six other languages, even as he does his mother tongue.'

In my mind I admonished Andre, for it seemed that he was praising Eisik's accomplishments as a way of justifying their friendship, and I suspected that Eisik may have been right in thinking that he had become prey to culpable sentiments.

'He is a follower of Maimonides?' the Dominican raised

his brows and narrowed his eyes.

'I believe so.'

There was a smile, 'Not only is he a Jewish dog then, an unbeliever, but also a heretic into the bargain!'

'A heretic in whose eyes? Some would say your order had no place in burning Maimonides' books. After all, he was not baptised and so not bound by Christian laws.'

'That may be . . .' the inquisitor dismissed. 'However, all books, especially those of the Jews, contain heresies that undermine the very principle of faith! Even the infidel,' he said with a grin turning up the corners of his mouth, as if to say to my master, 'I should be very pleased to see your infidel carcass upon a burning dais', 'even the infidel,' he continued, 'who is the Devil himself, as you no doubt know, preceptor, finds no affection for this animal. Intellectual pride, this is at the root of all evil!' he said pointing one finger at Eisik. 'Maimonides rejected the resurrection of the body, and said that we can prove neither eternity nor the creation of the world! Furthermore, he approved the saying that 'a bastard who is a scholar takes precedence over an ignorant priest' . . . That he who studies the law, is closer to God, than he who follows it!'

'He said this, Rainiero, at a time when Jewish priests had become decadent, lazy, and so ignorant of the laws which they enforced. No doubt *you* understand? However there is much to be said for a priest who does nothing more than what he is told.'

'Exactly!' exclaimed the inquisitor, thinking my master had finally come to his senses. 'Ignorance is a blissful state, preceptor, one obeys what one is told to obey. After all, obedience is the cornerstone of our rule, obedience! Learning, however, is the way to apostasy, the way to wilfulness and the gratification of self.'

There were whispers of acquiescence among the various delegates. The bishop and the others sat back with fraternal indulgence, patting their ample bellies in communal understanding.

'And yet,' continued my master, biting into a hunk of cheese as though he wished it were the inquisitor's neck, 'should one be forced to accept religion without reason?'

The Bishop of Toulouse frowned and leant over the table, his mouth framed by two huge, wet, lips. 'But it is the church that decides what is reasonable,' he waved a hand imperiously, 'and not the individual, preceptor, that is common and undisputed knowledge!'

There were nods and smiles, their faces aglow with the fire of wine that by now they had all consumed, despite their previous apprehensions.

'Then, your grace,' my master said, his dark, Arabic face filled with the thrill of restrained battle-anger, for his eyes shone a brilliant metallic green, 'I see how the church must be burdened.'

'Burdened . . . yes . . .' the Friar de Narbonne answered, in somnolent vacuity, and then frowning, as though suddenly confused, he asked, 'by what in particular, preceptor?'

'Why, burdened by a deep contradiction friar, namely, that the Roman church has come to rely so heavily on those learned men whom it despises, and on whose wisdom rests an entire body of theological material that has become the foundation of its own philosophy.' Satisfied, he bit into a dumpling, and waited for a reply.

'Why should this concern the church, preceptor?' asked the bishop, shrugging his fat shoulders, lacking a little, if I may say, in what the Greeks call intellect.

'Perhaps it should not concern the church at all. After all, the world is ruled by contradiction, nature itself is the greatest paradox . . . and yet,' my master paused, and I saw the churchmen move forward a little in their seats, 'it bears consideration. There may come a time when the canon lawyers and theologians disagree with the pope. One can only then imagine the dreadful circumstance, my brothers . . . Shall we have a pontiff whose weakness is ruled by the wisdom of earthly men, and not by the wisdom of God? Or shall we have a pope who ignores the wisdom of his theologians because he is ignorant?' My master then quoted Plato in Greek, saying, 'What is just or right means nothing, but what is in the interest of the stronger party.'

There was a confused silence, and to my delight I saw a congregation of frowns. The abbey's head librarian, Brother Macabus, a middle-aged monk with very curly hair, deep folds under both eyes, and a curiously small nose, answered my master, also in Greek, 'Is that which is holy loved by the Gods because it is holy, or is it holy because it is loved by the Gods?'

My master smiled. 'Indeed. Is that not a timeless question, brother?'

The pope's legation was silent. The only sound was that of men shifting in their seats with obvious bewilderment.

From my right there came a voice, 'The Greeks honoured the body more than the soul.' It was Brother Setubar, the old bent monk, speaking in slow deliberate words. 'They were fools! Learning is only good for the body, the soul nourishes itself with spiritual things. As a physician I knew this, and so I learnt only what was necessary and no more. It is only pride that moves a man to know more than he ought to know, and it is pride which makes him think that he knows more than he should! We are born and from that moment we are *depravati* . . . corrupt, a body that dies little by little, that is all we need to know, everything else is dung!' He ended, muttering something in his own German vernacular.

'And yet Peter tells us,' my master retorted, 'that one must travel through the barren desert of doubt to find at its end the green meadows of faith and comprehension. A faith that is enlightened by knowledge. Peter denied Christ and was absolved.'

'Peter was absolved, but Judas atones in hell for his sins!' the old man cried. 'Man should seek to know God! He should not seek knowledge of the world!'

It was at this point that I realised my master had manipulated the entire conversation in order to investigate the mysterious author of the note and I admonished myself for having thought ill of his intentions.

'God is knowledge, venerable brother, by definition, and he did indeed create the world as we are told in Genesis,' Andre said finally, almost a little heated now.

'Yes, preceptor,' Rainiero joined in, 'but knowledge of God and knowledge of the world are not the same thing! One must shun the world and its iniquity and live only for revelation, in contemplation of holy scripture.'

My master smiled a terrible smile, close to a leer. 'Then, by God! you have much in common with my Jewish friend, for he believes the same thing.'

We had come around full circle.

The inquisitor, full of malice, held his breath until his lips were almost blue. 'Jews are fomenters of dissent, responsible for infecting Christian heresies – which are in any case multifarious – with the devil of cabbala. And if that were not a most heinous sin, they allow their adulterations to land in the curious hands of Christians who eagerly consume their demonic formulas!'

'Formulas?' my master inquired, raising a thick brow.

'Everyone knows them, preceptor . . . the mystical meanings of mystical acts; numbers that are diabolically numerical; letters that are more meaningful than words, and words that have no meaning unless read backwards. Points and strokes, ciphers, acrostics and the unholy symbolic interpretation of biblical texts! Necromancia, astrologia, alchemia!'

When he finished, there was a hush, the other members of the legation looked down at their hands or their plates, shifting in their seats in an embarrassed fashion.

'Your erudition is remarkable, Rainiero!' my master remarked. 'You must have spent many moments studying these things!'

'You know being a man of war,' he answered caustically, 'that one cannot fight an unknown enemy. One must rather study an adversary's every move, every thought . . . even if doing so constitutes a perpetual affront to one's mildness and tranquillity of soul.' He then raised his face, and rolled his eyes in a heavenly direction. 'Often I am haunted! Haunted by those things that have come into my hands through the power afforded me! The most terrible works! The most heinous depravities! And yet I have forced myself to become familiar with the errors of the Devil, lest his falsehoods be mistaken for truths. I say, blessed is the man who is ignorant, blessed is he whose soul is protected from the weakness of his intellect!'

My master considered this for a moment. 'But your grace the evil one does not merely work, as you know, through primary causes, that is, in a writer's thoughts, but also through secondary causes, namely, in the disposition of the reader.'

The bishop filled his mouth with food, letting the juices run down the corners of his mouth. 'That is also true,' he confirmed and tore into the carcass of a bird.

The inquisitor huffed. 'You Templars are strange creatures. I have no liking for monks of your sort, I divine that you are doomed to die on the pyre for your heretic sympathies, and that to lead you to such an end would be a task most honoured!'

There followed a stunned silence at this open threat. My master smiled so calmly that I felt a terrible sense of foreboding, for I feared he might at any moment lose his temper.

'We *all* live in a permanent state of fragility, inquisitor, and the only immutable truth is that truth is capricious, and perpetuity uncertain. One thing, however, has remained constant throughout the eons of time, and I believe it shall continue to do so for many more, the evil of which I speak is ignorance. I believe it to be the worst sin, because it leads to all other sins . . . It was ignorance that nailed our Saviour to the cross that fateful Friday, and it would be ignorance that would burn him at the stake today if He were to threaten the power of the Church, in the same way that He threatened the power of Caesar.'

Alas, my fears were realised. All eyes enlarged and mouths gaped open in incredulity and I knew at once that my master had made a terrible mistake.

But the moment was rescued by the abbot, who invited us to be quiet and listen to the reading of the rule, which he said had been specially requested by the inquisitor. It consisted of an admonition to all spiritual fathers as to their teachings and the obedience of their disciples. We were told that any lack of goodness found in his flock would be accounted the shepherd's fault at which point the reader's voice broke a little and he gazed up from the holy book in the direction of the abbot's table. The abbot gestured for the reader to continue, though a worried frown graced his brow.

Later, after the customary formalities, we departed in silence through the great doors that led to the cloister and from there headed in the direction of the chapel in quiet procession. More than once I thought I caught the evil eye of the inquisitor and his men cast in our direction, and I prayed for God's protection, though at the time I did not know how much we would come to need it.

4

Capitulum

Completorium (Compline)

And so it was that the last service of the day began in the usual manner, after the sun had descended below the horizon. Firstly the abbot gave the master of music the signal to intone, *'Tu autem, domine, miserere nobis,'* with our response, *'Deo Gratias',* followed by the abbot's reply, *'Adjutorium nostrum in nomine Domini,'* to which we replied in chorus, *'Qui fecit caelum et terram'.*

This is the time of day when a good monk prepares to place his soul into God's hands. For sleep is a preparation for death, in which the external world is extinguished, and the world of the spirit is illuminated by the light of the soul. In this death, we are told, there is the promise of life and so, sitting in the shadows of the stalls, comforted by the warmth of many bodies, I was reminded that our life is not without end, that in the same way the orb of the daystar sinks into the bosom of the dark horizon, so too our bodies return to the earth. Yet it is from out of this darkness where things seem most hopeless that the sun journeys back to triumph. So too, we are told that man must triumph over death to find a new horizon awaiting him in the cradle of divinity. At this moment I wanted to believe that the world was good, that the captains and hallowed judges that formed the body of the Holy Inquisition (surely a reflection of God's infinite justice and mercy?) were righteous and pure. Why then was I assailed by sentiments so close to those I felt that day on the banks of the Nile? I looked about me at the faces of the congregation, trying to dispel my fears by reminding myself of my vows. Had I not yearned for a cloister? To be safely sequestered from the vicissitudes of a vain and depraved world, where one feels only an intense peace? Now I was realising that dangers lay not only in a battlefield, and I shuddered. I turned my mind to the intoning of the opening versicles and responses, '*Converte nos . . . Et averte . . .*' and '*Deus in adjutorium*' which were now beginning and determined to think no more of such things. Surely I was tired? Tomorrow a day would dawn anew and my fears would dissipate along with the darkness, which now oppressed my soul. Was not my master, who sat beside me, a bastion of strength, a fortress of wisdom? Moreover, who could contest the authority of the king? I realized that perhaps the inquisitor was right when he said that an ignorant man was a happy man. For ignorant as I was, I began to feel a little better, joining the many masculine voices merging respective tones and qualities into one. Entering that great animal whose individual members are only as perfect as the sum of its totality; the great body of the divine archetype, whose only purpose is the glorification of God.

As my lips intoned those first words, '*Hear me call, O God of my righteousness: thou hast enlarged me when I was in distress.*' I felt a calm sweetness. In humility there is constancy, I concluded, and in obedience there is also peace. Perhaps if my master were more obedient he would find calmness of spirit?

After the four prescribed psalms, the abbot took his place at the pulpit. He began with a short, eloquent speech in which he once again welcomed the pope's envoy to the monastery, declaring the innocence of the abbey, and further adding his unswerving belief in God's protection during the forthcoming inquiry.

And because Completorium was a time for reflection, a time for the examination of the conscience, as spiritual father, he also publicly forgave all those who were responsible for bringing the terrible calamity upon them, and cautioned the brothers of the order to take a moment to examine their hearts for any feeling of ill will that may have taken root there. He then announced that, for this reason, the reading would not be taken from Jeremiah, chapter 14, as was customary, but from the Book of Revelation which, he stated, should serve to remind us of our task against evil, of the battle that is waged in the soul against pride, and envy, and vainglory. He announced that Brother Sacar of Montelimar, the master of music, should give the lesson, and he stepped down.

I stifled a yawn as the monk climbed into the pulpit and began his sermon. Despite his subject – horrifying descriptions of hell and death – and despite his inspired phrasing – the phrasing of one accustomed to melodic formulas – my eyes, God forgive me, were growing heavy. The brother's words seemed to escape from his lips like phantoms whose natures were one with the spectres created by the light from the great tripod, and I fancied I could see many hovering above, tumbling and frolicking with the echoes of words deflected by the high vaults of the church. Not only did I see words, but also thoughts meeting those words! They danced along the arches of the temple, sliding down the columns like little children and coming to rest above the many cowled heads in the choir. Flames, each differing in colour and hue, rose from each brother. I saw pride welling up from the secret corners of the heart, forming (or so I thought) the shapes of animals. Before my eyes a lion entangled with a dragon, a serpent curled hissing around the form of an eagle, here a lamb, there a cow!

Above the inquisitor, I imagined an ugly little devil with two heads, clinging to his shoulders, each head whispering into one of his large ears. Above the Cistercian emissary sat a viper, on the friar a monkey . . . on the bishop a pig! Had I been awake (thank the Lord God I was not) I would have laughed. However it was in a kind of perfect dream-lucidity that I witnessed weakness, desire, and hatred, as a painter sees colours laid out upon his palette. Incredulous, I contemplated the likelihood of a young novice having such visions, but I remembered having heard that devils were responsible for many things. One monk wrote that they made him cough and sneeze in church, and that one troop of devils spent all their efforts weighting his eyes and closing his eyelids, and others snored in front of his nose, so that the brother next to him believed that it was he who was snoring and not the devils. Indeed, devils are said to make monks sing badly, for one tells of seeing a devil like a white-hot iron come out of the mouth of a monk who had started a higher note by mistake. And so, I wondered with detached calm if this monk speaking before me had created such spectres – by the aid of some infernal magic – to confound the inquiry? Perhaps it was a good thing that the inquisitor was here? Perhaps there was a terrible power at work in this abbey? I was weary, my eyes sought the solace of that moment of dark peace, and soon the world around me became drops in a pool, rippling, embracing and diffused, until I could no longer distinguish or define anything. I felt the flame pale to a comfortable glow, only to awake to a chorus of gasps. I looked around sleepily to find that Brother Ezekiel was standing at the end of the row of stalls. He uncovered his white skull with one translucent hand, and turned his gaze to a point in the distance above all our heads, perhaps to an imaginary landscape where his eyes saw an eternity of damnation . . . on the other hand, he may have been seeing the same visions that I had seen only moments before!

'Heed ye sinners! The antichrist is at hand!' There was a sudden terrible silence. 'And it was John,' he continued, 'the one whom Jesus loved, who beheld the beast coming up out of the earth with two horns like a lamb, and he spake as a dragon; and he exerciseth all the power of the first beast causing all to receive a mark on their right hand, or on their foreheads that no man might buy or sell, save he that had the mark, or the name of the beast, or the number of his name . . . Blessed is he who can name the number of the beast for it is the number of a man!'

There was a great commotion. The abbot stood, the inquisitor followed.

'He is here,' Ezekiel hissed. 'He comes to tear away your anima and drive you into the pit! You who have been dragged down into sin because your body is material, and material because it is sinful! You who have become food for the devil!'

Here he paused for breath, and the abbot, perhaps seeing his chance, called out, 'Brother Ezekiel! In the name of God!' he was trying to get past monks who had thrown themselves on the floor of the stalls moaning, but the man continued despite the command.

'It has been written . . . and so it shall be! Heed the word my people – *Audi populos meos!* For the seven letters have been sent! The seven communities have been warned! He will come, it is certain, but now he hides, *furtivus!* But while he waits, he feeds on cleverness! Fattening his belly with the beast of knowledge, waiting for the *secundum millennium,* when he will try to overcome the sublime Holiness! Then it will not suffice to turn your sorry countenances to the heavens and say; save me because you are merciful! *Convertere Domine, et eripe animam meam . . . salvum me fac propter misericordiam tuam!* For the Scorpion will have already found the iniquitous, *omnes qui operamini iniquitatem!* And all of you will be driven into that dark eternal flame of hell, because the world will have fallen into lawlessness and men will be blown hither and thither by the fetid breath whose magic will be blasphemy, whose name will be treachery, whose legacy is darkness! I am old, but I see you! You follow the beast! You are the fattened calf!' He pointed in the direction of the pope's men. 'You carry out his business, you believe the foulness of his words. And the

crown will join with the antipope, and like two snakes they cop-
ulate, they entwine in an evil union! Deceit, hypocrisy, violence!
You search for him but you will not find the *cuniculus* . . . No, you
will not find it! You will not rob him of the sacred, little jewel.'
Ezekiel then smiled hideously, for he had no teeth. 'Ahh but the
widow is wise!'

He grabbed at his throat then, in an anguished gesture.
All of us sat transfixed, so shocked were we to hear such things.
The abbot once again made a vain attempt to reach him, but
there was now a great commotion, a kind of hysteria had overtaken everyone, many had taken to their knees, crying and pulling
out their hair.

'You feed the genius of the demon! The genius of numbers! And the number is 666 the number of . . . SORATH!'

Monks wailed, covering up their ears as though assailed
by countless agonies. Some fainted, others, horrified, crossed
themselves, shaking their heads and thrashing their bodies about.
'Salva me!' They cried and moaned, eyes upturned towards the
vaults of the cathedral.

The old monk raised his voice once again in a terrible
shrillness, amid the horror and confusion. 'Sorath!' His face was
filled with a vision that only he could see. 'I am flying! Have mercy on me, Lord, *Miserere mei, Deus, rere mei, for my soul trusteth in thee*
. . . I FLY!'

These last words sounded hollow. He choked and
coughed in a terrible way, gasping for breath, and his eyes bulged
as he reached out one hand like a drowning man. Not long after,
the life seemed to drain from his body and he doubled over, his
limbs still twitching uncontrollably as he collapsed on the floor
of the stall. Someone shouted. 'There is a fluid coming from his
mouth!'

That was all I saw, for my master told me to go outside
and wait for him in the cloister, but later I was to see that the old
monk had died clasping the wooden cross around his neck so

tightly that the infirmarian could not prise his fingers away from it when he attempted to wash him for burial.

I waited for my master as I had been instructed, and presently, the abbot sent the brothers to their dormitories, and I was left alone in the darkness. Thankfully it was only moments before Andre returned from the church wearing a worried frown, and I hurried to meet him, as simultaneously the inquisitor intercepted us, flanked by the other members of the legation.

'Preceptor,' he said with gravity, his eyes falling upon my master with slight irritation. 'It is sadly worse than we could have imagined. The evil one has visited us, and we cannot ignore his diabolical signs. He has this night revealed his infernal face so that we may bring about an expeditious and orderly resolution to this inquiry.'

'How obliging of him,' my master said, his thick brows knitted. There was a pause.

'Merely fortuitous,' replied the inquisitor.

'But I find that almost always what is fortuitous is only so for the sake of convenience, Rainiero.'

The Bishop of Toulouse moved forward trembling, and in a whisper said to us, 'God has revealed the Devil's infernal face to us, preceptor, we cannot ignore his message, surely?'

My master did not answer him. From the folds of his habit he produced an apple and bit into it, chewing.

The party watched in disbelief, but the friar was the only one to speak, in a voice that sounded scared and at the same time bored, 'Preceptor, why should we think anything else? You were there, you saw the Devil take hold of that wretched man!' He looked around at the others. 'We all saw it!'

There was a general agreement.

'We must take care, dear brothers,' Andre replied after a lengthy chew, 'not to base our recriminations on the confused and distorted words of one dying monk.'

'Yes, words,' the bishop stifled a belch, 'heretical and heinous, spoken by a Cathar!'

'In any event,' the inquisitor dismissed, 'at this moment guards search his cell for proofs of his dissent and if we find this abbey has been protecting and harbouring apostates – as we shall soon know – it may also be guilty of other more terrible crimes. 'Let the ungodly fall into their own nets together . . . that they may not escape!'

My master raised his chin slightly and I saw adversarial fire in his eyes. 'Proverbs tells us that we must not boast of to-morrow; for we do not know what a day may bring forth.'

The inquisitor stared at my master in the way wild creatures stare before devouring their prey. 'Must I remind you of your position here? Think not that your authority surpasses . . .'

'Rainiero,' my master forestalled his next remark with a gesture of his hand, 'I am only advising a little patience. After all we have heard these ravings before. There are many who still await the prophesies of that poor abbot of Fiora. Indeed, there is far too much study of the apocalypse . . . and yet, this is not a crime, surely.'

'You say this, Preceptor,' the inquisitor said patiently, as though explaining some trifle to a child, 'because you have not seen the patient work of the Devil as it unfolds in all its subtlety before one's eyes . . . He spoke of the antipope, and he aimed his words at the legation . . .'

'But the man was nearly blind, Rainiero,' my master replied, 'he could have been aiming his countenance in any direction!'

'Even more diabolical!' the Cistercian gasped, his un-blinking eyes even wider than usual. The others crossed themselves in anticipated horror. 'A blind man sees through the eyes of the Devil,' he continued, 'who then consumes his instrument and seizes his immortal soul!'

All around there were disconsolate gasps, and with a hint of satisfaction the inquisitor raised his voice, 'This abbey is cursed! This I know!'

'Then it should be a simple matter to prove it,' my master said, using a tone, which implied that his part in the conversation was over. 'And since this is your task I will bid you a good night. Come, Christian, one prayer before bed.' He pulled me away from the legation, and I was glad, for I was a little overcome.

'I did not think Templars had much time for prayer,' the inquisitor retorted after us, 'only for killing and pillaging . . . one only wonders at the wisdom of a king who places so much faith in renegade warriors.'

'We are all warriors, Rainiero,' my master answered, turning around. 'Some of us, however, battle against the true enemies of the faith, while others battle . . . elusive ones.'

At this point there occurred a strange thing between the two men. I saw their dislike for one another turn into a terrible rivalry that raised its head like a beast between them. 'I will admonish you to stay *en garde!* Whatever you may believe, preceptor. For it is beyond speculation that in this place Satan's minions roam.' He paused, giving me his attention. 'Do you hear the moans of the succubus, my beautiful one?' I thought for one horrible moment that I could indeed hear them. 'They course through the abbey looking for their next victim . . .' He reached out his hand to caress my face. 'One may not be safe even in God's house.'

I felt a wave of nausea overcome me as he paused moments before touching my cheek. With a slight look of longing in his cold eyes, he withdrew his hand, but slowly, so that I seemed to hold my breath for a long time. 'Narrow indeed is the way that leadeth unto life,' he concluded.

'Thank you for your concern, your grace,' my master interjected. 'You need not worry, we shall be vigilant.'

The inquisitor's teeth glistened like diamonds between thin lips, and he drew his cowl over his face turning to the others in silence, and they left us, melting into the darkness of the cloisters.

We walked to the south transept door and I must have looked disturbed, for my master said soothingly, 'Your mind must not linger too long on other men's aberrations. As incredible as it may seem, it is known that there are those whose sentiments run to unnatural desires. Of all sins it is one of the most abominable, but there's no sense in crying over it. Come with me and think no more on it.' I could see his strong silhouette in the darkness, and I thanked God for his wisdom.

We made our way to the choir stalls in the shadow of the great tripod at the altar. I paused for a moment before it, and said a short prayer to keep the Devil at bay.

'You see, Rainiero has managed to accomplish much this evening,' my master said, annoyed.

'What do you mean?' I asked after I had crossed myself.

'It is the job of an inquisitor to instil fear into the hearts of men, and I must say Rainiero does it well. He has you and the others fearful of your own shadows, believing in untold evils, exactly as he intended.'

'I'm not afraid, master . . .'

'Christian,' he sighed,' you should never show a mad dog that you are fearful, for the moment he senses it he will attack without mercy . . . beware of the dog – *cave canem – Domini canes.*'

I frowned at his play of words. 'So what should one do, then?'

'You must hold his gaze, never swerve for a moment, and run like an infidel!' He laughed then, but I was not surprised, for I had observed this peculiarity before in men of eastern race; that they laughed at strange things, and so I changed the subject lest his impious comparison of the inquisitor to a dog result in some terrible heavenly retribution.

'What about the old monk?'

'He is dead, that must be obvious even to you, but the cause will not become apparent until we have had time to examine the evidence, namely the body. At this moment the infirmarian, our eager brother Asa, waits for me so that together we can execute a concurrent examination. Until that time I'm afraid we shall have to reserve our judgements, lest we desire to look like fools later . . .' He searched my face, 'Oh for heaven's sake, boy, one would think you had never seen a man die! He was old, how many have you seen die in the flower of youth, run through with a lance or a blade? To live beyond a certain age may seem a gift from God, but to many it is a curse from his infernal adversary. Though I will grant you it is far preferable to die sleeping, quietly and without fuss . . .'

'Actually, I have been wondering about the name the old monk kept calling out . . . the name . . .'

'Sorath?'

'A strange name. I've never heard it before, but it seemed to inspire such fear.'

'Of course you've heard it! The man himself told us as much; he is the sun demon.'

'So he is like a devil?'

'His name comes from the Greek vernacular, and so he is a pagan devil more wretched than Satan or Lucifer, we are told.'

'But I thought there was only one evil one?'

'Evil wears many faces, dear boy, like a body with many limbs through which works the one infernal intelligence.' My master smiled and I was afraid for his immortal soul.

'Don't look at me that way . . . I smile because here we have found another piece to our puzzle, like a hilt to a sword, it fits perfectly, that is all!'

'Another piece?'

'Sorath is a Gnostic devil, this is well known.'

And so it did not surprise me that I did not know it, for very often what he mistook for common knowledge was simply not so.

'And how do you know about him, master?' I ventured, perhaps a little impudently.

'I make it my business to know many things!' he fired at me. 'Now, stop asking me stupid questions, for you are interrupting the flow of my thoughts . . .' He cupped his beard in one hand and supported his arm with the other. For all his bad mood, he appeared to be well pleased. But I, dear reader, was miserable, because I could not forget the look on the old monk's face in that final moment; a face filled with so much pain that it seemed close to immense pleasure.

'Also,' he broke through my meditations, 'did you not hear what he said?'

'What he said?'

'By the sword of Saladin, boy, where are your wits?' he cried and his voice reverberated in the holy room, 'Did you not hear these words, 'They will not find the one . . .'?'

'But the who one, master?'

'Well, how should I know?' He seemed at the point of exasperation. 'It is not significant that we know whom, for that will come when we have discovered where and when, and this where could quite possibly be the cuniculus . . .' Seeing my blank face, he said, 'Come boy . . . the tunnel . . .'

'What tunnel?'

'If you had been asleep you might have a plausible excuse – though it would still be a poor one – for this lapse in observation. But as you were awake I must conclude that you were stupefied.'

'I'm sorry, master, but it all happened so suddenly and even if I had heard what he said, I would still not have understood it. What tunnel?'

'Precisely. That is what we must find out. It is again as I thought. There are tunnels under this abbey . . .' he muttered, 'tunnels . . .'

I nodded, feeling ashamed at not having come to the same conclusion.

Andre added, 'He also said something about a widow being wise.'

'But what has a widow to do with a monastery?' 'It points
to a sect called the Manicheans.' 'The who?'

'A sect led by Manes, known in the early centuries as the
'son of a widow'. Cathars, my boy, believe in Manichean ideals –
in other words, heresy. The inquisitor was right about one thing,
our dead brother spoke like a heretic.' 'So we know then, master,
that there are heretics here, and that there are also tunnels in
which, perhaps, some are hidden?' 'You have made up for your
lack of wits! Yes, that's it . . . for now that is what we know.' I
nodded a little pleased, though, to be honest, I remained confused.

We made our way through the stalls to that which had
previously been occupied by the dead brother. Here, on the
ground where the poor man fell, there remained a little pool of
brownish fluid.

'And the note?' I asked, looking away, trying not to imagine what it was like to die such an agonising death, 'Do you think
it has anything to do with the brother's death?'

My master seemed to ignore me, and began his inspection by picking up a small something, which I could not quite see.
'Raisins.' He sniffed it. 'Old men are always eating raisins, it helps
to restore the saliva . . . Now to answer your question: all things
are possible in the beginning. Let us progress through our chain
of causes, we shall then be in a better position to say many more
things with confidence. If the poor monk was murdered, the question we must ask ourselves is why? The note read that he who
seeks the light of knowledge dies in ignorance. What could this
mean? Let us ruminate. Could it mean that our Brother Ezekiel
was a seeker of knowledge? Or did he merely die in ignorance?
Perhaps he sought the light of knowledge because he was going
blind, or he may have been in possession of a knowledge that
someone wants to keep in the dark? Only the abbot knew that we
were about to ask him questions.'

'So the abbot is a suspect, then?'

'Right now, it is as though we were a good distance away from a friend, and in our eagerness we run to him and call out his name...'

'Only to find that he is not our friend at all, but one who bears a likeness to him.'

'So you remember Plato, well done! We will have deceived ourselves, because we were looking only at the general things, which, from a distance, are only ill defined; his height, his weight, the colour of his hair, so on. And not at the particulars which, on closer inspection, reveal his nose, eyes, the peculiar turn of his mouth. You see, from a distance, he could be anyone. And that is how we must think, until we come closer. We will then see with clarity, that is, one step at a time. Sometimes, however, one can see better from a distance, and at other times it is preferable if the object of our attention comes to us. Remember to follow outward signs is to be like the captive in a cave who believes the shadows cast by a fire to be the real world and not what lies above and outside the cave. So, as captives we must allow the nature of things to tell us their secrets. That means that we must listen carefully, and reserve our judgements for a later time. At any rate, at this stage all we see is a man who is not a man but a eunuch, throwing a stone that is not a stone, but a pumice-stone, at a bird that is not a bird, but a bat, sitting on a twig that is not a twig, but a reed!'

'You mean nothing is what it seems?'

'Precisely.' He bent over and retrieved something from the ground beneath the seat. He inspected it, 'Another raisin . . .'

'Do you think it was the inquisitor, then?'

'Hm?' My master looked up from his kneeling position. 'The inquisitor? The inquisitor what? What are you saying now?' He bellowed.

'Do you think he wrote the note?'

'Why should he have written it?' He continued looking about beneath the seats. I looked away, for it did not seem a very dignified position for a master.

'Because he does not want our interference.' I answered, 'he may have been warning us not to meddle in the inquiry.'

'Whoever wrote the note is clever, for he has a command of Greek, and the inquisitor knows no Greek at all, not having recognised my vulgar use of it at the dinner table this evening. No, I'll wager five hundred Saracen ducats that someone is playing a little game with us.'

'So, the librarian? Brother Macabus?'

'It is possible,' he nodded, 'because he has a good command of the language, however, we must not discount the possibility that there might be others who know Greek. I suspect that the author of our little note would not have been so imprudent as to announce his identity in such an obvious way. Then there is Setubar . . . but he cannot use his hands, have you seen them? They are so gnarled that he cannot pick up a spoon, let alone a quill . . .'

'Why Greek, then?'

'That is a good question. Perhaps the author wanted only those who knew Greek to understand it?'

'Perhaps he did so, master,' I added, 'to throw suspicion on the librarian?'

'Perhaps . . . though monks are rarely so clever in matters of intrigue. Now help me up.' I held out a hand to him and he took it. I knew his knees caused him endless suffering. 'Damn the Count of Artois to the bowels of hell for ruining my legs!' he said breathlessly, then, after a moment of recovery, 'Now, we shall hunt for tunnels, there must be catacombs somewhere down there.'

'Tonight?' I inquired, hoping that I sounded calm.

'There must be a crypt. A ghastly cold place . . . no, not tonight. My knees are frozen stiff and also, Asa awaits us in the infirmary.'

And so saying, we left the church, stepping out into the

cold cloister, and made our way to the aperture. We found, how-ever, that we could not exit through it because it was locked, so we tried the kitchen door. It was open. My master ventured to the larder from which he emerged holding two carrots, one of which he (most graciously) handed to me. Taking an audible bite of it, he tried the door that led to the garden, but it had been locked from the inside, forcing us to enter the church once more and exit through the north transept door which was customarily open throughout the night.

'Strange that the cookhouse has one door locked and not the other . . .' my master said, thinking out loud as he chewed.

The night was cold, but the sky was dotted with flickering stars. I noticed high above in the dormitorium the circa or night monk making his rounds and it occurred to me that his life must be very lonely, for he must pass the endless hours of the night alone, saying psalms. A moment later we entered the cheering warmth of the infirmary to see that Brother Asa had already begun his gruesome investigation by washing the body. Sitting a little way off, near a large fire of smouldering embers, was old Setubar. Everything in the room seemed moulded by his venerable will, including his pupil. But the old man's face, so often sour and impassive, beamed in a benevolent smile as he offered me a place beside him, and I wondered what had occasioned his sudden good humour.

'What have you found, Asa?' my master asked almost im-mediately, carrot in hand.

The man looked up myopically from his work, a deep scowl creasing his thin face. 'Nothing. I find nothing.'

'Well then, the poor man must have died of excitement,' my master concluded, 'and yet I can see why you look troubled.'

'You can? I mean . . . I do?' the infirmarian asked, as be-wildered as I.

'Yes, of course, and I cannot say that I blame you.'

'No? But . . .' Asa looked to his master Setubar for guidance. 'I do not understand, preceptor? You have not even seen the body?'

'I do not need to see it, brother, to know that you have a problem.'

'I do?'

'Of course. You have a problem, a most unfortunate, puzzling one, because you know that the symptoms this corpse displayed in the throes of death coincide precisely with death by poisoning.'

The man was shocked into silence and my master savoured his next words. 'A problem . . . and yet at this point we must be prudent, my dear colleague.'

'Prudent?'

'Yes, Asa,' the old man broke in, in the solemn way of Germans. 'The Templar preceptor, who is also a respected doctor as you know, is displaying wisdom. We cannot be certain, and so we must be very circumspect, for we do not wish to alarm our community nor disturb the inquiry with foolish assumptions.'

Asa's eyes held the old man's gaze for a moment. 'Master, perhaps . . .'

'Nonsense!' the old man exclaimed with authority, 'The monk was old, it was time he died, perhaps his heart ceased to beat?'

My master sensed that he had stirred up something between the two men, and this pleased him, for he took another bite and chewed his carrot smiling. 'Brother Setubar, you were the infirmarian before Brother Asa?' he asked, abruptly changing the subject.

The old man eyed Andre with a great, unreserved suspicion. 'I held this esteemed position for many years, though I did not particularly relish it. Now I am enjoying the accomplishments of my pupil, though he still needs a little guidance.'

'Was it you then that amassed this fine collection of simples?' he asked, investigating the shelves crowded with vials, earthenware pots, and jars of thick glass in which various coloured powders were distinguished by labels in strange vernaculars. He stopped more than once to investigate further, picking one out from the rest, opening its lid, and sniffing its contents.

'A small, though comprehensive, collection that you might find interesting,' the man said a little proudly, suddenly unguarded. 'Some were gifts from pilgrims travelling from every part of the known world, as repayment for lodgings and food.'

'And what lies behind this door?' my master pointed with his carrot to an aperture on the far wall to one side of the fire.

The infirmarian, without glancing up from his work, answered, 'The chapel, preceptor.'

I knew it was common practice for monasteries to have a small chapel near the infirmary for those whose illness prevented them from attending the services in the community church. However, I noted a lingering curiosity in my master's eyes.

'Yes, of course . . . and now, on another matter, do you keep poisons here or in the herbarium, Asa?'

'Any *potentia*, used incorrectly, may be said to be a poison, preceptor,' Asa pointed out.

'No, I mean a specific poison, something very potent, that only requires the smallest amount to kill.'

'We do have various substances, powders, derived from herbs we dry in our herbarium, *atropa belladonna, colchicum autumnale, digitalis purpurea, datura stramonium.* These compounds are very good in minute amounts for various treatments, but they are at the same time deadly. You don't think that . . .'

'I am exploring all possibilities, brother, and also I have to admit, all things curious interest me . . .'

'We are not here to satisfy your curiosity of insignificant things, preceptor,' the old man snarled.

'No, you are quite right, I shall endeavour to be curious only of significant ones . . . and as it appears significant, I shall ask you where you keep these herbal compounds. Not in the reach of any person who might wander in, I hope?'

'No, of course not!' Setubar answered. 'No one but the infirmarian and I have access to such things in the herbarium. We alone hold the keys.'

'A prudent decision.' There was a thoughtful pause. 'On another matter, do you supply the monastery with any other substances apart from medicinal ones?'

'We make our own ink,' Asa said, 'from the wood of thorntrees. I collect this wood for I am very often in the forest. However, the making of amalgam for applying gold leaf, the tempering of colours, and the production of glue, these things I leave to others who specialise in these arts.'

'Yes, I see.' My master then moved closer to the body on the great table, whose ashen features were troublesome, especially since there was a strange redness collecting on those parts beneath the trunk, lower arms and legs. Later my master was to tell me that when the heart stops beating the blood no longer circulates around the body, but collects in the areas where the body happens to be lying for a time after death, and this sometimes can indicate the length of time between a death and its discovery.

'There is no bruising?' he asked.

'No, preceptor.'

My master handed me the stub of carrot and proceeded to his inspection of the body, firstly the feet, noting that they were covered in a red mud.

'This is curious . . . clay?'

The infirmarian peered at the dead man's feet. 'So it is.'

'But the abbey rests on dry, rocky earth,' my master said thoughtfully.

'Indeed, though if one digs lower, as I have occasion to do in the garden, a moist red earth reveals itself.'

'I see.'

He continued working his way up the legs of the body, the torso, arms, and finally the fingers and hands.

'His hands are sticky.'

'Brother Ezekiel had a sweet tooth,' said the old man in reply.

'Ahh yes, the raisins.' My master then searched the cadaver's face, his ears, his eyes, and mouth. I looked away as he opened it and sniffed inside. 'Was the venerable brother suffering from any illness or disorder that might account for his death? I can see his blood did not circulate well around his legs for here we see evidence of past ulceration, am I correct?'

'Yes, if he were to bump his extremities in the slightest, his skin would tear, and within a few hours a terrible wound would develop,' Asa answered.

'And he was going blind, was he not?' my master said, looking up.

'Yes, for many years.'

'We are then perhaps looking at the body of a man who suffered from a disease known in the east whose designation escapes me . . .' He then quoted a medical text. 'Just as the *corpus* of a man does not respire *aqua*,' he said, 'and a fish does not breathe air, so do many innocent substances kill those whose organisms find them unsuitable. It is only conjecture at this point, of course,' my master stated, 'but much knowledge can be gained by using the art of diagnostics.'

'Yes, the skill of the Greeks,' said Asa, who then became very thoughtful. 'You remember his continual somnolence, Brother Setubar? His thirst, and constant need to relieve himself?'

Brother Setubar grunted a little in answer.

'Of course . . . I am a fool!' The infirmarian slapped the side of his face with one hand, then.

'No, it is not always easy to diagnose,' my master assuaged, 'and yet his breath could have secured your confidence in this hypothesis, for it would have been very sweet. Did his urine have the familiar smell?'

'Sweet?'

'No, caustic.'

'Caustic?'

'Caustic . . .' My master washed his hands in a bowl of warm water and took his carrot stub from me. 'One whose body is afflicted with this condition cannot dissolve the *materia* of sweet *potentia,* it remains in the patient like a *fermentum* and infects the entire *corpus.* The adepts from the far eastern lands have written a great deal about this complaint. You see, because the *corpus* is not able to use sweet substances in the process of combustion, it looks for other calcinated substances to replace it. And the remnants of these unholy dissolutions are excreted in the *urina,* leaving an acrid smell. I myself have come across it several times. Older men of large proportions, and likewise obese women, are particularly prone to such visceral aberrations. Still, I have heard of some who are born this way, though they die early.' He finished his morsel pensively.

'But this is caused only through the ingestion of sweet things, master?' I asked.

'No, all foods have a certain measure of sweet *potentias,* Christian, bread, for example, and wine. The venerable brother drank his share of wine tonight.' He pulled a sheet over the body.

'And yet we cannot be sure he did not simply die because he was old,' Setubar said, annoyed.

'You are correct. This unfortunately remains a hypothesis,' my master assented.

'Yes . . .' Asa nodded in agreement, 'whatever it was, we will perhaps never know.'

'And yet there is only one likely cause of death,' Andre said.

'You mean poisoning?' asked Asa.

'Nonsense, you fool!' The old man waved a hand impatiently.

'I believe,' my master ignored him, 'that if our brother

had died of this disease, he would have died peacefully, as many do, perhaps after a seizure or two, but he would not have experienced the violent spasms and other symptoms we witnessed tonight. And so I'm afraid that we still have a problem, a stubborn one.'

'Yes . . . his condition may have been incidental.' Asa frowned, washing his hands.

'And chance is incidental cause,' the old man quoted Aristotle.

'But if he was poisoned, master,' I said and was thrown a sharp look by Setubar, 'it is not likely that it was by chance, is it? The disease, as you have said, could have been incidental, but not the poison.'

'Christian,' my master answered me more patiently than was his custom, 'it could also be that the poison was incidental, or accidental, but we must take care not to suppose that purpose is not present because we do not observe the agent deliberating it.'

The old man stood, but he may as well have remained seated, for his back was so bent that he only gained a few inches. 'Stop all this absurdity, and let the body of our dear old friend rest in peace!' he cried, raising the stick he used to steady himself. 'He is the happy one now. Resting in the bosom of our Lord, in the arms of the mother whose milk will nourish him for all eternity. He prayed each day that it might be his last, and his prayers have been answered. You are young.' He looked at us with malice. 'You know nothing of the suffering of the old whose bones are brittle and whose teeth are gone, who piss all night and who cannot keep awake all day! The old smell death in their nostrils as young men smell flowers, their youthful form withers before the eyes, and the mind! The mind, once a joyous manifestation of erudition and wisdom, becomes a playground for delusions and deceptions. The old forget what they should know, instead of knowing what they should forget, and because of this they see the things that God reveals only *per speculum et in aenigmate,* that is to say, through a glass darkly, and call it wisdom. No . . .' he shook his head. 'Physicians want to cure every illness, bestowing long life to their patients. I know. I was once filled with such delusions, but now I understand this is merely the wiles of a vanity that cloaks its true intentions with the artifice of charity. The body is evil and so it must be endured until it can be shunned. To be rid of it is a blessing. Concern yourselves with the living. Our dead brother was old, and so he died, that is all!'

'On two points I am at variance with you, venerable Setubar,' my master replied, to the old man's surprise. 'Firstly I do not believe that the body is sinful, for it is only an instrument by which we make manifest the will that resides within and without it. Corinthians tells us, 'Know ye not that your bodies are the members of Christ?' And further, 'Know ye not that your body is the temple of the Holy Ghost which is in you?' and lastly, 'Therefore glorify God in your body, and in your spirit'. And secondly, that it is our holy duty as physicians to preserve this temple, this vehicle of higher truths, and to keep it healthy.'

'But you are wrong!' Setubar exclaimed in a shrill voice. 'The body is evil, evil! And easily seduced by sin, compelled by desires whose captains are the infernal legions of hell! Matthew tells us that it would have been good for man if he had not been born into the body, for only in his soul is he truly God-like. Only in death can man find the fulfilment of his true nature, preceptor. When he is alive, and particularly when he has become old and useless, he is nothing more than an animal, driven by hunger, cold and pain, like a child dribbling the food from his lips that others, who are young, deign to serve him!'

'I prefer to look at it as a return to a state of innocence, for Matthew also tells us that we must become like little children if we wish to enter the kingdom of Heaven.'

The old man gave a grunt, his bitter face stone-like. Only his melancholy eyes betrayed the intensity of his feeling, and these he directed menacingly at my master. 'Because I am old and too am nearing my own ultimate and blissful end, I can say with authority, 'Oh wretched man that I am!''

A heavy silence descended over us. The infirmarian dared to break it, though I sensed a quiver in his voice.

'Thank you for your assistance, preceptor.'

'It was a most enlightening discussion,' my master replied, and turning to the older man said, 'I hope I have not offended you, venerable brother, for this was not my intention. I am merely a seeker of truth, as we all must be.'

He pointed a twisted finger at my master. 'Beware of the truth, preceptor, for it wears many faces, as you may already know, but you have not come by it this evening. There is no conclusion to be drawn here, only suppositions and speculations that may lead us all into the pit of inquisition!'

'Perhaps you are correct,' my master said humbly. 'If you will pardon us, we will retire. It has been a very long day.'

Thus we left the infirmary and hurried to our lodgings. The weather once again turned disagreeable, with a cold wind sweeping up the gorges. My master retired to his cell, and I to mine, so tired that I did not light my lamp, falling onto my pallet fully clothed, as was our custom, but I found that I was unable to sleep, tossing and turning until a late hour. The old monk's death and Setubar's words coursing through my troubled mind, it was only after I drank a small draft of wine that peace finally overtook me, and consequently it was the sound of the night bell announcing matins, and the gentle intonation of the choir wafting through the compound, that finally woke me from an uneasy sleep. I thanked God once again for the wisdom of a rule that allows for the opening psalm to be recited somewhat slowly! I was able to join my master in the stalls at the saying of the words, 'Come and hear, all ye that fear God, and I will declare what he hath done for my soul,' before the closing of the great doors, and the reciting of the Gloria.

Thus this remarkable day would have come to an end in blissful contemplation of those dark hours just before dawn, if I did not first need to narrate something that occurred between the hour of my troubled sleep and the hour of the Holy Office. The first of many such experiences that, to this day, remains as vivid as it did that cold night in my cell at the monastery of St Lazarus.

IGNIS
THE FIRST TRIAL

. . . and your sons and daughters shall prophesy, your old men shall dream dreams, your young men shall see visions.
JOEL II 28

5

Capitulum

I Awoke flushed with perspiration, a strange feeling, not exactly fear and yet quite close to it, radiating to my every limb. It was cold, but from my cell window I could see that it had not snowed, higher in the night sky it was clear, and across to the east a starry script written indelibly in God's hand promised an answer to all my questions . . . but alas I did not, in my ignorance, understand its mysterious language. By the position of the moon I guessed that it must be sometime before midnight. Soon, the bell would toll matins. Down below, a light burnt and I wondered if the pilgrim was awake gazing up at the moon as I was. He had been in my dream, the pilgrim. I should go down, I told myself, and make his acquaintance.

I lay back on my pallet, pulling the sheepskin very high against my face, and told myself that I must sleep. I imagined the bitter cold outside. I would shortly have to rise and attend the services. What kind of scribe would I be if I were seen to fall asleep during the proceedings tomorrow? And yet, I felt an impulse to rise, and threw myself out of bed, annoyed – for it is never pleasant to lose an argument with oneself – and opened the door to my cell, venturing out into the cold.

Outside the moon offered me a little solace, illuminating the compound. I walked with quick steps past the graveyard, pulling the cowl over my head against the wind, hiding from the eerie light that made the gleam of the white crosses unearthly. I was relieved to see the *circa's* light making another round high up in the dormitorium, but I pressed on, not wishing to be seen. As I rounded the east face of the church I was taken by an unknown force and suddenly, without explanation, I found myself facing the great gate just as the doors opened before me. Outside, there was the scent of pine, and the ground was icy against my bare feet, but I found that it did not disturb me. How strange this all seemed! I followed the road through the battlements, and out into the forest, moving with the agility of a goat down a narrow path, which led through coarse vegetation. Then I was standing at the entrance to that little shelter I had seen on the day of our arrival. Inside I saw a man, a little short of thirty springs and of stocky build, and also another a little younger, though thin and tall, sitting beside him. They appeared to be in deep contemplation, little noticing my presence until I spoke.

'Happy night,' I ventured.

The younger man looked up from his dreamy world with the eyes of a doe assailed by a wolf. 'Who comes hither?'

'I come in peace,' I soothed, 'from yonder abbey.' I pointed upwards in the direction of the monastery bathed in moonlight.

The older of the two glanced up and fixed me with wisdom-filled eyes. 'You may sit with us for a moment, and share a little warmth before the bells.'

I felt large and awkward – and I was only of a slight build – entering their modest shelter. In the centre, sheepskins covered the earth encircling a little fire that provided only adequate warmth. It smelt of animals and smoke and incense.

'May we know the name of he who disturbs our pater noster, and our credo?' the man asked presently.

'My name is Christian de St Armand and I am a Templar

squire visiting the abbey with my master in the name of the king,'
I answered, finding that I was boasting.

'I see,' he nodded his head. 'Miserable sinners we may be,
but we follow the canonical hours, as should a Templar squire!'

'Yes, at any moment we will hear the bell,' I found myself
saying. 'I would have already left for the great gates, but . . .'

'Do not let us keep you from your duty, but you have
some moments. Sit,' he said, making room for me. He had a
broad sanguine face with thick eyebrows and tufts of brown hair
framing his tonsure. His eyes were a honey-brown, the same as
those of a young calf, and as they fell upon me they bestowed
instant calmness. The younger monk was paler, and his face had
the quality of chiselled stone, though he spoke animatedly, blink-
ing very often. He appeared as excitable as the other was calm.

After an awkward moment in which the two sat in silence
watching me and nodding, I ventured to speak. 'Would you like
me to ask the abbot if he will admit you as pilgrims? Certainly
you must be suffering the cold.'

The younger man smiled, fluttering his eyelids. 'One cannot feel cold whose heart has been enkindled with the fire of the
spirit, but we thank you for your charity.'

'Are you on a pilgrimage to Santiago de Compostela? Jerusalem, as you must know, has been taken long ago.'

The older smiled, nodding his head as though I had said
something mildly amusing. 'The Jerusalem we seek is not physical, but spiritual. I have come with my devout companion Reginald to find peace!'

'Oh, peace.'

'There is no peace in Paris, only disputation,' he continued, looking a little weary.

'Paris?' I was intrigued.

Reginald interjected, 'Thomas was asked to give lectures
in Paris on the Book of Sentences.'

'These two years in Paris have been difficult,' Thomas

continued, sitting forward and gazing clearly into my eyes. 'There has been strife and discord in the universities. The students and professors protest the powers of the chancellor, and there is a growing antagonism towards us . . . Our good abbot of St Jacques, being the wisest of men, has sent us on a journey away from these disturbances . . .'

'You are monks?'

He did not answer.

'But you are very far from Paris!' I exclaimed. 'Is there a Dominican house in these parts? And what of your habits?

Once more he did not answer me exactly, 'Yes, we are a long way from Paris, we have travelled on foot for many days, as did our beloved and sainted founder, called by a spirit voice. We needed no directions, no maps, we simply followed our hearts and the spirit has guided our sinful souls to this very place. Is it not wondrous? And since our arrival, I have had one dream that lasts even as the daystar rises in the sky!' he looked at me in awe. 'Even now I am within this dream, as you are within this hut. I see him . . . In this dream he leads me to the waters . . . Sometimes he is an eagle, sometimes he is a man. He says that he will lead me to the Temple, and there I will gain the knowledge that will allow me to proceed with my life's work, to reconcile Aristotle and Christianity.' He noted the interest in my eyes. 'You have heard of the Greek philosophers?'

'I thought everyone knew about them?' I answered truthfully.

The man smiled, 'They will . . . they will. Now I must write my Summa, and yet it is not always possible to say what one must say, you know . . . There is so much to do, and so many forces working contrary to the purposes of God! And yet here, I can be one with the eternal light that rules the world, and I can dream of a time when the minds of men will not be clouded by fear, a time when the mind will be free . . .' After saying these things Thomas became quite dull, as though he had lost his faculties.

Reginald moved closer, whispering to me, 'He has been this way since we arrived some days ago . . . He is in the throes of an ecstatic vision!' he beamed with deep admiration. 'On his face one sees sadness alternate with joy (there are moments in which his despair appears to be very deep, and other times he becomes joyful like a little child). He has passed these last days without eating or drinking and I must confess to having despaired that he was suffering from some terrible illness of the mind, for his estimative virtues have been disrupted; he cannot remember the day or the hour, at times he does not even recognise the face of his friend. And yet in moments of lucidity he assures me that he is quite well, and that he will soon return from the worlds which he frequents. Here there is peace for his work,' he affirmed.

I was astonished. This man Thomas, whose face was now filled with a saintly fire, had travelled here to find peace? I wondered what he would think if he knew of the events occurring behind the great gates.

'The brother needs to rest, you must leave.' Reginald stood.

Feeling very perplexed, I emerged from the hut, and almost immediately I heard the bell toll matins.

'Christian de Saint Armand,' a voice called out after me, 'life takes us on many divergent paths, and yet we shall meet one more time! Not in the flesh, but in the sun, man's home, *homo hominem generat et sol! In the sun . . .*'

I awoke as I have said, to the sound of the bells, still in my pallet. I had dreamed that I had dreamt.

6

Capitulum

After Lauds

The sun had only risen a half-hour before, and as we walked the cloisters in quiet meditation, we could see only a little sky that, through the arches, echoed its brilliance.

One had to appreciate these moments of rare stillness and beauty, for I was learning that at this altitude the climate was never constant or predictable, but in perpetual transformation. Even now one could see clouds chasing away the indigo blue, stirred by a high impetuous wind that signalled a storm.

My master sniffed the air pensively. We had so much to contemplate. Aside from the strange dream that I had not the occasion to mention, there were other considerations. The more we examined the unsettling course of events since our arrival, the more confounding they became. Not only because we were witness to the untimely death of a poor monk, but also because the rose cross, for instance, and the black Madonna in the church, signalled that this was indeed no ordinary abbey.

We walked, observing the monks engaged in various contemplative pursuits. How could they seem so untouched by events? Like the seasons, that irrespective of human vicissitudes continue to grace the earth with regularity, bringing order to chaos. I wondered what they thought of us. What else could they think of us, I answered myself, but that we were the messengers of their misfortune? I shuddered a little from the cold. Soon they would prepare to leave for the dormitories, to change into day shoes before a wash in the lavatory. And we, too, observing their custom, but for now we continued in silence, respecting the rule, until finally the bell rang and we were alone.

I determined to tell him of my nocturnal sojourn, though I knew my master gave little importance to such things, but I was interrupted by the good abbot, Bendipur, whose pursed lips and furrowed brows signalled his displeasure.

'I have just spoken to the infirmarian,' he said as he drew nearer. 'He tells me that it is your opinion that our brother died in . . . unnatural circumstances, and I must tell you that this is simply not possible.'

My master nodded his head. 'I see your point. But the facts remain as they are, abbot.'

The abbot looked disheartened and his usually ruddy cheeks paled. 'But Asa tells me the examination was inconclusive, and revealed no evidence of foul play?'

'And he was quite right, it was inconclusive.'

'Then why do you . . .?'

'There are only so many ways a person can die, your grace. Last night I was able to make an assumption on the basis of certain undeniable signs. Firstly, the nature of the old brother's death was not from some violent external event, this is plain. Secondly, although he seems to have had an ailment for some time, his behaviour in the church – that is, the paralysis, the abdominal pain, and so on, point to other causes. It is my belief, having seen the effects of such things in the past, that he was poisoned and therefore murdered.'

The other man looked a little amazed. 'But the infirmarian was unable to tell me what substance could have occasioned death, if indeed you are correct in your summation of events.'

'That is because there are an untold number of poisons or even combinations of poisons that leave no trace whatever.'

'Brother Setubar believes otherwise. Strange that you seem to be at variance on such a simple matter.'

'Simple things are often surprising in their complexity, your grace, but at this point, my personal opinion differs from his and nothing more. Moreover, if I may, there are other concerns . . . of a delicate nature, which we must now broach.'

The abbot became tense, and a little vein over his eye bulged slightly. 'Other concerns?'

'I do not wish to cast a shadow of suspicion on the poor soul of the deceased, your grace, but these circumstances demand that I imagine the unimaginable, so I must ask the question, as painful as it is to utter the words, namely, had you any reason to doubt his faith?'

The abbot looked at my master for a long time, then answered his question with another question, 'Why would you think such a thing?'

My master smiled a little, 'It is never an easy thing, suspicion.'

'What do you suspect, preceptor?' he asked.

'It is a delicate matter.'

The abbot shook his head. 'Brother Ezekiel was a man of pious confession, a dedicated, holy man . . .' He looked at me with narrow eyes. 'Might I speak with you alone?'

'Dear abbot, my scribe is bound to me by oath, he is like a son, there is nothing that he will divulge without my permission.'

The abbot huffed a begrudging assent, but I could see he was not convinced of my prudence.

'Then I shall be frank with you,' he continued quietly. 'For some time now, it has become apparent, preceptor, that something sinister lurks in God's house. And although I have not been able to discern its nature, I have been aware of its existence.'

'The wisest thing then, your grace, might be to inform the inquisitor,' my master answered.

'You know what that could mean, preceptor. You are a man whose wisdom understands the delicate nature of our situation, and I seek your help, and your prudence, not only because it is your duty to place them at my disposal, but also because it is in your nature that you must do so.'

My master's face hardened, but his voice remained warm and solicitous. 'My duty is to remain equitable and unbiased, to see that the inquiry is carried out with fairness. That is all.'

'And yet have you not questioned why the king has sent a Templar on such a mission? Come now, a man of your estimative capacities?'

'As a knight I have an autonomous disposition.'

'And who better to blame if things go wrong? Come now, we both know the tide is turning against your order. We are not the only ones in peril, preceptor, and so I beseech you, do not go to the inquisitor with your suspicions, at least not until you have verification of their exactitude.'

'If this is your wish, I shall endeavour to follow it.'

The abbot led us out of the cloisters through the small aperture that opened out to the outer courtyard. The sky looked turbulent and grey now, and the sun could be discerned only vaguely, somewhere in the east.

'It would be of benefit to all concerned if such things could be arrested before . . .' he shook his head, 'before . . . I dare not say it.'

'But have you considered that I might, in the course of my investigations, uncover something that is in any case doubtful?'

'That has occurred to me, and I admit that under other circumstances I would not desire such an intrusion. But with the inquisitor's presence in our midst we are faced with difficult decisions. After all, we are brothers . . .'

'We are all brothers since the fall of Adam, your grace, but I must point out that nothing can influence the course of justice.'

'No, indeed it should not,' the abbot agreed, 'but a matter can be handled delicately or indelicately, preceptor.'

We followed the abbot in uneasy silence, meditating on his last words. He led us to the highest point of the compound, near the graveyard. From this vantage one could see over the walls to the mountains that rolled eastward whose form could be seen faintly. We stood gazing out and for a brief moment the clouds above us parted, and through them a shaft of light descended over the abbey in a mystic blessing. For the first time since our arrival I saw the rugged mountains that towered above and beyond in majestic peaks and chasms. Undulating northward, they touched the sky's vast canvas only a little where clouds, suddenly arrested by the unearthly stillness, reached down from the heavens to caress mortality.

'From this great height,' the abbot said, 'one observes creation as a whole in all its generalities, raised above petty particulars to witness the boundless. Sometimes it is best to see things from a distance, to look at the whole rather than the part, the universal rather than the singular. We must look beyond ourselves and what we don't understand, preceptor, in order to see things clearly.'

'Sometimes that is so,' my master answered.

The sun disappeared then, behind the clouds, casting a gloom over us like a delicate shroud, and once again we were broaching dangerous things.

'You and I, preceptor, have much in common, united by the divine light of St Bernard. That is why I come to you now. Not because I wish to distort the course of God's heavenly justice (His authority will prevail despite our human machinations), but because there is much in the balance . . . You must not misunderstand me. Like you, I believe that to die in God's name is perhaps the most glorified sacrifice, and if there is suffering all the more so! But it is not death that I fear, preceptor . . . because as Ecclesiastes tells us, we must praise the dead who are already dead more than the living who are yet alive. What I fear, I cannot tell you. Such words my mouth dare not utter. I request that you seek what must be sought, before even greater catastrophes befall us.'

'Perhaps there is something else that impels you to seek my service in this desperate manner?' My master paused a moment. 'Perhaps this is not the first death under similar circumstances?'

Suddenly the abbot was robbed of the composure suitable to a man of his station. 'Who told you?'

'Why, you have told me yourself,' my master said calmly to the measure of the other man's distress.

'Do not play games with me, brother!'

'I do not mean to be impertinent, your grace, however yesterday you were clearly reserved when I asked if I could question the monks and inspect the abbey, and yet today you are most anxious that I do that very thing. In the first instance you behaved like a man who wished to hide something, in the second, like a man who knows there is no hope that it will not be discovered. My conclusions are only logical.'

There was an uneasy silence.

'But how could you know?'

'It is simple. You see, I noticed the fresh grave in the cemetery from my cell window the day of our arrival. Later I saw that, inscribed on the small cross above it, was the name Samuel. When I mentioned it to Brother Ezekiel, he was very fearful, saying the words 'The Devil will kill us all'. Your reaction, abbot, merely served to seal my hypothesis.' My master cleared his throat. 'In light of this I assume that you will give me permission to access the tunnels?'

'Tunnels?' The abbot was like a vessel assailed by one

great wave after another.

'The tunnels below the abbey, your grace .'

'The catacombs beneath the church are not to be approached. The tunnels that lead to them are very old and perilous and I have forbidden their use.'

'I see.'

'No, I don't think that you do. As abbot of this monastery I absolutely forbid you to enter upon this subject again.' His feathers truly ruffled, he tried to regain his composure by smoothing his grey habit over his ample belly. 'In any case,' he continued in a moderate tone, 'the combinations have been forgotten, and so it is for the best. Let the bones of the dead lie unmolested, they can do nothing to help you in your search.'

'May I at least attempt to . . .'

'Brother . . . *brother,* please!' he pleaded. 'There you will only find rats, but you will not, I assure you, find murderers. In any event, let us not frighten this poor child with talk of old bones, and tunnels. Many monasteries have catacombs and ossuaries below their abbeys. These passages are old, and I fear for your safety.'

'However, your grace,' my master insisted, 'I know of no monasteries where a murderer roams its hallowed halls, committing unspeakable acts against its community of monks.'

Suddenly the abbot turned to me, without answering my master. 'Do you like gems, my young and handsome scribe?'

I admitted that I did.

'Here then, you must have this as a gift.' He handed me a most curious rock, warmed by his touch, obviously a favourite. 'Have you not seen one before? It is a tiger's eye, a most exquisite specimen from the alpine mountains. The sword of St Michael.'

'The sword of St Michael?' I asked, holding the stone in the palm of my hand, appreciating its smooth texture.

'Yes, dear boy.' The abbot bestowed his smile on me from his great height. 'The yellow colour comes from the content of iron in the stone. The iron sword of St Michael that will one day vanquish the Devil, and banish him to the bowels of the earth!'

I became so thoroughly shaken that I dropped the gemstone to the ground. Why I should have felt this way I cannot say. My master gave me a bewildered look, and scooping it up in his large, powerful hand, returned it to me.

'Yes, by heavens!' The abbot laughed. 'It has startled you. Hold it tightly, for there is a power that lies hidden within, concealed until the day it can be revealed. But we must not forget that nature intends this to be so. Her secrets are not be divulged without a great effort. God commands that in order to see the heavenly, one must acquire heavenly eyes. And so it is the foundation of our life that we speak only when necessary, and like nature, remain prudently silent about those things not yet to be revealed. Like a stone by the wayside.' He smiled warmly at me. 'You will not divulge our conversation to the members of the legation, will you?'

I shook my head.

'I assure you that my squire is loyal.'

'Ahh, but the young are filled with great enthusiasm for noble deeds, preceptor, and this means that sometimes they are not discriminating. Dissimulation is a virtue taught at the school of experience; why should a young man have acquired it when he is only too eager to trust anyone because he has not himself been deceived by others? But I am not saying that we must be deceitful, no. Only that we must draw an honest veil over things meant for the ears of gods and not for the ears of those who would distort their essence. As a Templar you appreciate my position. Your order guards its secrets zealously. Also, having survived the ill-fated battle of Mansourah, the consequences of which have seen your order under some suspicion, you must know how easily things can be distorted. Such things can only result in nothing less than tragedy.'

'And as a Templar,' my master said, 'I give you my word

that I will see to it that this is a fair inquiry, your grace.'

'Come now, preceptor, the purpose of an ecclesiastical trial is not to establish the objective truth, we both know that it only exists to obtain a confession and to mete out punishment.'

Was there truth in his words? I sensed that my master felt there was. 'Lord abbot, you ask for my help, but if I am to help you, I must know everything, I must have access to the entire monastery.'

'Impossible! I have told you all I can. I believe you are a capable man, and what you know should be enough. Do not ask me any more questions. There is a seal over my lips no earthly man may break. You must remember that without death one cannot rejoice in the living, without the one perfect work, one cannot reach the final conclusion. This is our main concern, dear brother, all the rest is meaningless.' There was a momentary flash of defiance in his eyes and he turned, headed for the church, a grey figure in the vast greyness of the compound.

After this conversation, we followed in the abbot's footsteps but only as far as the graveyard. Here, my master became seized by a demon of motion. He paced between the crosses with his short legs, making little gestures with his hands, nodding now and then. I had seen him like this before and I knew he was in turmoil, caught in the chaos of opposing winds, so I waited for this mood to pass, watching him from the steps that led to the graves. It was very cold and I drew my cowl low over my face, huddling, shivering in my draughty attire. To keep from freezing, I drew my chin inside the collar of my scapular and blew warm air into my vestments, but this almost immediately turned to ice. I placed my hands deep into the wide sleeves, hugging my arms, but the wind had picked up and found its way to my bones through any unguarded opening. I considered a casual comment about the state of the weather, but thought better of it. Indeed, I feared my master's icy glare more than the icicles collecting on my nose. I looked up instead, at the sky's milky grey, only a patch here and there of very faint blue. It smelt like snow, I could almost taste it. Soon my feet would turn purple, indeed they were very numb. Oh, misery, I thought while I waited. Why couldn't my master think equally well in the warmth of the kitchen with a hot glass of milk in his hands? Further off, in the direction of the stables, I noticed the inquisitor shadowed by the bishop. They were going about the monastery asking questions of the monks. They stole glances in our direction and I wished that they were not seeing my master pacing up and down among the graves like a madman, for I believe they grinned, both shaking their heads as they walked off. A moment later Andre paused, remaining very still, and then walked resolutely in my direction.

'It is decided,' he said finally.

'Master?'

'I have made a decision, God help me, not an easy one, but a decision, nonetheless.'

'May I ask what it is concerning?'

'No, you may not. Now, I want you to go and find some refreshment in the kitchen, bring me an apple or something. In the meantime I will find the dead brother's room. I want to inspect it before the start of the hearing.'

'Do you think you'll find anything significant? Surely the inquisitor's men must have conducted their own search?'

'Therefore it is my hope that I will find something insignificant,' he said, 'because it annoys me to keep reminding you that it is the insignificant thing – that which may have escaped the eyes of the inquisitor's men – that may prove very significant to you and me.'

'I see,' I said.

'Good. I shall see you soon. Do not eat excessively . . . and do not be late!'

Thus he left me in contemplation of his foul temper, and the wisdom that directed my mother to leave me in the care of a madman. And yet, I consoled myself, I was given a moment of liberty, so I headed for the cookhouse, deciding that I would take the entrance from the garden. As I rounded the body of the cloister buildings tantalising aromas immediately assailed me and suddenly I forgot all my previous inconveniences and thought how good and kind my master was.

The cook, Rodrigo Dominguez de Toledo, was a giant, with big hands, and feet so enormous they poked through his ill-fitting sandals. He was a Spaniard of cheerful countenance, and of friendly disposition. So it was that as I entered the threshold of the kitchen he greeted me with a deep resonant voice and led me to an enormous table in the centre of the room where, amid a bustle of activity, he bade me to sit down and promised to prepare me a fine repast.

'Nothing but the best of foods for a guest!' he said, slapping me very hard on the back.

While I waited, I observed as numerous assistants under his vigilant eye prepared the meal. I mused that they looked much like infantry about to launch a cavalry charge on a mighty enemy, hence the preponderance of nervous energy, the quick pallid exchanges, and the sudden quiet loss of temper.

The kitchen was rectangular, with its two storeys buttressed by surmounting arches on all sides. The massive fire, dominated by a stone chimney, stood at the northern end, and this was the source of the delicate aromas that escaped through the adjacent door to the cloisters. A large hatch on the west wall opened onto the refectory whose strange position at right angles to the cloister was characteristic of Cistercian monasteries. The larder and buttery both had hatches on the eastern side, and the brew house, which ran north–east, had a bolted door near the east corner. Along this eastern side there were windows placed very high, capturing a good morning light that even on sunless days illuminated the entire room without the need of torches. The windows were fixed and the only ventilation came from the door through which I had entered, situated on the southern end.

I was to learn that this was always left open through the day, allowing for a moderate flow of air to enter the kitchen in strange bursts, so that one felt chilled one moment, and very hot the next.

I watched the cook with fascination. The air was thick with smoke and Rodrigo fired his orders like a commander, for an atmosphere of activity followed him as though it emanated as much from his own being as from necessity, 'More salt! Less water! Stir that pot!' he shouted in a mixture of Latin and the vulgar tongue of the Spanish. Luckily I was acquainted with Spanish because as a boy my father had taught it to me, saying that a Spaniard is a true gentleman, and that if one is to speak anything other than Latin – the tongue blessed by God – then Spanish was a fair alternative.

The cook told me as he went about his business that he was honoured to have me share his table. Remarking with a generous air, 'Es muí bueno! Good, good, sabes qué tengo debilidad por las órdenes militares . . . I very much like the military orders, very full of courage! Tenéis a petito? Hungry? Some fresh bread?' He went into the larder and came out holding a great golden loaf that he placed before me, along with a cup of warmed wine that I drank almost immediately, and a generous slab of cheese.

The man smacked his lips, 'Bendita Santa Divino!' he said, looking at the bread. I dared not ask him why, I merely ate it, and soon realised that it was indeed divine.

'The miel oh what honey! Is muy deliciosa ...!' he sighed. 'Our bees very much like the mountain, and this makes the honey light . . . sweet! Is like a good woman, yes?' he laughed, winking hideously and reached up with one long arm to a shelf near the fire from whence he brought a substantial earthenware pot to the table. A disturbed rodent scurried down from its hiding place behind the honey and fled across the room. This sent the cook into an instant agitation.

'Maldita mierda – Cursed dung!' he exclaimed with great

annoyance, giving it chase. But the furry thing was swift, escaping moments before he reached it through a tiny gap in the stone. The cook became enraged, aiming a volley of insults and curses at the bewildered assistant who, standing in the corner, cowered in the wake of his temper. In this mood he threw the knife in the general direction of the rat's exit, and spat a perfunctory wad of saliva at the stone floor.

'Cursed be the breast milk that thou hast suckled!' he bellowed, and the windows shook. I believe he then remembered me because he gave me a lame smile. *'Por favor* . . . I beg your pardon . . . I am the dung of a donkey! But they are, after all, so tasty . . .' He picked up the knife and wiped it thoroughly on his shirt before placing it in my hands, *'Estúpido!'* he said, pointing to one of the cooks. *'Idiota!'* he snarled at another.

I glanced at the soup bubbling with purposeful anxiety on the great fire and wondered about the rat. Seeing my concern, the man laughed. 'It was not for our food — *qué cosa buena, eh?* Good, very good. No, no, it was for the cat, you see?' He pointed to a spot above the fires where in a little alcove a honey-coloured feline slept unperturbed by the activity and the smoke. 'Don Fernando.'

'Why does he not catch it himself?'

'Oh, not Don Fernando!' said the other incredulously. 'He is afraid of them, *él tiene un humor muy delicado,* he is delicate, and lazy also. So, you come with the inquisitor, eh?'

I nodded.

'Ahh, Templar! I have not seen a Templar for many years.'

I flushed, swallowing down the bread with a good measure of wine. 'I am not yet a knight. When I turn eighteen I shall truly enter the order, for now I am a squire and a scribe.'

'Ahh ... you learn to be *un medico* — un doctor, like your master, eh?'

I said that I hoped so.

'Very good! U*n médico Templario! Muy bien!* Good, *bueno.'*

He clapped. 'Is good to be young, no? Is yours the world, yes? *El mundo es sujo, sí?* I was once strong like you,' he said with a grin, and then, like a man who has not had much occasion to indulge in conversation, he set about telling me his life's story.

'I travel much! Oh! What I have seen with these eyes!

But,' he lowered his voice in a circumspect manner, 'it does a cook no good to talk such things . . . no good with the inquisitor sniffing around eh? No . . . *Creo en el poder del papacy sí,*' he emphasised, 'I believe in the pope, the holy mother, *la madre* the church, *el Papa*, the mouth of God!' He crossed himself and kissed the crucifix that dangled over his dirty habit.

At one point the refectorian rushed in. 'Rodrigo, the bread!' he cried, then in a hushed tone, 'The brothers are seated.' On seeing me, he nodded solicitously, 'I will send the assistants in.'

The cook did not move. He seemed to become even more indolent. He exclaimed an 'Arrgh!' under his breath and, waving a hand, continued enlightening me on various recipes and preparations. At one point one of the assistant cooks asked about the wine to be served at the table.

'Not from the larder, fool, *ignorante!*' he shouted and the man cowered, 'I have told you, is not to be touched that one, on the old brother's orders.'

The monk glared at me, in a strange way frightened. 'But, Rodrigo, the boy's wine?'

Rodrigo frowned and took the empty glass from me, shaking his head, '*Idiota!* Only for the old ones!' then to me. 'It has powers for the health, *poderes curativos,* not for young ones, eh?' he laughed then, but I had detected a little nervousness in his voice.

Presently, once this little misunderstanding had been clarified to his satisfaction, and the assistant suitably reprimanded and sent to the church to perform penance for his carelessness, the cook continued, telling me that in Sicily one could procure many foods from the Africas and surrounding areas. He intrigued me with stories of fruits so sweet no honey could be sweeter and bitter herbs the likes of which burn the mouth and purge the senses. He told me that in countries beyond the scope of maps, the natives grew peculiar foods of unequalled aroma and taste. Strange herbs, he said, and even stranger wines, numbed the head and made one lose one's senses after just a glass, but even more intriguing were the strange concoctions that, when burnt over a slow fire and smoked, or even eaten as a paste, caused one to make communion with devils. I gasped as predicted and he laughed heartily.

'What wonders . . .' he told me in a husky voice, leaning his belly across the table. '*Is* your order brings such things in ships. Ahh, but you know, you have been in the Holy Land, no?'

I told him that Templar life was meagre and sparse on campaign.

'*Dios mío!*' he cried with emotion. 'Your master *matas moros*, he kills the infidel?'

I nodded. He raised huge hands high in the air, grabbed me in my seat, pulled me to him – very nearly crushing my bones – and kissed me on both cheeks, 'Deliver us from evil, *libera nos a malo. Amen!* I am your servant.'

I flushed, his foul breath lingering on my skin. 'But you were speaking of something else . . .'

'Eat, eat!' he interrupted me, 'I am your servant, I am your servant!'

So I did, not wishing to insult him. After a time, however, I began to feel sated and a little tired, so I leant back in my chair, patting my middle as I had seen the bishop and the others do the previous night. 'You must have been highly favoured for your abilities. Did you work for a king or a duke, perhaps a wealthy merchant?'

He laughed a great guffaw that echoed loudly because he was a lay brother and therefore not so strictly bound by the rule on laughter. 'Dukes? Kings? *Niño!* Boy, I say to you it was the great ruler of the empire!' He then hesitated and his face became ashen.

'Frederick?' I sat up so abruptly that I almost fell off my seat.

'O! My tongue is sinful!' he said. 'What I said . . . I did not mean, Frederick . . . I . . .'

'You have worked in the kitchens of the excommunicated emperor! Tell me, I am intrigued.'

He looked at me with sharp eyes, 'Are your lips wise, or are they as loose as a whore's?'

'They are wise, very wise,' I said anxiously.

The man moved from his position opposite and sat down beside me at the table. He smelled of onions and garlic. 'Frederico, he was *un buen hombre!* A good man, but you have heard the stories, no? A man with strong body and good brain, a hunter . . . a lover of women,' he said in a low, wistful voice. 'The emperor's court! *Qué maravilla!* I was a craftsman in his kitchen! My dishes were the delights of infidels, the ecstasies of magicians, the enjoyments of astrologers, the pleasures of mathematicians. *Poetas,* troubadours, concubines! What women!' He closed his eyes, seeing in some corner of his corrupted mind their superior form. 'Delicious like pears, lush, with the flesh of pomegranates, rounded, brown like berries and sweet like . . . Yes, what would they do with a little Templar like you, eh?' He laughed again, seeing me turn a violent scarlet.

'Why did you leave the emperor's court?' I changed the subject, putting an end, or so I hoped, to such talk.

'Is my luck that is good the nose, eh?' He tapped his large, veined nose, 'It smells when a stew is cooked, yes, yes. Sicily it came to troubles, pestilence and I left. *Frederico estaba muerto,* dead, and his son Conrad . . . coward! No like his father, no like him! Then the other son Manfred . . .' He lowered his voice, 'An illegitimate! *Un bastado* from the wombs of a whore! A whelp of a she-wolf!' He spat and smiled. '*Con perdo 'n* ... And now ... *Dios mío* the inquisitor has come, and we shall all be burned . . .' He blessed himself. '*Domini Canes* – the Lord's dog, not a man, a devil!'

'Sir! You are speaking of a representative of the holy inquisition!' I said indignantly.

'Ahh, si, but you do not think that only heretics are – how you say? – inspired from the Devil eh? Eh?' he pressed. 'No! *El* inquisitor *también* – also! He does not look for monsters . . . he makes them! Big ugly ones! With my eyes I have seen them. *Tiene miedo? Sí?* Are you scared? You must be scared, tremble and beg like an animal, *como un animal,* and the holy mother will let you die before the flames eat your flesh!' He began to howl like a wolf and I felt my stomach tighten into a knot and the food that I had so eagerly consumed became sour in my belly.

'With my own eyes I have seen it!' he asserted.

'And how does a cook know so much?' I asked.

'From a kitchen I see everything, life and death. You must be *discreto,* but the truth should be spoken,' he whispered, 'I know this man, *este hombre* Rainiero Sacconi . . . *un* traitor to his people.' He spat, and wiped his mouth with his sleeve.

'A traitor?'

'Well known is his history. You too must know it but I will tell you!' He moved closer and I could smell his sour breath. 'He was *un* Cathar, a heretic in *Italia* high in the Catharan Church. He taught *la doctrina.* Many *inocentes* followed him in believing that all laws were lies and laughing at *las reglas,* the rules of fasts and feasts . . . taking the *consolamentum.*' The cook leant forward, both hands on the table. 'Like the Devil in the garden, he seduced them.'

'How did such a man become an inquisitor?'

'How?'

At that moment two assistant cooks entered the kitchen, their eyes to the floor, cowls over their faces. One lifted a massive tray upon which an assortment of bread and cheeses was laid out. The other was handed an immense pot in which a vegetable broth had been cooking since the early hours. This the young monk placed, with some difficulty, on a wooden trolley. The cook handed him a ladle and shooed him out. 'Out with you! Out all of you!' he yelled, and as they scurried away, they reminded me of the rat.

He wiped both hands on his shirt, then gathering the folds of his vestments blew his nose loudly. 'Aaah . . .*sí* ... *sí*, this *herético* ... *sí*, one day he was *iluminado*, saw his errors and was *convertido!* A miracle – *un milagro – hágase el milagro y hágalo el diablo!*

I looked at him blankly.

'Do not they say 'if the work is good what matter who does it', eh? Rainiero entered the Church in Milan and swore to hold the faith of the fathers, promising to obey *el papa* in the order of the dogs! *Ole!* That is the end.'

'What do his former followers think of him?!' I exclaimed.

'They hate him! Is natural!' he said shrugging his shoulders. 'He mistreated his old *amigos* very much, very brutal since he replaced the old man Piero, Prior of Como . . . the martyr that was killed at the hands of the assassin Giacoppo della Chiusa. This man also tried to kill Rainiero at Pavia, but he was *estúpido* because he did not succeed . . . Rainiero is a clever man, *listo e despierto!* And now he is the pope's dog, an inquisitor with a heretic up here.' He tapped an index finger against a sweaty brow. 'Innocent was clever too, better if the smart ones are on your side and not the enemies, even more because on Italian soil there is conflict, *terrible,* the church fights against the emperor, and the emperor against the church. Now he is here and I smell flesh burning in my nostrils . . . it is the smell of pig! Poohf! But I will speak no more. Those with loose tongues die in this abbey, those who know too much die also. I want to be *ignorante*, my young one, so that I may live a long and sinful life!'

I asked the cook for an apple, and left.

I wandered the grounds feeling a strange sensation, a

kind of light-headedness. On seeking my master, I found him not in the dormitories, but in the scriptorium, leafing through a large book and having a most cordial discussion with the librarian, Brother Macabus, and a copyist whose present work (I would soon see) was filled with the most precious illuminations. I entered the enclosure of the scriptorium and made my way to them as quietly as possible, though a number of monks looked up from their work with barely concealed suspicion. Almost immediately, as if the sight of me caused them discomfort, they hung their heads over their shoulders and continued their work in silent rebuttal. But I took this rare opportunity to watch them discreetly, as they scraped away at an old palimpsest, or carefully marked the margins of a new one. Today I know this is how we have lost many a precious manuscript because a monk's work is less about appropriating and perpetuating wisdom than perpetuating appropriate copying. As we are told a busy monk is only troubled by one devil, while an idle monk is troubled by many. This philosophy has sustained copyists and illuminators alike for centuries, as they proceed day by day to work unhurried, as though all eternity lay before them, erasing the works of the most orthodox and revered Christian fathers to make palimpsests of relatively little importance.

Once again obedience.

Still, I must confess to having envied them a little at that moment, if only because their life seemed a truly satisfying one. A life of constancy, devotion and fidelity. Where work is carried out for the sake of continuity and of permanence, and not – as overcomes so much of human endeavour – to satisfy the sin of pride. Here there was peace, and order, and the goodness of the word, which is God. And I remembered what the inquisitor had said on the day of our arrival at the abbey, *magna est veritas, et praevalet*, that is to say, great is truth and it prevails.

Shortly my master drew me to his side, I gave him his apple, and his eyes told me that he would perhaps have preferred a dumpling. Even so he bit into the apple eagerly, and between mouthfuls, proceeded to tell me that despite the unfortunate circumstances (by this he meant that he had found nothing in Brother Ezekiel's room) he had passed a valuable morning looking through herbals and bestiaries provided by the librarian Brother Macabus. He then introduced me to the other monk, Brother Leonard, who was presently instructing him on the various inks and parchments used by him in his works.

'The skins of young lambs . . .' Leonard smiled, displaying prominent incisors, 'is the preferred choice for works of great importance because it lasts so well. One may also re-use it many times because of its thickness. We also use vellum when we are graced to have some on hand, and rarely papyrus, for as you know, preceptor, it is brought from the lands of the infidel and is, of course, very rare.'

'But where are your treasures, Brother Macabus, I do not see any bookcases?' my master asked, taking another large bite of his apple, looking perplexed, though many times I had occasion to observe that he already knew the answers to his questions.

The man showed no hesitation in answering. 'They are safely stored in the library, away from heat and humidity that can be so damaging to old manuscripts.'

'It must be a most comprehensive library, brother librarian.'

'Yes, it is comprehensive,' Macabus said, 'though, by most standards, very small. Still it is our life work. Our most notable pieces are on the medicinal arts, and music.'

'Ahh, then . . . I would very much like to see them.'

'And your order is so often maligned for its illiteracy!' he raised his chin in a suggestion of superiority. 'It heartens me to think that erudition can complement a soldier's life and yet I hear that you studied in Paris before joining the order, and Salerno also?'

'Yes.'

'How fortunate.'

'I do not believe in fortune, brother, only in tenacity. May I have your permission to visit the library?'

'Impossible! For that you shall require the abbot's permission, preceptor,' the librarian answered with the slightest hint of bitterness, 'there are not many who are given that privilege.'

'Oh, I see . . . but where is the library situated, I have seen no building . . .?'

The monk looked a little embarrassed and Leonard interrupted, by means of changing the subject. 'Have you been to the library at Bobbio, preceptor? Their catalogue is said to enumerate well over six hundred works. There is also St Gall. Have you heard that in Rhenish monasteries they are now using woodcuts?' Straightening his back proudly he said, 'I have seen one or two works of supreme excellence, but here we prefer the traditional use of stylus, reed, or quill, with inks and pigments unsurpassed in luminescence.'

My master was thoughtful for a moment, 'Yes . . . so you translate many Greek texts?'

'How did you know?' Macabus asked, a little amazed.

'When you said that your most notable works were on the medicinal arts, I assumed you meant the works of Hippocrates, and Galen.'

'You are correct,' the man said smugly. 'We have had, and do have, I believe, the finest translators in Europe.'

'Really?' my master nodded, very pleased.

'Oh, yes, indeed.'

'And who might be your most notable?'

'That would be Anselmo,' Leonard answered and was immediately sorry, for a dark cloud moved over his superior's brow.

'Yes,' Macabus said through tightened lips, 'a young man who shows great promise. He has not been with us long, but his father was widely travelled and the child knows many languages. A boy of many talents.'

'Are there any others who speak Greek apart from this boy and yourself?'

'Oh, yes, a library must have several, but none know it so well as the two of us,' Macabus answered.

'May I see the translator's desk?'

The man hesitated a moment, then, covering his initial reluctance with a smile, showed us to an immaculately kept table near a good source of light.

'He is presently working on various projects.'

'Does brother Anselmo presume to better Gerard of Cremona's translation of Aristotle?' my master asked, picking up a manuscript from the table, the half-eaten apple still in his hand. 'He must be exceptional!'

I saw the librarian gasp, observing the proximity of the moist fruit to the manuscript. 'He is, certainly, but his finest work to date was the entire works of Galen.'

'The entire works? *Mashallah!*' he exclaimed, I suspect intellectually overcome.

I saw Leonard and his superior exchange a meaningful glance.

'Is that Arabic?' Macabus asked looking down his nose at Andre.

'Why yes, do you know it?'

'A little. You speak it like a native.'

'Well, that is because I am a native.'

A disbelieving quiet descended over us.

My master smiled, pleased to have occasioned embarrassment. 'On another matter, how are the writing implements cleaned, brother librarian?'

Macabus narrowed his eyes. 'Various substances are used whose efficacy is well known.'

'Might I ask where you store such substances?' My master held the apple core out, and I reached for it, but instead of giving it to me, he handed it to Brother Leonard who looked at the article with distaste and handed it to a lesser brother nearby. He, in turn, held it with just the tips of his fingers and passed it on to another, perhaps lower in rank than he, and this man left us holding it before him, for the cloister.

'Along with gold, silver, lead and mercury used for the making of amalgams, locked away in a repository.' Brother Macabus fumbled in the pocket of his habit and brought out a large bunch of keys. Singling one out from the rest, he directed us to a spot away from the carrels, or library stalls, near a great map of the north seas. Here, set inside the stone wall, behind a large tapestry, there was a heavy iron panel no bigger than two hands across and three high. He opened the lock with the key, looking about him. Inside, the aperture revealed vials, ampoules, and a large glass flask containing a powdery substance.

Andre peered in. 'This powder does not appear to be labelled.'

'I believe it is a salt, somehow strangely related to mercury. We have no use for it though we know little about it and so we keep it locked away. It has been in the repository a long time, in fact, since before I arrived here. I simply do not know its name.'

'Thank you, brother. One more thing. Do you ever leave your keys in someone else's charge?'

The man thought for a moment. 'It is my duty to lock the scriptorium and the aperture to the cloisters each night, but I also hold the keys to the kitchen and the cellar. However, there is always some necessary work to be done in the kitchen after the supper and so the cook locks those rooms and brings me the keys after he is finished, usually before compline.'

'And no one else?'

'Why do you ask?'

'I am a curious man, brother.'

'Are we not warned, preceptor, not to be curious in unnecessary matters?'

'Yes, but as Syrus has said: necessity gives the law without itself acknowledging one. However, I would not quote the Apocrypha again, brother, not in earshot of the inquisitor. Now, as to my question . . .'

The librarian was visibly shaken – perhaps realising that peril awaited him at every turn – and answered promptly, 'Sometimes the hospitaller needs to replenish the wine in the abbot's rooms and I allow him the use of it.'

'Does either the cook or the hospitaller have any idea that on that ring of keys resides the key that opens this stronghold?'

'No, I don't think so, but why is that important?'

'You are quite right, it is of no importance at all, and I have been wasting your time. I humbly apologise. You see, you were right; the Devil of curiosity is a cunning one, for he leads us to contemplate marginalia. I thank you for your patience,' my master said, bowing politely and after the brother had locked the repository once more, we bade him our leave.

'That man is either very careless, or he is not very astute.' my master mumbled as we headed in the direction of the chapter house.

I was too caught up in my own thoughts – feeling that I now knew the identity of the killer – to answer him. 'The boy is the author of our note!' I said resolutely and unequivocally. 'He knows Greek!'

'No, I do not believe so, Christian.'

'But, master . . .'

'If the young boy is the best translator of Greek this abbey has, why should he make the obvious mistake we found in the note? And even if he were the author, you are assuming that this connects him immediately to the crime. This is not necessarily the case. In any event, he is right-handed.'

'But how do you know that, master?'

'It is very simple . . . a left-handed copyist, is more likely to leave smudges on the left side of a page than a right-handed one, because his hand in its labour travels over freshly written words. A right-handed copyist's hand travels ahead of the word. Moreover, left-handed copyists have a peculiar angle to their lettering.'

'Always?'

'No, not always, but mostly.'

'So the boy is right-handed. What about the author of our note?'

'It was written by a left-handed person.'

'Oh,' I said, suddenly excited, 'and as there are not so many left-handed persons it should be easy to find our note writer.'

'That is true,' he conceded, 'in fact there are not many left-handed people in the world. Perhaps because some believe it is an infernal trait. You will remember that Christian mythology tells us Lucifer sat at the left hand of God.'

'And is it an infernal trait?'

My master gave me an annoyed look. 'It is utter nonsense, of course!'

'What about the poisons?' I pressed. 'The lead and mercury, and the cleaning agent used on the instruments? Do you think one of them killed the old brother?'

'Perhaps, and for this reason I shall have to consult some books on the topic of poisons, but for now, it is only a possibility. Despite what Macabus says I don't believe that the repository of these substances is a great secret. After all, it is a small monastery . . . no . . .' he trailed off. 'But the powder . . . the salt could be a compound known as serpent de pharaon.'

'Is that a poison?'

'A very potent one.'

'Then Brother Macabus is our best suspect,' I said, changing my mind like the wind changes direction. 'For he not only speaks Greek, but he also has unlimited access to the repository.'

'Let us not forget,' Andre added with caution, 'how many others speak Greek and have also handled the keys.'

Just then the bells tolled, announcing the opening of the inquiry, and with these considerations weighing heavily on our souls we entered the chapter house, my head feeling even lighter than before.

7

Capitulum

Some time after Terce

Beloved brothers of the monastery of Saint Lazarus,' the inquisitor Rainiero Sacconi's words echoed in the chapter house. 'My colleagues and I have journeyed here at the pope's request, having come a great distance, as you know, to substantiate accusations of heresy which have been directed at this community of monks.

'Dear brothers, it is the duty of the holy inquisition to seek out even the smallest or indeed insignificant speck of evil. To root out the Devil wherever he is evidenced or, on the other hand, to bless and sanction those who walk according to God's laws. Do not, then, be afraid, my children, for the wrath of God is tempered by a powerful and fraternal love for his people. He seeks not to punish the innocent, but to vanquish the guilty. As a shepherd seeks to nurture his flock and keep it from harm, so it is for your good that we are here.' He motioned to the bishop and the other prelates of his legation who sat flanking him. 'Is it not better to die repentant than to live a life of sin?' He stood motionless. 'As you know, this legation is not bound by the precepts of ordinary law, and is exempt from all common jurisdiction. And although it is customary for those found guilty of crimes against God to be turned over to the secular arm, let it now be known that, because of this abbey's seclusion, I have been given a special dispensation from our lord pope to carry out all sentences in order to save the souls of innocent people, should this investigation lead to inquisition.'

'The scoundrel,' my master said to me in a whisper.

'Let it also be known that all those who recant, through fear of death, will be thrust into prison for life, there to perform penance until their last days. All communal property will be confiscated. Those who defend the errors of a heretic are to be treated as conspirators to heresy and will, therefore, suffer the same punishment!'

A low murmur went through the assembly.

'And as we punish ordinary people whose ignorance is no excuse for committing sin against the holy laws of the church, how much greater indeed should be the punishment of a monk who – having known the eternal light of heavenly laws – still chooses to offend the rules of his church. And so I call this inquiry to order, so that all matters called into question may be thoroughly investigated and I therefore summon all those who know of any matters of interest to this inquiry to come forward without fear, for we are the ears and eyes of God, and will listen with fraternal love, devoid of prejudice. Those of you who choose to come forward and confess their sinful heresy will be treated with leniency. Those who do not will suffer to the letter of the lateran canons.' He paused, and in his eyes there was an intentional hostility. He wanted all to know this: you are in my power, and you had best act accordingly. Then he smiled, 'Friar Bertrand de Narbonne has kindly travelled from the priory of Prouille to assist in these inquiries. He is, as you may know, an esteemed theologian.'

The friar stifled a yawn and nodded without standing.

'He will act as judge, along with father Bernard Fontaine, our emissary from Citeaux, whose wisdom is renowned.'

Bernard looked unblinkingly at the gathering, his square chin tilted up a little in a gesture of disdain.

'And finally, as there must always be two inquisitors at any trial, the Bishop of Toulouse shall aid me in this grave and yet necessary duty.'

The bishop stood. Looking like a bright ball in his purple robe lined with fur, he fondled a jewelled pectoral cross with short fat fingers and delayed a moment, holding out the other hand in an ecclesiastic gesture of pomp before sitting down with a heavy sound upon his seat.

'As it is the day of our Lord we will obey his decree by delaying the commencement of proceedings until tomorrow. On this holy day, however, may we search our hearts and meditate carefully, and may the Lord guide your consciences into the everlasting light of truthfulness.'

The abbot rose from his own ornate chair on its own dais to the right of the group. Pulling away his cowl, he spoke with the strength and dignity befitting an abbot whose duty now lay in sustaining his community.

'Brother Rainiero Sacconi, esteemed members of the legation, my community. It troubles a father's soul to know that a shadow has cast its evil greyness over the conduct of his children. A father's eye sees only good, never evil. Only righteousness, never iniquity. And yet, it is as a father that I must seek to illuminate this shadow with the light of truth, to renounce all evil words uttered against my children, and replace them with words of praise and love. This I know is God's will, as it is the will of the church to see justice done in His name. It is then my fervent wish that our community may assist this inquiry in every way necessary to this end. The preceptor of Douzens,' he said, surprising my master, 'whose skill in the medicinal arts is well known, will shed equal objective light on our methods of healing, and so we should grant him every convenience.'

I saw the inquisitor's eyes glisten with adversarial hatred.

'Remaining your modest servants,' the abbot bowed to the legates, 'may God grant the holy inquisition the wisdom to see these things to be true. In the name of our Lord Jesus Christ. Amen.'

The abbot then pronounced the benediction, and the legation left with grave and solemn ceremony.

That was when my head felt suddenly very light . . .

Once we were outside in the broad daylight of midmorning I felt a little better, warmed by the sun, and my master's company.

We walked around the compound, my master lost in thought and I in the misery of my shame.

'I am sorry, master, but I seem to be so light-headed lately,' I said lamely.

'Oh, it was only the heat in the chapter house . . . and that infernal man!' he snarled. 'Saladin was right when he said that he never saw a bad Saracen become a good Christian. That wolf in sheep's clothing may well have outwitted the king . . . and in this case us too, but we are obliged to see it through.'

'But how? It seems to me that he has taken matters out of our hands. If he has the sanction to mete out punishment here, then there is little we can do.' I shook my head, trying to dispel the strange sensation.

'Firstly we must decide what is of greater importance. Our orders from the grand master, or those from the king.'

I had not thought of it before. 'Are they not equally important?'

'Yes and no.'

'How do you mean yes and no, master?'

'What do you mean, how do I mean? It is perfectly obvious to anyone except stupid squires that, as an illness dictates a particular treatment, so too will circumstances dictate our actions. This is the only wise thing to do.'

'So what is our next step?' I asked, a little humiliated. 'Do you know yet?'

'No, but I'm sure it will come to me.' I believe he was then sorry, for his voice became gentler and he said, 'Now calm down, I did not say that we will not attempt to do those things asked of us. What I am saying is that we may not be in a position to do so and this begs a question that must at once be asked. Why were we chosen to accompany the legation? The abbot brought up a good point. Let us see what we can gather from what we know. Here we have a monastery whose land belongs to the Templar order, but whose monks are Cistercians. This, in the first instance, is strange indeed. Second, it has been largely unknown for many years. No one has so much as given it a cursory thought, until a bright star in the sky of the inquisition is sent here in the middle of some very stormy times in Italy. This sword does not fit its scabbard. Why not use a French inquisitor? Why not Bernard de Caux? It seems to me that there are far too many parties interested in so small a prize, and that leads me to suspect that perhaps it is not so small after all. Then third, we are asked to accompany the legation, though it is miles from our jurisdiction.'

'But we hold the titles, master.'

'Yes, so they say, but it is more likely that we were sent because we are expendable. Languedoc, my son, is a strange location of diverse alliances. Alphonse of Poitiers, the king's brother, who now possesses the sceptre of the south is an avaricious man, deeply political and (unlike our poor vacillating Count Raymond before him) staunchly against heresy. One might say his zeal is in direct proportion to, let us say, the profitable confiscations received by his province from inquisitorial persecution.'

'You mean that he is only interested in the money and lands he might receive from confiscations by inquisitors?'

'That is my opinion.'

'So he welcomes the pope's legation in Languedoc, but his brother the king is suspicious of it?'

'Alphonse may be hoping to receive something but the

king knows that he has not paid his taxes, and he knows that the pope can confiscate and keep the property of a condemned heretic. Did you not hear the inquisitor mention this fact? You must see to your ears, boy.'

'But monks are poor, master, they do not own property.'

'Individually they do not, my good Christian, but communally, communally they may be very wealthy. Many monasteries are richer than whole kingdoms.'

'What about the grand master? Why is he interested in the monastery?'

'Perhaps it is the case that the Cistercians, our order, the Romans, the king, and his brother are all vying for the same thing.'

'What thing?'

'That is what we must find out.'

'And if we do, whom shall we turn to, master? The king or the grand master?'

'Perhaps neither, perhaps both,' he answered, 'and if things go wrong we must not expect a legion of knights to come to our defence.'

'You mean our order will desert us?' I cried in disbelief.

Andre brought a finger to his lips. I had not noticed that I had been speaking loudly. 'Calm down. All I am saying is that there must be something here in this abbey which is of great value, but also in some way incriminating. The question is, what are Cistercians doing on Templar ground? Then also, why do we find a rose cross on the door, and furthermore, a black virgin holding a rose and a cross on the window in the church? These things are physical signs that may help us solve our puzzle but to be sure of more things we must somehow get a look at the great book in the chapter house, the one which catalogues dates of deaths, admittances and so on. This may help us to find out where these monks came from, and perhaps why they are here.'

'Why do you not simply ask the abbot, master?'

'He will not tell us, his lips are sealed, as he told us. Perhaps there is a vow that he cannot break? Or he has learned something in the confessional. No, I am afraid we must find out for ourselves.'

'But what obliges you to go poking around in the abbey's business, master? Are we not here simply to see that no injustice is done by the inquisition?'

'The abbot has done what he could by asking me to seek the 'evil roaming the abbey', whose words echo those of Ezekiel that day before his death, if you will remember, and yet, in the end, nothing obliges us to do anything we will not do willingly, out of a desire to *know*, am I right?'

'So our next move is?'

'I would say that at this point, with all that has happened, our first priority may be to prevent the inquisitor from using our bones as faggots – but you will be glad to know that, among all these questions, we do know something, and that is, that there is a tunnel beneath the abbey that no one wants to mention and that the abbot seems anxious to safeguard. There have been two deaths, not one, and under similar suspicious circumstances. I don't yet know what one thing has to do with the other – perhaps nothing, perhaps everything. But we must remember that if we know these things it is only a matter of time before the inquisitor also learns of them, that is, of course unless he has known about them all along . . . in which case this abbey is doomed.'

Having said these things my master lapsed into a pensive silence and it was some moments before I had occasion to tell him of my conversation with the cook. He listened quietly and then rubbed his hands together, very pleased, 'Good,' he seemed cheered, 'he may be of great help to us.'

'Really? I don't see how a cook can be of any help, master, after all, how much could such an ignorant man know?'

'Why, you are a stupid boy!' he looked surprised. 'A living dog is better than a dead lion! We must not confound learning with intelligence for here is another who says those with garrulous tongues die in this abbey, and we had better start listening.'

'And what shall we hear?

'Something that will point to where we must investigate. I shall question him later . . .' saying almost to himself, 'but for now, we must look about us, and as Peter has said, we must be sober, we must be vigilant.'

'What must we look for, master?' I shivered.

'Everything and nothing at all!'

'But how does one go about looking for nothing?'

'Christian, must I explain what should be as apparent as the colour of my skin? Nothing is only anything devoid of everything, or rather, a something lacking, which can be just as significant as its opposite.'

'Oh,' I said, absolutely perplexed.

'Sometimes we must look, as I have told you, not only for things of substance that add weight to our hypothesis, but also for things that, on the surface at least, may seem unimportant, so prosaic that they incite suspicion. Only a good physician hunts down the less evident symptom . . . that peculiar movement of the hand, that little tremble of the lip. All such things also apply to our investigations, because it is often the small, undetectable things, that point to deeper truths.

The sun seemed higher now, but one could neither see it, nor feel it. We walked past the church, and in the daylight I realised that it rose far higher than I had previously thought, reaching dizzying heights, as though its architect had in his design attempted to echo the awesome elevations that surrounded it.

All around us work carried on as usual, for even on Sundays a monk's duty had to be performed. The animals had to be fed, there was bread to be cooked and ale to be brewed. Those whose tasks lay in less manual work engaged in fruitful intercourse. Some read the scriptures, while others prepared for mass. Still others sat in contemplation, meditating on the lives of the saints.

We headed in the direction of the stables where our animals resided. Here, where the garden separated it from the kitchen, life was manifest in all its peculiar forms, in all its diverse movements, sounds, and smells: A young monk brought sour-smelling scraps from the cookhouse and threw them out to waiting chickens. Another set out from the great gates to collect kindling. We could hear the brother blacksmith straightening a horseshoe on the anvil. I rejoiced. There is nothing more wonderful! Nothing holier than devotion to work that sustains a community. Nothing more blessed than the study of the divine word through the daily ritual of life. Even under such difficult circumstances men went about their business as if it were any other day, and not the day in which the inquisitor had made his intentions clear. As we reached the garden, I reflected on the idea of the paradox, on inconsistencies and disparities, infinite universes of differences and similarities, that were at once distinct and yet the same, and in a state of confusion, I could not refrain from questioning my master further on the subject of heresy.

'Master, I am confounded.'

'That does not surprise me,' he said, pausing to observe the sky above us. 'Life is complex and confusing and yet if it were a simple matter, we would all be gods, for our life must be a simple matter to Him. What confuses you?'

'Our enemies confuse me, master.'

'Ah, I see. So, you are confused because here in France our foe is not who he seems to be,' he said winking. 'But our foe is seldom who we think he is.'

'But an inquisitor, once a heretic, now burns those who follow the doctrines that he himself once believed? It sounds . . .'

'Contradictory?'

'Yes. Contradictory.'

'And that is where one relies on one's powers of good judgement.'

'If that is the case, then I must surely have none,' I said,

135

'for I do not know whom I should fear!'

'My good Christian,' he said patiently, 'you should fear all those whom you cannot like. This is always a good rule. Because it is likely that they do not like you.'

'But what if you are faced with having to fear even those whom you *should* like . . . Why must there be so many contradictions?'

'Contradictions are the way of the world! Listen to me. In the course of your life you will hear many things and occasions may arise when you will be tempted to allow your foolish heart to hold sway over your head, as you are now doing, and I tell you that you must never do it. Never decide even the most insignificant of things without first undertaking a fully reasoned deliberation.'

'Is that what you do, master? Do you never feel a thing passionately?' I asked.

'It is better to say that I choose to be dispassionate. Because a man who wants to live to a full age, to gain the respect of his equals, and the envy of his enemies, must never allow sympathy and antipathy to rule his reasoning. My advice to you is to remain unhampered by the trifles and trivialities of an emotional disposition and you will be a happy man. Rational thinking is the key.'

So says a man, I thought, whose temper is often foul. 'I'm sorry, master,' I said aloud, 'but heresy does not afford occasion for rational thinking.'

'Everything in life, my impertinent young rogue, affords one with occasion for rational thinking. Life is not simple, life is perplexing and convoluted, as is the question of heresy.' He paused in deep reflection and I knew he was thinking a great many things. 'In the East, you knew the enemy because the differences between you were more obvious, am I right?'

'Of course. That is it, exactly.'

'The infidel denies Christ, he believes in Mahomet. His

skin is a different colour and his customs are infinitely at variance from yours, and though as human beings you share a common physical law – as do all living creatures – that is all you share. Here in France, however, the enemy is far more deceitful, far more cunning.'

'Because the enemy here professes to believe what I believe?'

'Yes, his customs, too, are your own, and he has your complexion, your colouring. He may be your neighbour your friend, even . . . your priest. He is not who he pretends to be.'

'Who are you speaking of, master? The inquisitor or the church or the heretics?' I asked.

'All of them! Because even the faithful shepherd, whose task it is to guard the sheep from the hungry wolves, may be anticipating a good lamb stew! But we must begin at the beginning, if there is such a thing, for God had six days in which to create the world and how are we poor sinners to elucidate it in a few moments before mass?'

We entered the stables into the wonderful world of smells that are earthy and good, but murderous on my nasal passages. I sneezed twice in succession.

'Now then, heresy,' He sought Gilgamesh and found him in the stall next to Brutus. From a little repository in his habit he produced, as always, a morsel and fed it to him, patting the animal affectionately. 'You have heard no doubt of the dualists?' he continued, as though I should know what he was saying, 'such as the Cathars, for they were renowned in these parts (as you have found out of late) and are the very form of heresy that we suspect here at this abbey in one form or another, but there are many more . . . and we do not want to be here all day! You see, one must also consider those who have diverged, even from the essence of heretical doctrine, and call themselves by other names, or no names at all!'

'But that would mean that there are heretical heretics?'

'Something like that.'

'But how is one to tell one heretic from another when they are so similar that even the heretics become confused?'

'It is only from a distance that they may seem that way because human nature is both complex in its distinctions and similar in its simplicity. From a distance one plant looks very much like another, and yet one may be poisonous, while another may be harmless. You see Gilgamesh? Is he not in substance a similar creature to Brutus?'

'No, master, Gilgamesh is fiery of spirit, gallant, and speedy, while Brutus is slow, obstinate and exceedingly loud,' I answered.

'Yes, but you are only describing particulars, and not universals. If you were to see them from a great distance you would be hard-pressed to say that they were different.'

'It would have to be a great distance,' I retorted.

'Let us look at it another way. They each have four legs, a neck, a tail. They both eat oats and grass, they breathe air and drink water?'

'Yes, master, but Gilgamesh is a beautiful beast, high and slender. Your sight must not be as good these days if you can compare the two creatures.'

'But, my boy!' he cried, I believe exasperated. 'That is not the point! Both creatures are in substance similar and yet different in temperament, and in particular qualities that distinguish them even from other animals in their own breed.'

'And so you say that some heresies like Gilgamesh are better than others like Brutus?'

'No, that is not what I meant!' He sighed deeply. 'I mean that one heresy, from a distance, may be similar to another by virtue of its body of dissent, but not, in proximity, by virtue of its accident.'

'But they are both heresies. They are, like Gilgamesh and Brutus, of the same substance.'

'Yes. All heretics have fallen from the one true way, but some have fallen further than others. Finally you understand!'

'I think so, I see now that all heresies are evil and detestable.'

'Ahh, but if we believe Aristotle when he says that the endeavour of a human being always aims at some good, then we must surmise that there is an element of virtue in all human thought.'

'But if there were any measure of virtue in their heretical ideas, surely the church would not persecute them?'

He brought out one more morsel, popping it into the horse's mouth, and proceeded to a thoughtful pause. 'What is good and what is evil? Therein lies the key,' he answered finally.

'But that is plain and unquestionable.'

'Is that so?' my master asked, raising one eyebrow very high, and I knew that I had made a mistake. 'Then perhaps you would like to elucidate this age-old problem for me and all the great philosophers who are now basking in heavenly glory and for whom this very question was never answered? No, I think not! You have far too much confidence in your own perspicacity, and this will, one day, lead to your undoing!'

I nodded my head demurely.

'Now, if I may continue,' he cleared his throat. 'Plato tells us that a man cannot *be* good, for that is a privilege of the gods, and that he cannot *be* evil for those same reasons. He can *become* evil or good, but he therefore cannot *be* evil or good.'

'Well, if man can be neither good nor evil, what is left to him?'

'The middle state which, Plato says, is preferable to either. Perhaps it is the natural function of man to seek the middle way and this is the cause of heresy.'

'But tell me, master, for I become more and more confused, what makes the Cathars different from the Waldensians, and the Waldensians from the Spiritualists who seem to be so similar to the Franciscans?'

'It is all a matter of how far they have wandered from the middle way. Cathars, my boy, believe in a Manichean ideal of evil which rests on the belief that everything created in the material world – including man himself – is the work of the evil God. They deny the cross, for they do not believe Christ died upon it and they do not believe in the sacrament as it is given in the Roman church. St Augustine confesses to having been a Manichean before he was converted.'

'And what of the others like the Waldensians?' I pressed.

'The Waldensians do not seek doctrine outside the church, but their downfall rests in that they abhor wealth, believing it to be sinful, condemning rich bishops and priests of being corrupt and so not worthy to give the sacrament. A pious ideal when applied with temperance, but a terrible weapon in the hands of the poor and hungry, or those of extreme propensity whose violence leads to murder and plunder. These sects then become, after a time, like old encumbered trees whose branches are laden with fruit, whose seeds cause new trees to grow . . . perhaps birds carry the seeds a very long way from their place of origin . . . and thus, when they are carried to many diverse places, the trees they generate are different, because they are influenced by this or that; climate, soil, etc so that they become almost unrecognisable. This makes it exceedingly difficult for the church, as you can imagine, for her captains are constantly facing new strains of the old heresies.'

'So what can be done?'

'Not too much. Here in Languedoc we see that even when the rivers are awash with blood it is impossible to stem the tide of dissent because it is characteristic of the human spirit that it is infinitely resilient. You may quash a movement here and before too long new movements linked with the old can be seen springing up there. Like those seeds we spoke of earlier, having become estranged from the mother tree, they develop independently, and often in confusion, for they consist of members that had perhaps belonged to the Cathars or the Waldensians, or Bogomils from the *ordo Bulgariae* elsewhere. Often these men bring with them no subtlety of doctrine, only simple moralistic ideals. The accidents of one then are attributed to the other, and they are seen as one and the same, though initially in principle they were very different. It is a being that comes to life through a mixture of elements.'

'So you are saying that it makes no difference what heresy it is because they eventually intertwine, and so all must be equally punished?'

'No, that is not it.'

'But ...'

'No, because what a man confesses when persuaded with a hot iron, my boy, may far exceed the extent of his sin. One can never be certain that one hears the truth under torture.'

'But why lie? How could one confess to terrible crimes if they are not true?' I asked because I did not know, at that tender age, that the flesh is weaker than the spirit.

My master shook his head in dismay, and at that moment he looked more like a Saracen than a Christian. 'Firstly, we are not all born to endure a martyred end, my boy, otherwise we would all be saints! When one is tortured – and we must remember with what zeal an inquisitor pursues his victim – one will often confess to anything in order to die and in order to escape pain and humiliation. A person will often confess to the most remarkable things . . . Then too there is a strange phenomenon, something not explained by medicine or science, that occurs between an inquisitor and his captive. An unnatural, unholy bond that sees the accused confessing to greater and greater sins in order to please the inquisitor. After a time even the accused believes his own lies. It is a terrible thing.'

'And yet,' I retorted, 'if a person confesses to having committed a sin that he did not in truth commit he is then compounding that sin with an even greater one!'

'You say these things, Christian, because when one is young, one believes very simply, as you have said before, in black and white, right and wrong, good and evil, but just as nature adorns herself in manifold colours, so, too, are there various shades of virtue, as there are various shades of depravity.'

'How must I differentiate to what extent one evil is greater than another, and one good is less good than another good, master?'

'One must look into the heart of it to see what is heresy. In its most extreme case it is a noxious weed which seeks to strangle the good plant, but we must eradicate this weed wisely, for as we know, some poisons are not only harmful to the weed, but also to humans and horses and others only to cattle or dogs.'

Seeing my blank look, Andre considered another explanation.

'In my opinion the only true heresy seeks to take Christianity as a living spiritual reality, and transform it into a dead animal, one that only seems to live, but is decayed and lifeless . . . theoretical.'

'Do you mean, like the theologians do?'

'Yes, but they have the help of the Arabic philosophers who interpret Aristotle in such a way that man begins to lose sight of the spirit.'

'Master,' I interrupted, seeing my chance, 'I had a very strange dream last evening, in which I –'

'Did you? Well, you must tell it to me sometime . . .'

'But it concerned this very subject. A monk called Thomas and his companion were living in the shelter outside the abbey.

This Thomas spoke about a task that he had to perform, he said something about Christianising Aristotle.'

'Indeed, your mind works wonders in your sleep!' he exclaimed and I knew there was no point in pursuing it further. 'We were speaking of the heresies.' He scratched his greying head and pulled at his beard. 'Come outside.'

We turned away from Gilgamesh, leaving the comforting smells of the stables and walked to the garden, now blanketed in snow. Andre glimpsed a bush, now covered in the smallest leaves, and picked one or two. Rubbing them between the palms of his hand, he sniffed the scent lightly. A moment later, he remembered me and continued as before.

'To begin with, we must consider Christianity. Since the holy death in Palestine things have changed, Christian. In the first centuries men still had a knowledge of Christ, but this knowledge became corrupted. Some began to doubt that a God could have died on the cross, that is to say, Christ could not be born nor could He die since He could not have lived in a mortal body whose very essence is, to their way of thinking, sinful. You and I know, however, that Christ did indeed die on the cross, but his cross signifies life, not death, as the church would have us believe. As time passed, Christian, men have become dull of spirit and clearer of mind, and this means they need to make everything comprehensible, in a tangible way. So the church comes up with all manner of dogma and stupidity to explain things that cannot be explained. It tells us that Jesus was born to a virgin, when it is well known that Mary was inspired by the heavenly Sophia who comes from the region of the Virgin in the starry heavens! The church no longer knows the meaning behind the sacraments, or the reason behind the partaking of the wafer and the wine. It has lost the knowledge of why the monstrance is decorated with the sun and a sickle moon. The Cathars have a sentiment for this, you see? They have come into contact with an old Gnostic wisdom that understands what the church has forgotten. They know that Christ has come to us from the sun and that we partake of wafer and wine to remind us of that, because the wafer and the wine are products of sun forces. The monstrance depicts the forces of the sun, or Son, Christian, as they gain victory over the old forces of the Father, or the moon wisdom of the Jews.'

'But master —'

'Listen, they have become empty rituals now, and the church seeks to protect itself from what scraps of wisdom still exist in the world.'

'In the name of power?'

'Yes, Christian. There is a vast empire to protect and the pope has become its new caesar. He is the new *pontificus maximus,* you see he even retains the name! It should not surprise me if in the future he makes himself a god, infallible. Is he not almost a god? When the pope tells us that a black cross is the symbol for Christ, then we must accept it, is that not so? Or else prepare our carcasses for the pyre.'

'So we do not believe in the black cross, master?'

'Our cross, as I have just told you, is a red cross, it is a living cross, Christian! It tells us that Christ *lives* in our blood.'

'And so you are telling me that the heretics know more about Christ than the church and this makes the church despise them?'

'Cathars know many things even if their wisdom has become distorted as we have said, and it is worth keeping that in mind. There is distortion everywhere, it is inevitable.'

'Then everyone is wrong and the world shall fall into ruin.' I was crestfallen, my heart weighed down and my mind filled with thoughts like an anthill is filled with ants.

'In time man shall forget that there was ever a Christ and shall remember only Jesus.'

'I cannot believe that, master.'

'Now, now, there is hope, Christian. As men become clearer of mind they begin to question everything. They seek to know the reasons for things, the fundamental principles. Perhaps their questions are not always the right ones, but the important thing is that they question! The church struggles because it has no answers. It has forgotten the old wisdom and interprets everything wrongly. Then it gets into further trouble by expounding lies in order to cover up preposterous things. You see, that is why in the end it comes to despise men who strive after truth, it seeks to destroy them.'

'But God is the embodiment of truth. Is that not what you have always told me?'

'Yes, but the church believes that only it may say what is true and what is not. It wants to rule men's minds. It has forgotten about God altogether! You heard our conversation at the table last evening? It does not limit itself to the heretical orders, it also persecutes the educated men in the universities because the church believes, as we have heard, that knowledge breeds discord and doubt. The church condemns the search for knowledge because to see the truth leads one to discern it from what is untrue, and that is why lay people are prohibited from owning copies of the Bible.'

'But master, where do lay people find copies of the Bible when most can hardly read?'

'Those who can read have been known to make and disseminate their own translations. The council of Narbonne had to pass a law forbidding this practice by the Waldensians. You see, the church seeks to prevent men from questioning.'

'I think it is wise, for how can the ignorant man know anything of doctrine? If what you say is true and the old wisdom is lost, then only error can result.'

'Man must regain wisdom, perhaps in a different way than before.'

'But if you educate the ignorant man he will be like those learned men who are also condemned of heresy!'

'That is so, but I believe it is far better to suffer in knowledge than to suffer in ignorance . . . or perhaps it is worse? I don't know.'

'But I am a little wiser now, and yet I find myself knowing very little.'

Andre smiled with affection. 'Wisdom is gained in a lifetime, Christian. Even the greatest fathers of our faith have been known to have felt this way because they knew that man himself is imperfect! They understood that man carries within himself the polarity of good and evil, and so is bound to all that is divine and noble, and yet bound to dogmatism and opinions that may be erroneous. Remember our discussion that first day I warned you that in the coming days you would hear many opinions. Only trust what you know truly in your heart. Augustine himself has said that he would not have believed the gospels were he not constrained to do so by the authority of the church.'

'But master!'

'Do not look so surprised! Only four hundred years ago the pope himself allowed a form of heresy to enter into the matters of doctrine.'

'How?'

'He denied the spirit, and so he allowed a form of Arabic thinking to enter into the body of belief.'

'But man has a soul, is that not spirit?'

'No, Christian. The spirit is something higher. In this revelation, the pope decided that he should deny the spirit in man. He did not think clearly, however, because if you deny the spirit in man then you also deny the possibility of revelation through man, for it is the inner spirit that can, in turn, recognise the outer spirit, *et par conséquent,* what is revealed through it. Do you see how ridiculous it is?'

'I am once again confounded, master. Why should he deny it?'

'It is merely that he had lost the ability to see it, Christian.'

'Then who is right and who is wrong?'

'Right and wrong, like good and evil, are rarely what they seem.'

'I see . . . So it is the Devil's deception that makes good men seem bad and bad men appear good, so that even pious men are fooled?'

'Yes. Believe only what is in your heart, and yet it must come from a deliberation without emotion, for more often mistakes are made when men are driven by a feverish zeal . . . on both sides.'

'As in the case of Eisik?'

'Unfortunately, yes, for as Alcuin tells us, the righteousness of a crowd is always very close to madness. That is, often times there is a kind of frenzy enjoyed by men in the anonymity of a crowd. That is why the inquisition was formed in the first instance, to introduce a logical and practical way of dealing with such things! Without laws we lose the ability to hold together savage men in a society of civilised human beings. However, even as I say this, there are also those whose zeal is ignited by singular power. Inquisitors are not immune to such things.'

'And yet I remember a Scythian prince having said that 'Written laws are like spider's webs; they will catch the weak and poor, but would be torn in pieces by the rich and powerful.''

'Very good, Christian. Religious fervour requires a fine balance. This is true of both heretics and the most devoutly orthodox men who call what they approve, good, but what they do not approve, evil.'

'What then, master? Will we see justice done?'

'I don't honestly know. As men of science, however, we must not look at what is good or bad, wrong or right, we must rather search for the facts, find the cause, and treat the disease. And so too if we are to take the right path to solving our mystery.'

'Like you knew the right path the day of our arrival?' I offered.

'Yes!' he cried jubilantly, 'which only goes to show that I am usually right.'

'But not always,' I dared to say.

'Well, my impertinent boy,' he fired at me so suddenly that I nearly reeled, 'perhaps I should leave it all to your illiterate and clumsy faculties . . . Where would we be then?'

I looked down, knowing I had indeed been impertinent.

'Come on then, boy,' he said then, seeing my distress, 'it may be that I prove not so worthy of praise. This, too, remains to be seen.'

I stood, chastised, shuddering as something cold fell on my face. I looked up and the sun had disappeared and a greyness had overtaken us. It was now snowing lightly and I followed my master to the church, feeling tormented by doubt, watching as more and more snowflakes floated gently onto the ground before me.

8

Capitulum

Mass

A young man is ruled by antipodes. He either loves in abundance or he hates vehemently, his spirit glides confidently on a joyous breeze of hope one moment, or is plunged into the gulfs of despair and doubt the next. He is guided, we are told, by exalted notions because life's artistry has not yet humbled him or shown him his limitations. Now as an old man living by memory rather than by hope (could the little life left to me ever compare with the long past now gone and yet lovingly remembered?) I tend to smile, feeling a little pity for that poor young man, for I was in morbid contemplation of discrepancies and inconsistencies which threatened to overwhelm me.

The more my youthful-self reasoned, the greater my doubts became, like an object that casts a darker shadow the more one sheds light upon it. My master, because he was a man in his prime and, as Aristotle tells us, not guided so much by what is solely noble, but also what is useful, had during our discourse challenged many things that I had previously accepted unquestioningly – things that formed (albeit unknowingly) the cohesion of my existence – and I believed at that moment that I understood the origins of dissent and the metaphor of the seed. A little knowledge, I now surmised, was food for this odious germ which then only requires a suitable medium in which to thrive and to grow until it becomes a tree of suspicion and mistrust. I felt that perhaps the inquisitor was right. What good is learning if it drives one away from the grace of God's love?

And so, it was in this mood that every word of the Sunday mass, every ritual, every formula posed a question: is this the work of God, or only the desire of man, in his vanity, to mimic him? As the abbot ascended the altar and we sang *'Judica me Deus'* from Psalm 42, kissing it as the sacred repository of saintly relics, I wondered from what inexhaustible source were so many relics recovered? Indeed how many fragments of one holy cross could there be? Andre once said – I believe to shock me – that five churches in France pledged they held the one genuine relic of Christ's circumcision, and that the churches of Constantinople purported to have some hairs of the Lord's beard. When I asked him about the heart and body of the martyr St Euphemia, kept at 'Atlit by our order, he told me that it was said to have miraculous properties, and that it drew in many pilgrims. Raising one brow he then added that it was exceedingly good business too. How could one keep one's faith from crumbling like so much dust?

Before too long I found myself joining the others in reciting the *credo in unum Deum* and I wondered how I could sing it? *'Credo in unum Deum,* that is, I believe in one God.' But did I truly believe?

At some point the abbot consecrated the wafers of bread and the chalice of wine into the body and blood of Christ, and was bidding us to lift up our hearts to God; *'sursum corda',* I heard myself answer *'abeamus ad Dominum',* followed by the triple *Sanctus,* the *Agnus Dei* and the *Pater noster,* with a special emphasis on 'deliver us from evil', and I thought that these words must have been meant for me alone, for I was once again faced with further cause for distress. What if my master was right? What if there was no magic that allowed a man to turn bread and wine into the body and blood of Christ? Moreover, what if the one whose duty it was to perform this monumental and awe-inspiring task, was tainted with sin, corruption and irreverence? Did this result in the failure of the ritual, or did the blood and the body become tainted with the stain of his sin, so that all those who partook of it became stained also? Perhaps the Waldensians were right when they refused to take communion from those whom they saw as impure? Oh, what anguish! It was only by the barest margin that I managed to keep from shouting out 'no!' Then, almost overcome with guilt, I prayed for the Lord to pacify the ravenous, unrelenting beast that consumed my faith, with a sign of his universal omnipresence, his eternal and infinite goodness. God, I was convinced, was aware of my pain, and in his benevolence could restore my faith by rallying the elements to do his bidding. Soon, I was certain, a bolt of lightning would shatter the abbey, cataclysmically tearing asunder the church in an arc of blinding light that, landing squarely on the altar, would irradiate with its illuminance the void that was now my faithless heart. I would then know that God dwelt in heaven and on earth and in every place, and that he heard the feeble cry of a young, confused novice.

I waited, but God remained silent.

In that moment of deep despair my master leant in my direction a little and whispered, 'A pair of organs.'

'Organs.' I was shaken out of my misery for a moment.

'The instrument, boy, the instrument,' he said jerking his head towards a massive structure of pipes to our right and behind us. I had not noticed, but a young monk had been playing it, accompanying the service.

'Oh,' I said, 'but I only see one, master.'

'Don't be a goose, Christian, they are called a pair because they reproduce the operation of the lungs.'

'It is very large indeed,' I whispered back.

'Large!' he replied amused, for this afforded him the opportunity of instructing me further. 'I have heard of such an instrument at Winchester cathedral so majestic in size that it has no less than four hundred pipes! Indeed its keys are so large that the organists are forced to strike them with fists protected only by padded gloves!'

I smiled despite my anxieties, because it is characteristic of the young that although they suffer a great deal it is only for the shortest time, unlike the old, who for a long time do not feel their passions so intensely. And so it was that my master, being the cause of my misery, was also albeit unknowingly its alleviator.

After the *benedicamus Domino,* we answered '*Deo gratias*', and the brothers filed out in silence. We remained seated and, once alone, my master drew my attention to the master of music.

The brother stood by the altar, going through some musical element of the liturgy with a young acolyte, both engrossed in their duty.

'Yes,' I answered, remembering the spectres that I had seen when he gave his discourse the night Ezekiel had died, and so for this reason I eyed him suspiciously.

'*Mashallah* . . . he is a genius,' Andre said, and I wondered if he intended this to be complimentary, for not unlike his outward demeanour whose characteristics were often contradictory, he would sometimes say one thing, where he meant its exact opposite.

'He is a musical genius. Come . . .' He stood, tugging at my arm, and as we walked to the altar, at that moment, the young acolyte began to sing.

What a voice it was! It was as if all the choirs of heaven had been embodied in one individual. I stood transfixed. My master also paused to listen as the boy sang in a voice whose liquid perfection was almost intoxicating to the ear.

The master of music had his back to us, his arms outstretched, swaying gently to the waves, the flow of currents created by the holiest of human instruments.

The young man was singing the first responsory of Advent Sunday.

'Beholding from afar, lo, I see the coming power of God, and a cloud covering the whole earth. Go to meet him, saying: 'Tell us if you are the one who will rule over the people of Israel.''

To which the older man responded. *'All you men of earth and sons of men, both rich and poor . . .'*

Without turning, as though expecting us, and, in anticipation of our approach, the master of music then said, *'Dulcis cantilena divini cultus, quae corda fidelium mitigat ac laetificat.'* With this he turned to greet us, fixing my master with his energetic blue eyes filled almost to the brim with tears. He was slight and tall, with fine features though his nose was more prominent than classically acceptable. His every movement seemed strangely fluid, in harmony with some inner music.

'Jubilate Deo, omnis terra servite Domino in laetitia,' my master replied, quoting eloquently from the great book.

'Amen,' the brother concluded.

There was a pause in which we further listened to the sweet voice, and then my master added, 'The sound of singing does indeed make one glad . . . as you have said, even during such difficult times.'

'Especially during such difficult times, preceptor,' he said with a shy smile. 'It is truly a blessing and a miracle that man imbibed with the spirit, can so humbly express it.' He interrupted the singer, commenting on the inflection of a note with firm and yet kind authority, then waved the boy on and once again turned his attention to us.

'You are the master of music?' my master asked.

'Yes. I am brother Sacar, and this,' he gave his singing pupil a truly loving look, 'is my finest student, though he be my only one. I have been humbled by the grace of our abbot, who has entrusted me with the music for our convent. I must tell you though that my predecessor was the most learned, and indeed inspired, master of music. If I know anything it has come from those venerated lips,' his voice trembled a little.

'I ask because I mean to express my admiration for your work,' Andre said, 'your music seems far more beautiful than any I have heard.'

'Ah . . . you speak of our harmonious melodies . . . yes . . .' he smiled, 'our voices do not traditionally accompany the tenor voice as other choirs you may have heard. Our voices seek other harmonies through notes not following the cantus firmus.' He moved closer to my master, animated, 'We sometimes hear complex weaves of singular melody whose diverse but concordant strains cross and merge in waves of harmony! Oh yes . . . it is truly beautiful.'

'You use notation, I see.' My master was referring to a manuscript which the brother held loosely in his hand.

'Indeed! Indeed!' He showed us the strange figures. 'The discovery of notation by our brother from Cologne was truly a miracle! And since the addition of the musical staff by the learned Guido – who should be sainted – music can be experienced with the eye! Yes, it is a triumph! My predecessor was the one who

introduced this abbey to such wonders.'

'Very interesting. What was his name?'

The man's pale face became paler. 'Brother Samuel of Antioch.'

My master frowned, his eyes narrowing a touch, 'Samuel of Antioch?'

'Yes, a holy man from a holy land . . .' He paused, perhaps remembering his master's face with fondness, and his eyes became once again a little moist and I wondered if this was the monk Samuel, whose grave my master saw on our first day at the abbey.

'I see also that you have an organ.'

'Oh, yes . . . it is so like the voice, do you agree?' He held both hands together in a gesture of praise.

'A magnificent instrument. Is it operated by air or water?'

'You think too highly of our little community, preceptor, we are not so fortunate as to have an air-operated instrument. This one is very old and operates by the aid of water whose flow works the pump. We are lucky to have the service of an underground spring which runs below the abbey and we are able to divert its energy to a heavenly purpose.'

'So the abbey was constructed around the existing channel?'

'Yes and no. We have had to alter its direction slightly. Our beloved forefathers constructed a wonderful arrangement of drains that follow a course beneath us.'

'That is ingenious. And the water is diverted by what means, brother?'

The monk paused for a moment, seeming unsure of what to say. 'I am told that it is a miracle of engineering.'

'Surely from time to time these tunnels must be visited for practical purposes?'

'All I know is that the abbot has forbidden it for reasons of safety. We are told they have become . . . unstable. One brother nearly lost his life many years ago during an inspection.'

'So it has been visited in recent times?'

'Many years ago, though that brother is now dead, and our general father, the abbot, has imposed a silence on the subject. I feel uncomfortable discussing it, preceptor.'

'I am sorry, brother Sacar, it is merely that Abbot Bendipur has requested my help in the matter of Brother Ezekiel's death –'

'Do you think that the tunnels have any bearing on your investigations?' he interrupted a little anxiously.

'I must say that I do not know. I am by nature a curious man,' my master answered with equanimity. 'Curious things intrigue me. In any case your music is quite exceptional.'

Sacar was noticeably relieved to conclude the uncomfortable inquiry and to return to his beloved subject. 'Thank you, preceptor, and yet it is the spirit that sings!'

'I agree . . .' my master acknowledged, 'the voice is the bearer of the soul.'

Sacar beamed, his face almost radiant with pleasure, 'I believe, dear brother, that everything natural has its supernatural counterpart, do you agree? Even here in our modest church . . . The door which faces east is none other than Christ, through whom we enter heaven, the pillars are the bishops and doctors who uphold the Church, the sacristy is the womb of Mary, where Jesus put on human flesh. You see everything physical, has its spiritual counterpart.'

'A reflection of the order and number of the universe.'

'Music,' Sacar continued, lost in thought, 'music and prayer, the marriage of two complementary gifts. *Omnem horam occupabis, hyumnis psalmis, et amabis* . . . Music, being the greatest expression of the diversity of God through man and prayer ... *tenere silentium, super hoc orationem diliges et lectionem nutricem claustralium* . . . the expression of man's unity with the saints who, on our behalf, deliver our lamentations at the foot of the Christ and through him directly to God. Could there be anything holier?'

'Indeed.'

My master seemed far too amiable, and it struck me that he was biding his time before tackling unpleasant matters.

'Tanners invoke St Bartholomew, as we know. St John, plunged into a cauldron of burning oil, is the patron of candle-makers. Our St Sebastian is well known to be mighty in times of pestilence. St Apollinia heals toothaches, St Blaise cures sore throats, St Corneille protects the farmer's oxen, St Gall his chickens, St Anthony his pigs!'

My master smiled. 'Yes, though I have to wonder, dear brother, if these sainted men had intended their torment to be the vehicle by which a chicken lays a greater number of eggs, or indeed, the obesity of a pig is profitably increased.'

I knew my master frowned upon the ritual worship of saints which, in most instances, only replaced the worship of pagan gods, and tended to exceed veneration for the Lord himself.

The master of music seemed to miss Andre's point, however, and looked around him, absently motioning his pupil to his side. The boy stepped down, and made his way to his teacher. He was no older than me, though shorter, with thick black hair encroaching upon his tonsure. He did not smile, but fixed me with an unusually intense stare; perhaps curiosity, perhaps dislike.

'This is Anselmo de Aosta, our monastery's voice.'

The boy bowed humbly, crossing himself devoutly with his left hand.

'He is also not without talents as a translator. It is a fact that I may lose him to the library. Obedience . . .'

'Anselmo,' my master bowed his head with respect, 'you are named after one of the finest doctors of the church, may you honour him. So you are not only a fine singer, but also a translator?'

'I am also composing a new mass in honour of our Lady,' he said in his lilting voice.

'Exceptional!' Andre exclaimed, obviously impressed and I, God forgive me, felt a twinge of jealousy.

'I saw some of your works this morning. Your translation of Aristotle is enlightening! Where did you learn Greek?' my master asked, cunningly.

'My mother is Greek, and I have studied the classic pagans since I was old enough to read.'

'I see.'

'We have been fortunate to have had two young geniuses,' Brother Sacar added.

'Two! That is fortunate indeed, in such a small abbey. Who is the other?'

'The other . . . is unwell I'm afraid.'

'Oh, the novice! Yes of course.'

The monk gave him a blank look, 'Novice?'

'The young boy who was not at the dinner last evening.'

'Oh . . . yes, yes,' he hesitated a moment.

'Is he also a fine singer?'

'Well . . .' the brother trailed off, 'he was a very special child, weak, but gifted.'

'You say, was . . .?' my master asked. 'Has he died?'

'Oh, no!' Brother Sacar explained, in an anxious way, 'I mean, he was special as a child. He is now a young man, not much older than your scribe, though his qualities remain exceptional, even as a young man. That is what I meant.'

'Yes, I see,' my master said, then hastened to add, 'perhaps I might have a look at him in a medical capacity?'

'Oh, that is indeed a most generous offer,' he appeared ruffled, 'one that is sure to be welcomed by Brother Asa of Roussillon.'

'The infirmarian?'

'Indeed.'

'Of course, Asa. Well then, I shall seek him out,' my master concluded, rubbing his hands together. 'Where may we find him at this time of the day?'

'In the infirmary or the herbarium. Sometimes he goes out in search of plants in the forests around the abbey. Other times you may see him tending his garden. Here in this abbey we are never idle, preceptor.'

'Thank you, brother. I have enjoyed our conversation, and may I end it by saying once again that I believe your music to be truly remarkable.' In a grave tone, 'May God see fit to end this inquiry quickly and expediently in your favour.'

The monk nodded, 'Thank you, preceptor. No one knows the ways of God, but God himself. However, I must tell you that your words soothe my uneasy spirit.' He moved in the direction of the south ambulatory but something stopped him because he

turned around as though he had forgotten something. 'Preceptor,' he said, 'the death of our dear Brother Ezekiel has shaken
our community, but there have been other things . . . no doubt
the abbot has told you.' At this point he sent the boy away, watching him leave before continuing more desperately than before.
'Perhaps I am committing a sin against the rule, but I am afraid.
I am afraid for the future of our community.'

My master was intrigued. 'What is it, brother?'

'Before you arrived, preceptor, another monk . . . in fact,'
he lowered his eyes, 'my predecessor, Brother Samuel, was found
in the church. He had been . . .' he swallowed hard, as though
these words were bitter in his throat, and his eyes welled with
tears, but my master, whose interest had increased ten-fold, cared
little for sensitivity.

'He had been what, brother? Murdered, perhaps?'

The other man blanched and his eyes widened as though
he had seen a devil. 'You know?'

'Tell me!'

'He was in the church. He was found dead.'

'Who found him?'

'Brother Daniel of Albi, they were inseparable.'

'Another old monk?'

'Yes, he found my master lying at the foot of the virgin,
near the entrance to . . . Go speak to Brother Daniel, you may ask
him anything about the abbey, he knows it very well.' He looked
down for a moment. 'I have to go now, God bless you and keep
you safe.'

With these words the master of music left us, with many
questions unanswered.

I asked my master how he had known that the young
novice had been missing from dinner.

'If you will remember, the hospitaller told us on our first
day that the abbey had only two novices, and since I could see
only one at dinner I assumed that was whom he meant. I simply

made a hypothesis, assuming the English and not the Greek interpretation of the word.'

'The English interpretation?'

'The English understand a hypothesis to be something that may be true, but needs testing whereas the Greek say it is something assumed for the purpose of argument.'

'I remember now. The hospitaller was very suspicious of the novices, saying they drank too much and ate too much.'

'Yes, it is the curse of the old that they conveniently forget they were ever young.'

'And the curse of the young, master, that they don't always remember what they should,' I said a little dejected.

'Very good, Christian! We'll make a philosopher out of you yet, even if it kills you.'

9

Capitulum

Before Nones

We searched the abbey, but it was not until later in the afternoon that we found Brother Daniel in the north transept chapel. A slight figure in grey, he was almost indistinguishable from the stone around him. He lay in profound meditation at the foot of the Virgin of our sorrows, and did not turn at the sound of our footsteps as we approached. It was only after we had been kneeling beside him for a very long time that he raised his head and cast a bewildered gaze upon us, like a man alighting on the shores of some distant and unfamiliar place.

'She is purity and serenity,' he said finally.

'The countenance of virtue, brother,' my master answered.

'You have good eyes! One whose eyes look upon the virgin with love and adoration will want for naught else! I am glad of your presence, preceptor, it has been many years . . . How are things in the holy land? Have we lost Jerusalem? Oh, I am a senile fool! I remember now . . . yes, perhaps better than I remember what I ate this morning.' He smiled warmly, and taking my master's hand in his, stood with difficulty. 'Youth is beautiful

. . .' he touched my head only slightly with warm, nervous fingers, 'but this world grows old with ugliness! Poor brother, he was a man who could see. There are so many who see and yet are blind. Am I the last now, I wonder?'

'How do you mean the last, brother?' my master asked.

'The others are . . . but that is another matter. What year is it? No, do not answer, it does not concern me.' He began to pray, *Dominus illuminatio mea, et salus mea, quem timebo?* – The lord is the source of my light and my safety, whom should I fear? – but what was I saying? Oh my feeble, feeble mind . . .' He shook his head.

'You were about to tell us, venerable Daniel, in what way you were the last.'

'Was I? *Should* I tell you? I am old, and I therefore distrust everyone and everything. Perhaps that is why I am old?' He laughed a little. 'I am the last of the first, and yet, no, I am wrong, Brother Setubar was also one of us, though much younger . . . thank God for Setubar, the milk of human kindness runs through his veins . . . Did you know he was a fine physician once? He cured me of phlegm! In any case, that is all you need know . . . shhh!' He looked around him. 'I sense his presence. Somewhere in this abbey *he* waits!'

'Who? Brother Setubar?'

He looked aghast. 'No, the antichrist, of course! He is everywhere . . . he is stubborn, and so he is patient.'

My master nodded gravely. 'Where have you seen him in particular?'

'Do you not know?' he searched my master's face closely. 'Why, in the human soul, in the soul, my sons, and in our midst, in this abbey, though disguised.'

My master paused, wording his reply, 'Is he in human form, venerable Daniel?'

'Of course, how else? He has chosen a monk, perhaps there are two . . . tarnished with unmentionable crimes . . .' in a soothing voice then, 'Oh, now I have frightened you, my child. I know, I know, but do not fear unwisely, fear is only a good thing if it instructs us to be attentive and uneasy. Ease is his servant as you know, the love of comfort, his willing vassal.'

'Who is *he,* venerable master?' I asked because I saw in his kind eyes that he had given me this sanction.

'*He* is old, older than time, and wiser still . . . he is infinitely persistent, he follows a design and is easily recognisable. Our dear brother, now gathered to God, had the *arcanum!* He knew the secret of the evil one who will come again in the second *millennium.*' The old man placed a milky hand over his forehead as though this thought taxed his mind. 'We must prepare, for the battle is nigh! But I am weary, so weary.'

My master said humbly, 'You mean the first *millennium,* brother, that is yet to come?'

The old man looked at him as though he had not understood his words. 'No, not the first, but the second!'

'Venerable master,' Andre said softly, throwing me a look that conveyed his pity for the older man, 'some days ago you found a brother dead in the chapel.'

The old man's face creased with pain. 'No! Must I speak of it? Who told you?'

'Brother Sacar.'

'Sacar has a good ear, but a loose tongue! Yes, he was choked, his face was blue – the Devil sucked out his soul. Oh . . .' he convulsed, 'mortify the flesh, rid it of sin and make your souls transparent for the love of Christ, or he will find you also.'

'Where was Brother Samuel when you found him?'

'Here, at the foot of the lady. Please, I do not wish to speak of it again, I am tired, so tired.'

My master continued with tenderness, 'Before Brother Ezekiel died, he spoke of a holy one, whom he said the antichrist and his followers awaited, something about a sacred jewel?'

'Yes, yes,' he replied, 'they are cunning . . . but they will not find him. Oh, Lord! Have I not tried to escape the world beyond these sainted walls? Have I not sought freedom from the dominion of worldly things? And yet,' he raised his eyes to heaven, 'in penance, in exile, it continues to seek me out.'

My master changed his tack, 'You have been at this abbey for many years?'

'Years?' he looked amazed. ' I do not remember years . . .'

'Where did the first founding monks come from, brother?'

'Founding monks?'

'The ones who built the abbey?'

He shook his head. 'We must not speak of such things.'

'I only mean to praise their work, for this is indeed a fine abbey. Were they all Cistercians?'

'Cistercians?' He looked a little confused.

'The brothers who built the abbey?'

'Cistercians. Yes, white monks. Oh! They were brave men, but there are no longer brave men in this world, only cowards. In times long gone, men were full of wisdom, now they are filled with egoism, in the past they were vehicles of grace, now they are merely empty vessels.' He sighed deeply, 'The church falls into the pit with each new day, distorting the teachings of the sainted fathers, so that they have become a pale shadow of a brighter vision.' He looked at me, his eyes veiled with tears. 'The sun rises on the genius of man, but at the same time it sets on the living spirit, and my heart longs to be gone from this place. I remain only for him. When he departs this mortal prison, I will pray for the moment of death, be it quick and painless, or agonising and martyred, only death will be my final absolution.'

'You say, venerable brother, that you remain for him. Do you mean Brother Setubar?'

'Good heavens, no!' he chuckled, as though Andre were out of his mind.

'Someone else in the abbey, then?'

'Of course! Have you not been listening? That is why they have come! Naturally.'

'You mean the pope's men.'

'They are learned men, but they believe all manner of erroneous things, all elucidating . . . none *knowing*. All seeking paths that lead them to the abyss. The poor want to be rich, the rich want a simple life, the church condemns them all, because she places money and power on the altar of God! Transformed into a harlot who will lay belly to belly with the Devil for a sackful of gold.' At this point I blushed most severely, but the old brother seemed lost in this vision and did not notice me. 'They know that he is here, the synagogue of Satan has found the little rose!' I gasped, and he turned, mistaking my gasp for fear of his words, but it was his reference to the rose that had astounded me. 'Do not look so alarmed, my dear . . . sinning is not a privilege of the weak and ignorant. Some day you will come to know that the line that divides wickedness from saintliness is often more indistinct than that which separates erudition and stupidity . . . the inquisitors, my sons, smell of luciferic dung! Ahh but then one sees the Virgin! Though she is marred by my feeble sight she remains the object of all things beautiful and noble, and once again I am almost prepared to believe that there is goodness in this world. The pious little mother whose daughter is the church and yet the daughter mocks the mother with her temerity, offering to feed her the daughter's milk . . . but was it the patriarch who said it or was it the pope?' He became a little vague, growing tired, then he spoke in a fragile voice. 'In any event you are faithful, praying to her for guidance.'

'We pray for peace, venerable master.'

'Ahhh, peace!' he nodded and then added, a little astonished, 'but you are a man of war?'

'I pray for inner peace from which, one hopes, sprouts the seed of the outer.'

'Yes, yes, one hopes! If peace be your request none other

can intercede on your behalf with as much influence as our lady.'

'Venerable master, you are a wise and prudent man.'

'I should be prudent! My life has taught me many things, but we old ones desire most what we need most urgently, and what I need most urgently now are some raisins. My mouth tastes of death. Perhaps I am dying, perhaps I am dead? If only Jupiter would bring back the years. And yet soon . . .' He was suddenly exceedingly lucid and I marvelled at the convenient frailty of his venerable mind. 'So you want to know about the tunnels?' he said. 'I know this is why you have come.' He looked around him. 'He told me not to tell . . . but the world will soon know everything, is that not so?'

'Who told you not to tell?'

He lowered his eyes, like a little child caught stealing sweet cakes. 'That I cannot say . . .' Looking around him once more suspiciously, 'What do you want to know?'

'The catacombs, are they reached through the tunnels?'

'That is common knowledge, preceptor. The secret does not lie in *where* they are reached, but rather *how*. In any case,' he narrowed his eyes, 'what do you want with the catacombs?'

'The abbot,' my master said patiently, 'has asked me to investigate the recent terrible murder.'

The old man looked at my master anxiously. 'You know then that the evil one works through a monk who has ignored the *interdictum* – the prohibition?'

'You mean someone has entered the tunnels?'

The man nodded, closing his eyes.

'How do you know, Brother Daniel?'

'I know because it is the duty of every monk to guard his fellows, to keep them from sin. Had this been observed perhaps much would have been prevented. In any event, the crypts are unsafe . . . a labyrinth of tunnels and channels of water. Anyone going there would never return. Only the Devil could find his way out, that is why this monk must be the Devil himself!'

'But how does one enter it, brother?'

'There are many entrances . . .' he grinned and answered in Virgil's words, *Facilis descensus Averno* – that is to say, easy is the way down to the underworld . . . but to retrace one's steps and to make a way out to the upper air, that is the task, that is the labour. It has only one exit.'

'Perhaps I should have asked regarding its exit.'

'But there is the abbot's prohibition . . .!'

'I understand but the monastery is endangered, venerable Daniel, by many foes. The inquisitor will make a judgement, perhaps not favourable – more monks may die . . .'

The man fell silent. Indeed, I thought that he had fallen asleep, for he hung his head on his chest and made snoring noises. He then spoke, lifting his eyes to meet my master's with gravity. 'I will tell you, only because I fear for those brothers who are innocent, but I will tell you without telling you,' he said with a sigh, 'so that I do not sin against the rule. The combinations you must calculate for yourselves. I am old, my mind is weary . . . the signs . . .the planets, it is too difficult.' He pointed to an area to the right of the Virgin, near the exit to the graveyard. 'There, *Procul este, profani!* But you must not enter!

Spirits guard the tunnels. They follow the seven letters in number and order, but he who would seek to go against the seven churches . . . he will perish!' Drawing his cowl, he said, 'Look for vanity in the one who commits these heinous crimes, this one sin begets all others. You may pray for Brother Samuel, my dearest friend, for Ezekiel too, and also for me if you wish . . . but you must be vigilant.'

'Thank you, brother, we will use this knowledge wisely.' My master prepared to leave, but at that very moment Setubar entered the Lady Chapel. It seemed to me that he was following our every move, listening in on our conversations. Such was the feeling he instilled in me when his eyes cast their hot, piercing gaze on us.

'There you are, dear one, I have been looking for you.' He removed his cowl. Fixing Daniel with a stern look, he handed the old man something.

Daniel beamed like a little child. 'Ahh, you remembered.'

'As always,' he said benevolently. Turning to my master, he asked, in an amiable way, if we had found the abbey interesting. 'I have seen you wandering about, asking many questions, observing, as does any good physician.'

There! I had indeed been correct. He had been following us.

'I find your abbey exceptional, Brother Setubar. Only today I have learnt so much.'

'Have you indeed?' The old man raised his brows and narrowed his eyes a touch.

'Yes . . . and one thing puzzles me.'

The man leant solicitously in my master's direction. 'If I may be of assistance?'

'This is the thing, venerable brother, abbeys for the most part display an immeasurable preoccupation with past accomplishments which, at times, you might agree, tends to border on the sin of pride. Here, however, no one can tell me much beyond one or two generations, much less who founded the abbey and when.'

'As you can ascertain from your own lips, preceptor, we Cistercians are not vainglorious like those Cluniacs you may know in the large cities. We walk the hallowed halls built by our forefathers and we sing God's praise in the stalls built from their sainted hands, and we pray each day in our venerated church that we might preserve our humility and our temperance. What else is there to know?'

'It is only that I am intrigued as to the origins of your monastery.'

The old man nodded his head thoughtfully. 'As is always the case, thirteen brothers – the mirror of Christ and his twelve apostles – set out to find a lonely place, a place where they could

feel the spirit of God most readily; a place far from the temptations of a wicked world. The rest you see before you. It is simple.'

'Yes, you are indeed so secluded that, in fact, not one of
your abbots has ever attended a meeting of the general chapter.
To some this might appear strange.'

An evil look passed over the old man's face. 'It is very
difficult for an abbot to leave his monks, there are too many
considerations, there is the weather, and time of year, for as you
know we are very often not able to travel the road that leads out
of the forest. And there is also the distance, as you have seen
for yourself. In any event, the things that are discussed at such
gatherings have little to do with our small community, preceptor.
They are only for those whose motivations are governed by political considerations, those who live in the shadows cast by kings
and popes. We, on the other hand, live in the shadows cast by the
great mountain that feeds us and quenches our thirst.'

'Yes, that is another thing that I have learnt today, venerable brother.' My master cleared his throat and at the same time
changed the subject. 'So you have lived here all your life?'

'What has that got to do with anything?' he answered.

'I was hoping that you could tell me, for I also am a lover
of architecture, how long it has been since the new additions
were made to the church.'

The old man frowned, 'Additions?'

'Yes, surely you must remember. For I was only speaking to Brother Macabus today on that very topic, only I forgot
to ask him . . .'

'Ahh, yes, yes. I'm afraid my mind is becoming addled.
The additions . . . it was so long ago. Forgive me,' he shook his
head.

'It is of no consequence, once again curiosity. Perhaps
the abbot might help me. In any case we must not take up any
more of your time, Brother Daniel needs his rest,' my master said
very quickly.

'Nonsense!' said Brother Daniel with emotion.

'No Daniel,' Setubar affirmed. 'The preceptor, who is also a physician, can see the pallor on your cheeks. Come and I will read to you from the gospels.'

'The pallor on my cheeks!' the man said indignantly. 'Am I a maiden that I must wear a sanguine expression?' Then, 'Are there any more raisins?'

'No more today, as I have told you before.' Setubar locked Daniel's arms into his and directed him to the ambulatory, but before they could enter the south transept, Daniel called out to us without turning,

"Let the hymn baptise you with the nine resonances of water. Beware, the antichrist is at hand!'

We remained for a little while in the Lady Chapel and then strolled out into the graveyard through the north transept door and into the cold winter day, meditating on Brother Daniel's revelations.

'So, brother Setubar did not remember the church alterations. Is that significant?' I asked.

'It would have been more significant if he had.'

'How do you mean?'

'What do you mean how do I mean, boy! There were no alterations . . . I simply made that up, so when he suddenly made excuses for his lapse in memory I knew that he was not being truthful.'

'But you said Brother Macabus —'

'I know what I said.'

'But then you have lied yourself!' I said aghast.

'Dear boy, lies are an abomination unto the Lord!' he exclaimed fervently, adding without even the slightest hint of guilt, 'but a very present help in times of trouble!'

'So what did you find out by lying?'

'Christian, you must learn to think with the head God gave you. Setubar, a man who can quote word for word from the old book, a man whose eyes are as sharp as his, is not in possession of an addled mind. Besides, the old are known to have very fine memories of distant events, even though they cannot remember what they had for breakfast, as Daniel has admitted. Setubar should have remembered something so significant as the alteration of a church. No I do not know as yet why he lied, but I have my suspicions.'

At this point it began to snow, not lightly as earlier in the day, but a heavy, pregnant fall, more appropriate to winter than to spring. I patiently followed my master as he walked among the graves whose positions were denoted only by white crosses. My master, who had always been unperturbed by death, whistled as he inspected every cross and there were indeed several.

I drew the cowl over my head to protect it from the snow, which even now found its way into the collar of my habit and down my back. Suddenly I heard my master say 'Aha!' with such exuberance that I slipped on the icy ground, and narrowly escaped falling face down onto the grave of Sibelius Eustacious.

'Eureka!' he exclaimed.

'Master?' I asked, a little annoyed.

'Eureka,' he said, amazed that I did not recognise it. Then impatiently, 'Archimedes . . . Eureka! In other words mon ami, I've got it!'

I shook my habit of snow and said, not too politely, 'What do you mean, you've got it?'

'Look at this!' he pointed to a headstone of moderate height. It was situated nearest to the mountain wall that cradled the abbey, quite a distance from the others. I walked over to it and my master grabbed me by the arm in his excitement and said, 'What do you see? Come now for I am cold and we are losing light.'

I looked at it closely. It was a rectangular stone upon which only the shape of a sword was carved.

I told my master what I saw and he looked at me and

said with irritation, 'Dear Christian, I too can see! No, I do not mean that you should describe it to me, I mean to know if you recognise it.'

It was as though I had suddenly become blind, for the more I looked the less I saw.

'Dear boy!' he exclaimed. 'How can you not know it? It is a Templar grave!'

'A Templar grave?' I said, stunned. Why should I have recognised it? In the East men were buried in haste, with rarely a wooden cross to mark their remains.

Kneeling with some difficulty Andre removed a portion of the shallow layer of snow covering the grave. 'This is an old grave. It must have been an important monk, for no other head-stone can be found here . . . very interesting.' He stood looking around. 'This is perhaps finally making some sense.'

'But that would mean . . .'

'Do not make assumptions, Christian, it may be the grave of a wealthy knight who, on his way to the holy land – partaking of the generosity of the monastery – died here of something or other.'

'But ...'

'We must wait before committing these things to our hy-pothesis, we must first take a look at the great book in the chap-ter house. Come, lest we draw attention to the headstone.'

So we left the graveyard and as we rounded the court-yard, passing first the abbatial church then making our way to the cloister buildings, we came upon the bishop ambulating toward us. My first instinct was to turn and walk the other way and I could tell from my master's momentary hesitation that he too felt the same, but we could not avoid him.

He walked towards us with unsteady gait, for walking was not a simple matter for the bishop. Not only did his considerable size impede his progress – I dared not imagine what layers of fat must be hidden beneath his ecclesiastical vestments – but also a vacuous haziness that I suspect was the result of a good deal of monastery wine.

On our journey to the abbey, my master had commented, rather unkindly, that the bishop was like a man who wore ill-fitting clothes. I noted his sumptuous ermine and velvet, his absurdly huge pectoral cross, catching the meagre light and throwing it back in brilliant colours, and I realised that my master was right. For all his regalia nothing served to soften the troubled expression that had long ago settled on his blotched face, leaving deep furrows and wrinkles, clouds of mistrust and disdain. My master enlightened me that his appointment in France made him an outcast at the king's court, as he was seen as a papal infiltrator, sent to spy on France. He, in turn, viewed everyone with derision, perhaps feeling that he deserved a better position than an inconsequential bishopric, miles from Rome, and further still from any chance of career advancement. Whatever the case, he was a man capable of the deepest hatred, so it seemed to me, a man envious of all men, as though he moved inside a storm; his mere presence appeared to signal bad weather.

The bishop reached us huffing and puffing and paused, catching his breath and patting his paunch as a pregnant woman pats her belly, lovingly.

'Dear preceptor,' he said after a moment, in his voice a suspicious magnanimity, 'I have been looking for you in every place!' In a lower voice, 'I must speak with you on matters of extreme delicacy.'

'I am your willing servant,' my master bowed with humility, but in his tone I noted some annoyance.

'Yes . . . yes . . .' he looked about him with a frown of importance. 'Last night we were witness to an abominable crime. The inquisitor was right. The Devil roams these evil corridors and none are safe who seek the truth in the name of God.'

'Those whose eyes look for evil will find it in every place, your grace, even in God himself,' my master said calmly.

'Come now, preceptor, we must not be careless! There is an evil working here that is more powerful than you know. Rainiero has warned us to keep *en garde*. The next to die could be one of us, therefore I am here to advise you that we are to travel in pairs and stay in our cells as much as possible, until such time as these proceedings are dispensed with.'

'And did the inquisitor also advise you to wear a garland of angelica as named by our Brother Linaeus to be efficacious as a safeguard against evil?'

'No.' The man was wide-eyed, not knowing, as I knew, that my master was commanding the tool of Aristophanes. 'Do you recommend it, preceptor?'

'Only when the moon is full, your grace.'

'Oh,' the man said gravely, nodding his head, and, looking up at the deeply overcast sky, added, 'Most wise. One never knows . . . We are told of men who conjure up demons to exercise power over inquisitors. Incantations which, when recited several times, can put an enemy out of the way! Keep an eye on that Jew, preceptor. It is, after all, common knowledge that Jews are responsible for everything of a diabolical nature. Much can be attributed to their designs. Have we not all heard of the terrible acts committed in Saxony and other places, where they regularly steal the host in order to use it for their own evil purposes, causing it to cry out in agony – as it is tortured and is made to relive Christ's sufferings – and to produce miracles of every kind!'

I gasped and my master gave the bishop a reproachful look. 'Your grace, let us not frighten my young scribe with such stuff, none of which has been witnessed, nor proven. We all know that whenever a genuine inquiry was held into these accusations its findings always exonerated the Jewish community. A learned man should be above superstitions which occupy the feeble minds of the wretched and the poor.'

'Indeed,' the bishop squared his shoulders, his voice icy as the wind, 'the fact remains, preceptor, that even those of the converted species, in their heart of hearts, reject the purity of Christianity. That is why they steal the host, and also why they kidnap Christian boys and murder them in fiendish rituals . . .'

I could see that Andre was becoming exceedingly annoyed. The bishop, not altogether dull in his senses, saw it also and changed the subject with a diplomatic flair. 'But, of course, I sought you on another matter, a matter of utmost importance, as I have said.' He said this last line with a flourish of his hand, and his amethyst ring flickered in my eyes dazzling me, the spell only broken by the gloom of the cloisters as we entered them through the arched aperture. Far away I heard a bird cry out, perhaps an eagle. Otherwise the day was strangely still, the air frigid and damp. I longed for a warm cup of ale to gladden my heart.

'How may I help you, your grace?' my master asked when it seemed that the bishop would not begin.

'I wish to speak to you about the proceedings.' The Benedictine paused for a moment, I believe unsure of how to broach the matter, he then placed his plump palms together in the manner of prayer and slowly, with deliberate wording, began, 'I am deeply concerned, brother Templar, that you may not be aware of the difficulties faced by the church in these very difficult times. Indeed, the entire continent, of which France is but one small part, has been a hotbed of intrigue and I fear you may not understand the importance of our duty to the pope, in the matter of . . . in the matter of, the abbey.'

'My lord, I am always conscious of my duty.'

'Yes, no doubt,' he cleared his throat, 'but while you were away – fighting valiantly on behalf of all good Christians – many things have changed.'

'Perhaps you should enlighten me, your grace.'

'I shall. Firstly, as you may know, the church has been occupied with the unholy works of the *guedes* here in France, whose character is not unlike the *Ghibellines* of my own country, and whom everyone knows, seek only to fatten their coffers with the blood of Christ. They are supporters of imperialists. Helped by Louis and his brother, they collude to weaken the power of the papacy by reducing the privileges of the church and refusing to pay taxes! We must watch the fox and the wolf with diligence, lest we lose the vineyard!' He moved his vastness in the direction of the large arches overlooking the central court, and fixed my master with a pained expression that on his face looked absurd. 'I fear the king supports those responsible for the death of one pope – God rest his soul – and the dismemberment of Italy.'

'I think you are confused, we are not speaking of *Ghibellines*, only merchant guilds, craft guilds.'

'Ahh . . . but the king supports them, like Manfred supports the *Ghibellines*, because he wants power . . . Louis grows stronger by the day.'

'But it was the pope, your grace, who handed Languedoc over to him, knowing him well enough. In return the church was promised the end of heresy. But our lord pope was wise for another reason, for he allied himself to a powerful throne, a champion, in the event that his power was once more threatened. It is after all Louis' brother, Charles of Anjou, who stands at the ready, waiting to ensnare Frederick's son, Manfred, before he can take up his father's sword against the church! The pope seems to ally himself with whomever it pleases him, dear bishop. Has he not at this moment the *Ghibelline* Ottaviano governing northern Italy because this man's family is very powerful in Bologna, whose geographical position is highly strategic?'

The bishop gave a grunt, perhaps because he hated *Ghibellines*, or perhaps because he thought that he should have been given this position. Nevertheless he defended his pontiff. 'The pope's designs are the concern of God, how am I to question his wisdom? However, you must concede that his supreme authority must remain flawless. How can we perform our duties when the king and the consuls continually erode our power? It is no wonder that we must find intricate and devious ways to exercise our jurisdiction . . .' he trailed off as if to leave much to the imagination.

'But is it not also the inquisitors that threaten your power, your grace? The Dominicans who presume to know more than the wise Benedictines.' My master knew the antagonism that existed between the orders on this matter, and I believe he was using it as a divisive tactic.

The other man narrowed his puffy eyes, 'Yes, there are men who unknowingly function as the enemy's tool, but we must keep in mind our duty to the faithful. That is what is most important. For instability always leads, as is well known, to heresy. Look at Languedoc! You must remember, so many here, even those whom the church had trusted, were 'questionable'. The battle is difficult, but all of us must fight the holy war together, even if sometimes we do not always agree as to the methods applied!'

'No war is holy, your grace,' my master said sadly, 'it is only war.'

'But you are a man of war! Do you say that the wars you have fought have not been for a holy cause?'

'I am a Templar, a knight, but also a doctor. What I have seen has not pleased my soul.'

The bishop assessed the meaning of my master's words and chose, for the moment, to ignore the entire matter, 'In any case, with a new pope we may see things return to normal, we might forget the stink of the false emperor!'

'A false emperor that was crowned by the pope.'

'But what choice did he have? Tell me! Philip of Swabia was dead, Otto of Brunswick was an underhanded mercenary.

Frederick was his only choice. Besides, there were agreements, promises . . . He sought to lie like the Devil until crowned, and once emperor he began his campaign to establish complete imperial authority! Do not confound the truth with lies, preceptor, he was excommunicated at the council of Lyons because of his treason and you, a Templar, should have no reason to side with the likes of that fox! Did he not retain Templar property in Italy? Did he not shame your order by forming an alliance with the Saracens, managing to secure the Holy Land single-handedly, where your order and others were disastrously unsuccessful? We have seen your incompetence in your terrible defeat at Mansourah.'

My master blanched. 'Frederick may have secured the Holy Land,' he said with vehemence, 'but such a bargain was procured at the expense of papal interests, as well as the interests of other European states. However, peace is peace, and I believe one has to measure the success of his diplomacy on those terms.'

'Many have been deceived by that snake's artful ways. Many still believe the false emperor to have walked according to truth, but it is plain to anyone that he was a devil, pretending to be a pillar of God in order to disguise his devious plans. It is common knowledge that he embarked on his crusade merely to elevate himself in the eyes of those around him. Once in Outremer, however, his zeal for sacrifice became tempered by a desire, nay, an obsession to serve his own interests and not the interests of the Holy See! He became infected because when you lie belly to belly with pigs you smell like pig, because sin begets sin . . . that also is common knowledge.' Wagging a finger at my master agitatedly, as though he had forgotten something of great importance, which he was now about to impart, he said, 'Rumours abound that your men at Acre were influenced by Cabbala and Islam, the seed of heresy! There are many who believe that your order has for too long walked a path that is not so straight.' He moved closer in a conspiratorial way, 'Even your dear Louis made your grand master kiss the hem of his tunic as penance for his arrogance. And then there are the rumours, which connect your order with necromancy, sorcery, and all manner of foulness, which I dare not repeat, for doing so would distress my quiescent senses. These rumours may be the result of malicious conspiracy,' he added. 'Nevertheless, we live in delicate times, preceptor, the memory of heresies and bloody massacres is still fresh. Do we not remember Avignonet? So much bloodshed! The new pope knows that you defended the heretics of this region, that you harboured Cathar nobles and their families, aiding murderers and adopting their doctrines . . .'

'If you speak of women and children,' my master said with polite hostility, 'imperilled by blood-thirsty animals, if you mean the elderly and the infirm, then those rumours are true. We have always maintained that the only true Crusade is the one against the infidel. Must we recall the terrible crime that saw women and children massacred in the churches?'

The bishop smiled with malice. 'The antichrist makes no distinction between sex, nor age. That is well known. And neither should those, whose place – in the divine order of things – is to root out such loathsomeness. Kill them all! God will recognise his own!'

'God forgive the bishop of Citeaux, I believe he did not know what he was saying when he uttered those words,' my master said bitterly.

The bishop looked at him curiously, as though this reply was beyond his understanding. 'The bishop of Citeaux was a practical man, as I am. Even now there still exists a stink about the place. We must stamp out any seedlings before they resurface, and we can do no better than to start with these monasteries whose influence and wealth surpasses that of any secular organisation, whose abbots feel themselves autonomous and unconstrained. These false clerics, we know, side with emperors and kings against Rome. They call secular rulers their masters, quoting our beloved St Ambrose and St Augustine and using their divine words to further their own selfish aims at independence! Praise God that the pope has commanded a review of all monastic practices in this area! It is time we root out all those who stray from the regulations of the Apostolic See.' He then proceeded in a fraternal way, 'Take care that your order is not next!'

'We are sanctioned by the pope, your grace.'

'I confess, you have been useful,' he answered as we rounded the south walk and the scriptorium, now empty and silent. 'But do not make the mistake of thinking that we will look the other way if your *brotherhood* transgresses the teachings of Christ. Consider this . . .' He moved closer, 'There are many who, from the start, have had misgivings about your order's duplicity. I, for one, and many others like me, are watching you and your kind with the utmost care. St Bernard may have been your most devout advocate, but I feel sure that he looks down from the blissful non-existence of divinity, in rebuke. His valiant knights, behaving like Jews!'

'I would hope that in heaven there is less distinction between race and creed than we find here among sinful mortals. However, if St Bernard gazes down upon our brotherhood, it is with love and approval, for it is not the Templar order that should be closely scrutinised, your grace, but all the small parishes which are in the hands of dubious priests, and perhaps the larger diocese, run by greedy bishops.'

The other man's face matched the colour of his amethyst ring.

'Even in his life,' my master continued, 'St Bernard could see avarice blooming like weeds in the hierarchies of the church.'

'Master Templar! How dare you say such things!'

'I am merely saying that even the faithful dog must be closely watched by the shepherd.'

There was an awkward silence. The bishop spoke then, with restrained anger. 'The Synod of Toulouse is quite clear! And it is my duty to uphold it! It is the responsibility of all citizens to search out heretics, to root out lasciviousness and its followers, patrons or protectors. No one is exempt, as you say. Not even the Militia of Christ!' He stared at my master, a look pregnant with unspoken hostilities, and it was then that I knew that we were being openly threatened.

'Not even the pope himself, one hopes.'

There was another terrible pause. Incredulity did battle with dislike for supremacy on the bishop's face. 'The time will come, preceptor, when your order will have outgrown its usefulness. What will become of fighting monks who have lost their *raison d'être?* Will you continue to barter and trade, staining your hands with money and blood when it is meekness and mildness in the service of God that you should seek! Your order is no better than these irreverent monasteries. No better than this Manfred devil, for you have become a law unto yourselves. It is your own empire that you seek, autonomous, independent, owing allegiance to none other, least of all the pope. In effect, you take for yourselves a power that not even the emperor dare claim! Even kings are in awe of you! Be careful, you have made yourselves indispensable, that may be true, but you are also hated, for it is no secret that you are the bankers for every throne in Europe . . . and kings with empty coffers have very short memories!' In an attempt to calm himself, he wiped his brow with a handkerchief and continued, 'Remember usury is an abomination in the eyes of God and the church.'

'Yes, usury has many names. When bishops borrow from the city consuls they call it a *dono.'*

'I will not have you say such things! What impudence! Donations are necessary for the life of the church! How else could we maintain our place in the world?'

'But our Lord, your grace, died on the cross, naked.'

The bishop's eyes widened, irritated and bloodshot. 'Jews and merchants line their purses with the sufferings of others. The church, on the other hand, provides fraternal service to its children! For charity, not poverty, is the basis for the perfect life. No,' he continued, out of breath, 'we do not pretend to be paupers, nor do we live a sybaritic life! And although there is pride in wealth, preceptor, there is also pride in poverty! A hypocrite stands before me preaching the value of poverty when it is no secret that your Paris preceptory holds treasures beyond comprehension!'

'What we have accumulated for services beneficent to the countries we inhabit is used to maintain our militia, so that we may best serve the pope, and so, naturally, God. And if you speak of charity, no other order has such strict charitable obligations as the Templar order, my lord.'

The bishop laughed, 'You make an excellent diplomat, preceptor, I can see why the king holds you in such high esteem. Your tongue is smooth and obviously illuminated by learning. I hear Alexandria, where you were born, preceptor, is the centre of heretical learning. I am told it is a hotbed of gnostic wisdom, cabbala, sufism and all manner of sin.'

'It is a great place of learning, your grace, as you have said. As a matter of fact, the Christians of Alexandria were foremost in interpreting the ascetic teachings of the early fathers, the founders of the monastic life.'

'So you say, because you are half infidel, preceptor, and I begin to wonder which half of you takes precedence.'

'The half that counts, your grace.'

The other man looked at him blankly, 'Yes, and yet, was it the Christian half or the infidel half that was compelled to leave the university of Paris? Perhaps you thought you could hide your past from us? Your strange methods were not considered ... shall I speak delicately? Your methods were not considered pious. Today you might be burnt at the stake for such transgressions. In any event,' he paused, savouring his words, 'after so many years you do not seem to have learnt the error of your ways. Remember the maxim? *Chil paist, chil prie, et chil deffent.*'

'This man labours, this prays and that defends . . .'

'Precisely . . . Listen to me, this is not your war, return to your preceptory, leave the work of rooting out the disembodied enemies of the faith to the inquisitor!'

'I cannot do that, your grace.'

The man sat down on a stone bench facing the central garth and sighed, suddenly tired. 'What has happened to the world? All over Europe Christians struggle with Christians, heresy sprouts up to poison the calm waters of wisdom . . . In truth, politics do not interest me, it is not my concern if the classes struggle one with the other, that is the king's business. Only when it affects the morals of my community, only then does it come under my authority. In such cases, mark my words well, I would use all the power afforded me to see to it that the laws of the church are upheld whatever the cost! I will not allow patricians, nor indeed these defiant monasteries, nor even the privileged classes, to cause the ruination of the faith of my community.'

'But what is faith to a man who does not make distinctions between right and wrong, but simply between living and dying?'

The bishop shook his head stubbornly. 'I do not profess to know the solutions to all things, preceptor. I am a simple man, unlike you . . . however, even you must not fall prey to pity. You must rather see through the disguise of poverty and obedience to what lies secret, and obscure. Namely, greed and wealth!'

The bell tolled and my master helped the bishop to his feet.

'Tell me, how is your friend Jean de Joinville on his return from the Holy Land? I believe he has become quite the hero fighting alongside the king.'

'I believe he is well, recuperating after some four years at the hands of the infidel,' my master replied.

'Hmm . . . the battle of Mansourah, a terrible thing. So many men captured, so many dead . . . but you and your squire escaped?'

'Yes.'

'How fortuitous. Some would say too fortuitous for a

half infidel,' he said, watching my master closely. Seeing no sign of anger on Andre's face, he continued a little disappointed, 'The life of a Templar knight in the East is certainly a dangerous one. But the life of a knight in France is also fraught with hazards. I hope you will take some advice from an old man who has seen many things in his life: there are two certainties in all this, one is that the mouth of an inquisitor speaks with the pope's tongue, and the other is that his jurisdiction is absolute. Do your duty, see to it that justice is done! These are days of strange affiliations, preceptor, and we must stand together as men of God, despite our differences. *Oportet inquisitores veritatis non esse inimicos!'* That is to say, there should be no enmity among seekers after truth.'

The bishop left with a swirl of his robes, but it would not be long before he would do disservice to his parting words . . .

It was later, during supper, as the weather grew more and more turbulent outside the refectory, that a discussion broke out which ignored the observance of silence, and resulted in a debate among the legation which, because of the anxiety felt by all, assumed a confused and distressed character. I would lie if I did not say, dear reader, that I was a sad witness to a tempest of tongues inappropriate to grave and responsible persons whose composure should mirror the qualities of still waters. My master sat back strangely amused, having started the entire incident with a careless remark that I shall now recount to you, by way of illustrating further the enmity that existed in those dark days among men of God. It seemed to speak to me, that moment almost comical if not also at the same time terrible, of the vanity and pride of men. That even the noble and the holy are apt to debase themselves to the level of peasants at the slightest provocation.

It began when my master observed that the exquisite cross hanging from the bishop's neck was dangling a little in his soup. The bishop answered by removing it and cleaning it with a moistened napkin. Andre then remarked that it was a beautiful work of art, marked by intricate gold filigree and studded with the most precious stones surrounding one great ruby whose dimensions were that of a small walnut.

The bishop smiled, holding it timorously in his hands and as he brought it to his moist lips he said, 'What better way to express one's veneration, preceptor, than by using nature's gifts. The ruby, as we know, suggests the countenance of the archangels, the gold is the sublime reflection of Christ whose radiance is only implied by its splendour. See the amethysts? See the diamonds? It is true . . .' he said, lost in reverie. 'They echo the marvels of the universe! Indeed, all the powers of the heavens are vested in the miracle of the stone in whose depths hide many levels of knowledge. In truth I feel a holy communion every time I hold it to my lips, subjugated by its secrets.' He seemed to be speaking a little like the abbot when he had told me about the tiger's eye, and yet differently.

At this point, the Friar de Narbonne rolled his eyes in irritation and mumbled loudly, 'How can one stand to hear our Lord's cross depicted in this vulgar manner! Next you will say that his manger was stuffed with gold thread and not straw!'

The bishop turned his vastness then, in the friar's direction. 'I do not expect a mendicant friar to understand these things, for they require a little erudition and subtlety of education. However your founder was not so simple-minded, for he knew how to seduce the pope to his bidding.'

'Your grace!' broke in the Cistercian by way of defusing the problem. 'Surely you do not suggest . . .? Francis was a holy man! On this all agree.'

'No doubt his nuns attested to his manhood!'

'You irreverent snake!' cried the friar, aghast, lifting himself a little out of his chair and banging both fists on the table. 'How can you say such a thing against a most venerated saint of your own country? And his nuns! Those sainted women are as virginal as the holy mother!'

The bishop smiled, 'They are all virgins, you fool, until

they become nuns.'

'Brothers, please!' The abbot moved in, but it was too late, each man was now at the other with escalating hatred.

Below the dais all stopped eating, their mouths gaped open at the spectacle before their eyes, for now the friar, his face a deep crimson, shook his hand menacingly in the bishop's face.

'You vessel of greed! You filthy swine! You simonious thief! Whose wealth is gained by imposing penances that you overlook for a small fee!'

'Shut up! Innocent should have listened more attentively to Cardinal Albano,' the bishop spat, at the apex of anger, 'who advised him to keep the mendicants down below the feet of the lowest priest!'

'Yes, and the same day he died of a broken neck!' the Franciscan cried.

'Therein lies your guilt!' the bishop shouted. 'You murderers . . . you steal the food from the mouths of the poor because you are not only as dumb as asses, but as lazy! Because for all your talk of poverty and austerity you smell of money, along with your wealthy Cistercian brothers whose preference for sheep is well known and has made them rich!'

'And your order, Otto,' the Cistercian stood, his face purple and his body shaking with rage, 'recalls a fat pig lolling about in its own excreta, opening its mouth to whatever is thrown to it!'

'Is that so? You patron of depravity!' the Bishop of Toulouse shouted. 'Defender of Fransciscan dung! Have you forgotten that William St Amour said they are beggars, flatterers, liars, and detractors, thieves, and avoiders of justice! How should I allow myself to be insulted by a smelly old goat who knows nothing of the greatness of the Benedictines! If you could read you would know that our divine order was established when your founder's grandfather was not even a seed in his mother's belly. We were here before you and we will exceed you in wisdom, years, and numbers.'

'Perhaps, but only because you receive your own bastard sons as oblates to plump up your diminishing population!' cried the Franciscan triumphantly. 'How many nephews do you have, bishop? You are, of course yourself, a nephew . . .'

'You profane devil!' The bishop lunged forward, trying to grasp the friar by the scapular.

'Brothers! Brothers!' cried the abbot, standing between the two men, avoiding a volley aimed at the bishop who, snarling, prepared to land a punch squarely on the friar's weak chin.

'May the Devil take you!' yelled the Franciscan from behind the abbot, his animated face contrary to his nature. 'It is no wonder there is so much unrest in Italy! I begin to sympathise with the Ghibellines of Umbria!'

This struck the bishop better than a blow. 'Traitor!' he vociferated, breathing heavily and waving his fat fists about. 'I can see why even the heretic Frederick would not allow your kind into Sicily, for you give off the odour of a woman!'

'I would rather give off the odour of a woman than to be the son of a whore!'

'And I would rather be a good son, even to a whore, than to slip into your lice-infested habit each miserable day!'

'Mind your tongue, you desecrator of saints!' broke in the Cistercian, waving his knife at the bishop. 'You Benedictines are a bunch of idolaters who build your grand churches stuffed with gold and silver so that you can seek your own greedy reflections on every surface!'

'And your order's bare walls are only a reflection of St Bernard's buttocks; pale and exceedingly dull!'

My master cast a look of victory at the inquisitor, and again I noted that the Devil of rivalry that existed between the two men was almost at the point of embodiment. I began to wonder if the bishop had been right – if the infidel in my master's blood was stronger than the Christian, since it seemed that he took pleasure in division and confusion as much as the inquisitor took pleasure in fear and pain. At that moment, it appeared that they had much in common.

'Venerable brothers!' the inquisitor shouted, raising his arms in an effort to stop the blows and cries. 'Peace! Peace!' He frowned at those responsible, and continued only after he was certain that they had each calmed down, 'I pray that we might sit down and collect ourselves before it is too late. Might I remind you of our sensitive mission here, and of the great peril that faces us? Surely this is the work of the Devil who seeks to divide us, so that we may not come to a judgement, for if I have ever seen him, I have seen him tonight, snarling from out of the mouths of pious men the most odious and disdainful words! Let us be filled with contrition, let us pray for guidance and also for forgiveness. The enemy is among us and we feed him with our dissension and our hatred of one another.'

He sat down and silence reigned once more but, in truth, it was an unhappy silence, because once a word is spoken it has the ability to alter things, create things, even destroy them.

Now, only the wind outside could be heard beating itself against stone, making the candles flicker about, casting ominous shadows on the walls of the refectory. I wondered as I looked at all the now solemn and frightened faces around me if any here was without sin.

AQUA
THE SECOND
TRIAL

'And he dreamed..'
GENESIS XXVIII 12

10

Capitulum

I was in the midst of a storm, alone within elements that burst forth in the most violent manner. Thunder shook the world, and out of a bolt of lightning, these are the things that I saw.

Behold a door was opened in heaven and emerging, a throne, surrounded by four creatures. I saw four and twenty seats upon which sat four and twenty elders, dressed in white raiment.

'Give Glory and honour and thanks to Him that sitteth upon the throne who liveth forever and ever!' a voice cried. 'Woe be unto him that followeth the foulness that is spewed from the belly of the underworld.'

Suddenly I heard a grumbling coming from below, and from out of the penumbral night, a crack in the earth thrust out lava whose sulphurous light illuminated the firmament, revealing waves of mud, smoke, scum, and dung. Creatures of every kind in bursts of liquid fell upon mankind, the multitude who, like little ants at first congregated, dispersed as the progeny of demons sought them out. Vipers, minotaurs, salamanders, serpents, hydras, lizards and vultures, gryphons, crocodiles and scorpions, became one boiling convulsing substance – a thick oily matter that, ignited by the first rays of a black sun, descended upon a convention of discord, an assembly of abominations, a cohort of transgressors. They tore eyes from their sockets, ripped souls from out of mouths, stripped the flesh from naked bodies with sharp, jagged teeth.

At this point, I could see a giant eagle, ablaze with stars, so that in its luminous wake other beings followed, lured like drunken moths. The creature whose brilliance was an offspring of the celestial bodies that clot the sky, descended through the dark area of mountains possessed of such fury and determination that I felt a sudden rush of air escape my lungs. He began by darting at the loathsome creature with seven heads, whose form only now emanated from the schism. The battle had begun.

The beast curled in fury, winding its body around itself, each profane mouth emitting whole chromatic scales, shrieks, and whimpers. Craftily it dodged the eagle, but the great bird aimed at his mark with care, and in one swift slash of a long, sharp talon, he tore out the heart of the creature, whose cry of agony rose to the great heights of heaven. The dismembered parts were then flung to the four corners of the earth, and thereupon four temples appeared. From the beast's heart, a red blood, thick with life – as though in it convulsed a multitude of reptiles, abundant in the power of transmuted creation – surged, forming a river. And I saw this river divide into two, then the two became four, each branch finding its way to one tabernacle. Along its banks, where gleaming sandy beaches wound around peninsulas, canyons, and valleys, there appeared blood-red roses whose upturned petals praised the great primordial power of the universe. Stars fell then, from the great galactic desert, burning holes through the mantle of the night, uniting with each temple. And a voice said:

'Glory be to Manes for he has seen the power of good and evil. Glory be to Zarathustra for he has seen the sun in its divinity. Glory be to Buddha for he has experienced the starry light. Glory be to Scythianos for he raiseth the Temple to the highest summit.'

The eagle transformed itself into the countenance of a man, and brandishing a blade, with one swift move, he pierced the dismembered belly, out of which spewed forth seven books, bound in red. These he placed at my feet and with a voice like that of thunder he spoke these words:

Take these seven books, for they are the gifts of cosmic Intelligences.

> For all time these books have belonged to me,
> Now I must forsake them for the sake of humanity.
> Be ye their guardian, that whosoever,
> Out of a purity of thinking, feeling and willing
> Can tread the long steady path to intelligence,
> Let him eat of these books and be saved.

Suddenly I found myself falling into an abyss. Devoid of self, suffused with a sense of selfless union, I plunged into the synthesis of the universe; expanding, growing into all that was around me, until within me I beheld unintelligible constellations, celestial deities, whole worlds residing. I was a cosmos, and all around me concealed nature became exterior form; organs were as macrocosmic satellites mapping out their course through the microcosm of my planetary being. I saw with awed reverence, a liver circumnavigate a spleen, whose own revolutions around a heart whispered astrological philosophies, profound harmonies. It was a rhythmic oscillation and vacillation, a universal school, where cosmic secrets murmured to the sweeping orbits of distant suns.

'That which is here spread out and around thee, thou art that!' I said to the orbs at the perimeter of my existence.

'I am a god, and thou art my people,' I said to the internal cosmos that I now embraced.

What was intrinsic was also extrinsic, within, and without,

form became formless, and the formless embodied. Soon, Christian de St Armand would cease to exist, his sun eclipsed by the light of a moon whose effulgence was far greater than his own. Then the twelve became seven, and the seven stars appeared.

11

Capitulum

At this point I awoke, and yet I knew that I was still asleep, for before me stood the figure of Plato. You may find this curious, but far more curious was the fact that I did not find it curious at all, but quite the most natural thing.

Herein lies the difficulty,' Plato said, 'that I may never solve to my satisfaction.'

'What is it, Plato?' I asked.

'I ask myself what is the meaning of this dream?' he said, pacing my cell, long Grecian robes rustling in the still, dead of night, one slender hand cupping his chin in a remarkable manner, a little reminiscent of my master. 'Are we to say, then, that you have dreamt a vision?'

'A vision,' I considered, 'a vision of what?'

'The battle between good and evil?'

'Indeed, that may be so,' I nodded my approval.

'A vision also of a kind of knowledge . . . whose guardian you shall become . . .'

'It stands to reason, Plato,' said I, 'but what knowledge is this? And why have I been chosen?'

'My art is in examining your thoughts – as my tutor, Socrates, would have said – and not in promulgating my own. You must not see me as an originator of ideas, for I am like a midwife who in her barren wisdom, can never bring forth. It is you who must give birth, you must labour, and I will see to the delivery . . . Come . . . what could this knowledge be? If it were known to all men it would not be vouchsafed to you, am I right?'

'I should think not,' I affirmed.

'So it is a secret thing . . . and so not easily learnt or attained?'

'Following this line of reasoning,' I replied, 'quite rightly.'

'It is not of a practical nature, for it would not be called an intelligence, it would be called wisdom.'

'But wisdom is the same as intelligence. Is it not?'

'You forget my friend that I am ignorant, you are the person who is in labour.'

'But I am in pain!'

'And so, I will comfort you. Do we call a man wise, whose nature is prudent?'

'Of course.'

'And from whence does the fount of prudence spring?'

'From practical experience.'

'Excellent! And what of intelligence?'

'From understanding?'

'Yes! It is the understanding that enables you and I to grasp the first principles – as my pupil Aristotle has said. And, as an outpouring of the gods, it is therefore divine. Prudence, on the other hand, is merely the result of the practical use of this understanding, and therefore human. So we may say that the knowledge vouchsafed to you is of divine origin?'

I nodded.

'Then we are in agreement,' he said.

'But what does this have to do with the monastery?' I asked.

'It is clear from our discussion that this intelligence is

mysterious, and now we also know that it is divine. Am I right in saying that opposite natures and substances attract?'

'I suppose so.'

'Then nothing attracts a great evil more than a great good. If this knowledge is a great good, it shall attract a great evil, and so the battle will ensue. The monastery is merely the battleground.'

'But how to find these books and therefore unlock the secret?'

'Like the act of birth, all understanding is preceded by a little pain. This you must undergo with courage, but it is only the beginning, for when one learns a thing, it leads one to desire to know other things, and questions give birth to other questions, and so one conceives afresh. I, Plato, on the other hand, am dead.' He sighed, 'Having delivered too many men when I was alive . . .'

'Alive . . . Come alive, boy!' I heard these words echo through a darkened consciousness, and I found that my body was being shaken violently . . .

12

Capitulum

Some time before Matins

At first I could see nothing, but I then realised that my master was standing over me, a black shadow that I recognised instantly.

'Master?'

'For the love of God! If I were a Saracen you would now be singing discordantly in the great choirs of heaven.'

Half asleep, and a little hurt by the word 'discordantly', I fell into a broody silence, but as I readied myself I told him because I could not hold it in any longer. 'I had a dream, master,' I said very quickly. 'First there was a dragon and an eagle . . . Plato said it was the battle between good and evil.' I held the little gem, given to me by the abbot, hotly in my hands.

'I say it was too much mackerel at dinner. Now up with you! Tonight we search for a mystery. Come along, look alive!'

'But master —' I began to argue with him, but seeing his mood, thought better of it, for he was rubbing his knee.

'Curses to all ignorant Frenchmen!' he mumbled. 'Damn the Count of Artois. Are you ready? Do not forget the lamp, boy, we are not bats!'

I nodded, and taking the lamp in one hand and tapers in

the other, joined him outside.

It was snowing lightly. I pouted, feeling a great frustration. My master sniffed the air, pausing, and for a moment stood very still. 'Tomorrow it will storm,' he said emphatically.

Who would have argued differently?

We entered the church, and hid in the shadows behind the rood, waiting long moments. I thought of Eisik, who was usually praying at this time, and I wondered how curious it must be to be a Jew believing in only one God, and awaiting a Saviour who had already come. I hoped that he was praying for our safety, for I was afraid. Not of what we might see, crouched as we were like thieves, but rather of what we might not see, for it was my impression that the evil one in his infernal wisdom works invisibly, and therefore unknowingly. My master seemed unperturbed, even excited and in a very good mood. I must say that this worried me more than anything.

When Andre deemed it safe, we moved past the choir stalls and to our right, in the direction of the north transept. Moments later we were in the Lady Chapel, at the altar of the Virgin of our sorrows. My master motioned for me to light the two lamps from our rooms on the perpetual flame of the bronze tripod. This I did, and on my return we began to inspect the area behind the great red curtains, near the exit to the graveyard, for this was where brother Daniel had pointed saying Virgil's words, *'Procul este, profani!'* Here there were stone panels around three or four paces square, and my master determined that there must be a device hidden somewhere. In the dim light we could see very little, but we continued looking for anything. Soon, however, I found that I was assailed by a desperate desire to sneeze, and it was as I attempted to emerge from behind the dusty curtains that I became entangled and fell. Luckily I held the lamp firmly, otherwise it would surely have set the curtains alight. It did, however, cast the lamp's brilliance upon the lowest panel that, from my position near the stone floor, became visible to me. I could see something, at first only vaguely. My master was about to help me to my feet when he saw it also. He dropped painfully to his knees then, bringing the lamp closer, exclaiming perhaps a little louder than he should have, 'Oh defender of the holy sepulchre!' He must have hurt his knee, and in a strangled whisper said, 'Hush!' as though *I* and not *he* had uttered these words.

Producing a parchment and quill, from the little repository inside his scapular, he copied the inscription quickly, but then we heard something that we later realised were footsteps headed in our direction. My master with presence of mind pushed me out from under the curtains, saying, 'Quickly, through the door!' and I was suddenly dragged to my feet and thrust out of the north transept door and into the cold night.

'Master –' I began in a bewildered whisper but was forestalled by the smell of damp and death that pervaded the graveyard.

'Hush! Follow me, and don't ask stupid questions!' he said, putting out our lamps, and pushing me around the body of the church, past the crosses and to the east door, whose aperture remained open until midnight.

'What are we doing, master?' I asked, put out.

'We are spying on the Devil,' he said, and I thought I could see a devilish grin on his face, but it was too dark, my imagination was having its way with me. Even so, I had never seen my master so excited, and I feared he was fast becoming Aristotle's model of an intemperate man whose desire for what gives him pleasure is insatiable, and draws its gratification from every quarter. What pleasure, though, could a normal person derive from scampering in the dark in graveyards? I shuddered to think and admonished him for his terrible curiosity.

Presently we found ourselves moving down the nave with the instinctive movements of a fox training its nose to the hunt, and it was only a matter of moments before we were once again on the other side of the screen, dashing quickly in the shadows, to a place behind the choir enclosures. That was when we saw the figure of a monk moving silently past the great bronze tripod, not too quickly, for he was carrying something. He was headed in the direction of the Lady Chapel. I surmised that he must have stopped to pray before the great altar, otherwise we would not have caught up with him. A devil that prays? We followed him, coming upon the arch that separated us from the transept. My breath pulsated before me in time with my racing heart.

'For God's sake! Breathe quietly,' my master whispered harshly into my ears and moments later the figure disappeared behind the curtains.

'He is going down into the catacombs!'

'Who, master?'

'How should I know?'

After a brief moment the monk's shadow came out into the pale light, but we did not see his face, covered as it was by a cowl, and he disappeared into the inky gloom of the ambulatory.

'By God's bonnet!' my master cursed, and moved hurriedly to the chapel, lifting the curtains. 'By my hilt! Nothing!' Pausing a moment, he said, 'Stay here, wait for the bells. I shall soon return.'

He left hurriedly, and I, fearing the Devil himself around every corner, huddled in the shadows of the ambulatory, praying many paternosters, thinking that my master must return at any moment. But matins came and went. There were whispers.

'Where is the preceptor?' they asked in fearful tones, glancing at his empty seat. I waited as the last of the brothers filed out. What could have happened? I was becoming exceedingly worried, but being very weary, and not wishing to disobey my master, I huddled in a corner, anticipating his return like a dutiful child, and in this way I fell into an uncomfortable sleep.

13

Capitulum

Before Lauds

When I woke, the light in the church seemed brighter. I rubbed my eyes, and resolved to find Andre. Perhaps, I thought in dismay, he was dead, a victim of the antichrist! Would I come by his twisted, poisoned body outside the church? I could see him now, drenched in sweat and blood (for he would have fought the Devil like a valiant knight) with his face distorted in that now all-too-familiar way of poisoned cadavers. Alas! I once again wondered at the wisdom of a mother who leaves her only child in the care of so careless a caretaker! And yet if I found him alive I told myself with a shiver I would soon forgive him, not only because I loved him, but also through relief at not being left alone in this terrible place of murder and of evil. Thinking these things, filled with a deep anxiety, trembling at the knees, I stepped out of the choir enclosures and through the aperture in the pulpitum to the other side of the screen, but I was not prepared for the light whose sharp rays assaulted my eyes.

At first I thought that it must be the great burning star of heaven which John calls 'wormwood', whose poison kills the iniquitous, but after a moment of blindness, I realised that it was the daystar rising over the eastern buildings, storming through the east door, and invading the temple. I then remembered the orientation of the church with some relief and watched it move (as though controlled by some invisible hand) beyond me and upward to the crucifix . . . and, oh, what magnificence did I behold! Whose majestic splendour, even now I am pressed to relate, dear reader, using words that are inept and unsuited to describe things sublime! That moment was possessed of a beauty whose dwelling is the light of rising suns that now breaks, or now directs its rays to chase away the dead of gloom. Scaling the heavens it recalls the resurrection, the beginning. It is the blossoming of innocence that urges the flowers to awaken, and man to prayer. So caught was I in this mood that I did not notice the brothers return to their stalls, and begin to sing *'Deus qui est sanctorum splendor mirabilis. Iam lucis orto sidere'* – expressing the beauty of light that is God, so that it reverberated sweetly in the nave, magically disembodied.

My meditation disturbed, I re-entered the chamber between the rood and pulpitum, expecting to see my master seated at his usual place, for the sun had risen and with it came hope. I searched among the brothers in their stalls, passing their matching shadows with my eyes, until they fell upon that empty spot and my heart sank. He had not returned. I was seized by a sudden panic, excited perhaps by a lack of sleep, the events of these last days, and my still burgeoning mysticism. So I ran. I ran from the church and out into the compound and headed in the direction of my master's cell. Thinking a great number of terrible things, I burst through his door and found him lying on his pallet.

I thought him dead, for he lay very still. However, I realised that he was breathing and, with a measure of trepidation, I ventured closer. Had he, too, been poisoned? I thought in dismay. Did someone suspect that we knew about the entrance to the tunnels? Was it the inquisitor? The librarian? Or the Devil himself? I said a shaky paternoster, possibly omitting words, before placing a trembling hand on his shoulder. That was when he bounded from the bed with such swiftness that I let out a loud and immodest yell, having been scared out of my wits.

'By the curse of Saladin, let me get at them!' he bellowed. Placing a hand on his head then, he moaned and sat back down.

'Are you hurt, master?'

'Who are you?' he asked, gazing at me myopically. 'Are you a heathen? I will smite you . . . where is my sword!' He reached out with his hands and then, I suspect because of the pain in his head, he came to his senses. 'Christian? Is that you? I can barely see . . . someone . . . my head . . .' He handed me a parchment that lay crushed in his right hand, whose contents were written once again in Greek.

'Except the Lord build the house: their labour is but lost that build it,' I said out loud.

'Help me up, for God's sake, boy . . .' He sat up wincing. I could see a very large bruise on his forehead, and a graze on his cheek.

'Are you all right?' I asked, feeling a little weak myself.

'How say you? A knight who survives the battle of Mansourah in which so many good knights died can surely survive a small blow to the head.' He growled in very bad humour.

'Did you get a glimpse of who did this to you, master?'

'No, by Saladin! I came here to fetch my compass in case we should need it, and when I entered my cell I saw a shadow; something struck my head. I must have lain here for a long time. What hour is it?'

'It is lauds, even now the services are in progress. I think he hit you with your helmet.' I showed him the helmet, which I recognised as his, beside him on the floor. There was a dent at the right eye-slit.

'Blast!' he cried with annoyance. 'Was anyone missing from the service?'

I was too ashamed to say that I had closed my eyes, and

in the time it took to say an *Ave*, the service had finished. I shook my head.

'Blast! In any case, I shall have to see the brother blacksmith, but not just now, firstly you must take me to Eisik . . . By St Peter of Spain! That savage monk nearly cracked my skull in two!'

'You say 'monk'? So you did see him?'

'Who else would it be but a monk, Christian? We are in a monastery, after all. Besides, I only saw his shoes.'

'Oh, that is good,' I said, 'were they singular in appearance?'

'No . . . just shoes, like any other shoes,' he snarled.

We walked to the stables slowly. It had been snowing heavily and the ground was covered in a thick layer of powdery white – a detail that I had not noticed in my anxiety to find my master. Now my feet were numb and the hems of my habit wet. What misery!

Eisik was in his little cell above the animals reading the *Talmud,* absorbed in the content of talmudic lore, when we entered.

'Oh, holy Abraham!' he exclaimed, immediately deserting his precious scrolls to come to us. 'What has happened?'

'Do not fuss, Eisik! I need you to see that I have not cracked my skull, for I cannot tend to my own wounds. By God, if only I had a mirror!'

Eisik was horrified but also angry. 'Oh, by the beard of Moses, someone has hit you with a sharp object.' He inspected the cut and the lump that was now quite blue and sizeable. My master showed him his helmet, and Eisik was seized by a second, terrible anxiety. 'You are lucky to be alive!'

'I don't believe luck had much to do with it, Eisik. Whoever hit me was not in the mind to kill me, otherwise he could easily have done so. I merely disturbed him in his work.'

'Do not tax the faculties of an old Jew. What work did

you disturb?'

'He was leaving another note in my room when I entered, looking for my compass, and he hit me rather hard in order to get away. Elementary.'

'Oyhh!' Eisik slapped his forehead, his big black eyes widening with fear. 'No! Do not tell me what the note said! I do not want to know it! I do not want to know anything, nothing at all.' He walked over to a basin of water beside his bed, moaning dire omens under his breath, and soaked a clean cloth in it. After placing the cloth on my master's bruise, he continued, agitatedly. 'I swear by the Talmud, Andre, this will come to no good! You should have listened to me from the first.'

My master ignored Eisik's comment and said, 'We found the entrance to the tunnels.'

'I do not want to know, I tell you!' he reiterated, and dressed the wound with a little square of muslin cloth, but after a long moment he asked – because I believe he could not help himself – 'Well? I suppose you think that I want to know who told you . . . but I am a Jew, and if a Jew knows anything, it is that he is wise if he knows nothing.'

'Brother Daniel told us.'

'Another old brother?' He raised his thick black brows in unison and became thoughtful, 'I suppose I cannot stop you from telling me what you found?'

My master grinned. 'I thought you didn't want to know anything, Eisik?'

'And I do not . . . do not tell me anything . . .' He waved a hand, shaking his head, but a moment later, 'How is the accursed thing reached then?'

'That is the mystery. There is an inscription. A kind of coded formula which when deciphered will, I am hoping, open a panel. All is possible.'

'Yes . . . yes . . . it is very common for such panels to lead to a crypt or an ossuary, that is to say, the place where bones are kept for all eternity, beneath the graveyard.'

'I believe so,' my master affirmed.

'But do not tell me the inscription. I do not wish to know it . . . there is nothing more foul on this earth than an inscription. Evil things . . . however, if it is encrypted it is true that perhaps only I can help you.'

My master showed him the parchment on which he had copied the strange symbols and words carved on the stone of the panel. Eisik looked at it reluctantly, but I believe that he was fascinated.

Mors Fiensque

D C

and beneath, a strange wheel of sorts.

Eisik became excited, *'Mors Fiensque* . . . You know, in such cases letters are more than symbols, they are vessels, manifestations of concealed virtues!'

'How do you mean, Eisik?' I asked.

'My son, all the wonders and sanctities of the law and the prophets result from combinations of twenty-two letters, letters that stand for numerals, and numerals that stand for letters.'

'Like the ciphers and acrostics mentioned by the inquisitor that night at dinner?' I waited for an acknowledgement of my acumen but there was none – perhaps I, too, was falling prey to the sin of pride?

'There are,' Eisik continued, his eyes shining like lamps, 'many rules and permutations, all holy methods by which one can evade the scrutiny of the uninitiated. Do you know, my young one, that the Bible was written from such coded messages? The oral law became a written law . . . but it is at most an incorrect interpretation of the sacred Cabbala. In all, there are three methods that are known. In the first each letter . . . no, no . . . let me see, that's not it.' He thought for a moment, tapping his head. 'It is the *sum,* the sum of the letters . . . yes! The sum of the letters that compose one word, are equal to the sum of the letters that compose various others, and so certain words come to mean certain things. Then again one may construct words by means of the first or final letters of several other words, but that is too complex. In truth, my son, all codes are not simple, and it is a fact that many are impossible to decipher, especially where words are transposed according to certain rules, that is, one divides the alphabet by halves, or is it quarters? One then places one half above the other in reverse order, so that A becomes T, or T becomes A. Lastly there is another code whose indiscriminate substitutions and permutations are obtained by forming a square of numbers, subdividing it by 21 lines in each direction into 484 smaller squares . . .' He trailed off, lost in contemplation.

'And one can always work out the meaning of codes by the use of one of these methods?' I asked, amazed.

'For centuries men have pondered the sacred art,' he nodded, 'but to answer your question, no. One is almost never succesful, for there are too many to choose from.'

'And,' my master interjected in an annoyed fashion, 'since we do not have centuries at our disposal we shall have to guess as to which method may have been used.'

'What say you, Nazarene?' Eisik looked up from his vague calculations as one who had just been wrenched from a deep sleep. 'I have never guessed a thing in my life! No, no, it is impossible! Do you know how many variations there are on a single word? We must work with strict principles. Strict principles!'

'Yes, but Eisik, we don't have time to test all such systems, that you have just said are too complicated, so by the sword of Saladin let us try one!'

'This illustrates to me why gentiles will never come to know the truths contained in the old texts . . .' He closed one eye, measuring my master with the other. 'Such matters cannot be attended to in haste. However, if I am to be forced I shall start by adding the letters, or the value of the letters together, this is the simplest of all systems and so one likely to be used by a gentile . . .' Eisik added, giving my master a caustic look. 'Now then, in this system A is equal to one, B to two, and so on, so on . . . and if we follow this principle we find that the sum of your code's numerical value comes to . . . one hundred and forty.'

'Is that a good number?' I asked excited, not immediately realising that the closer we came to solving the puzzle, the closer we came to inspecting the tunnels.

'No, child, it is very bad!' Eisik shook his head with pessimism. 'Any number that is not significant is bad, though many significant numbers are also not good. However, this number is not without merit, for it can be divided by seven which is perhaps the most venerated of all numbers, and by four, the number of the unpronounceable name. And although one can divide it by the number of gospels, and by eight, the number of the perfect tetragon and by five, the five world zones, it is not significant.'

'Yes, yes, Eisik,' my master sighed impatiently.

'*Mors Fiensque* . . . death and become. No, that's not it . . . become is spelt *fiesque* and it should be becoming, not become! Even so I believe that is it, my sons! Death and Becoming. And underneath it . . . D and C,' Eisik trailed off, closing one eye again, as if the vision in the other eye became sharper as a result.

'*Deus ... Christo,*' my master answered almost by reflex.

'*Deus Christo . . .* the numerical value of D and C together is, of course, equal to seven,' Eisik said, thoughtfully nodding. 'A venerated number.'

'But why *mors?*' my master said. 'Why not *moriens?* Dying and becoming and why the mispelt *fiesque?* Further more, why use a noun and not a participle? That is, unless . . .'

'May the gods praise an unworthy Jew who is also, as luck would have it (for luck is all a Jew has) exceedingly astute! It is because we must count the sum of letters and not in this case the sum of their numerical value. You see, it was a little clue!'

'I see,' my master said, smiling, 'so that they make twelve.'

'Of course! There are twelve! Twelve and seven, a holy concord of numbers!' Eisik clapped both hands as though about to sit down to a great repast. 'Now perhaps the curious wheel will reveal its arcana . . . here,' he pointed to the parchment. 'We see two interlocking wheels, the larger is divided into twelve, ordered by twelve Zodiacal signs, the inner smaller wheel again divided, only this time by seven, with the seven little planetary symbols inside each little division. Very curious . . . seven and twelve.'

'Make it such that the twelve become seven, and the seven stars appear,' I said absently, remembering my dream.

Eisik gasped. 'What did you say, my son?'

I told him that I had dreamt these words and he gave my master a sideways glance. 'The boy has had a prophetic vision where he hears the words of John! What else did you dream, child?'

'Come, Eisik, we have no time for dreams now,' my master blurted out impatiently. 'What of the wheel? Could it work in the same way as a sundial? With the twelve divisions being symbolic hours?' He paused for a moment, as though on the verge of something very important. 'I have an idea . . . But, of course! This is may be our guide to unlocking the panel.' He showed us the page. 'You see, firstly we have twelve divisions which correspond with twelve star signs, but also hours, that is twelve is north, three is east, six is south, and nine is west. Twelve and seven become the seventh hour which corresponds to Pisces at the twelfth hour in the outer circle. What corresponds with the seventh hour in the inner circle? Which planet is the seventh in the sequence of planets?'

'Let us ruminate,' Eisik said. 'In my tradition, the days are numbered, from Sunday, which is the first, to the Sabbath, which is the seventh.'

'And the Latins, Eisik, also named the first day after the sun, *solis dies* or *Dominicus dies,* the Lord's day. Now, the second was named after the moon, the third after Mars, the fourth after Mercury, the fifth after Jupiter, the sixth after Venus, and the seventh after Saturn, or Saturnday, your Sabbath.'

'That may be, my son,' said Eisik, narrowing his eyes, 'but as a code, were they not most commonly found in their celestial sequence?'

'Yes,' said my master, 'however even in the celestial sequence Saturn is still the seventh. This means that perhaps you are right, and this little fox has dreamt our answer, that is: 'make it such that the twelve become seven and the seven stars appear'. Pisces points us to the twelfth hour in the outer circle, and Saturn to the seventh planet in the inner circle.'

'How wonderful!' I exclaimed. 'But master, why are the Zodiacs in reverse sequence?'

'Because in this case, Christian,' my master said, 'the author of our code uses the Zodiac to allude to angelic hierarchies. That is, Pisces represents man, for Christ our Lord was the fisher of men, Aquarius represents the angels, Capricorn the archangels, and so on and so on, instead of the traditional sequence given to us by Isadore of Seville . . .'

'We have the answer then, master, all we need do is . . .' I paused. 'What *do* we do with Pisces and Saturn?'

'Either depress them or align them. We shall have to try many things.'

'But that is not your only problem,' Eisik commented morbidly, 'the real puzzle lies within the catacombs. I told you I did not wish to know anything and now I know what is in the note, the formula . . . holy Jacob!' he exclaimed, horrified that his curiosity had got the better of him. 'You have infected me with your sin . . . and those who know too much die, in this abbey!'

I left them to their arguing, labouring over these revelations, pondering, and reflecting, speculating and postulating various formulas for getting out of tunnels, none of which sounded practical. I knew that he would want to sojourn there tonight,

and now I was filled with dread, when before I had been so excited.

Lost in thought, I wandered into the horse enclosures.
I gave Gilgamesh a good brush, making soothing sounds as I
stroked his smooth coat. I checked that his shoes were in good
order, and placed a blanket over his back. Collecting some oats
from a large basket, I then fed him and Brutus. While I waited,
I glanced through a narrow aperture in the cubicle that revealed
glimpses of the great forest to the south-east. Above the horizon
the sky threatened an impending squall, casting a pallid gloom
over the landscape. My master had been right, today, or perhaps
tonight, it would storm.

I bent my neck in an awkward angle to the right, and found
that I could just see the encampment below. I saw that the fire was
still burning, for the smoke rose high in the stillness. If I went
down to that spot, would I meet Thomas and Remigio? Had I
really only dreamt that meeting? Had I dreamt my discourse with
Plato and the battle between the eagle and the dragon? How could
I have dreamt the answer to the code? At that moment I felt a
presence behind me. I looked around and found the small figure
of the singer Anselmo casting a strange shape at the door. His
eyes, however, shone out of the darkness of his Grecian face,
and we seemed to stand looking at each other a long time, neither
of us wishing to be the first to speak, when finally he smiled or,
rather, smirked.

'Is it your horse?' he pointed his chin in the direction of
Gilgamesh.

'No,' I answered, wishing that I could lie a little.

'I did not think so. He is too fine a horse to be a scribe's
mount.' He reached into his pocket and brought out an apple cut
diagonally. With his left hand he brought it to the steed. Immediately Gilgamesh deserted the oats that I had given him.

I tried to hide my annoyance, 'Do you have a horse?'

'No,' he answered as though nothing mattered, 'but the

abbot sometimes lets me ride his . . .' he pointed to a most beautiful stallion whose name I was told was Sidonius. 'So, where is your mount or did you travel like a slave, on foot?'

'I ride a mule.'

'A mule? A fitting mount for the likes of you,' he laughed, tossing another apple up and down in one hand, 'but there are ways that a man can improve his circumstances, that is, there are men whose wisdom can turn even someone like you into a respected person.' He threw the apple high and caught it standing on one leg. 'Your master will marvel at your erudition, at your acumen and skill, and he will think you so indispensable, so necessary to him, that he will offer his own horse to you.'

'What are you talking about?'

'It is simple, done with potions I believe, incantations and spells. I am told those who have mastered the art invoke the planets, and the zodiacs, the power of demons.'

I blanched. 'How do you know this?'

'Come now, a Templar must know of such things, surely?' he continued. 'Indeed, I have heard that your order is a brotherhood of sorcerers.'

'No! You are wrong!' I answered, losing my temper.

'I am never wrong . . . Your master is an infidel, word gets around. Ask him, I will bet you a ride on Sidonius if he does not know of these things. In any case, I would not ride such a vile thing, if I knew the formula by which to make myself worthy of that other horse . . . he is beautiful.' He lowered his eyes a little, and looked up at me from out of their narrowness. 'Unfortunately, beauty is little appreciated in this abbey – erudition likewise – and yet, I find myself talking when I should be making my way to the chapter house. I wonder what sins the inquiry will uncover . . . Well, I shall see you there.'

He threw the apple at me and I lunged to catch it, almost losing my balance.

'I would not let the inquisitor hear you say such things if

I were you!' I warned disdainfully. 'Or else he might burn you at the stake!' I was drowned out by his laughter, and then he was gone.

Almost at that moment Andre descended the narrow steps that led to Eisik's cell. I wanted to tell him what had just taken place, but what should I say? That the novice with the beautiful voice was possessed of an ugly soul? Or rather that he had read mine, and perhaps knew more than he should? He would have thought that I was exaggerating, or worse still, that I was jealous. So I said nothing, and obediently followed him out into the sombre day. I covered my head, and we walked in the silence of disquietude, in the direction of the blacksmith's building where he was to supervise the repair of his helmet.

He left me outside, and I sat down on a little bench opposite the garden, waiting for him. And it was here that I turned Anselmo's words over in my mind with distinct uneasiness.

That morning the courtyard seemed a hive of activity. Monks were moving to and fro in agitated preparation for the forthcoming meeting. I saw the inquisitor walk toward the aperture, in deep conversation with the bishop. Following behind them, the friar and the Cistercian with evil looks conspired one with the other. Obviously a great schism had developed between the two groups since the torrid events of the last evening, and this even I knew could serve to complicate matters. I was no sooner absorbed by these matters than I caught sight of the cook, looking like a man who did not wish to be seen, scurrying around the church and across the courtyard to the infirmary. Moments later he and Asa, the infirmarian, were headed for the herbarium where Asa opened the lock and allowed the other man passage. The infirmarian looked about him anxiously until the cook emerged carrying some herbs in his hands, then they split up; the infirmarian entered the cloister through the aperture, and the cook made his way to the kitchen. I concluded that the cook had been in need of culinary herbs, and chastised myself for my suspicious nature. It seemed I was becoming distrustful of everything and everyone and yet I was not the only one, for distrust appeared to be on every face. Indeed, every eye no longer knew if it was cast on friend or on foe.

14

Capitulum

Between Terce and Sext

Monks were already filing into the great rectangular room as we arrived. The scribes, assistants, judges, and armed men of the papal commission, sat on wooden benches flanking both sides of the dais, on which stood a great oak table. Here sat the senior officials and the inquisitor. The abbot was seated on a raised chair of red mahogany, carved in the most elaborate manner, at right angles to the table on the right side of the room. Next to him was his sacristan, with the rest of the obidientiaries dispersed on the benches along the walls.

We found a place among the general population of monks, facing the abbot and his men, so as to better observe both the defendants and the inquisitor. It was time, the inquiry was about to start.

I watched the inquisitor closely, noticing how his entire manner radiated certainty. Was he so pure that he should think himself worthy to judge and to condemn others? As he adjusted the papers on the table, a look of satisfaction mingled with profound gravity on his face, communicating the conscious dignity afforded him by power and position. On our way into the inquiry

I had asked my master how an inquisitor knew that he was right in his judgement. He told me that it was not an inquisitor's place to be right, only to be sure of the error of others. He told me that many times an inquisitor is not guided by the noble sense of truth that you or I might think is the epitome of justice, as much as he is guided by the usefulness of a lie.

As I sat in the chapter house I resolved to think no more, and to listen intently, not only out of a desire to record these events faithfully and with clarity, but also because I was curious to see if my master was correct in his assumption.

Suddenly there was a hush. Rainiero Sacconi, towering in black, a graven image of austerity, looked down upon us all from his great height. After a long moment, he spoke firstly about his duty and that of the judges to seek the truth; about the forces of good which must always overcome the forces of evil, explaining that the following proceedings were to remain an investigation until such time as evidence of guilt could be established. He pronounced the opening formulas, but not before saying that, besides the accusations of heresy which he intimated to be many and varied, the monastery was tainted with other crimes. One brother was at that moment awaiting burial, and the evil one roamed about the abbey. No one, he cried, was safe until those responsible were apprehended! As his first witness he would call the Abbot Bendipur to answer the accusations levelled against him and his order of monks, for whom he was responsible.

The abbot sat erect. His eyes I could see never once moved from those of the inquisitor, who, with a theatrical flourish, produced a parchment from which he began to read out the accusations:

'Let it be known that monks of the monastery of St Lazarus, of the order of Cistercians, stand this day in the year of our Lord 1254, accused of . . .' he held the document close to his face, 'healing the sick by methods other than those authorised by the church or ecclesiastical authority: that is by the use of magic

Cabbala or by other devilish means perhaps not known to this inquiry. Harbouring heretical tendencies and conducting rituals that have been deemed heresy by the Lateran councils. Harbouring and aiding Cathar heretics to escape God's justice during the Albigensian crusades and, as such, defending them and their cause. Tainting their own souls with their heresy. Indulging in necromancy, astrology, alchemy, and other infernal practices which are too varied and multiform to name.' He paused, and gave the abbot a hard look, a look that conveyed much, and served to increase the tension in the chapter house if that were possible. The abbot returned the stare though, one must say, being careful to convey an air of trust and humility. These are my sheep, his eyes said, I am the faithful dog, and you are my shepherd.

The inquisitor told the judges of the tribunal that they would now proceed with the hearing. There was another pregnant pause whilst he shuffled more documents, and a moment later he started to question the abbot in a friendly tone.

'Abbot Bendipur, please enlighten this hearing with an account of the practice of healing conducted by the monks of this monastery.' As though he had forgotten this vital warning he continued, 'We trust that you are aware that this council is a council of God on earth, and that all you say will stand as testimony in the eyes of His judges also, therefore I need not remind you of the necessity for absolute honesty. You must tell this court all it needs to know, and further, even that which you may not consider important.'

'I am your willing witness,' Abbot Bendipur answered calmly.

There was a smile, 'Please tell us a little about your order, the faith it holds, and your personal beliefs and, if necessary, I shall require you to swear.'

'I am the abbot of the monastery of St Lazarus, of the Order of Cistercians. From the beginning our community has been dedicated to duties deemed worthy by our founders. Healing the sick is only one of the many tasks which we conduct in all humbleness, in the service of our Lord. We believe in God, the Holy Spirit, Christ our redeemer, and the church whose likeness is His reflection on earth,' said the abbot with ardour. 'We stand before you innocent of the accusations which have been levelled against us and I ask the venerable judges to open their hearts to justice and fairness. How are we to be accused if the accuser does not appear before you, so that he also may be subject to interrogation?'

'Dear abbot, witnesses are to be held in secret, as you know. You may, on the other hand, make a list of your enemies and we shall see if the two coincide.' The inquisitor displayed his white teeth and I could not help but compare them to the sharp teeth on the devils in my dream. 'It should be sufficient that the pope has considered these allegations serious enough to warrant these inquiries. I trust you do not presume to have a greater wisdom in matters of dissent?'

'It is my duty to believe whatever the pope would have me believe, your grace, as any good Christian.'

'Yes, but what, dear brother, do you consider constitutes a good Christian?'

Even I sensed the inquisitor was preparing a trap for the abbot and it did not escape my master either for he whispered in my ear that this was the standard line of questioning used on Waldensians who, he said, had been taught the correct ways of evading questions of this kind.

'He who believes with fullness of heart in God, His son and the Holy Spirit, and the teachings of the holy church,' answered

Bendipur.

'I would like to know what you mean by holy church?'

The abbot paused, slightly confused. The inquisitor found this to his advantage, for he immediately launched into his attack.

'Do you not know what is meant by the holy church?' he

asked, moving off the dais and walking around the centre of the room.

'I believe that the holy church is the means through which God works his purposes on earth, the priesthood handed down to the apostle St Peter who was the regent of Christ.'

'The holy Roman church over which the lord pope presides?'

'If it upholds the laws of God, yes.'

'If?' He looked around incredulously, 'Why do you say 'if'? Do you not believe that it does?'

'I believe.'

'Please, abbot, I am confused. Do you believe that it does, or that it does not?'

'I believe that men do what they can to interpret the will of God.'

'But the pontiff is the reflection of God on earth, is he not?'

'Should I not indeed believe this?' he asked, and I noticed that his answer was formulated in such a way that the inquisitor could not affirm whether he did or did not believe it.

'I ask not, my dear abbot, if you should . . . but if you do!' the inquisitor cried impatiently.

'My belief is the same as yours, the same as all men of the church.'

'I pray, dear abbot, that you are answering my questions in this way because of your innocence and not, in fact, because of your guilt!' He turned to the judges, 'As our illustrious brother Alain of Lille has dictated in his treatise, Enchiridion Fontium Valdensium.'

There were a number of communal nods of support from the legation, though they did not dare look at one another. They merely looked at the congregation with grim faces, bearing down their condescension.

My master whispered to me that it did seem as though

the abbot was well versed in the rules of interrogation, but I could not believe it. I liked the abbot.

'In any case, my beliefs are not in question here,' the inquisitor dismissed, 'I will advise you to answer my questions simply and without dissimulation.'

'In all ways possible.'

'I sincerely hope so, Abbot Bendipur! Now, please, illuminate us on your healing methods.'

'We pray over the sick, we use what we know about the healing properties of plants and minerals. We anoint with oil and holy water.'

'Where do you do this work?'

'In the infirmary. After a diagnosis and treatment with medicaments prescribed by our brother infirmarian, the patient is anointed and blessed.'

'Where is the infirmarian?' Rainiero Sacconi looked around the room. Asa rose slowly, head bowed. When he drew his cowl I thought his face looked thinner than before.

'Abbot, you may sit down for the moment. Now, brother infirmarian, please inform us about the curative treatment of your patients.'

'What information would please you?' he asked meekly.

'Generally speaking . . .' he waved a pale hand in a suggestion of boredom.

'There are no general rules, your grace, every patient must, and should be assessed for a specific treatment.'

The inquisitor smiled, indicating his magnanimity and his remarkable patience. 'Give me an example.'

'Let me see . . .' The monk frowned, 'Would you like me to name various treatments for a specific disease, or one specific treatment for various diseases?'

There was a puzzled silence. 'Just tell me anything, anything at all.'

He thought for a moment. 'Well, in that case I shall start.

We use hot mustard and borage compresses for consumption and ailments of the chest.' He paused and the inquisitor waved him on. 'A paste made of foxglove for conditions connected with the region of the heart, garlic poultices for stubborn wounds, valerian for calming the nerves. We also use the organs of animals. One may occasionally prescribe the powdered horn of deer, the bile of vipers, the semen of frogs and animal excrement, such as ass' dung – which is very fine for promoting fertility. Though I have not had occasion to use it.' He paused, and there was a faint humorous murmur around us. This did not please the inquisitor, for he waved the infirmarian on, this time with annoyance.

'And of course, *Theriacum* . . . by far the most used drug in many infirmaries, a mixture composed of some fifty-seven substances of which the chief element is the flesh of poisonous snakes. Of course, there are also other methods such as purges, baths, cautery, surgery of which the Eastern infidels were masters. Is there anything in particular that you would like to know?' he asked, squinting a little.

Raising his arms in an exaggerated gesture of incredulity, the inquisitor said, 'From whence does your inexhaustible knowledge spring? Have you studied medicine in Paris? Or are there other means of procuring such information?'

There was a shy smile, 'I have not had the good fortune to attend formal training, but as I showed a natural propensity in this field when I was a novice, I was encouraged to study under Brother Setubar, my predecessor. Also there are many treatises available on this subject, as you know.'

'Brother Setubar?'

'Yes, but he is now retired to a contemplative life, though he assists me at all times.'

'I see. And did he too rely on these treatises you have just mentioned?'

'Of course.'

'And from whence did you procure these manuscripts?'

'Brother Macabus supplies us with what we need from our library, we need only to ask.'

'I see . . . I see, and was brother Ezekiel, that is the brother who was brutally murdered, also a past librarian?'

'He was a translator, although we have not established that he was murdered, your grace. He was old, like our Brother Samuel.'

'Brother Samuel?' the inquisitor paused. 'Who is Brother Samuel?'

There was a nervous pause. 'He was the master of music.'

'And where is he?' the inquisitor glanced about the chapter house. There was an uncomfortable stillness. 'Well?' he pressed.

'Brother Samuel died some days ago,' Asa answered, after a momentary hesitation.

Rainiero Sacconi turned once more towards the dais and said, 'And how did he die?'

The infirmarian became ashen-faced. 'He was found in the church, gasping for air and he expired shortly after.'

'What do you believe caused his death?'

'I do not know.'

'Could a poison have led to his untimely demise?'

'Perhaps, some poisons leave no trace. It would be difficult to say.'

'What poison could have caused his symptoms?'

'There are poisons that have the effect of cutting off breathing by paralysing the muscles of the lungs.'

'But what are these poisons?'

'There are any number of poisons, your grace.'

'And Brother Ezekiel? Could he have died as a result of being poisoned in the same way?'

'It is possible, but I did not say brother Samuel was poisoned.'

'No, all we need to know is that this is possible,' the inquisitor appeared pleased, 'and yet it is of no interest to this inquiry how either of the poor unfortunate brothers died, for we know the evil one works in manifold ways. What does interest us, however, is the use of heretical texts for the purposes of extracting cures through sorcery and black magic! Perhaps someone at this abbey has invoked the Devil, and now does not know the formula by which to release him, and so he continues to wander about killing monks.'

There was a loud murmur. I looked around and found a face in the crowd staring at me. It was Anselmo. I looked away, pretending that I had not seen him, certain that the singer was of evil disposition. Who else would smile during an inquiry?

'Perhaps Brother Samuel was strangled by the Devil,' the inquisitor said, 'after all, he was found gasping for breath!'

'I do not know. But I did not say that he was . . .' The brother shook his head. 'He was old . . . should the devil leave marks on his neck?'

Rainiero raised his brows. 'Are you saying that there were marks, or that there were no marks?'

'No . . . no marks!'

'Ahh, but it may not have been the Devil, but the Devil's own who has committed these heinous crimes . . . perhaps our pious brothers found out what you were doing with these manuscripts of yours, and you put an end to them before they could take matters to the abbot?'

'No, no!' Asa exclaimed anxiously, for the first time realising his peril.

'What manuscripts are these, then? Tell us and we shall judge if they be good or evil.'

'Medical manuscripts, your lordship.'

'Tell me.'

'There are many . . . let me see . . . the works of the *Doctor Admirabilis,* Avicenna and his canon of medicine, Averroes . . . many . . . many! Dozens of works of supreme importance in this field.' He added, trying to convince the man before him of their significance. 'Hippocrates's *Corpus Hippocraticum* is a wealth of knowledge for any young aspiring physician, there is also the classic works of

Roger Salerno and his *Practica Chirurgiae*. As well, the wonderful works of Galen of Pergamon, Aulus Cornelius Celsus, who wrote entire volumes, the physician Pedanius Dioscorides who became the first medical botanist – a man whom I humbly hold as a model – Rufus of Ephesus renowned for his investigations of the heart and eye . . . and there are many more.'

'You see! All works of pagans, infidels, and heretics!' he shouted in a sudden outburst that shook the congregation.

'Your grace,' Asa answered, wrenching his hands, 'if that were so, then why are there copies to be found in the abbey of Monte Cassino where the good doctor Constantine has translated into Latin from Arabic many Greek classics. As did another by the name of Albertus Magnus. And if so impure and loathsome, why can they be so easily found at the medical school at Montpellier or the University of Paris?'

'Do not seek to mask your guilt by quoting translations over which there have been grave misgivings. One day all these works will be branded heresy and condemned, along with those who found them exceedingly fruitful.'

'But these are fine books, they have provided many with immeasurable and illuminated knowledge. I have always thought that one must distinguish a man's faith from his wisdom.'

'That is not possible, one is dependent on the other.'

'Perhaps, but a man of science, your grace, must lay aside all other concerns, and work from natural laws.'

'Another heretical statement! What can one expect from a man who reads the thoughts of devils and infidels. These natural laws of which you speak are nothing other than precepts for committing necromancy and witchcraft!' There was a stir and the inquisitor, not one to miss an opportunity, seized his moment. 'Yes, witchcraft! Do you not call forth all the chiefs of the infernal legions to assist you in these miraculous healings?'

'No.'

'Is that not why monks have been dying at this monastery? Because there have been monks practising abominable acts? Is that what you mean by 'natural laws'?'

'Natural laws are the eyes through which we see a divine will at work in the world around us,' said Asa, 'and can measure and calculate its existence. Knowledge is God and God is knowledge. In the words of the loving Brother Vincent of Beauvais, 'The mind lifting itself from the dunghill of its affections, and rising, as it is able, into the light of speculation, sees as from a height the greatness of the universe containing in itself infinite places filled with the diverse orders of creatures', and Ephesus tells us, 'Gather together in one all things in Christ, both which are in heaven and which are on earth', and again, 'The spirit searcheth all things. Yea the deep things of God'. In Proverbs we are told to, 'Take fast hold of instruction; let her not go: keep her for she is thy life'.'

'I see you are also accomplished in ways to justify your heresy through your own diabolical rendering of holy words! Another impudent trait!' He bounded with agility onto the dais and brought his fist down hard on the oak table before shouting. '*Is it not true* . . . that you read these heretical manuscripts so that you may practise the *perverse* rituals dictated therein? *Is it not also true* that these rituals call for the use of astrology and alchemy and other abominations such as the calling forth of devils and demons and the eating of mummified cadavers?'

Brother Asa answered with a tremor in his voice 'There *is* such a thing as you have described . . . *Mumia,* though it is very rare, and I am afraid I have never seen it, though I believe such a thing to be filled with the forces of destruction. We have not called on such procedures, as you have just now mentioned, your grace.'

'Your impertinence would astound me, had I not been exposed many times in the past to the fox-like ways of the heretic! You evade my questions thus because you know there are so many diabolical procedures that I, a man who knows little about such things, cannot point to any one method in particular, and so it will go on and on, you will deny them all until I, by chance, name one you have used . . .'

Brother Asa said nothing, and this fuelled the inquisitor's anger.

'Do you then swear that you have never learnt anything contrary to the faith which we say and believe to be true through such manuscripts?'

'Willingly, your grace.'

'Then do so.'

'If I am commanded, all I can do is swear.'

'I do not command you, but if you wish to do so I will listen,' he said mildly.

'Why may I swear, your grace, if I am not commanded to?'

'Why . . .? To remove the suspicions that have been brought against you and your fellow monks that you are heretics, and as such, believe that all swearing of oaths is unlawful and sinful!'

'I am innocent!'

'Then you have nothing to lose by swearing,' the inquisitor's lips curled in a terrible smile.

'I swear by the holy gospels that I have never learnt or believed anything contrary to those same gospels.'

'And does that include what the holy Roman church believes and holds to be orthodox?'

'Does the Roman church follow the holy precepts and laws as they have been given to us by the great fathers of the church, your grace?' Asa asked humbly.

'Of course!'

'Then inasmuch as they do, I swear.'

'You writhe like a snake, SWEAR!

'I swear!'

'And yet you may well swear a thousand oaths and I will

not believe you, as I know heretics are told they may swear any number of times and it means nothing, inasmuch as they do not believe in the swearing of oaths!'

And in this way the interrogation came to an end.

We remained in the chapter house after the procession of solemn-faced monks left. Lingering in the shadows like thieves, we hoped to have a look in the great book of life.

On a lectern facing the abbot's throne was the large manuscript bound in goatskin over thin wooden boards. Once again, the rose cross adorned the central panel, stitched elaborately over a gilt parchment background.

'It reminds me of coptic binding, Egyptian,' my master said to himself.

Inside the book was made of the most exquisite vellum, with the perimeter of each page gilded in finest gold. All matters of importance were recorded in this book in endless rows of dates and names. I did not know what my master was seeking exactly, but he seemed to know because it did not take him long to make some remarkable discoveries. The first was that the commencement of the book was marked with the date 1187. This was interesting, my master said, because it coincided with the fall of Jerusalem. I did not understand the connection between the two, but he was convinced that there had to be more to the grand master's interest in the abbey. Could it be, he argued, merely that our preceptory held the titles to the land? No, he was sure there were other reasons, and too, he reminded me of the Templar grave we saw in the cemetery. Merely a coincidence?

So we continued looking through the old book searching for any more strange connections with our order that might lead to an elucidation of these things. When we finally arrived at the end, my master closed it and turned to me with a bewildered look.

'There are four names added only recently,' he said.

'How recently, master?'

'Only ten years ago.'

'Then they must be novices, but how could they be when there are only two novices?'

'There are four entries; Amiel, Hugo, Poitevin and I could not make out the other, the lettering is smudged . . . no other details are given. We should expect to see where they were from and their ages and so on . . .'

'A clerical error?'

'No. It is not likely. Everything else has been chronicled very precisely. Why omit the origins and ages of four monks? Besides, the names of the only two novices in the monastery are accounted for, Anselmo, and a certain Jerome.'

'Come to think of it, I have not seen this other oblate.'

'Very odd . . . it is a mystery,' he said, I believe annoyed.

We left the chapter house, looking about us a little anxiously, now knowing with a little more certainty that things were not as they appeared, and I was glad when we were out in the common grounds.

The weather had not improved. An ominous greyness had descended over the abbey, befitting the mood of the community. Soon the bell would toll the little hour of sext, and about us monks sought refuge in the comfort of daily affairs. To the scriptorium, or the stables, long, sombre figures moved. Everywhere monks would raise their cowls a little to steal glances at one another, perhaps seeking recognition and justification for an anxiety felt, but never expressed. My master and I sought out the infirmarian. We knew that he had left earlier in the direction of the infirmary. As we walked with quick steps past the graveyard, I saw two monks digging Ezekiel's grave, its dark depths contrasted starkly with the purity of the snow. Tomorrow, after the office of the dead, the old man's mortality would be immersed in the cold ground, to sleep the eternal dreamless sleep in which the silence of divinity resides in the chalice of peace, and I pondered on the words of Job, 'Man that is born of a woman hath but a short time to live, and is full of misery', and I was caught between despair for the monastery, and a grave fear of the antichrist.

We entered the infirmary where there was a good fire in the hearth, and as we stepped across the threshold, we saw that Brother Asa was hurriedly replacing something of large proportions in a velvet pouch.

'Preceptor . . . you have been injured . . .' he said, frowning a little, holding the pouch behind him. 'I see that you have dressed the wound.'

'Just a little graze. I should be more careful getting out of bed,' he smiled, fixing the infirmarian with one of his silent stares until the man began to look about him nervously.

'I wanted to tell you, but . . .'

'What did you want to tell me, Asa,' he asked him, 'about Brother Samuel's death? That you saw him dying, but did nothing?'

'How do you mean?' The infirmarian became distressed.

'At the inquiry you said Brother Samuel was found in the church, gasping for air, but when we spoke to Brother Daniel, he said that when he found the monk he was already dead. So logically we must assume that you came across the poor man before Brother Daniel. Am I right!'

The man fell to his knees, 'No! I . . . that is, I did not . . . you have to believe me!' he cried.

'That you did not kill the brother? Or that you were the first to see him and did nothing to save his life?'

'I will tell you . . .' Asa sobbed into one hand, but my master did not wait for him to regain his composure, and pressed him to go on by helping him roughly to his feet.

'I went to see Brother Ezekiel,' he pleaded, 'on the matter of a book. Being the translator and possessing a very good memory, Brother Macabus suggested that I see him. I was told that prior to nones he was always to be found at the foot of the

Virgin, so I went there, but he was not alone. He was having a heated argument with Brother Samuel. Lord forgive them, they were raising their voices in the Chapel of the Lady of our sorrows. Not wishing to intrude, I waited in the ambulatory.'

'What you mean to say is that you waited in the shadows, hoping to hear their argument.' The man was silent, lowering his eyes, and my master waved him on.

'For the most part I did not understand their conversation,' he continued, 'then I heard something which drew my interest.'

'Yes?'

'They were discussing something . . . they called it a 'final conclusion'. Brother Samuel said he must go down, and see for himself, Brother Ezekiel disagreed vehemently, saying that it was not the right time, he was not sure that any of them were pure enough . . . that it would depend on the others . . . I do not know what he meant by this . . .' he shrugged his shoulders. 'Brother Samuel then said that Daniel had given him the formulas.'

'What were they discussing? Tell me!' my master cried, his eyes ablaze.

'I don't know, I swear to you!'

'Now you swear!' There was a pause. 'What is this place they should not visit? The tunnels, perhaps?'

'I don't know, but I do know it has something to do with the boy.'

'The boy?'

'The novice, they mentioned him.'

'What novice, Anselmo or Jerome?'

He looked surprised, even shocked. His lips began to quiver and a faint perspiration appeared on his brow. 'No, not them, but another . . .'

We were both bewildered. 'What other . . .? Tell me about him.'

'I cannot . . . I don't know . . . no one has seen him, not

since he has fallen ill.'

'Tell me who he is.'

'He came to this monastery as an oblate of no more than seven. But no one has ever seen him. They say he is down with the ghosts, but no one goes there! No one! It is forbidden.'

'In the tunnels? Come now, there are rules that apply to monks, and others that apply to the abbot and his obidientiaries.'

'But it is not the abbot's regulation, preceptor, that prevents monks from venturing there . . .'

'Whose then, Setubar's?'

'No,' the man looked about him circumspectly, 'it is the admonition of the spirits!'

'Come now, brother —'

'There are spirits in the tunnels. It is *their* admonition.'

'And yet I have heard that someone has broken the interdict,' my master said, 'did he return?'

The infirmarian shook his head, and lowered his eyes once again, tears flowing down his face. 'He disappeared a few days ago, Jerome is his name, he has not yet been found. You see, preceptor? It is infernal. Here above, we sing like the choirs of heaven, and yet down below us, the maws of hell are open.' The poor man trembled with fear.

My master looked puzzled. So there were three novices!

'Could Jerome not have absconded?' my master ventured, 'this has been known to happen in monasteries.'

'No, no. I do not believe it. Absolutely not! He was my apprentice, a fine student,' the man broke down in sobs. 'He and Anselmo were the only novices at our monastery apart from . . . they were good friends, always together . . .'

'I see . . . and what of this boy? Were they friends with him?'

'Oh, no . . . he was kept apart from all the others. Treated with special care . . . please, brother!' The man cried suddenly stricken with emotion. 'I am afraid . . . Brother Setubar will not be pleased that I have spoken to you.'

'It seems all are more fearful of Brother Setubar than they are of the Devil?'

The man pulled his cowl over his face, perhaps ashamed of his fear, perhaps so that we might not see, and therefore judge, his expression.

'Tell me what happened after the argument,' my master said, giving me a strange look.

'Brother Ezekiel left, seeking his way through the church, for he knew it well despite his bad eyes, walking straight past me saying something about Setubar overhearing their conversation, but he did not see me. I was about to follow him, but I was intrigued by Brother Samuel's behaviour. He took a candle from beneath the Virgin, and disappeared behind the red curtains, but after a few moments I saw him return struggling to gain his breath. He was convulsing and coughing, and that was when I rushed to him, but there was nothing I could do!'

'Why did you not raise the alarm? Why did you walk away and leave someone else to find him?'

'I was afraid . . .' he pleaded, 'but I must tell you of something that did not immediately occur to me until the night of Brother Ezekiel's death. Before brother Samuel inspired his last breath, he said . . .'

Alas, at that moment the door flew open and a burst of frozen air and snow rushed in, violating the warmth of the infirmary.

It was Regino of Naples who, in an agitated state, hurried into the room pointing to the cloister buildings and exclaiming between gasps.

'Fire! Fire in the cookhouse! The cook! The cook is dead!'

I saw Brother Asa place the velvet pouch in a drawer before leaving.

When we entered the cookhouse the fire had already been put out by various monks with buckets. The cook lay prostrate on the muddy floor, and there was a smell of burning oil and fish that in my anxiety I mistook for burning flesh. Asa reached the man before us, carried by his supple legs, and we found him kneeling over him. He inspected the cook for burns or any other injury and produced from a pouch around his middle a small vial. He removed the lid and passed the vessel beneath the cook's nose – later I was to learn from my master that it was fennel juice – in any case, the man was instantly aroused. He opened his eyes, and with the face of a little child – a look that contrasted sharply with his great size – said from out of his moist mouth, *'Madre mia! La Virgen! La Virgen!'*

My master moved closer and the cook wrenched at his habit hysterically. 'I saw *la madre santa,* in the flames . . . she was beautiful! She said Rodrigo! Yes . . . she said my name! She said Rodrigo this is the sign!'

There was agitation in the crowd that by now had gathered in the doorway to the refectory.

'The sign!' someone shouted, 'for the fire hath devoured the pastures of the wilderness, and the frame hath burnt all the trees of the field!'

'No! No!' cried another.

There was confusion. Some were saying anxiously that the age of advent had come and that Joachim of Calabria had been right, even though, by his calculation, it should be the year 1260.

'Brother cook, were you cooking fish?' my master asked loudly, adding his voice of reason to the matter.

The man looked up at my master incredulously. What did it matter if he was cooking fish, his eyes said, he had seen the Virgin! My master repeated the question, and the cook said that yes, he had been cooking fish. Andre then walked over to the great fireplace beside the large oven. The fire had caused little damage because of the stone wall that surrounded it, but when he looked down, he noticed, as I did, a lump of charred hairy flesh, barely recognisable. 'What is this?' Andre asked, poking at it with a stick.

The cook looked in the direction of my master's gaze. At first uncomprehending, he realised suddenly, and gave out a loud, painful bellow. 'Fernando!' he cried, weeping into his hands. My heart sank. It was the cat.

After inspecting the surrounds, my master said, 'Now everything is clear.'

He asked the cook if the cat regularly rested in the alcove above the fire. Even I knew the answer to this question, but the cook was weeping into his burly hands and saying in soft whispers, 'Fernando . . . Fernando.'

Others joined in until many were weeping for the unfortunate cat.

It was then that Andre noticed something else, a dry, brown bunch of burnt leaves, perhaps herbs, hanging from a string above the fire. My master crumpled some of the charred remains in his hand, and bringing it to his nose, sniffed lightly. He nodded, returning to question the cook once more when, at that very moment, the abbot entered the cookhouse, followed by the inquisitor and the other members of the legation.

Surveying the scene, the inquisitor approached the giant on the floor who, in his present state of grief, did not notice him.

Rainiero gave my master a disdainful look and slapped the cook hard across the face. There was a collective gasp. The man's head turned from side to side, and he looked up wide-eyed as though he did not comprehend what had just happened.

'Mi poor Fernando,' he said shocked. 'He, too, saw la Virgen Santa!'

The inquisitor ignored this and turned to the other cook for satisfaction, but before the man could speak, my master broke in with his usual alacrity.

'It is simple, Rainiero, the man accidentally spilt oil over the fire while immersing fish for the meal. It ignited the herbs drying above the fire. Understandably he stepped away from the flames but, in so doing, he slipped on the floor, whereby he fell, knocking his head. The unfortunate cat,' he pointed to the burnt remains, 'in his surprise, leapt from its abode above the fire – a natural place for a cat, as they are known to hate the cold. It should have escaped misfortune, as we know cats land only on their feet. In this instance, however, it was its undoing, for one of its legs caught the side of the cauldron and it landed in the fire. Most unfortunate,' he concluded, and finding a radish hanging from a basket took a bite out of it.

Someone behind me said, 'What a marvel.' Another whispered, 'It is the Templar acumen.'

And as one might expect this did not please the inquisitor who looked on at my master's casual manner with incredulity. 'Very well!' he exclaimed, enraged. 'You seem to have things in hand. However, as I am the inquisitor, and not you, preceptor, I demand that you allow me to continue my investigations without interruption!'

'By all means,' said my master, stepping aside as a sign of submission. Rainiero raised his chin and looked down his nose at the cook. 'Now then,' he began, noting, however, that my master had stolen his thunder. 'Cook, what say you?'

'It was *la Virgen!*' answered the man beaming, 'She came out of the fire to take me to heaven. I was flying! *Et ne nos inducas in tentationem, sed libera nos a malo. Amen!* – Deliver us from evil. Amen!'

The inquisitor came forward until he stood very close to the cook. 'So, you saw the Virgin! The Virgin appeared to you? I see . . . a greasy cook has a beatific vision? Should we venerate you as a saint? Or perhaps as the devil that you are!'

'*He visto a la Virgen.* I have seen her . . .' the cook said softly.

'Or was it that perhaps you were casting a diabolical spell on the fish with some poisonous herb with the intention of harming this legation and those who seek the truth about this abbey? Come now, we all know the body of Satan is comprised of several plants! That his evil eye is henbane, his beard is the snapdragon, his claws the orchid, bindweed is his gut, mandrake his testicles! You have conjured up the Devil disguised as the sainted mother by sacrificing a cat. You see! All of you are witnesses! All of you know that the cat is the embodiment of Satan, whose urine is said to bring about the death of those who drink it. Whose ashes, when ingested, secure a man's soul! It is you that I suspect of being the killer of two monks, whom you have poisoned at the bidding of the Devil! Guards! Seize this man!'

There were confused cries of 'No!'

My master then, thankfully, interjected.

'Rainiero, I am certain this incident is an innocent one. The man hit his head and has become stupefied, that is all. Murder has not been established, Rainiero. I believe there is another agent responsible . . .'

'Really?' The other man was angry now, and his face was turning the colour of my master's radish. 'Pray enlighten us all, preceptor, perhaps I should defer to your wisdom, for you seem more adept in such matters than I.'

My master ignored him and continued, vegetable in hand, 'I believe the cook has somehow partaken of a poisonous herb, perhaps the same that killed Brother Ezekiel .'

'Why then is he not dead?' the other man argued, turning blue.

'I have not figured it all out yet, but perhaps it is because he did not ingest it, he only inhaled it when the herbs were set alight.'

The cook merely gazed from one man to the other. 'No! No! *La Virgen!*'

'And so how is it that you know what poisonous herb was used, preceptor? That is, unless you are in collusion with heretics!' he cried, 'The wolf and the fox are cunning, but the lamb is wise!'

'You are the wolf!' the cook exclaimed. 'Death to the wolves!'

And then he howled like a madman.

Rainiero's mouth twisted in an evil grin. 'Aha! Now we see the true nature of the beast! Death to the wolves! The cry of a *Ghibelline!*' He turned to the abbot. 'Not only do you harbour men who deal with infernal powers, but you also protect imperialists!'

The abbot frowned, lost for words. Once again my master ventured his opinion, 'The man does not know what he is saying, he is still under the influence of the herb and the blow to his head. You fail to see that there is more here than meets the eye.'

The inquisitor laughed a terrible laugh. 'Tomorrow we shall see what he says under oath! Guards, seize this vermin and take him to the room provided us by the abbey.'

The guards took the cook brutally by both arms. He cried in sudden desperation, realising the gravity of his situation. They dragged him out of the kitchen through the door to the gardens in the time it took to say one amen, and I felt a terrible sense of powerlessness.

'Infirmarian, you are to stay in your infirmary until I learn what part you have played in this terrible business, a guard will be posted at your door with orders to allow no one in without my sanction. And you.' He glared at my master. 'I'll have no more of your intrusions in the affairs of the inquisition, preceptor, your duty lies as a watchful servant of the king and nothing more. If I catch you sniffing about I shall have no other recourse but to have you and your apprentice seized until the conclusion of this dreadful inquiry, which is fast running a straight course toward inquisition.' Turning to the captain of the guards he ordered that he post archers at all known exits out of the monastery. No one was to enter or to leave without his orders. He also ordered that all food prepared for the members of the legation must first be tasted, and that this included all the wine. After this he left, amid the wails and moans of monks.

15

Capitulum

The storm came, not suddenly, but quietly. We were sitting in my master's cell, Eisik, my master and I. Having heard the commotion Eisik was unable to contain his curiosity, and had made his way stealthily to the pilgrims' hospice where we sat, deep in thought, as the wind began to rage outside the window. In the beginning it was nothing more than a gust, slowly, however, it became violent, pounding on the stone walls of the building with enough strength, it seemed, to carry a man. The sky, nearly black now, looked heavy with snow clouds that sequestered the mountain, and announced a heavy fall. Soon, up in the higher reaches, the peaks would become dangerously congested, like a pregnant woman longing to give birth to its excess – I fervently hoped, not on the abbey.

Avalanches were not extraordinary, so a brother told us when he knocked on our door to announce that the meal would be delayed. He had brought us a tray of nuts and bread and while he set it down he told us that this phenomenon was the consequence of unusually wet winters and that only ten years before, a brother, while crossing the grounds to the stables, was asphyxiated under an enormous mantle of snow that had loosened from overhead.

'He was not found until the next morning,' the brother said

in a thick vulgar accent, one eye permanently closed. 'When they dug his carcass out of the snow we prayed for his soul, God grant him, soaring lightly in the heavens, even as his testicles were as heavy as glass.'

Now we could see almost nothing except snow from my master's window.

Andre lay stretched out on his pallet staring into nothingness, his mouth working the nuts that he, from moment to moment, popped into his mouth. Eisik paced the floor like a caged animal and I sat on a chair impassively.

'Master?' I asked.

'Yes?' He raised his chin.

'What are you doing?'

'I am thinking, boy.'

'About the deaths?'

'Yes, that too.'

'What are you thinking?'

'I am thinking that there are far too many things to think about, nevertheless, I believe we are progressing in our hunt.'

'To which hunt do you refer, master? I must admit I no longer know whether we are hunting for murderers or for ways to get into tunnels or for . . . final conclusions, or monks who disappear . . .'

'We are hunting all those things,' he answered calmly.

Eisik shook his head from side to side. 'And the hunter shall become the hunted . . . mind what I say, Andre! Holy tribes of Israel! What a predicament you have found for us!'

'Firstly,' Andre said, ignoring his friend, 'in the matter of . . . we shall call them murders . . . we have two dead monks whose deaths are preceded by similar symptoms, at least one had, at the moment of death, a curious sensation of flying.'

'But a sensation of flying, master? Is that not also what the cook said?'

'Yes, he has come into contact, though only slightly, with

the poison. I have read something, somewhere, about a certain compound . . .if only there was order to be found in my poor confounded head!' He sighed. 'In any case, we must cheer up, we must think . . . What do we know? Firstly we know from our conversation with Asa that Samuel was seeking to go down to the tunnels to see something, though he was warned by Setubar against it. We then learn that a young novice, a friend of our Greek genius, has gone missing, having broken the interdict and ventured where no man must go.'

'Too many loose ends! There are too many!' cried Eisik, jubilantly pessimistic.

'Precisely, and so we must tie them all together, but not too soon. Let us not be overcome by it all, for there are many things to consider, and if we act in haste we may indeed tie the wrong ends together!'

'But the dying are piling up, master!' I said impatiently.

'Hurry not, learn deliberation! Remember that an Arab horse makes a few stretches at full speed, and breaks down, while the camel, at its deliberate pace, travels night and day, and gets to the end of its journey. Now let us ponder things a little, shall we? What were the similarities between the two dead monks?'

'They were both old enough to know many secrets about the past of the abbey?' I ventured.

'Precisely, old enough, as we have seen, to know something of the tunnels, and what is hidden therein.'

'Perhaps the killer wants these secrets to remain secret, master? Perhaps the killer did not want them going down to the catacombs?'

'That would be the less taxing explanation,' he answered, 'but just because something is plausible that does not make it probable. In any case, first let us examine the profile of our killer from what we know of him.'

'But we do not know anything, master, only that he knows Greek and that he is left-handed.'

'Nothing, he knows nothing!' Eisik thundered, waving his arms about. 'And still he meddles . . . The inquisitor hates him and still he baits and taunts him so that, in his sleep, the Dominican dreams of pyres whereupon he burns innocent Jews and Templars. In truth, Arabs are renowned for their arrogance, and you are the proof. Say nothing, think nothing. Do nothing more than what is asked of you.'

'What do you say? One impatient and one reticent?' my master said, sitting up a little. 'My lord, if you are not the most empty-headed . . . you *are* human beings therefore you can think! *So* think! If we are surrounded by enemies we must alter our management of affairs and change our strategies to keep the enemy from recognising them, that is all. One moment we are submissive, the next we are forceful. One moment we act, the next we wait. We must secretly guard our advantages.'

'Which are?' Eisik raised a black brow.

'That we know a great deal.'

'Do we, master?'

'Of course, we can construct the murderer's character as one constructs a house. Each brick is a little scrap of knowledge that we have of him, and even that which we don't have, and can only hypothesise. Firstly, we must venture a *propositum* of his motives because motives are closely tied to characteristics . . . We do what we do, Christian, because of who we are, is that not so?'

'That is so,' I agreed.

'Now, what reasons could a man of God have for doing away with his fellow monks? And notice I don't just see him as a man because he is not any man, he is a monk whose life is devoted to relinquishing sin. Either he is not a good monk – which we may say at the outset is most likely – or he doesn't see these murders as sinful, he justifies them in some way, as holy necessities. Let us consider what kind of monk would do such a thing, shall we?'

'A man who hates another, obviously,' Eisik contributed,

'and considering the powerful hate of a gentile . . .'

'All that aside, Eisik, hate is a strong motive, and usually a passionate one. In such a case the crime would be more violent, less . . . planned.'

'Greed, fear, jealousy, vanity, power?' I ventured.

'Very good, very good,' he nodded his head.

'But which one? Which one, for the love of Israel?' cried Eisik, overcome with an access of emotion.

'Perhaps a mixture of all of them, my friend. Let us see, he has succeeded in his crime, so he is clever, and those who are clever . . .'

'Are envious of others whom they suspect of being more clever than they, this is well known,' Eisik finished, pacing the room.

'We must remember that a community of monks is like a mirror of the world, only many times smaller,' Andre said.

'You mean that monks are no better than those peasants in the village who are envious of each other, who blaspheme and who go about their greedy business?' I asked aghast. 'Master, how can that be so?'

'There are not many men, be they monk or peasant, who are not this very day performing penance for some sin of pride or vanity. In any case we must continue by surmising that our killer may be envious, but why is he envious of older monks?'

'Perhaps the killer was envious of another's wisdom, master, because he is ambitious to be thought wiser.'

'The boy is brighter than you credit him,' said Eisik, 'for he sees that either the killer is young and therefore despises the wisdom of the old because it is not new, or he is old and envies the young whose fresh new ideas he detests, or perhaps he envies his equals because he falls a little short of having what they possess. This is usual in the case of envy, especially among learned men.'

'But that brings us no closer, Eisik, for he could be any

age at all!' I cried.

'Precisely,' answered Eisik, 'but knowing nothing is also something, for now we can surmise that he is also vain. You may ask me how I know this but I will tell you that only a vain person will kill another to possess more knowledge than he already has! There again we see the avarice of learning.' He threw my master a pointed look.

'That is assuming envy is at the root of it,' my master replied serenely, 'which, of course, it may not be. What else? Oh, yes . . . fear! If you have done something horrible or perhaps not horrible, but punishable, would you be terrified that those with a knowledge of your secret might one day betray you?'

'So you are saying, master, that the old monks knew something about the killer? Some terrible secret from the past? What about the cook? It is possible that he told others of his time in Italy.'

'On the other hand,' Eisik's face took on a reflective seriousness, 'the killer, God forgive him, may have done something to someone else who may be in a position to do something to him, and so he forestalls him . . . perhaps his motive *is* fear?'

'I do not think so,' Andre retorted, 'the killer must be confident. Who else but the most confident of men would go on a killing spree when the abbey is not only crawling with men at arms, but also a temporary home for the inquisition? Either he has never experienced brutality, or his experience gives him the means to deal with it. Those whom we do not fear are either weaker than ourselves or we have more supporters than they.'

'So there may be more than one killer?' I asked, so caught up in our puzzle that I momentarily forgot the seriousness of our subject.

'In truth, we must not discount this. The one who hit me on the head today was able-bodied, for this was shown by his quick actions, he is also shorter than I.'

'How do you know that, master? Because of the angle of

his strike?'

'No, and you may take some credit for this, my good Christian, because you asked me about his shoes which drew my attention to his feet whose dimensions were small. It is only natural that people with small feet are generally shorter than those with large feet.'

'So the demon is short and able-bodied . . . Oh son of David! That is why he is not afraid of the old, fragile monks. He must be young or in his prime. These are always the most dangerous men.'

'That we may assume with confidence, Eisik. In any event that only tells us the physical characteristics of the author of our note, and he may not be our killer. We must take care not to assume too much, not unless some other piece of evidence tells us otherwise.'

'What else do we know, master? Do you think that he is motivated by greed?'

'Yes, greed. Our killer wants everything, or maybe only one thing, but it must be of great importance.'

'Yes, my sons, the desire to have what one may not have is a strong one.'

'So those whom our murderer kills may be denying him something, or impeding him in his aim at something and this brings to mind something else . . . What if the killer is after the same thing that has brought us here? Have you thought of that?' Andre said.

'But what has brought us here if not the king's command, master?'

'Yes, I know, but I speak of whatever it is that has compelled his command, something valuable, powerful . . .'

Eisik shivered, groaning deeply, 'So, what you are saying, Andre, is that the old brothers were not mere innocents. You are saying, and it will be heard in the four quarters of heaven, that they were in possession of something . . . something terrible!'

I must have paled for my master became annoyed and he muttered some profanity in his native tongue which I shall not recount.

'Perhaps they are in possession of something, or they know how to come by it, and will not tell? Or perhaps they are ready to tell others about it, thereby denying the killer's sole ownership if he already knows it,' Andre finished, and popped another nut into his mouth with a gesture of defiance.

I was silent.

'Now, to the deaths . . . What is the rule? The poison, the note. Let me see the note.'

I searched in the repository inside my habit and produced the note. My master snatched it from my hands and proceeded to read it: 'Except the lord build the house: their labour is but lost that build it.'

'What is he trying to tell us, and why?' My master thought deeply for a moment. 'Brother Ezekiel was the old translator, and what do translators translate if not the knowledge of others?

Could we then call him a seeker of knowledge? It could be that the killer is forewarning us . . .'

'You mean telling us the identity of his next victim?' I asked, suddenly enlightened.

'Exactly! Whoever built the house will be next.'

'You mean whoever built the monastery?' I corrected him.

'An architect, the builder of the *house* may be a metaphor for something else, such as some *thing* to be accomplished, or some knowledge of the building, the configuration of something.'

'Perhaps it is the measurements of Solomon's Temple, that which was, before it was destroyed by pagans and idolaters,' Eisik offered.

'This knowledge could be the conclusion that Asa mentioned?' I remarked.

'Perhaps,' my master said.

'We know that the author of our note is the killer master, otherwise, how could he know the identity of the next victim?'

'Perhaps he is privy to this information, but does not have the courage to tell us face to face?'

'Why doesn't he write down the name of the killer, master, instead of using riddles?'

'I do not know,' Andre said, pensively, 'perhaps he is prudent.'

Eisik raised one brow. 'Perhaps he likes toying with fumbling Templars.'

My master glared at Eisik and laid his head back on his hands, now in a bad mood.

'But what about the cook, master?' I continued soothingly. 'He must know something.'

'I shall have to speak with him, but that is now difficult. At least we know many things, and I am beginning to think that my assumptions are correct. There are two monasteries, Christian. One that lives and breathes above the earth, and one that conducts its business below.'

'Is that not what the abbot said? That what is above is like that which is below?'

'Yes. Everything points to the catacombs, and I believe there must be something of great importance hidden there, perhaps important enough to occasion murder, and I aim to find out what it is. Now, away with you, and let me think! Tonight, after all are in bed, we visit the panel. We shall meet after compline in your cell, Christian.'

16

Capitulum

*'Let the bridegroom go forth of his chamber,
and the bride out of her closet.'*
JOEL II 16

I was in a magnificent garden. Around me nature seemed as fresh as the very first day of creation. Everywhere I saw His fingerprint upon the most sublime hues, and the most resplendent colours. Cool, limpid pools of emerald and jade in their innocence cascaded down to a stream whose origin seemed to be in some distant place, dissolving into an indistinct horizon. Here light played upon everything, dancing on the gauzy wings of a breeze, resting upon flowers of every kind that lay outspread like a blanket at my feet. They seemed like disciples whose grace and simplicity were singularly beautiful, their little faces upturned in the piety of their vestments.

I could have been in the paradise of Palladius, or high atop Parnassus, or even above the hills of the Isthmus, for it was an ecstatic vision of purest peace and concord the likes of which I had never before experienced. I sighed with deep contentment, gazing up at the blueness above, desiring nothing but that moment, knowing that God in his beneficence and unfathomable wisdom had bestowed this array of supreme beauty for me alone. For indeed I was alone . . . until I saw her . . .

. . . and she was much lovelier than I had imagined. How disarmingly beautiful she was! How divinely constructed were the bones of her face, how brightly shone her eyes and the jewels of her mouth. She was like mineral springs at their source, like cinnamon and saffron, like frankincense. She was illuminated, radiating all the colours of the spectrum. Like the world contained in a drop of rain; she was intrinsic and extrinsic, diaphanous and crystalline. All that she was, lay clearly before my eyes . . . Isis unveiled.

It was then that I became afraid. Perhaps because of what I had heard about the noon-tide devil; that woman being a feminine creature – and therefore diabolical – was the oldest and most powerful tool of Satan. Perhaps I was afraid because deep inside me I knew this not to be true and therefore could only blame myself for the impurity of my thoughts.

Proverbs tells us that 'stolen waters are sweet, and bread eaten in secret is pleasant', and it was indeed pleasant to remain transfixed, desiring to understand this most exquisite and enigmatic creature better. I found that if I could empty my mind of all the trivial little things about her, I could in a sense feel her essential being in a curious way stripped bare before me. I saw that she was good. She was lovely. I feel at a loss, patient reader, to explain why, or rather how, I sensed these things, but they seemed to me as natural as inhaling the brisk mountain air, observing how its crispness enters one's lungs, purifying them. A kind of fleeting knowledge, an intuition passing over the soul, and finally, oh sweet melancholy . . .

She passed by and in her wake there was the faint scent of jasmine as it is given forth from the hanging gardens of Babylon. Her mouth beckoned me, redder than the wines of Cana, adorned with teeth whiter than milk, each one like a little pearl.

She walked as straight as the towers of Lebanon that looketh towards Damascus, her breasts like unto apples, for their scent was sweet, and her eyes like the tranquil waters of Heshbon by the gate of Bathrabbin, for they conveyed peace.

'Come down, my beloved. Why tarriest thou?' I heard myself say. 'O beautiful maiden, rising over the horizon like the moon over Jerusalem. Vanquishing the darkness, and warming the senses like a radiant fire!' I felt a pang . . . Oh, sweet sweetest love! What miseries dost thou bestow upon a man! I knew that she must be the work of a cunning craftsman for I felt feverish. Who is this woman who, in her necklaces, hides precious fruits shining like the sun? Who, with one blush, could shame all the stars of heaven? I found myself at once relieved and also anguished, lured to the infernal gates of hell.

'Come to me, my groom!' she said, for her voice was like honey and it tasted sweet in my mouth, but was bitter in my belly. And my hands became gold rings set with beryl: my belly as bright ivory overlaid with sapphires. My legs were as pillars of marble, set upon sockets of fine gold: my countenance as Lebanon, excellent as the cedars.

And then she spoke, her voice like the waters of the Nile.

'Marry the bride with the groom, oh, my beloved! Marry the fire with the water, for thy mouth is most sweet . . . Set me as a seal upon thy heart. As a seal upon thy arm: for love is as strong as death.'

Together we entwined, and like the best wine that goeth down sweetly, causing the lips of those that are asleep to speak, so we, like the waters that merge into one fierce body, like a river breaking its banks, rushed together with one objective. Hastening towards one end we plunged into a sea of molten fire, licked by a flame, consumed by its coolness. Oh, Solomon! Is this the beloved of your songs? I thought, and like a desperate man, climbed upon the peaks of her mountains to see the contours of her country, the formation and symmetry of her kingdom, for she was Jerusalem, the bone of my bones, flesh of my flesh. With great care, I went down to the valley, caressing each little hill, drowning my thirst in her estuaries. There I smelt her earth, and stroked it tenderly, moulding it between my feverish fingers, kissing the fruits that, from out of the fertile belly sprouted, like berries, red and delightful. Then I tilled her soil, and reaped her corn, I gathered her roses and drank her milk, and when the storm threatened to tear my country asunder, I found sanctuary within her ample bays, waiting for that moment, the supreme moment when I would be as Moses before the burning bush.

Suddenly there was a great glow, a sudden shiver, a little earthquake shuddering beneath me, and she was my sister, my mother, my love, a dove . . . pure, undefiled. And the molten gold flowed from the *aludel, prima materia* – the original matter, flooded, unrestrained into the land, and . . .

The twelve became seven and the seven stars appeared.

AER
THE THIRD TRIAL

*Easy is the way down to the Underworld: by night and by day
dark Hades' door stands open; but to retrace one's steps and to
take a way out to the upper air, that is the task, that is the labour.*
Virgil Aeneid book 6, v. 1, line 126

17

Capitulum

I sat up with a jolt. Perspiration ran rivulets down my back and I was breathing heavily, my heart galloping like mad stallions. What had I done, I asked myself? I stood, and shamefully changed out of the habit that was soaked in my unchasteness, and dressed in the other garment the hospitaller had given me. Heavy of heart I then knelt, shivering from cold, fear and humiliation, and said one paternoster after another until I heard my master open my cell door.

Andre must have known something was amiss, though he said nothing, I only sensed that he was stealing an occasional glance in my direction. Perhaps he was working his peculiar logic on me?

We waited for Eisik, but he did not come, so we made our way to the church. I dived down into my cowl hoping to escape my master's scrutiny, and I little noticed how cold it had become, or how the compound lay shrouded in a ghostly white blanket. I thought only of the dream, which, like an inner fire in my chest, God help me, warmed my being.

We entered the church through the north door and made our way cautiously past the Lady Chapel to the altar where we lit our two lamps at the great tripod and returned once again, by way of the ambulatory, to the north transept where, immersed in gloom, we waited.

'By God's bonnet,' whispered my master harshly, 'where is that confounded Jew?'

Time was passing and my master signalled that we should proceed to the Lady Chapel stealthily, in the shadows.

You must imagine, dear reader, the two of us crouched behind the curtains that adorned the walls, feeling a mixture of excitement and trepidation. It was with such sentiments that I re-cited a paternoster once more, as my master made ready to open the panel. My heart was heavy, weighed down by a thousand weights. Brother Daniel's admonition, 'Beware the antichrist is near', ran through my mind like a chant and I wondered if per-haps I had encountered the evil one in my dream, disguised as a woman, for I knew that he was skilful and ingenious. I remem-bered hearing discussions in lowered voices, among the young attendants and stablehands, they said that a man could become intoxicated with a woman, not only through her smell, which works like a potent magic, but also because of the colour of her lips, whose moisture and softness were like that of new wine that begged to be drunk with pleasure. A man, they said, was seduced by the slightest thing; the rise and fall of an ivory bo-som, the milk and honey of a nape, the soft velvet of flesh . . . and by this infernal deception, induced to forget the holiest of vows to the mother church, to the order, and to God! Had I not been a witness to such things, even if only in a dream? I found I was breathing heavily, and my master gave me one of his odd looks. He, I knew, had always said that nature was the daughter of God and woman, as the daughter of nature, could be nothing less than divine. Now, as I looked on at the Virgin's image in the chapel, I wondered how one could venerate her and not, at the same time, respect the same bond of femininity that binds the mother with all women. Yet it was a woman, or the image of her (in some ways even more diabolical), that had induced me to sin.

There was no denying it, and for this I felt a great guilt. I needed to confess everything to my master, my mouth even opened to say those terrible words, but as fate would have it just at that moment he depressed the two necromantic signs: first, Pisces, and then Saturn, and my mind was gratefully wrenched, if only for a brief time, from the sorrow of my guilt.

'By the sword of Saladin!' my master whispered harshly, 'that's not it!'

'But master,' I thought a moment, 'you and Eisik were speaking of a celestial sequence '

'What did you say?' Andre turned to me. 'Of course! The sequence! Good boy, Christian!' he whispered jubilantly. 'You need to depress the sequence of planets with Saturn as the seventh, not Saturn alone!'

Andre tried to depress the sun sign but it would not move. 'Why not?' he whispered angrily. 'For the love of all the saints, why did it move before and not now, by God?'

'May the twelve become seven and the seven stars appear,' I said, risking his rebuke.

'Of course, I must be a donkey! The twelve and seven, Christian! They must go together, even you knew it.'

He depressed Pisces and held it down while he depressed firstly the sun, then moon, followed by Mercury, Venus, Mars, Jupiter and finally Saturn. There was a metallic sound and the panel began to move as though on a cushion of air, opening into a small antechamber only big enough to accommodate the two of us.

I waited for him to congratulate me on my acumen, but he merely paused before the door of the chamber, sniffing the air with suspicion.

'We must not forget,' he said, 'Brother Samuel died from his carelessness. A sweet musky smell . . . but not a poison, in this case something else . . .' He searched about with his nose, but seemed satisfied that no deadly poison awaited us, and so stepped inside, though he kept a vigilant eye about him. On the door ahead we illuminated with our lamps a sign inscribed into the wood that my master told me was the necromantic symbol for Saturn. To my right, a water stoup made out of stone dug into my thigh. No doubt it was filled with holy water for the ritual ablution. In this corner I also saw a number of strange long objects, and realised after a moment that they were torches, such as are dipped in mutton fat, and I was about to observe these further when my sandal touched upon something small though soft, and I looked down to see that it was a rat. I uttered a muffled cry, and my master shushed me, saying none too softly:

'By God, boy, you cannot scare it away, the odious thing is dead!'

'What killed it, master?' I asked, thinking that it must be a terrible omen.

'Perhaps the same thing that killed the old brother,' he replied thoughtfully.

'Shall I take one of these torches with us?'

'No. Touch nothing unless I tell you. These places are places of deception and, as we have seen, murder. Now, to open the door . . .'

He pushed it and it opened with little difficulty, revealing steps that led down into a pit of darkness. Just then I felt a presence behind us and turned expecting to see the hideous form of the Devil, instead it was Eisik, carrying a lamp of his own.

'Thy word is a lantern unto my feet: and a light unto my paths,' he said.

'For the love of all the saints, what happened to you?' my master whispered, taking Eisik's lantern.

'There are guards everywhere, Andre,' he said, hunching his shoulders in expectation of further evils. 'I had to use the cunning of my forefathers. I told the assistant cook I needed a lamp so that I might read the Talmud, and that I would say a prayer that he be spared by the inquisitor if he would be so kind as to oblige. But I will tell you, Andre, I am only here because you have asked me, and because I do not wish to outlive you! Something tells me that this is foolish and yet,' he sighed, 'it is the destiny of an old Jew that no man will listen to him, though if he did he would doubtless live longer.'

So it was that cautiously we embarked on our journey into the unknown, down a long, and seemingly endless, flight of steps, leaving the panel in the first antechamber slightly ajar, as a precaution. The steps were damp, and spaced unevenly; some were broken, some worn smooth, and it was only by a small margin that I managed to maintain my balance. After what seemed an eternity we secured solid earth beneath our feet, but this was only a temporary comfort, for we would soon enter an exceedingly narrow passage that angled obliquely to our right. I made a calculation that this must bear north-east because the steps that led us to our present position were in a westerly direction, as the panel had been on the western side of the transept. This passage, being many feet below ground, smelt ancient and putrefied, and was so narrow that, if I diverged even slightly, I could touch the damp walls on either side with my shoulders. The light from our lamps played on the surface of rock and I thought I could see the faces of numerous devils on the crevices and forms created by different mineral substances.

I trembled.

Why must there be tunnels? Why also curious masters?

At last we entered through an arch and found that we were inside an antechamber. Its three doors were set at the oddest angles, somehow giving one the impression of having suddenly changed direction. I knew that it must be a clever trick. To add to this phenomenon the chamber was also diminutive and that meant that we had to stand very close at its centre, our breaths puffing out in unison in the still, dank air. We raised our lamps to inspect the walls, and noticed that above the doors — that no doubt led to other tunnels — there were torches such as

I had seen on the floor of the first chamber, but these were not lit. Our lamps, however, were adequate in illuminating a number of strange signs carved into the rock above the doors. Directly ahead, the heavy angular aperture had above it the sign of the crescent moon, as well as the word 'Pergamos'. To our right, my master elucidated the necromantic sign for Mars and the word 'Thyatira'. On our left another crescent moon, and again the word 'Pergamos', and behind us 'Ephesus', and the sign for Saturn.

'A labyrinth of tunnels!' my master exclaimed. 'Now what Daniel told us makes sense. He who follows the seven letters in number and order will enter the kingdom of heaven, but he who would seek to go against the seven churches will wander the earth till the moment of death . . . This must surely mean the seven letters of the apocalypse, to the seven communities or churches . . . we must follow them precisely or find ourselves food for rats. Now, what was the first letter . . .?' my master asked Eisik.

'Smyrna . . . no, no, Ephesus . . . that's it, Ephesus.'

'Of course Ephesus . . . 'I am the Alpha and Omega, the first and the last; and what thou seest, write in a book, and send it unto the seven churches which are in Asia; unto Ephesus, and unto Smyrna and unto Pergamos, and unto Thyatira . . .' Blast! What comes next?'

'Unto Sardis, and unto Philadelphia, and unto Laodicea,' Eisik added.

'Eisik!' Andre exclaimed suddenly. 'You know the gentile Bible better than the gentile!'

'Why should I not, my son?' he said, but my master ignored him, for he was muttering other things under his breath.

'And since this is our first chamber, we should surmise that our next should be *Smyrna*.'

"To him that overcometh will I give to eat of the tree of life which is in the midst of the paradise of God',' Eisik quoted.

I was the first to look up at the vaulted ceiling where, at

its apex, a circle enclosing a smaller one could be discerned with Smyrna written in a semicircle at its perimeter. I pointed this out to my master and Eisik excitedly, but it only seemed to confound them all the more.

'If we are in Smyrna, the first was that little chamber before we entered the tunnels. In this case it stands to reason that we should take the door marked 'Pergamos', for that is the subsequent letter. However, there are two of them!'

'Oh, holy fathers . . .' Eisik whispered, wringing his hands, 'which door to take?'

My master looked in this direction and that, pulling on his beard. 'A good question . . . perhaps we are best advised to try one. Shall we?' He moved forward a pace.

'No!' I cried, and felt immediately ashamed. 'There might be something hideous waiting for us on the other side of the wrong door, master.' I reminded him of the story of the Minotaur of Greek legends, and he paused for a moment, nodding his head a little. 'Perhaps then we shall make him a very fine dinner.'

Eisik came to my defence, 'Andre, the boy is right, we must be careful, tunnels are evil places wherein one may become hopelessly lost not only in body but also in soul.'

'That is why I have brought a piece of charcoal and a parchment on which we shall draw a map.' My master handed me the articles that included a strange device set inside a bubble of glass. 'This way our bodies may find a way out, and hopefully our souls will follow.'

'What is this, master?' I asked, rolling the circular thing.

'That, my dear boy, is the instrument I have often mentioned to you and yet never shown you, it is called a compass.'

'Oh, yes, the reason you returned to your cell . . . What does one do with it?' I placed it against my ear tentatively, but I could make out no sound coming from it.

My master smiled. 'It seeks north.'

'Take it away!' Eisik whispered harshly. 'It is wicked, an

astronomer concentrated his thoughts on it for many years and his thinking is said to have created a wicked force, as it might create also a good one, and this force seeks the pole star, because proceeding from it is a great emptiness that sucks this force into itself. It is said to have also sucked into it the soul of the astronomer! Take it away!' He brought his hands up to his face as if to defend his soul.

'Sorcery, master?'

'I suppose it is,' he said, and then, seeing that I was about to drop the object in my horror, he steadied my hand. 'Don't be a goose, Christian! *Mon dieu!* It is most delicate, and may indeed be the only one of its kind on the continent. Although it may be a kind of sorcery, it is also a wonderful one, invented by the Arabs . . . It was a present given to me by a great Saracen convert . . . an Islamic scientist who credited this knowledge to the courts of Haroun al Rashid.'

'But are we in peril of our souls, master?'

'I shall tell you quickly how it works and you will see that it is merely scientific. A strange stone,' he said, 'whose curious properties are not known, is passed over the metal of the needle. The needle, in turn, is said to acquire the same properties as the stone. After this the needle will always seek the northerly direction by pivoting on its axis.'

I was thoughtful, turning it around many times. 'I see, that explains the markings denoting east, south and west. No matter which way you turn it, the needle always points to the north and in this way one may know in which direction one is travelling.'

'Very good!' I believe he was proud of me.

'Then it is a marvel!' I cried, elated at this interesting discovery.

'It may help us. It seems to work this far below the ground. Do not lose it now!' he admonished.

Presently, Eisik held the lamps high above us and my master pushed the door to our left. We were surprised to find that it opened easily onto what looked like more steps, and to my great relief revealed no terrible creature. My master moved forward, preparing to descend ahead of us, when something stopped him abruptly. He shone his lamp into the void.

'*Mon Dieu!* ' he exclaimed in a whisper, 'there are three steps and then . . . nothing!'

'By the blood of all the tribes!' Eisik murmured.

'Where does it go, master?'

'Down, and so would you or I or Eisik, had we descended those steps in haste.' He pulled the door closed and moved to the other. It too opened in the same way, but this time led down some steps to solid ground. My master went through first, then Eisik, mumbling prayers, with me going down last. I held the little stone the abbot had given me in one hand – for it was fast becoming a kind of amulet – and the compass and articles in the other as I proceeded down the perilously steep steps. Before I let go of the door, I was assailed by a terrible rank odour, and I sneezed. This, in turn, caused me to lose my footing and I let go of the stone, dropping it behind me as I fell the entire length of the stairs. Luckily, the bones of the young are supple and strong, and I did not fracture any part of me. I did, however, have a graze on both my hands, though somehow I had managed to hold on to the compass. Eisik helped me to my feet, at the same time inspecting me for any sign of injury. My master, now at the top of the stairs, called to us in a relieved voice, 'Thank the armies of God and all His angelic hosts! *Mon ami,* your sneeze has saved us!'

I collected the parchment and charcoal and made my way painfully up to where my master stood, and there I saw the meaning of his words. The little gemstone had landed between the door and the stone frame, wedging itself there and effectively preventing it from closing. My master pointed to a spot on the edge of the door. 'Look here, Christian, this is the mechanism.'

He showed me a metal device attached to the frame where it met the wall, pointing then to a hole in the wall in which this device resided when the door was closed. 'You see? Because of this apparatus one is able to push the door open from the other side with ease. On our side, however, there are no handles, and one is unable to pull the door open because it is perfectly aligned with the wall. Had you walked through, allowing it to close behind you, we would not have been able to open it again! Now what Daniel told us about these tunnels becomes clear: there are many entrances, and only one exit.'

'But master,' I said, now thoroughly afraid, 'these tunnels may continue infinitely, and we are bound to come across a trap that we shall not be able to anticipate.'

'Infinite qua infinite,' my master said because at that moment he chose to despise generalities. 'This is impossible. This labyrinth cannot be indefinitely long, for what is infinite in multitude or size is unknowable in quantity, and what is infinite in variety of kind is unknowable in quality, and so on and so on . . . The earth itself is not infinite, on this all men of learning agree. And if the earth is finite, one of its components cannot be infinite, but must also, following this rule, be finite. It is a simple matter of logic . . . as is the fact that a thing cannot be knowable in all its parts and at the same time be unknowable in its whole.'

Eisik had been muttering prayers, but not one for ignoring a chance to refute my master, he responded, 'The sages (men who have been known to hold infinity in their hands, and who create being from nonbeing) tell us that we may see the tail of a lion beneath some bushes and mistake it for a snake, Andre, or a snake mistaking it for a lion's tail. Knowing a small part does not always lead to knowledge of the whole. To know a half circle we must know the circle.'

'Yes, yes, but firstly, to hold infinity in one's hand,' my master said annoyed, 'is to know its quality and its quantity, in which case it is no longer infinite, but finite. Moreover, dear

Eisik, Aristotle tells us, everything that is manifest must arise either from what is, and as it is impossible for a thing to arise from what is not (on this all physicists agree),' he said, 'things must then come into being out of things that exist, that is out of things already present, but perhaps imperceptible to our senses.'

'You see even your dear pagan believed in invisible things!'

'Yes. But because we cannot see a thing, Eisik, does not make it invisible,' my master corrected. 'Perhaps if we had smaller eyes, or indeed larger ones, we might see the eternal element that underlies everything.'

'You mean eyes that are able to perceive the spirit,' Eisik ended, triumphant.

'Yes that is what I mean, however I did not say that to know a part is to know the whole, I meant that it may be the sign that points to an idea which surfaces in one's mind as an image which in its purest state may lead one to the full reality of a thing, whether it is something spiritual or material . . . but that is another matter, and we diverge further and further, as we are apt to do when discussing the blessed laws of physics . . . However, in this case when a whole consists of a substance divided into parts and we have learnt some of the parts we can then surmise the substance, ergo, one chamber of the labyrinth may help us to construct the rest. Now, let us proceed and have no more of this talk!' my master ended the conversation abruptly. Perhaps he too had become confounded?

'By God, I long for an apple,' he said.

'So if this tunnel is finite,' I said, trying to use his logic, 'it stands to reason that we must one day reach the end, and so find our way out, master, is that not so?'

He smiled, and I was heartened, 'Just as surely as these tunnels have a quality,' he said, 'they also have a quantity. Just as they have a beginning, they have an end! Whether we find this end, or wander about until our death, is another matter. This unfortunately is the logic of labyrinths which is all together different from any other kind of logic.'

Eisik moaned. I was fast becoming suspicious of logic. However I must not dull your mind, dear reader, with the discourses that ensued as my master helped me to begin constructing a plan of the tunnel and chamber. I will continue, rather, by telling how some time later, after we retrieved my little gem, seeing that it had not broken, we left a rock in the way of the door, so that it could not close, and found ourselves back where I had so gracelessly landed.

Seeking the way in a downward slope, not knowing what lay before us, I began to feel exceedingly cold and tired and it was in this mood that I recalled the reading in the warming room the previous evening.

'A man should keep himself in every hour from the sins of the heart, of the tongue, of the eyes, of the hands and of the feet! He should cast aside his own will and the desires of the flesh; he should think that God is looking down on him from heaven at all times, and that his acts are seen by God and reported to him hourly by his angels.'

Those words now pierced my heart profoundly, as though they had been somehow intended for me. But I knew that this was illogical. The service had been prior to my dream and how could Brother Setubar have foreseen my misfortune? It was impossible. And yet I also reminded myself that I had not as yet confessed my indiscretion. My master did not have the power to give me absolution as laid down in the rule by St Bernard. Only under extreme circumstances, such as in times of war, or the absence of a priest, could a Templar confess his sin to another. I wondered if my master considered this a time of war where secrecy must prevail? I felt a deep and powerful guilt seize me, and still I could not forget the beautiful girl in my dream whose voluptuous limbs entwined with mine in a sin most foul, and yet most sweet. Can a man take fire in his bosom and his clothes not be burnt? Reason, my master so often told me, is the natural revelation of truth, so I tried to use its power to release me from my sorrow. Is a monk deemed worthy if he abstains only from physical love I asked myself as we walked the long, narrow passage, or is love of the mind as sinful as its twin? If God was omnipotent, as the Apostles inform us, and resides in our every thought, He must also reside in our dreams! If this is so, I sighed dismally, He must not be well pleased with me. And yet, how can one be held responsible for the ruminations of one's mind? Are not dreams independent of the will? And then I immediately concluded that if my dreams were truly prophetic, as they had been up until that moment, I would experience in my waking moments what I had dreamt, and so, as a result, I would commit my sin twice! I told myself perhaps one's life of dreams is not prophetic at all, but merely the product of one's waking life, in which case all I had to do to redeem myself was confess, but what a confession it would be! I shuddered, for the passage deep in the ground was a reflection of my own sad soul, and I wondered if even with numerous formulas handed down by the wise fathers a monk finds himself unable to control evil lusts, what other recourse is there left to him?

Eisik peered at me in the gloom, perhaps seeing on my face a sign that inside my belly there had been a fire (so like the infernal fires of hell) that a man feels when in waking life he is flushed with a lustful fever. I blushed immediately, and looked down, pretending to be consulting the compass. In reality I was thinking that if I did not at once admit my transgression I would soon expire from guilt.

It was while I was consumed by such considerations that I noticed we were coming upon another door. Once more we found ourselves inside a second antechamber, identical to the one we had just left. Three doors again were set at oblique angles marked with signs. This was the Pergamos chamber denoted by a crescent moon.

I noted everything that I saw down on our little map, with

the small piece of charcoal.

'What now?' I asked perplexed, trying to keep my mind from wandering.

'And he that overcometh, and keepeth my works, unto the end, to him I'll give power of the nations,' Eisik said, pointing to the door on our left, 'Thyatira'.

This aperture opened in the same manner, but this time there was no devilish device. It led directly to a deep tunnel whose pitch again descended down a slight slope. The light from our lamps reached up as far as the height of two men and after an oblique turn to our left we walked a little distance and my master pointed to an area in the wall of the cavern high above our heads.

'The false door in the second chamber! *Mon Dieu!* ' my master exclaimed, his voice echoing in the dampness. 'You see there!' he pointed, and I could just make it out. 'We have been ascending and descending, there have been steps and inclines, it appears that these interconnecting tunnels twist and wind their way beneath and above each other! Ingenious!'

Ingenious indeed! We continued ahead, in a south-easterly direction, the tunnel becoming quite narrow and low, we were walking beneath the chamber of the sun or Smyrna. I noted this down. We made another oblique turn then, and the compass read north-east as we came upon another chamber. Again we were faced with three doors. Above the one directly ahead of us, we could see the strange symbol for Mercury and the word 'Sardes'. This was also above the door to our right. Behind us, as we expected, Pergamos. To our left Ephesus, so this meant that we had travelled in a kind of figure eight pattern, although on different levels. My master cupped his beard in his hand and viewed my plan of the labyrinth thus far.

'Now, Christian,' he said, looking around him, 'if you look closely at your map, you will see a pattern emerge. The door through which we enter the chambers is always marked with the name of the preceding chamber. Above us we have the chamber we are presently in. There are always, to this point, two doors marked with the same symbol, in order to trick the unwary, but they may not be the same doors every time. In any case we must now take the door marked Mercury, and if I am not mistaken, it is the one facing east,' he concluded.

'But how do you know that, master?'

'Have you not noticed that before each correct door the stone has been worn down from use?' He showed me, and I was astounded, for he was right. The stone immediately in front of the door where one stepped before descending the stairs on the other side was indeed smooth and polished, a sign that the abbot had not been honest with us. These tunnels were in use quite often.

'And here,' he pointed to the other door, 'we must conclude is another false exit. We have been climbing since the last diversion, and so this tunnel therefore passes over another, as did the first. Let us see if we are indeed right, shall we?' Slowly he opened the aperture, but closed it almost immediately, before either of us could see anything.

'They are there!' he exclaimed in a harsh whisper.

'They?' I said, shivering a little as we opened the door very slightly. Below in the tunnel that ran beneath the present chamber I observed several white forms illuminated by lamps, floating, it seemed, in single file towards the tunnel below us.

'Oh, burning bush of Moses! The spirits of the dead!' Eisik moaned behind me. 'Holy fathers preserve our wicked and curious souls!' Then he thumped my master on the back as a form of remonstration.

'The ghosts, master, the twelve ghosts!' I whispered back, alarmed, because fear, like laughter, is contagious.

'Nonsense, they are men, and no more ghosts than you or I. Did you not see their breath puffing out before them as they walked? Moreover, if they were ghosts, they should not need the use of lamps,' he concluded, and I knew that he was right, for it was common knowledge that ghosts do not breathe, and that they prefer to roam in darkness, having no eyes.

'Perhaps they are headed in our direction, master, along another route, in which case we should leave before we are discovered.' I knew my logic to be flawed, but I wanted to flee to the relative safety of my cell. My master, however, would have nothing of it.

'Do not be a goose, Christian,' he said calmly, 'they were headed south, and that is why we shall head north, and soon another chamber will have us travelling in their footsteps. Come!'

We left the chamber through the door marked 'Mercury', walking along another tunnel, and in my ears the sound of water, dripping, dripping, dripping, all around. I guessed that it must be the underground channel that operated the organ. I walked a little behind, feeling very much alone in my misery, despairing at ever being worthy to climb the ladder of which one side is our body, and the other our soul whereby a good monk ascends to heaven. I did not feel like a good obedient child, but rather, since our arrival here, I confess to having indeed attempted things too high for me, my heart had indeed been haughty, I did not go about my day quietly! It is only now with the passing of the years that I know how it is the misfortune of every young man to suffer so. Pity God does not bestow wisdom on a man before he is too old for it to be of any value!

But for now I must return to that moment, when my master disturbed my inner misery and wrenched me back to the equally miserable present.

'The sound of water . . .' he said. 'Somewhere close is the underground spring that supplies the abbey. We are close, very close.'

'I could have told him that,' thought I, sinfully.

We continued in silence, frozen to the bone. I could no longer feel my feet, I only knew that they must be there for I was walking. Above black shadows loomed and I wondered what good it would do to die in this deplorable labyrinth, even though death seemed a preferable alternative to a life of guilt. At this point we came upon the Sardes–Mercury chamber with two doors again heading in separate directions to Jupiter, or Philadelphia. We paused to look at our map once more.

'You see here,' my master pointed to the map, to the second chamber of Pergamos, 'this door reads 'Jupiter' also,' he pointed to the north door, and also the east door. 'See this, Eisik?' But Eisik was not with us and we turned around to find his pale countenance directing us to something behind what we guessed must be the false door.

'Holy Jacob! Holy Abraham!' he whispered, his face like that of a man who looks on death with mortal eyes. When we walked to him and followed the direction of his gaze, we saw what had caused his distress.

I closed my eyes, made the sign of the cross, and prayed, trembling violently.

18

Capitulum

Slumped to one side inside the small chamber we found the body of a young monk, his eyes open in a look of terror. There was a faintly sweet, sickly smell. My master reached down and touched the body.

'Cold. Dead for . . . three days, maybe more. This must be our curious young Jerome who broke the interdict only to find himself trapped inside this chamber. At least the poor boy did not die alone.' My master shone the light around the room and we could see the bones of other unfortunates scattered about. I looked away in pity and disgust.

'Strange . . .' Andre remarked after a short inspection of the body. 'He, too, must have been poisoned.'

'Why do you say that, master?' I exclaimed. 'Is it not more likely that he was trapped by the same mechanism we have encountered on the doors and expired?'

He gave me a look that was not altogether benevolent. 'If you found yourself locked up in such a place, what would you do?'

'Naturally I would try to find a way out.'

'Naturally, now tell me, after a time of this with no result, would you become quite desperate?'

'Almost certainly,' I answered.

'And as a last hopeless measure you would attempt to claw the door open, would you not?'

This thought made me feel deeply sympathetic for the poor wretched boy, and all I could do was nod.

'Of course you would, it is quite natural, and perfectly obvious to anyone but stupid squires and yet, do you see any signs of this? Where his fingers should be bloodied and his nails torn, they are impeccable, as any good apprentice physician's hands should be. No, this poor monk died shortly after entering the chamber, before he reached such a stage of anxiety . . . and I believe holding onto something . . . something long and cylindrical in shape. Note his hands have contracted in position around whatever it was. Someone has removed it after he had been dead for some time. There are no other signs, no blood, no wound, only that terrible anguished face.'

He walked over to a lamp similar to ours lying discarded on the floor.

'Short of wick and oil,' he concluded. He looked troubled and then nodded his head slowly. 'Sometimes there is a simple explanation . . .' He lifted his lamp up to chest level to the wall opposite the door. Something glistened in our eyes, as though rays of the sun were escaping through a gap in the stone, but I knew that this was impossible, we were too deep in the earth for that.

'Oh, Jacob! A terrible magic! Glittering like the eyes of Lucifer!'

'No, Eisik, it is only a mineral within the rock that reflects the flame of the lamp. Jerome's lamp must have caught their sparkle and he, perhaps curious, or dazzled, wandered in. It is a trap for the unwary.'

'The body then?' Eisik said. 'Holy land of our fathers, we cannot leave it here.'

'We shall touch nothing,' my master replied in a matter-offact way. 'Nothing can be done for him now, and if we move him where shall we take him? After all, it is impossible to take him back up. No, we shall simply close the door.' He made the sign of the cross over the poor monk, saying a paternoster, and did just that.

After a solemn silence, my master showed Eisik the diagram. The old Jew peered myopically at it for a moment. 'Holy Fathers!' he exclaimed suddenly, 'the star of David! The symbol of the heavenly union of man and God. The upper and lower triangles meet in the centre.'

My master had drawn, by calculating the directions given by the doors, the remaining unknown portion of the tunnels and the whole thing was indeed shaped in a star, the star of David.

Following my master's calculations, we emerged from the chamber, descending once more, entering another, only to leave through the door facing east, above which I could just make out the mark of the last letter, 'Laodicea'. After making an abrupt turn to the right, we were, as my master had earlier foretold, headed in a southerly direction.

'Ohh . . .' Eisik was muttering to himself, 'I am an old man, my feet hurt, and my bones ache with the damp! Must I take with me to eternity the sight of dead monks and ghosts? Why must I follow you, Andre, in your hungers and raptures, in your thirst after a knowledge that has little to do with a righteousness that we can scarcely formulate because we are covetous! May the God of our fathers forgive me. I should have stayed safely in my bed, with the Torah, and the sounds of animals to lull me to sleep.'

'Firstly, Eisik, you are not so old, and secondly, you came here because, like me, you are a curious man.'

'May God forgive me.' Eisik bowed his head.

We entered a passage whose walls and floors were lined with bones and skulls piled up, one over another in a gruesome collection.

'This must be the ossuary,' my master said, fascinated, picking up a skull and inspecting it before setting it down casually and continuing on.

Just then, as if prompted by the toothy grins of those long dead, Eisik's lamp went out, having run out of taper, and we were forced to proceed with only two lamps.

'Soon the catacombs,' my master commented almost to himself and in a reassuring way to me said, 'Do you know that the first Christians worshipped below the ground in catacombs to hide from the Romans? They buried the bones of their dead there too, and so the divine services were held over graves. Now you see why there are the relics of the bones of saints in our altars.'

'I see,' I said, wishing to talk of anything but dead bones.

'The Christian prays over the forces of death and destruction,' Eisik commented, 'which is a fitting thing since that is their foremost occupation.'

My master gave Eisik a black look. 'Bones cannot hurt you, Christian.'

'As I believe in the rebuilding of Zion so too do I believe,' Eisik repudiated, looking around him with a grim expression, 'that deep in the earth lie spirits whose existence is tortured by demons . . .'

'Eisik!' my master admonished.

'Listen, if you will, to this old Jew whose race is prepared for every effort of evil! We are told there are powerful forces in the nether regions. Here forces of ancient ethers, frustrated in their efforts to find the light, smoulder, calcified and crystallised. The sages tell us of ground where the bodies of the dead, Andre, are rejected, and one hears strange rumblings coming from the bowels of the earth when one disturbs the soil, because in doing so one releases elemental creatures, whose natures have been trapped for thousands of years. Evil is their function, and I feel it in my bones, as I am sure they felt it in theirs.' Eisik pointed to the heaped skeletons.

I shuddered, uttering a formula against the evil eye that annoyed my master.

'This powerful force of which you speak, Eisik, is merely the force of attraction, or magnetism. It is . . . scientific,' my master asserted.

'Scientific or not, it is evil. One does not change a thing by denominating it,' Eisik said dismissively, as he walked.

'And yet,' my master argued after him because I suspect he always desired to have the last word (even as death loomed above and below in the way of corpses and ghosts), 'this science has been useful to many, including mariners who have used it since the beginning of our century to navigate to many countries of the far East and West by using the compass. A force that attracts iron to it, enabling one to find the northerly direction and therefore other directions as we have done. However, there must not be much of this stone in the earth around us, or we would not be able to use the compass as it would spin round and round . . .look!' he said then.

Near the forthcoming shallow tunnel, there was the false door from which we had seen the twelve ghosts. I realised that we had thus followed in their footsteps, as my master had said, penetrating into the earth before entering what we presumed was the last chamber.

This time, the door behind us was marked *'Aer'*, to our right we read *'Aqua'*, to the left *'Ignis'*, straight ahead *'Terra'*, that is, air, water, fire, earth. But no *Laodicea!*

'This is the last antechamber,' my master remarked. 'This must lead us to what we are looking for, but which door?'

'Behold I stand at the door and knock,' Eisik said, 'if any man hear my voice, and open the door, I will come in to him.'

'Surely you are not suggesting that I knock on the door?' my master said, pulling at his beard.

Eisik smiled. He often showed the greatest wit at the

most awkward moments.

'Let us think,' Andre said, almost to himself, 'what did Daniel say that day? He who follows the seven letters in number and order will enter the kingdom of heaven, remember the words of the hymn for they will baptise you with the nine resonances of water . . . Water!' He moved forward in an agitated fashion, and opened the door to our right, which read *'Aqua'*. It was appropriately named, for now we could see the source of the water that we had heard and had felt through some of the tunnels.

It sounded like an underground river, but I believe it was the echo resonating from the walls in the narrow cavity that gave one this impression. My master lifted the lamp that was, I noticed, running out of taper. It illuminated a channel of fast-running water, lined with stone on either side, effectively forming a kind of purpose-built conduit. It continued into the darkness, barring our way to the door on the other side of it that, as luck would have it, read 'Laodicea'.

'And he showed me a pure river of water of life, clear as crystal, proceeding out of the throne of God and of the Lamb,' Eisik said.

'How deep would it be?' I asked.

'I do not know,' my master said, vexed, 'and, as I cannot swim I will not venture to find out. Brother Sacar told us the builders redirected the stream to suit the purposes of the monastery, flowing through channels diverted here and there. Let us not forget that the organ is operated when the water is diverted,' he said absently, 'perhaps when it is diverted further up the channel, one is able to pass over to the other side.'

I was about to confess to knowing how to swim when I was gratefully interrupted by a terrible sound whose thunderous roar echoed through the narrow passage. We hastily withdrew into the antechamber, not knowing what this sound would bring. Another sound, a haunting, terrifying screeching, had us rushing out the door through which we had only moments ago entered. Seized by panic, fearing the legions of hell, I ran, holding the parchment to my breast with one hand, and the compass in the other. I could hear Eisik panting behind me. My master carried the lamp ahead of us. We turned sharply to our left, not knowing what we might find ahead of us, and continued for quite some time past the tunnel lined with skulls, making another left turn until we were back in the previous chamber. My master's taper was almost at its end, so with great agitation, lest we find ourselves without light, we proceeded, according to my map.

When we finally returned to the antechamber where we had left a rock in the way of the door, hoping to light the torches we knew were hung upon the walls, my master's taper ran out. Thus we were in utter darkness with no possibility of light, and with the antichrist at our heels.

We heard footsteps coming from the direction of the tunnel behind us, but also (alas!), from that which led to the north transept, namely, ahead of us. We were trapped. My first instinct was to try another door, maybe there was a tunnel beyond it in which we could hide? Images of the inquisitor followed by his archers danced before my eyes, and I believe this prospect was infinitely more frightening than whatever might be lurking behind any door. We stood together in the centre of the room. From memory I knew that somewhere to our right lay the false door but that we had not tried the door that must be to our left. I mentioned this to my master and after a moment of deliberation, in which the sound of footsteps seemed closer and indeed louder, he cautiously felt to the left and found the door.

A strange smell like that of putrid eggs came from this entrance, but seeing that we had no other recourse, my master once again felt with his hands and found, after a quick inspection, that there was a flight of ascending steps.

With a stone once more in the way of the mechanism, we crossed another tunnel. We seemed to be going up, and perhaps would soon surface again at another point, but we made laborious progress in the darkness, not knowing if we might come upon a chasm or a shaft. I tripped several times, one such time dropping the compass, that – thank our Lord – I was able to find before my master noticed. If the tunnel diverged it was difficult to tell without light, for I could not see the compass, and so we proceeded at the mercy of the passage. It would lead us wherever it desired.

We arrived at another, this time very small aperture, measuring only three or four paces in height. My master felt with his hands.

'A skull marks its centre, with the words, *Procul este profani*' carved below it. Keep far off you uninitiated ones,' my master said, 'and *Aer*, or air. Now, to open the aperture, as Archimedes has said, 'Give me but one firm spot on which to stand, and I can move the earth'.'

He pushed, but it did not come away. 'Ahh the Devil take you!' he exclaimed, and in a fit of temper hit the door or rather, as he was to tell me later, the skull. Suddenly there was a snapping sound and my master began to push it open, and this occasioned a terrible creaking that echoed loudly and made us jump.

'Master, we shall be heard!' I said alarmed.

'Nonsense, we are too deep in the ground, besides, we either go through this door, creak or no creak, or we take our chances and go back the other way. Which do you prefer?'

I knew he was right and said nothing. A moment later my master slipped through the opening, and we behind him, not knowing what we would find.

We entered into a room of generous proportions with five sides. Only one lamp, much like the ones that we had brought with us, stood on a bracket, illuminating the darkness, casting long shadows along the pentagonal apartment. We saw that four out of five walls were of a red colour, and covered in shelves holding hundreds of bound *codices* or books. In the centre of the room two long wooden benches, one longer, one shorter, formed the shape of a cross, or *tau,* and on this various curious items could be discerned in the dim light. Receptacles of glass, held by metal brackets so that they were perched over unusual lanterns, were placed here and there and beside them unfinished parchments and other assorted paraphernalia; quills, pumice stones, and inks. Also, glass receptacles filled with liquids and powders, vials, and ampoules, mingled with large volumes that had been haphazardly scattered about. There was no other door that we could see ahead of us.

Eisik, who until now had been muttering unintelligible things under his breath, became even more morose. My master, conversely, became exceedingly excited. He found some tapers on the table, lit his lamp, and began inspecting volumes, one by one.

Numerous books resided side by side, denominated by the classification of *Ars Aeris, Ars Aquae, Ars Ignis, Ars Terrae.* I wondered, as I walked along the shelves, how many hands had leafed through these countless pages? How many tired copyists had laboured, sometimes an entire life, so that the knowledge of one book could be passed over to one more generation!

'I will wager that many sins have been forgiven here,' my master remarked, reading my thoughts.

'Sins?'

'In order to keep monks from tiring, Christian, they were told that God would forgive them one sin for every line they copied. In fact, Ordericus Vitalis informs us that one monk escaped the fires of hell by the narrow margin of one single letter!' He paused, looking around. 'Marvellous!'

I was taken a little by his contagious excitement. And, perhaps because knowledge is a seductress that promises a man false comfort and security, or perhaps because there is something wistful, even familiar and friendly about the smell of books, we felt immediately at ease, completely forgetting that moments before we had been in peril of our lives if not our souls. Eisik was right when he admonished us to beware of learning's artful ways, for very soon we would come to regret our carelessness. But I speak prematurely. Instead I shall tell how presently my master took a large book off a shelf from the *Ars Aeris* denomination and cried out in ecstasy,

'Here there are several works on Greek astronomy . . . and one on Arabic mathematics. Very fine specimens . . . and,' he cried once again, 'an astronomical text written by Abu'l Fraghani of Transoxiania, this is a treasure! And another, in which we find the measurements of planetary movements, and the study of the spots on the sun!'

Moving along to *Ars Terrae* my master brought out a manuscript. 'A book of plants written by Abu Hanifa al Dinawari, a Moslem biologist whose works were based on Deioscorides, Christian, but adding many plants.' My master's face was afire with excitement and I wondered, looking at him, if my sin was any worse than his. He seemed to experience as much pleasure from discovering such repositories of the intellect as another man would draw from undressing his wife! A moment later I felt truly ashamed and humbly asked God's forgiveness for my foolish thought, reminding myself that there was indeed a great difference.

'If the infidel is so learned, master, why does he not believe in the highest wisdom?' I retorted, because I was angry with myself.

'He believes his own wisdom to be higher, that is all.' He paused, replacing the book and taking out another. 'Oh! Ten treatises on the eye by Hunain ibn Ishaq. And *Liber continens,* the Latin translation of Kitab al Hawi!'

'Arabs may be infinitely wise in the healing arts,' Eisik moved towards us, drawn, despite himself, by the medical books, 'but very often, even you have to admit, Andre, they do not follow strict principles.'

'I disagree, many times their methods have proved successful,' my master retorted. 'Such as the case of Jibril ibn Bakhitisha, who is said to have cured his Arab ruler of a persistent illness by prescribing that he should learn to play chess.'

'Impossible!' I said sceptically.

'It is a mystery . . . but in a few days the man discovered that his cure was commensurate with his propensity to win, which was considerable. It is true that he felt such relief that he rewarded the physician 800,000 dirhams! But the man also had to teach many of the Arab's servants how to play the game, making sure that they always knew discreet ways to lose.'

'I see!' I marvelled. 'The power of mind over matter.'

'No Jewish physician would ever have prescribed such a treatment,' Eisik sniffed.

Now in an excited state, I browsed through other books. 'Here is another by that same author,' I said, taking an enormous volume from the shelf, 'Why Ignorant Physicians, Laymen, and Women Have More Success than Learned Medical Men.'

'Ahh yes,' he said, taking it from my hands with a smile, 'no one could say that the man did not have a genial side. Come, Eisik!' he waved a hand to the old Jew. 'So many treasures!'

But Eisik was lost in thought, inspecting the articles to be found on the table.

'Look here!' my master cried in jubilation, bringing a large manuscript down off the shelf. I wandered over, and peered inside at a page containing a frightening illumination of the human body dissected, revealing the inner organs being attacked by devils. I winced and my master, seeing the cause of my distress, laughed a little. 'Medicine is not for the faint-hearted, my young squire. Now, what do we have here,' he continued. 'A treatise on drugs used to induce sleep . . . hashish . . . mandrake . . . aha! Poisonous herbs . . .' he gasped, 'in this treatise, mandrake is denoted for being a subtle poison. The victim, it says, agonises for three days before dying. Here we see the antidote which consists of all these together, honey, radish, butter, oxymel, rue, sweet wine, castorium, dill, borax, leaves of watermint, absinthe, assafetida . . . Then, if all this were not enough, the victim should have his head bound, and rose oil poured into one nostril. Furthermore, it goes on to say, should this fail to restore him, a tea of mint and leaf of almond is poured hot over his head while he sits in a bath.'

'I would consider it preferable to suffer the poison!' I said, and my master laughed.

'But wait,' he continued, 'here we have a number of concoctions which use poisonous herbs, and a mention of a substance used by witches. By my sword! Now I remember!'

'What, master?'

'Devil's ointment! That's it! At the time I was in Paris, Christian, attending university, I heard the trial of a Cathar woman accused of communion with devils. It was a terrible, public affair!

The woman, after many days of questioning before the judges of the tribunal, and also much humiliation, and many nights of horrible torment, was persuaded to confess to flying into the arms of Satan with the aid of an ointment. I do not know if she really used this ointment, but when asked what was contained in it, she gave a perfectly scientific explanation for her symptoms. It was a compound of atropa belladonna, and wolf-bane mixed with wheatflour, and (so she said) the fat of a still-born child.'

I cringed, 'Surely not?'

'That might explain Ezekiel's last words, and the cook's delirium . . . atropa belladonna!' He walked over to a shelf denominated *Ars Ignis,* still mumbling to himself, and came upon another discovery. 'Look here! Several volumes devoted to musical subjects; Al-Kindi, al-Farabi, Avicenna, and others! A treatise, *Ars cantus mensurabilis* by Franco of Cologne, laying down a system for indicating the duration of musical notes. He opened another book and I heard him say with veneration. 'Ah . . . Guido of Arezzo . . . here . . .' he pointed to a passage, 'he names the first seven notes of a musical scale by taking the first syllables of each half-line of a hymn to John the Baptist. *Ut queant laxis, Resonare fibris, Mira gestorum, Famuli tuorum, Solve polluti, Labii reatum, Sancte Johanne . . . Ut* or do, *resonare* or re, *mira* or mi, *famuli* or fa, *solve* or sol, *labii* or la and *sancte* or si!' he explained.

He browsed through another manuscript, like a starved man who eats a little of this and a little of that, not able to eat everything in sight but desiring to nonetheless. 'Notket Balbulus together with Odo, Abbot of Cluny, used the Greek device of naming notes using the first seven capitals of the Latin alphabet for the first octave of a scale.' He closed the book.

Eisik spoke from his position at the table. 'Now it is I who have found something interesting . . .'

'What?' my master looked up from his various meditations.

'There is a manuscript here,' he held the vellum close to his face. 'The last date entered was today, they have even included the hour, which is nones . . .' He read to himself for a moment, and continued aloud, 'When finally the solution is taken out of the *Terrestriaet,* and is strengthened by long digestion, it is set free from the *Crudae Materiae*, and is prepared and reborn in the most subtle form . . .'

My master walked over, shining the light on the Jew's pale funereal face. The two men seemed to know what these things meant. I sensed that some fascinating secret had been discovered and I wanted to ask many questions, but something in their demeanour told me it would be best not to interrupt them.

My master took the manuscript from Eisik's hands and read aloud, 'The raw material or *crudae materiae,* cometh from the *astris* and constellation of the heavens into its earthly kingdom, from which is then drawn the universal spirit or the *spiritus universi secretur* . . . amazing!' My master was now in a frenzy. 'Look, come here . . . come here.' He waited for me to bring the lamp to him before proceeding to read,

> 'He lies hidden in the grave
> The spirit stands near
> And the mind comes again from heaven
> Take care at all times
> That the mind is elevated,
> And again return from above
> To that which is below.
> Thus it unites the friendly powers of heaven and of earth:
> And with its rich gifts
> It will bring the body to life again.'

'What is it master? Some terrible magic?'

'I do not know exactly,' he answered, perhaps as per-plexed as I was. 'It could be that our monks are . . . Look here,' he said, pointing to a date on another page.

'But master, this date must be wrong, it reads two days away.'

'Yes . . .' he said, reading the entry under this date.

> 'In our heavens stand
> Two beautiful lights:
> They indicate the great light
> Of the great heaven.
> Unite them both
> As if woman were led to a man:
> So that the marital status be induced . . .'

The blood drained from my limbs. With all the excite-ment of entering the library, I must confess to having forgotten my sin, and I must have swayed, for my master steadied me, at the same time, shouting, 'Christian! What has got into you today?

Pay attention, boy!

'The sun and moon
Are husband and wife
And they too,
Multiply their kind.

Ex deo nascimur,
In Christos morimur,
Per Spiritum Sanctum reviviscimus.

In God we are born, in Christ we die
In the Holy Spirit we are reborn
He will rise on the fourth day.'

'I had a dream, master!' I cried suddenly, tears welled up
and were set free, and I recounted the dream, omitting nothing.

'Calm . . . calm . . .' my master stroked my head lightly, 'so
that is why I found you saying paternosters . . . Don't be alarmed,
no matter, no matter.' Seeing that I was in need of more comfort, he added, 'Christian, I do not believe as others do that such
things are evil, at least no more evil than . . . say . . . the desire to
eat when you are hungry or to drink when you are thirsty. We are
monks, and so we abstain from many things. However, it is never
easy. A man who fasts can no more deny his hunger than a man
who shuns physical love can deny his desire for it. And as far as
that goes I cannot help reflecting that as God, in his wisdom, is
continually replenishing this gift to . . . procreate, that he might
also find ways for any excess to be . . . dissipated . . . for instance,
an overabundance of matter within the earth erupts in volcanic .
. . no that's not it . . . like a dam that is overfull bursts . . . Ahh!' He
sighed. 'Christian, one cannot help it at times.' His voice faded
and he seemed at a loss. Perhaps he had embarrassed himself. 'It
is more the case that those who enjoy deprivation derive a certain
pleasure from pain and humility and the adoration they engen-

der. One must work on one's soul slowly; this is also true, though you must try not to do it again . . . I absolve you. And before you say anything, these are special circumstances,' he said, putting a hand on my forehead, making the sign of the cross, 'But you must ask for the Lord's confirmation.'

No sooner was he finished than Eisik grabbed me by the shoulders excitedly. 'If you will forgive an old Jew, my son, but you have dreamed of the marriage . . . the marriage!'

'The marriage?'

'In the secret tradition of my forefathers the mystery is called 'Shekinah'. The mystery of man and God, and the relation between things above and things below, of the intercourse of earth and spirit.' He looked upwards in a heavenly direction, his features taking on a peaceful expression, and at this moment I saw that when he was not contemplating disaster, he was indeed younger than he appeared. 'But this is a celestial union,' he continued, 'not a physical one, my son.'

'Of course!' my master vociferated.

'The great work of the alchemists,' Eisik continued. 'She is one time the daughter of the king, another time she is described as the betrothed as in the Song of Solomon, the bride and also the mother, or the sister. She is the beloved who ascends towards the heavenly spouse. This is called the final work!'

'This is precisely what Asa said the two brothers were discussing at the chapel, before Samuel died . . . the final conclusion . . .' my master added, his eyebrows working furiously.

'But why did *I* have such a dream?' I asked because now it seemed that my dream had become more important than my sin.

'I will tell you that you have had a vision,' Eisik beamed proudly. 'A vision . . . and why? We are told that when one is worthy one receives Ruach as a gift of grace. This is the crown of Nephesh, and leads to illumination of the spirit by the light from superior regions. This allows one to discern the laws of the secret king.'

'There have been other dreams,' I said, almost in a whisper.

'Others?' Eisik queried.

'We have no time for dreams now, Christian,' my master said in an annoyed fashion because I knew he preferred to ignore the illogical direction our conversation had taken.

He perused things on the table and paused before a large manuscript on an elaborate lectern. Feeling better now for having unburdened my sin, I accompanied him, and seeing the intrigued look on his face, moved closer to get a better look. Inside I saw the most curious symbols. A triangle apex down, a triangle apex up, circles with crosses, crosses with circles. Also a beautiful vignette depicting, what we now came to expect, a cross with a circlet of roses at its centre, and the words *Dat Rosa Mel Apibus* or the Rose Gives the Bees Honey. To the right side of the cross a bee, its wings dipped in gold, and four beehives. To the left two spider webs within a wooden frame.

'Wisdom and industry,' Eisik said, moving closer, 'it is also a marriage. The union of calm waters of wisdom with the fire of industry. The union of soul and spirit.'

'We see this cross with roses everywhere,' my master said. 'It is on the east door of the church, on a window and on the cover of the book of life in the chapter room,' he remarked, picking up the thick manuscript and turning over its fragile pages to reveal beautiful illuminations. Strange animals became transformed, or rather fused into the flourishes, hairlines, and hooks of gigantic letters. The margins, too, were filled with mysterious necromantic images and biblical quotes.

'*Tabula Hermedis!*' my master read.

Eisik blanched, and his eyes seemed to enlarge, while his mouth gaped open.

My master continued, '*In profundo Mercurii est Sulphur, quod tandem vincit frigitatem ...*'

'No!' cried Eisik, placing both hands over his ears. When

my master paused Eisik tore the book from my master's hands, and opening it himself read with tears in his eyes, 'What further miracles do they have stored here?'

But it was I who, having found a some parchments showed them to my master and caused by way of it, the greatest commotion.

'In the fine airs of heaven, was written the Eternal Gospel, and the Gospel was with God and Gospel was God. All things were written therein and without it there was not a thing written that was written. It speaks of the life, the life that is the light of men. This light that shines into darkness and is not understood by men is Christ, the true light, which enlightens every man. Christ came into the world and Christ is the Gospel and the Gospel was made by Him. But the world has understood it not.

My master looked at me, 'This is written in Langue'doc . . .'

'The language of the Cathars, the heretics?' I said aghast.

My master was then overtaken by an intellectual ecstasy. 'This is extraordinary! This is remarkable!' He seized me by the shoulders. 'Do you know what you have found my little goose? You have found the eternal gospel!'

'Eternal gospel?' I said, half laughing, happy to have achieved something of note, in his eyes.

'Epiphanius,' Andre explained excitedly, 'has listed a number of works, not apocryphal works, but works written shortly after the crucifixion that were on the church black list, like the gospel of the Hebrews, the gospel of the Egyptians, Ebionites, the gospel of the Nazarenes . . . the secret Gospel of Matthew! These have all disappeared, sequestered behind locked doors by a few pious, or if you like, impious, keepers of knowledge. However there has long been a rumour of an eternal Gospel, a pure gospel, so holy, it had to be kept from profane eyes. Some call it the *Fifth* Gospel because it reconciles all four canonical gospels! It is rumoured to have been written by the Sophia and kept safe by the Cathars who moved it to a safe place before the seige of

Montsegur. This is the first time I have seen any proof of its existence.'

Eisik huffed, 'Proofs! I suppose that next you will be wanting God to prove Himself!'

'That would be most beneficial,' Andre said. Then, because he was thinking of the gospel, he remarked. 'This must have been translated from Coptic or Greek, and so there must be an original...where could it be?'

At this point he began to make a feverish search among the parchments and Eisik, seeing my frown, took pity on me and explained,

'Egyptian Coptic is the Egyptian language written in Greek.'

Time, however, was against my master's search and when no trace of the original was found he resolved that we had better get back, before the bell tolled the vigil of matins, if it had not already done so.

He rolled up the Gospel parchments and secured them in the belt that held together his mantle and we began to look for our way out. I was about to say that I thought this somehow impious, when our, or rather my, grave mistake erased any concerns for impropriety from my mind. It was now evident that the panel through which we had entered the library had closed behind us in the now all-too-familiar fashion, meaning that we would not be able to open it from inside. In my state of intellectual abandon I had, as it were, imprisoned us.

'Confounded secret doors! Damn the Count of Artois!' My master shouted, and with an access of emotion kicked the panel quite hard with his foot. I believe the pain sobered him because calmer now he walked to the far wall opposite to the way we came in and said, 'The monks of this abbey have been exceedingly cunning, and we must be equally so. What direction is this wall?'

I consulted the compass. It lay in an easterly direction.

'Easterly, you say?' He looked puzzled. 'But we seemed to . . . am I losing the order in my head? I could have sworn we changed direction, very gradually, but even so . . . very well, that means that the infirmary must not be far off, though I surmise that we are still too deep in the ground for it to be directly beyond this wall. There is no doubt a secret exit. Now we must search the room for clues.' He began by tapping the stone, anticipating a hollow sound, but there was none.

I could hear my heart in my ears. We were trapped like that poor monk Jerome! 'What if there is no other opening, master?'

'Then we shall die exceedingly erudite,' he answered.

Eisik inspected the shelves, and I the floor, but neither of us had any luck. I leant dejectedly against the wall where a sturdy oak frame was fixed. I noticed that it contained a large map of distant lands and oceans, perhaps the *fons paradisi* of which many books tell, so large as to be the height of a man and the breadth of two. It was illustrated with terrible sea monsters, sirens, and ships. One ship in particular was portrayed beached atop a large fish which the sailors in their ignorance, due to its gigantic proportions, mistook for an island. It felt familiar to me, where had I seen this map before? I asked myself. Beneath it were the words: From the end of the earth will I cry unto thee, when my heart is overwhelmed: Lead me to the rock that is higher than I.

I said these last words aloud, without really thinking about their significance, but my master heard me and moved quickly to where I was standing.

'What did you say?' His eyebrows were raised very high as he came toward me. I thought I had committed some terrible sin, and so I was unable to speak. I pointed to the map and the words below it. It was then that he slapped me so hard on the nape of my neck that it nearly sent me reeling in the direction of some unknown sea.

'By God! There is our clue!' he cried jubilantly. 'The rock

that is higher than I? Higher than the map, I'll wager!' He reached up with difficulty (for his height was not much greater than mine) and with a reddened face from his efforts, pressed a stone panel, which he noticed seemed to be of different hue to the others surrounding it. This moved in an inward direction, unlocking a device that made a loud snapping sound, and the entire segment of the wall, map included, pivoted open.

It was through this door that we entered another tunnel rank with the smell of mould and rotten vegetation, and a flight of steps ascended to another door that this time my master opened with ease. We did not, however, come out as we thought in the infirmary. We came out in the scriptorium! Our bearings utterly confounded, we entered through an identical map to the one through which we had left the library moments ago.

My master shook his head, taking the compass from my hands. 'By the curse of Saladin, boy! How long has the needle been stuck on east?'

I lowered my head, and said all that I could say; that I did not know, but that I had dropped it in the dark in the last tunnel before the library.

The door that led out of the cloister was locked, so we made our way stealthily to the church. As we were about to enter the south transept, however, I noted that my sandals were soiled with a reddish mud, so I cleaned them on the stone flags before entering – lest I leave tell-tale footprints on the church floor. My master viewed this with a pensive frown, saying that interestingly his shoes and also Eisik's left no marks because their soles were smooth. Mine were sandals given to me by the hospitaller, and were indeed the same as all other monks in the abbey. They were patterned, and therefore less slippery, but they also allowed much dirt to gather in the grooves. He said nothing further, only continued to frown as we said goodbye to Eisik, who scurried into the darkness of the north transept, his robes flapping like the wings of a bird. The hour was near, so we waited in the church for the intoning of the bells, and this gave my master further opportunity to inspect the organ.

The instrument was surmounted by no fewer than twenty pipes, and it was through these that one heard melody when the organ was played. On the upper level there were ten pipes in the centre with the rest flanking either side a level lower. The entire wooden structure was supported by little columns, with a console of keys equally divided on two separate levels. A beautifully carved seat was placed before it, and some papers with musical notation resided on a little rest made of wood, directly above the keys.

'If, as Sacar says, this organ runs on the water channelled beneath the abbey, it may have some connection to the tunnels. A switch of some kind must divert the water to the pump that drives it, as our brother intimated. The question is what to look for?'

I watched him for a time, a slow feeling of tiredness overtaking me, and to keep awake, I asked him if he believed there was something magical about this 'Final Work'. Perhaps, I ventured, it was a relic endowed with special powers, a stone or a cup, as portrayed in the romances.

'Romances fill your head with nonsense and are not recommended reading for monks. Relics, on the other hand, exist, that is quite natural, and the way of the world,' he answered.

'But it must be something of great significance, valuable, even holy, to be secreted in such a way, master, with so many tiresome puzzles and traps to protect it?'

'Relics are usually highly venerated, but we must not speculate on what we are to find, nor on its efficacy,' he said, looking up from his work. 'You think too much, and too much thinking often leads to error.'

'And so you do not believe in magic?'

'I believe in the magic of science, *mon fils,* and in the magic of nature, but never in the magic of men. Very often the language of magic is merely a symbolic language for something else.'

'But you do not deny that a potion made from dragon's blood destroys devils?'

'Firstly, I have never seen a dragon, have you? Secondly, have you ever wondered, as there are so many potions to kill and ward off devils, why their population never seems to decline? Remember what I have told you about knowledge and opinion.'

'But –'

'What you call magic,' he interrupted, 'is nothing more than a clever suggestive art, that uses fear and superstition as its loyal agents. Of course, much can be accomplished by its use. Let us say that you come to me (the magician) because you want something very badly. I would tell you that you must pick a certain herb from a cemetery every night at midnight.' He paused for a moment to inspect beneath the keys of the large instrument.

'And, where was I? Yes, I say you must pick a certain herb at midnight and lay it on the steps of a church. If you were to follow my instructions precisely as I have told you, getting up at midnight, going to the cemetery, pulling out the herb, and so on, it is more than probable that your longing for achievement and your faith in such instructions will bring about what you desire. If you omit even one night of this ritual then I, the magician, cannot be blamed in the event of failure.'

'So you say that magic is only in the mind?'

'A man is so constructed that when his desire is strong enough, Christian, he will find the means of realising his objective. This is quite natural, and not in the least magical. In many cases it is science that is mistaken for magic because, you see, even learned men have not yet lifted their minds out of the dung heap of superstition.'

'But a physician is a scientist as you have often told me.'

'And that is why a physician must be as prudent in his cure as he is in his failure to cure.'

'So you say that it is better not to cure an illness if it will be seen as something diabolical?'

'No, that is not what I said.' He stood, and straightened his bad leg with difficulty. 'What I meant was that a cure often engenders more suspicion than a failure to cure, and so it must be approached with care. Do you know that there are several ailments that can be healed almost immediately? If one does so, however, one risks many things, not the least of which may be one's skin! So one must bring the patient to health, so that his state of wellbeing comes about gradually. One chants many prayers, one cauterises, and bleeds the patient, advising him to visit his priest very often for confession. In this way after a few weeks he is cured and believes it to be God's grace, and so, quite natural.'

'So you keep your secrets to yourself, like Brother Setubar seems to keep much from Brother Asa?'

'Here is another thing . . . When we surpass the world with our knowledge, we must be careful whom we allow to share in this knowledge. This is the art of prudence.'

'But this art you call 'prudence' sounds like avarice, master, covetousness. Surely the world should have a share in a wise man's accomplishments. Those who imparted their knowledge in the books we have just admired must have felt this way.'

'They are truly wonderful books, and deserve praise to their authors, but as you have seen, they are hidden from public view, and quite wisely, for there is more wisdom in a prudent silence than there is in a thousand books.'

'But I thought you loved books, I thought you believed in knowledge?' I asked, confounded as always.

'I do, I do . . . but it is important to know when and how information is to be distributed. In this way something good cannot be mistaken for something evil, and also misused by those of evil disposition. Look around you at this abbey, whose cures have brought it to the attention of the pope. Need I elucidate further?'

'But is that not in essence what the abbot said on our first day here, about drawing a veil over things not understood . . . but then you disagreed with him?'

'I disagreed with him because there is a distinction between the arcana – the mystery – of nature (whose celestial seal must not be broken irreverently) and the arcana of men, whose accidents may lead to heresy, and as we have seen, to the death of others.'

'So what you are saying, master, is that there is no magic at all, only science, but that we must not allow others to know this,' I said sadly.

'I am afraid so . . .'

'There is not much use in looking for something that has no magical or holy powers, is there?'

'And yet we cannot discount that whatever lies beneath all this intrigue may indeed be something magical.'

'But you do not believe in such things!' I was becoming annoyed, believing that he was taunting me.

'That has nothing whatever to do with it!' he replied, astounded at my ignorance. 'The fact that others believe is an important tool in solving our riddle. It is the riddle that concerns me, as it should interest you if you are to be a good physician. A good physician must first and foremost have a strong desire to solve riddles.'

'What riddles do you speak of? There seem to be so many.' I looked at him boldly, and he seemed pleased. He moved around the organ, with a curious smile on his face, and I heard his voice echo from various points behind it.

'The greatest riddle of all . . . the riddle of man! The complex mystery of the universal human being as he stands within the threshold of universal laws. This is the most fascinating puzzle! Every riddle starts with a question. For instance, one might ask: does this organ exist?'

'Of course it does. I can see it and touch it.'

'So you say because to satisfy any inquiry in a scientific

way we must first hypothesise, and we do that by either affirming as you have or by denying, as I shall . . .' he said, moving around to the front of the organ, knocking some musical papers from their place over the keys and onto the floor. 'But our inquiry does neither alter its existence, or its nonexistence, it serves as a starting point from which we set about proving our postulation. As the Greeks tell us in their profound wisdom, 'the beginning is everything'. You saw me pacing the graveyard on our first day, after our conversation with the abbot. You were as annoyed with me as you are now . . . am I right?'

I lowered my eyes. How could he read me so well?

'At the time, Christian, I was asking the 'first question' . . .'

'So what was the answer?'

'I did not say that I answered my question, I resolved to let the nature of things speak their truth to me, even if at first I denied an absolute truth.'

'But why would you want to deny an absolute truth?' I asked, because such an idea seemed ludicrous.

'Because there are no absolute truths, except the existence of God, and because sometimes a man must begin with doubt, in order to end in certainty.'

'Oh,' I said, no further enlightened.

'In any case, as Hippocrates tells us, observation holds the key to success in all such cases, and so observe we shall, and reserve our judgements. By the son of Apollo, boy, what has got into you today? You are taxing my mind! Now I have forgotten what we were doing!' He picked up the papers, and holding them in his hand, uttered his thoughts aloud. 'Some device, some key, redirects the body of water, and I believe that was the sound we heard, the loud sound in the last chamber. Someone diverted the water flow in preparation for entering the tunnels and that is why we heard footsteps coming from the direction of the church . . . Perhaps the same monk we caught the other night sneaking behind the curtains?' my master said pensively. 'Where would the clue be? Where to place a formula? Somewhere you would read-ily see it. If I was about to play this instrument . . .' He sat down on a stool before the complicated conglomeration of pipes, keys, and knobs. 'I would need to simply see it . . .'

This could take forever, I thought dismally, yawning so hard that I almost displaced my jaw.

'Look here, boy, for your eyes are better than mine, to the spot where these papers reside. What does this say?' He pointed to an engraving on the wooden surface, barely distinguishable in the dim light. It read in Latin, *Cantus Pastoralis* – the shepherds' songs – and beneath a set of Roman numerals.

CL: IV
CIII: XIX
CXLII: IV
CXLIII: VI
XC: XII
CXLIV: IX
CVII: XXXIII

That was when the bell rang for matins, rhythmic and peaceful. I noted down the numerals on the back of my map and replaced it hastily within the folds of my habit. Soon there was the sound of many footsteps coming down the night stairs, and the long procession of monks made their way, cowls drawn, into the church.

We took our place in the darkened stalls before anyone could see that we had been inspecting the organ. Brother Sacar intoned *Domine labia mea aperies,* and we replied *et os meum annuntia-bit laudem tuam.* My master noticed Brother Daniel missing from his place beside Brother Setubar in the choir and whispered in my ear that I should expect the worst. Later, when the reader announced that the homily would be *lectio sancti evangelii secundum Mattheum xxi,* and began the words in *illo tempore,* and there was still no Brother Daniel, we saw the abbot call a monk to his side, and after some anxious whispers the brother hastily left by way of the south ambulatory.

After the prescribed lessons we did not sing the *Te deum* because of the proximity of Easter when songs of jubilation are not appropriate. Instead we prepared to intone the previous responsory by replacing our cowls and standing. My master and I, noting that all the others had their cowls drawn and could not observe us, glanced in the direction of the organist, Anselmo, as he prepared to play the instrument. He sat down and placed his hands over the keys but we could see nothing else because of the angle of our seating.

I heard my master utter some terrible thing under his breath and I sang a little louder so as to disguise his indiscretion, *'Domine Deus auxiliator'*, praying not only that my master might be wrong about Brother Daniel, but also asking God to release me from the bonds of all my doubts and anxieties when, at that moment, the monk entered the church, his face struck with terror.

He made his way to the abbot who calmed him with a gesture, but on hearing what the man whispered in his ear, his face, too, became very pale, and he rose, rushing out of the church.

The singing stopped abruptly, and my master pulled me to my feet, but by now others had done the same, and we found ourselves pushing our way through a group that seemed on the verge of hysteria.

On our way up the night stairs Andre pushed me past many monks until we were beside Brother Macabus, and asked him if he knew what had happened.

'Brother Daniel of Carcassonne,' he whispered loudly as we neared the last step, and the landing, 'dead!'

My master shook his head. I felt my stomach tighten into a knot.

We were at once in a darkened hallway, dotted with apertures leading to small individual cells. Arriving at an open door, we followed the librarian, the inquisitor, and the abbot, leaving the others, including the members of the legation, outside.

The room was bare and small, though the ceiling was high, having a large inset window facing east. We could see very little until a monk entered with a lamp. As soon as there was light, a terrible sight assailed our eyes. There on the floor lay the poor brother, in a pool of blood, his face contorted in a horrible grimace. His head had been badly beaten, but there seemed to be no weapon about. The circa was telling the abbot with a trembling voice, that his last round had been at the tenth hour and at that time he had helped Brother Daniel to the latrines and back to his room. Thereafter he had neither heard nor seen anything suspicious.

Many monks now peered through the door, over the heads of others, and soon the room began to fill with the sound of their voices. I forced myself to look at the body clinically, concentrating on the stony face, the eyes open, perhaps with a look of surprise. My master walked over to the body of the old brother and I saw him pick up the man's foot. He removed a sandal and inspected the sole, but said nothing. He simply replaced it, leant over the body, felt for a pulse, and finding none, closed the man's terrible eyes and pronounced him dead to a chorus of gasps and strangled whispers.

My master then turned to the inquisitor who had been ordering his archers to search the compound for a weapon. 'Now you can see that this is not the work of the cook nor the infirmarian.'

'I do not see that at all, preceptor!' he answered. 'It is well known that sorcerers can kill from a distance by the use of their infernal powers.'

'This is clearly a case of violence, Rainiero, otherwise you would not be wasting your men's time looking for a weapon,' my master said exasperated. 'Somewhere the murderer has left his indelible mark and I believe it is a physical one.'

'Physical or metaphysical, it matters little. The ways of sorcerers are many and varied. No, this death only serves to emphasise the urgency of appropriating guilt and carrying out punishment as soon as possible.'

'This one differs from the others . . . Brother Daniel was killed by an instrument, a sharp instrument, we see that here . . .' he pointed to some substance on the ground which, to my horror, looked like fragments of brain matter, ' . . . it has penetrated his skull. The others, I believe to have been poisoned . . .'

At that moment, Brother Setubar entered the group. His tortured frame moved awkwardly to the body of his friend and then he let out a groan that seemed to emanate from the pit of his soul. He made the sign of the cross and turned, bestowing a look pregnant with fierce malevolence on all of us.

'Satan has struck us once again!' he cried, as though he himself had been struck on the chest by a blow. He steadied himself on the abbot's arm and continued a little out of breath, 'God has turned his countenance away from us all. Brother Daniel, architect of our destiny, venerated brother and friend, dies because this very night the Devil's instrument has once again penetrated the sanctuary where no man must go!' This was followed by a great agitation. Setubar shook his head. 'Now God will turn His rage on all men and as Joel has warned, He will make it that the sun shall be turned into darkness, and the moon into blood. The earth will tremble, and the stars shall fall to the earth, and the earth shall shake with His anger and when men hide themselves in the dens and in the rocks of the mountains then we shall cry to the mountains and rocks to fall upon us and hide us from the face of Him that sitteth on the throne, and from the wrath of the lamb!

You!' He pointed a deformed finger at the inquisitor. 'Sanctify ye, call a solemn assembly, gather the elders and all the inhabitants of the land into the house of the Lord your God and cry unto the Lord, alas for the day! For the day of the Lord is at hand, and as a destruction from the Almighty shall it come!'

The old man was led away by the abbot who encouraged the assembly to disperse, and the poor body was taken to the infirmary. My master, having been given permission to inspect the room before it was summarily cleaned, remained. He paused before the doorway, and kneeling on the ground, investigated something that he could see on the floor.

'Red dirt.' He brought the clay-like substance nearer to his face. 'But why not on the brother's shoes?' He paused, thinking. 'Of course!' he exclaimed. 'Not on his shoes because not he, but another here tonight, has entered the tunnels besides us. That is why Daniel's death is achieved by a different means.'

'We may have partially solved our mystery then,' I said, 'we can surmise that the red dirt has something to do with the deaths.'

'Do not place too much faith in syllogisms. It is true the other three may have had red dirt on their shoes, but you also had red dirt on your shoes, and you are not dead, moreover whoever stood here tonight with red dirt on his sandals is also not dead. This leads me to postulate that merely entering the tunnels has not caused the demise of the other three, but plainly something else . . . some substance in the cursed place with which neither you nor I, nor indeed the killer has come in contact. This death satisfies the assumption that it was a desperate act of violence. Furthermore I would like to know how our venerable Setubar knows that we entered the tunnels tonight, for he said someone had broken the interdict once more?'

'He also mentioned that Brother Daniel was the architect of their destinies, that is close enough to builder, is it not? If so, then our note has once more been exact in its prophecy.'

'Excellent!' He patted me on the back, in a good mood. 'You are learning. The author of our note has once again been correct, and we shall see if he tells us any more secrets, only then shall we know that he is not one and the same as our poor brother. Did you see Anselmo in the crowd of faces?'

I shook my head.

He walked around the room, setting straight a small table that had been overturned. 'We see evidence of a scuffle.' He pulled absently at his beard. 'This adds weight to our argument . . .' He looked down at the bloodied floor and at the wall behind the pallet, splattered in strange patterns of dark red. 'The killer will have blood on his clothes and on his shoes, therefore, we should see some prints on the floor . . . yes, here we see the print of a day shoe, perhaps belonging to the monk who found him, perhaps belonging to the killer. We cannot discount that they may be one and the same person, for there is also a little of our red dirt surrounding it . . . but that could have been there before his footstep, at which time the two combined. It may have belonged to Daniel himself from another time . . .'

'So we are still no closer to arriving at the truth.'

'We are always closer. In the next few hours we must notice any dark stain on the shoes or clothes of any of the monks. But one moment!' He paused suddenly very still. 'We heard those footsteps in the tunnels around an hour before the holy service, that is some time between the tenth and the eleventh hours.'

'Why do you say an hour, master?'

'Because we had enough time to investigate the library and to make our way back to the church before matins. The circa says he helped Daniel to the latrine at about that time, so he was still alive, though he could not have been the one we heard coming towards us in the labyrinth, for he was too frail, the footsteps we heard were those of a youthful monk.'

'Because they were strong and steady of gait.'

'Precisely. If this imprint of dirt belongs to the killer then the murder must have occurred after the killer returned from the labyrinth with red dirt on his shoes.'

'So the murder must have been committed sometime while we were in the library or on our way to the church, and not after, otherwise we would have seen the suspect leave the labyrinth, for he would have had to come out of the Lady Chapel.'

'That is true, or perhaps he left the tunnels later by way of the scriptorium, the same way we did, in which case the murder was perpetrated between the time we left the scriptorium, and the bells for matins, that is, while we were inspecting the organ . . . On the other hand, there may be other exits . . . and then again, perhaps others who come and go from the tunnel, and that means our hypothesis is shot! We must find out where our Brother Setubar was during the time of the murder.'

'But does Setubar know Greek?'

'That is the second thing we must find out, assuming that the author of the note is the same monk who has commited these crimes.'

We made our way down the night stairs, intending to leave by way of the aperture, but when we walked past the scriptorium we noticed Brother Macabus sitting at his desk.

His figure cut an ominous shape in the dim light from his lamp. Surrounded by shadows he appeared to be in deep concentration. I followed my master until we were almost upon him, giving him a start, and causing him to stand up abruptly. I saw him cover his work with a sheet of vellum as he greeted us with a saddened expression that appeared not altogether genuine.

'Such dedication,' my master commented amiably.

A pale smile moved his thin lips, 'I find, preceptor, that when I am disturbed, it is best if I apply myself to some work. Tonight I fear that we are all disturbed . . .'

'Yes, and to what work do you apply yourself?' My master lifted the sheet of vellum to reveal pages of what looked like Hebrew, and alongside this, another sheet where he had begun only a few lines in Latin.

'You are translating the Old Testament directly from Aramaic?'

'Yes.' The man looked a little nervous. Everyone seemed so

nervous.

'Extraordinary. I know very little in comparison with true men of learning such as yourself. Why not from Greek?' My master asked.

'The Semitic language was, of course, the original language of the Old Testament, preceptor, it was only much later that it was translated into Greek.'

'However, Moses, having been raised by Egyptians, could have used the language of his keepers, could he not?'

'There are differing schools of thought on this subject. This could be the case, some translations may have been from Egyptian into Hebrew and also, later into Coptic, however, Aramaic was the Semitic language of the people, and incidentally the language of Jesus. Hebrew was the language of the priests. I prefer to think that Aramaic is the purest. At least it is purer than the pagan Greek language which has corrupted everything . . . Saint Jerome, God Bless him, translated the Bible from Hebrew to Latin, but it is fraught with errors. Moreover, the Greek text is known to have included a number of books not present in the texts used by the Hebrews, Saint Jerome did not include them and called them 'apocryphal'.'

'You mean . . . heretical.'

'Actually, it means hidden,' he said with a grin, 'The Apocrypha has been embraced by some, others believe it to be inspired by Gnostic philosophy.'

'And what of the gospels? I have heard there are a number not included in the New Testament. The gospel of Thomas for instance, and others like the secret Gospel of Matthew?'

The librarian turned an ash-grey, 'The Gospel of Thomas, Matthew? Yes, I have of heard them.'

'Curious, is it not? Though one can hardly believe that such things exist.'

The librarian moved closer. 'Oh, but they do, preceptor!' The man betrayed himself. 'We are told they were not found to be canonical, firstly the gospel of Thomas does not mention the crucifixion and other important events while the secret Gospel of Matthew . . . better that the world not know of their existence, we must leave these decisions to those wiser than we.'

My master smiled a little. 'Ah, yes, but think what a dull world it would be if one always deferred knowledge to wisdom. Still I know that you are right. One cannot help wondering, though, what such gospels might tell us . . .'

'Yes, one can only wonder,' Macabus narrowed his eyes, 'and yet what can one more gospel tell us that we do not already know, preceptor?'

'Indeed, I suppose we shall never know.' Then my master made a gesture that signalled that we were about to leave, and the other man made a noise, a kind of clearing of his throat as though he were about to say something.

Dear reader, you may ask why brother Macabus embarked on the following conversation when there was no outward reason that he should do so. All I can say is that perhaps the sin of the intellect is best nurtured in collusion, because instruction is like an act of seduction that one man uses to gain advantage over another, or as in this case, to affect a semblance of importance. It seemed that the circumspect librarian, given the first opportunity, was about to divulge many things.

'There have been rumours,' he said.

'Yes?'

'Rumours that we . . . that we have these same gospels here in the abbey.' He held a hand over his mouth suddenly, as though he had uttered a blasphemy. 'Held in the treasury as a relic given to us by a generous benefactor.'

'Is this true?' My master managed a look of incredulity that would have fooled anyone, no less the man standing before him. 'And yet surely if such a precious item existed in the abbey it would be at your disposal?'

The man smiled a little wanly, 'That is a logical conclusion and yet we do not live in a world ruled by logic, preceptor, but one ruled by obedience.'

'Yes, however, as librarian you must have access to all the books belonging to the library, is that not so?'

The man straightened his shoulders. 'No, in fact Brother Ezekiel alone was sanctioned to enter the library proper . . . Now, we must await the abbot's decision . . .'

'Oh, I see . . .', he gave me another one of his peculiar looks, and I was coming to realise that they were meant to signal me to attention. 'This must have been a source of much anguish on your part. An erudite man is by nature curious . . .'

'You do not know preceptor . . .' the other man said, opening up as a flower does to the warm rays of the sun, 'how many long nights I have contemplated my shortcomings, I have mortified the flesh seeking the reasons for my exclusion, and yet . . . 'I am a worm and no man: *adversus eos qui tribulant me*'.'

My master gave the man a look of warm commiseration.

'And yet it is the worm that makes the earth fertile, brother. No one could blame you for becoming so overwhelmed with emotion that you would do almost anything to hold those precious codices in your hands, at the very least . . . to see them.'

Macabus eyed my master shrewdly and raised his chin in defiance. 'Not anything, preceptor, I would not lose my virtue, nor would I kill for it, if that is what you mean.'

'Oh, no, no, of course not, but I wonder, has anyone seen these gospels? Or are they speculation on your part?'

'There is one, though he is not worthy.' He lowered his eyes, but not before I saw a deep resentment in them. 'These last months, because of his weak vision and sudden frailty, Brother Ezekiel had been working on a project of great importance with the young translator Anselmo. He was working on the translation of a certain...gospel.'

'Is this true?' My master smiled, cunningly, as though the man were not serious.

'Yes,' he said, 'he was given the sanction to accompany the brother to the library.'

'No!' my master exclaimed with indignation. 'Yet you, the librarian, have never been there? That is absurd!'

The other man's eyes softened, 'My very sentiments, preceptor.'

'But how do you know this was their task?'

'Anselmo told me, perhaps to make me feel even more inferior. In any case when the brother heard that Anselmo was puffed up with pride, he ended his work with him.'

'No doubt that upset the boy.'

The brother looked about. 'He was very calm, as is his nature, but his eyes grew black with hate.'

'I see . . .' my master said thoughtfully.

The man, perhaps sensing that he had been imprudent, said, 'Now, if you will excuse me, preceptor, soon the bell will toll, and I must make ready. I hope you will not mention what I have just told you to anyone . . .' he trailed off.

'Your words are safe with me, brother librarian. Thank you for a most erudite discussion.' My master bowed and we began to leave when he suddenly remembered that the aperture would be locked as was customary. 'Oh, Brother Macabus, if you will be so kind as to let us out?'

The brother searched his vestments. 'The cook's assistant must still have the keys, preceptor, I gave them to him when the poor cook was . . . detained. You will have to leave via the north transept door.'

'I see,' said my master with a smile.

Moments later, after entering the church, my master said that it was a pity that our investigations of the organ would have to wait, but it was far too dangerous to pursue this matter with the inquisitor roaming about. Instead we left through the north transept and found ourselves within the stormy elements, at the perimeter of the graveyard.

'So is Macabus a suspect now, master?'

'It is possible. He was all too ready to incriminate Anselmo, perhaps to save his own skin by diverting us . . . To be librarian and have the library denied you, especially when it is purported to hold such treasures, and to have one much younger and less experienced given the sanction to use it, must have caused him a great deal of shame. Never underestimate this emotion, for no man is more capable of hatred, Christian, than a man who feels he has been unfairly or shamefully treated. We also know that he had access to poisons, and that he knows Greek . . .'

'So if he does not know it as well as Anselmo, that may explain the errors in the note?'

'Yes, you could be right, and yet I am not convinced of anything. Did you notice that he was right-handed?'

'What about Anselmo? He also had a motive.'

'Yes . . . too many possibilities too little time . . .'

'Master?'

'Yes, Christian, what now?'

'I am confounded. Greek, Hebrew, Aramaic!'

'Firstly we must differentiate between the Old and New Testaments.' He winced, for the wind assailed us. 'The New Testament was given to us in Greek from the first. The Old Testament was handed down to the Jewish people in Hebrew, and then translated into Aramaic and Greek. Macabus was correct, however, in saying that Greek may have corrupted the original intentions of Moses and other Hebrew writers of the Old Testament, because a translation is never an easy thing. If we take, for instance, the word 'soul' and translate it into Greek we arrive at the word 'psyche', a very good word as words go, but also one that has been given a meaning by the Greek philosophers that was not intended by the Old Testament authors. You see to the Greeks 'psuche' or 'psyche' also includes the function of the mind and reason, in Hebrew the equivalent means only soul as a spiritual entity.'

'It is such a fine distinction, master, for thinking is a function of being that constitutes the soul.'

'Yes but a distinction is most significant when it is least obvious.'

'So when translating one cannot escape the distortions produced by one's philosophy and politics?' I said.

'Precisely,' he answered.

'It is all much clearer now . . . but master, before when you were speaking to Brother Macabus, you sounded as though you knew very little about translations.'

'Yes.'

'But now it appears that you know a great deal?'

'It is always best to seem ignorant when measuring another's wisdom, Christian.'

'Why? It seems to me that an honest exchange of knowledge can only further us in our investigations.'

He rolled his eyes heavenward and I am ashamed to say that he uttered a blasphemy in Arabic. 'Have I taught you nothing! We are not at a university exchanging pleasurable views on varied topics of interest. We are conducting an investigation where our goal is to test a suspect's knowledge when his guard is at its lowest.'

Once again I thought he sounded very much like the inquisitor.

'So your empathy was another formula to loosen his tongue?'

'There's nothing better . . . Once a man senses that you understand him, that you too think the same way, he will say almost anything . . . Many have fallen by the edge of the sword, Christian, but not so many as have fallen by the tongue.'

Once at my cell door Andre bid me to take a rest, for he said lauds would be a most unhappy service this day.

'Keep your door locked,' he said, 'and your ears sharp! The inquisitor is a fool. Indeed, I know there are murderers at large and they are as real as we are.'

Entering my cell in silence I discarded my shoes and lay down in a foetal position, fearful. I huddled in my pallet, praying silently.

Qui sedes ad dextram Patris miserere nobis . . . Thou who sittest at the right hand of the Father, have mercy on us.

TERRA
THE FOURTH TRIAL

The full soul loatheth an honeycomb;
but to the hungry soul every bitter thing is sweet.'
PROVERBS XXVII 7

19

Capitulum

I dreamt that I was surrounded by bees. They entered the cavities of my ears and I could hear the word as spoken by the fathers, the interpreters of scripture, of whom it is said that they make the honey of the spiritual understanding of the word of God. They penetrated my mouth, and I spoke forth words of majesty and splendour! They whispered profound mysteries through the continual movement of their wings. They told me that individual freedom was the future of mankind, that heresy wears two faces, that violence is evil and love conquers above all human emotions, that poverty was the ideal but sacrifice was greater. Below me on earth, I saw the inquisitor, but his eyes were the colour of blood, like the eyes of a devil, and his mouth became like that of a serpent, and he was about to swallow the monastery whole, when a light from out of the depths, from out of the catacombs, shone out all around and into the cosmic spaces where the angels rejoiced! This light was indeed the brightest light I have ever seen, and inside this light I saw a figure, and I knew it to be the sick boy. The one that the monks would not discuss. The elusive dying novice. A voice then rang out through space, and I heard it say,

'Have you sufficient oil in thine own lamp? Make it such

that the twelve become seven and the seven stars appear.'

I woke and found myself sitting up on my pallet, trembling from cold, and perspiring profusely. Another vision! Would I never escape this torment! Outside I could hear the wind, as a faint light heralded dawn through my window. I would not be able to sleep now. There were too many things to consider, so I resolved to ready myself for prime and, putting on my sandals, I ventured out into the gloom.

The wind had whipped up the freshly fallen snow, making it difficult to see, especially as I had no light to guide me, for I had to ask the hospitaller for more oil and tapers and I knew that he would become suspicious were I to do so. A groaning whistle met me as gusts circled the abbey, swirling and surging around the bell tower. Coiling and entwining, the wind encountered the hardness of stone and was deflected in countless directions. I heard other sounds, too. Sounds that were almost human, and I realised, to my great relief, that the noises were coming from the direction of the stables. The awful night had disturbed the animals. I changed direction and headed there to see that they were safely tied and had enough water. This took me some time, for I seemed to be taking more steps in a backward direction than in a forward one. By the time I entered the building I was cold and exhausted.

The stables afforded one little comfort from the conditions outside, and I did not remove my cowl immediately but walked inside, patting my sides and stamping my numb feet. I found old Brutus, whose whining began the instant he saw me. I gave him a morsel that I had procured from the kitchen the day before and looked for Gilgamesh. The beautiful steed raised his head when he saw me, and as I neared him he edged forward, nudging my arm with affection. I must confess to having saved him the best morsel and this I gave gladly, patting his long graceful neck and smoothing out his mane.

I resolved not to tax my mind with unnecessary thoughts.

If nothing else, these last days had taught me to be economical with my emotions, for I was sure to need them in ample measure in the not-too-distant future. Instead I decided to delight in the quietude and peace of familiar smells; well-oiled leather and animals, dung, and hay. I would forget the tunnels, and the Cathars, the girl in my dream, the bees.

I entered the cubicle in which Gilgamesh resided, and from his saddle found the brush with the ivory head that my master had procured in the East. I brushed his fine muscular body with long strokes, making comforting noises that seemed to soothe him. Looking out beyond the abbey, through a small aperture in his cubicle I could see a faint dullness over the eastern mountains. The daystar would not be discerned today, there would be thick grey clouds above. Below, a fierce wind, and a brilliant whiteness. Everything moved in time to the impetuous weather. There was, however, no smoke from a fire that I had come to expect, below the abbey.

Suddenly from behind me I heard a voice.

'Be ye not like unto horse and mule, which have no understanding; whose mouths must be held with bit and bridle, lest they fall upon thee.' I jumped, and a gasp escaped my lips. Gilgamesh twitched in alarm, sensing my fear.

My terrified eyes located Setubar sitting low on a chair to the far right of the stalls, his angular frame drowned by his voluminous habit, his eyes wrinkled and wickedly intelligent. He nodded, lifting his long tapered hands to beckon me to him. 'Come, come, my beautiful boy . . . Why art thou so full of heaviness, O my soul, and why art thou so disquieted within me?' He laughed a little, 'Have you put thy trust in God? Oh, the young never trust God,' he answered himself, waving a pale hand in the air. 'They trust only in their youth! But youth is fleeting . . . You see me? I was once red-blooded and sinewy, like you.'

I stood motionless, not knowing what to do.

'I see you love your horse, after all he is beautiful and

strong,' he continued, 'but he is a creature of pleasure and all pleasure is rooted in evil . . . The mule is unpleasant to behold, and though he is stubborn, he is loyal. The mule is a creature of service.' He nodded his head, and a faint trickle of saliva escaped his mouth.

'Yes, venerable brother,' I answered, very frightened, 'but he is not my horse, he is my master's.'

'Ahhhh,' the old man hissed, 'so it is that you covet your *master's* horse?'

I felt a cold sweat snaking its way down my back and I shuddered. This man seemed to be the Devil himself. 'I confess to having a fondness for him, master.' I trembled.

'Oh, a fondness! Yes, when one is young one is fond of everything. Everything is new and wondrous, but as one grows older those very things that one thought wondrous cause us the greatest anguish, for as Ecclesiastes tells us, 'He that increaseth knowledge increaseth sorrow.'' He leant forward and waved me over to him. 'Come, tell me what gives your youthful face that pallor . . . I am old and my teeth are nearly all gone . . . I will not bite you!'

Oh, dear God, how I feared that man! Yet I knew that my desire to know the truth should outweigh all other considerations. It was my duty, I told myself, as a soldier of Christ, or very nearly so, to get close enough to the old man to see if his shoes were stained with blood or clay. Determined, I made my way out of the stall, walking timidly what seemed an eternal distance between us. I could see his grey eyes, sparkling malevolently beneath his cowl, drawing me with their intensity. What else could I do but follow his wish? Should I kneel at his side? I wondered. No! I thought in sudden terror. Once I was within reach he would caress me with his cold fingers, as was the custom of older men, what if I should flinch? He would suspect that I knew the truth! I bit my lip. I was no coward, this was my opportunity to find out if he was indeed the cunning murderer. He was not physically strong and so, easily overpowered, and yet, I realised, placing one foot ahead of the other, his victims had not overpowered him! But they were old, ahh . . . but what of young Jerome?

The door to the stables creaked open for a moment allowing a cold gust to invade the relative warmth, then it banged shut with such force that I gasped, jumping out of my skin, as they say. Indeed, it must have been a comical sight, for it occasioned a chuckle from the old man.

'Come, come . . . You think I am a wicked old man, don't you?' he asked.

How could he know? I resolved that he must be a sorcerer, in league with the Devil, how else could he know my every thought? It is only now, after much reflection, that I know Setubar's power not to have been diabolical, it lay rather in observation, the quiet skill of every good physician. His was a strength born of many years studying faces, hands, gestures, inflections, tones, to arrive at a diagnosis of the state of a man's inner as well as outer being. But it also vested him with the ability to penetrate the soul and wrench from it every human desire, thought, passion. In this respect he was indeed formidable.

'Did you know that once they burnt those whose complexions were as pale as yours?' he grinned, waiting.

I said nothing.

'The pale ones were naturally suspected of being Cathars, for Cathars do not eat meat . . . They did not know that the old are cold and therefore always pale, because they treasure a life which they know they will soon forfeit, and this paves the way to cowardice that leaves a kind of pallor on the skin.' He touched his face absently. 'Youth is warm-blooded and brave. You are not afraid of me, are you, my boy?' He searched for my face, and I thanked God that I had not removed my cowl.

'Of course not, master,' I said a little nearer.

'So your pallor beneath that cowl suggests something

other?'

'I –'

'The Arab philosopher,' he interrupted, 'on the other hand, believes that there are two reasons for pallor . . . infatuation with those feminine creatures,' I lowered my eyes, 'because this sin never leaves one satisfied, but rather, by virtue of its heinous nature – that one may never in truth apprehend – leaves one insatiated and melancholy. The other reason escapes me . . . Ah, yes, discontentment. Confusion.' He left his mouth open, waiting for my response. When there was none, he huffed, shrugging his shoulders. 'You are confused because life is complicated, is that not so . . .? Or are you perhaps in love?'

'I am not in love, venerable brother.'

'You are confused then. Yes? Love, confusion and discontentment are one and the same. One may be discontented because one is confused about love, and then one may be confused because his love leaves him discontented, still one's confusion and discontentment may lead one to seek out a love that will ease his pain . . . The young love so easily.' He smiled. 'So trustingly . . . but the old love as though they will some day hate and hate as though they will some day love, as Aristotle tells us . . . but we do not speak only of the temporal malady, my fair one, which is inappropriate to those who have chosen to live their lives in the service of the Lord, but also the love of God can be tainted by unholy sentiments.'

'In what way unholy?' I asked, almost at his side, and he ordered me to kneel with his hand in an impatient way.

'When it falls into disorder, for disorder is to be shunned as a tool of Satan, because it leads to discord and discord leads to confusion, and soon one does not know the difference between the good love and the bad . . . You see? Your mind is in disorder, you no longer know what to believe, is that so?'

'Master, I . . .'

'Beliefs and unbeliefs . . .' he dismissed, 'we must learn

to forget and unforget, to remember, and unremember! Because when we grow older those same beliefs, like our faces or our hands, change.'

'But our belief in God does not change?'

'Ahh . . .' he wheezed, placing a cold hand on my wrist, and I felt like snatching it away, for his skin felt moist, 'perhaps not our belief, but the way we believe changes. Our belief of what is good, and what is evil, changes, or perhaps it is not our belief that changes but our faith in that belief,' he said. 'And yes, this finally is wisdom, my boy . . . not as many young men think – a knowledge bestowed from above when one reaches a venerable age. Wisdom is knowing that life is not a path to perfection, but a path to recognising our imperfections . . . You have had a dream? You are a dreamer?'

I blushed violently, worried he was referring to my sinful dream, and buried my head deeper in my cowl. Seeing that I was trying to hide, he snatched it off my face leaving me exposed to his scrutiny. Before I could make a move he took me by both wrists with his sticky fingers, and in horror I realised that he was looking for a pulse.

'Did you know, fair one, that the heartbeat changes when one is not telling the truth? Avicenna was close to discovering this, but he was not clever enough. You have a vernicular pulse, my boy, either you are in love or you are frightened of me . . . Tell me, for I know that you have had a dream. Did you dream of bees?'

I swallowed a gasp and he eyed me shrewdly.

'Ahhh, yes. Do not despair, a peasant from the village of Vertus was also tormented by bees in a dream. They entered his body through his private parts, stinging him horribly as they made their way out through his mouth and nostrils. He said they bid him to do things possible only for devils, so the wretched man went to the village church and desecrated the crucifix! Therefore he was burnt. And yet, the bee remains a symbol of purity, mes-

senger of the word, as Bede tells us. But the purity of its message depends upon the recipient of that message. Do you follow,
child? Like the purity of the wine is dependent on the vessel that
carries it . . .' He paused, somehow finding this humorous, cack-
ling like an old hen. 'You see, in the case of the poor unfortunate, the bee's good function was reversed because of the man's
iniquity, so that it became a messenger of evil, entering his body
through a shameful gate.' He sighed, a little tired. 'One man may
have a dream in which bees herald God, and another may have a
dream in which it heralds the beast!' He looked at me pointedly.
'The Lord clothes his messages to suit his purposes . . . you see?'
He stroked my head as though I were a favourite cat. 'I have been
young and now I am old, you too will be old, and the old are
best dead! Because you begin to care less about what is good and
more about what is useful, and the useful is only what is good for
oneself, it is rarely what is good absolutely, and that is where the
danger lies. Would you like a raisin?' he asked changing the subject so abruptly that it took me by surprise. I thanked him, but
declined his offer, fearing that it might be coated in some poison.

'Oh, no matter,' he said. 'More for me. I like raisins, they
all did . . . It makes the mouth moist and conceals the sourness
of death. They are soft and sweet and innocent, like a nubile
virgin whose innocent, plump, little body has matured, warmed
under the caresses of God's hands . . .'

'Do you come here often?' I blushed but thankfully he
did not notice.

'Hm? Oh, yes, I come here to get away from them,' he
said coldly, pointing in the direction of the cloister buildings with
his walking stick. 'Sometimes an old man needs the company of
animals . . . They do not ask so much of me.' He looked at me
then as if suddenly seeing me for the first time. 'Yes, you remind
me of *him*. You are beautiful, as he is, but you must remember,
the beast likes the beautiful ones best of all. He lures them with
vanity, for he knows that a beautiful boy provokes the most lust-

ful of desires, the most unholy of sentiments . . .' His hands were like ice on my head, did I have a fever? I longed to be gone from him before those hands seized my throat. 'Your beauty, child, is your sin, a sin for which you must atone each day. Mortify the flesh! Better to be ugly and scarred than beautiful. Far better to be abhorrent, because then you will not be responsible for the downfall of your fellows! Beauty only hides what lies beneath it, ugliness, falsehood and evil!'

'But master,' I said, confused and angry despite my fear, 'we are told that man is created in the image of God and this image must therefore be true and beautiful and good.'

'Ahh, but what you do not know is that it is created by the evil God in His own image, and therefore repugnant, offensive and ugly! Pity, my boy, arouse pity in others, even disgust, and you will be assured of a place on earth and in heaven.'

That was when I noticed his shoes. The left one was stained with the red colour of mud from the tunnels!

I stood to leave, and he gripped my arm with surprising strength. 'I have upset you? I, too, am a sack of dung, a sinner, I detest myself!' Then he let go of me and I left very quickly, not once looking back.

I ran to the cloisters. A faint pink glow, diffused through thick cloud, promised another cheerless day and I entered the cloister buildings through the kitchen door, which was now open, feeling as though the old brother had drawn a veil of filth over me.

One or two assistants were preparing the daily meal. After wishing them a good morning, and refusing their offers of warm milk, I entered the south walk, hearing as I did so the office of lauds echoing through the stillness. The beautiful sound intoned the youthful message of praise for a new day. The world may indeed be evil and ugly, I thought defiantly, it may be soiled with sin, but I also knew that when a man lifts his soul up to the vaults of heaven, reaching seraphic heights with the power of his voice, he becomes an eagle soaring, an instrument of the Holy Ghost. I paused, thinking about Sacar's words on music that first day, and listened to the phrasing of the voices as they paused, continued, paused again, and I realised that this rhythm, like the beating of the heart, is nurtured by that one brief moment of uncertainty, that ever-present space, that remains silent, awaiting the unknown. In this pause, in this interlude there is no fear, no anxiety, for it is this moment of silence that is the key to all re-generation. The moment in which the divine can leap across the silence to the new word, the very next beat. Man then becomes like the heart is to the body; the voice of the cosmos made manifest in the earthly realm, and the rhythm from which all earthly rhythm is created. Perhaps this and nothing else was the secret of creation? The mystery of the pause, that, like a seed, appears small and insignificant, but from it grows the tallest tree? Now I understood better Sacar's words to us that day in the church and these thoughts gave me a little comfort, dispelling my misgivings, as I entered the lavatory. I needed to wash the old brother from my skin and from my heart.

The two walls were lit by small torches, leading to a great fire on the far side of the rectangular room. On the fire I could see some water in a bulging cauldron boiling. I thanked the monks of the abbey and prayed for their health and longevity, as I filled the bath closest to the crackling warmth. I immersed myself in the water, wishing to feel clean again, trying to forget the old monk's unpleasant and uneasy words. But soon I found myself taken by a second and more horrible terror. Perhaps Setubar had followed me? Moreover, perhaps he did not commit the crimes himself, but instead, as the inquisitor had said so many times, sent his devils to do his work!

Suddenly every shadow, every noise, no matter how slight, heralded the appearance of the evil one. My hair stood on end.

In such instances the mind is an enemy, for it recalls best what it fears most, and so I remembered with remarkable vividness a story where a sorceress killed in a most violent manner an unwilling lover, though she was leagues away in another village. Another tale told of a man who lured devils to his aid by the use of one single word, ordering them to scour the countryside for children whom they would kill and bring back to him. I sat transfixed. There might be beauty and goodness, angels, in the world, but there were also demons and devils. And I imagined hell, as it is given to us by the church fathers, where Satan is said to be bound to a burning gridiron by red-hot chains, his hands free to reach out and seize the damned, whom he is said to crush like grapes with his teeth. At the same time his assistant demons with hooks of iron, we are told, plunge the bodies of the damned first into the fire, then into ice and afterwards hang them by the tongue, or slice through their viscera with a saw, or boil them so that their flesh may be strained through a cloth! And here I was naked, with the boiling water only steps away!

Long moments passed, or perhaps it was only a short interval – for time stands still when one is so terrified – where I was certain that at any moment I would meet my fate. Brother Setubar need not move from his seat in the stables, his demons would do his bidding, and an hour from now, someone coming in to wash his hands would find me dead, drowned in my own blood! Or boiled, or skewered over the fire! I could hear my master's voice saying, 'But there are no identifying marks?'

At that moment, I heard a sound coming from the door to the cloisters, a piercing cry whose shrillness echoed down the hallway and into the lavatory. I stood up, preparing to jump out of the bath for my clothes, when the singer Anselmo came in, dragging a large bag of firewood. The sound I had heard was merely a branch that, poking through a hole in the sack, scratched the stone floor as it was dragged over it. Heaving a great sigh of relief, I barely realised that I was naked. It was only his amused expression that gave rise to my awareness, and I immediately sat down.

Anselmo said nothing, he dragged the bag behind him until he reached the fire, and then proceeded to replenish it with some larger logs. I climbed out while his back was turned, and dressed quickly. When I had finished, he turned to me with a sardonic grin.

'You must be very brave, bathing on your own this day. The Devil himself has been seen lurking in the corridors. Soon he will have killed everyone who knows . . .'

'Who knows what?' I asked.

'But how can I tell you? Would you like to die, too?'

'So you know something?'

He ignored my question. 'You will soon find him. Your master is a capable man.'

'Find who?'

'The murderer, of course . . . but I suspect that it is *he* who will find *you,* and when he does, you had best recognise him first,' he laughed.

'Come, Anselmo, tell me what you know.'

He moved closer, conspiratorially, saying in perfect Greek, 'I know that someone else has broken the interdict, and whoever it was, is responsible for Daniel's death . . .'

'Maybe it was you?' I ventured.

His eyes creased and he laughed out loud. 'Me? Your bath has softened your brain. There are far bigger fish in this pond, my friend. Bigger and tastier . . . I will not insult your intelligence by naming names, no doubt you have your own suspicions . . . but I will give you one clue . . . the infirmary chapel.'

'Why are you not at lauds?' I asked as he turned to walk away.

'It is bathing day, and on those days it is my duty to see to everything, the blades for the leaching, water etc. What about you? Should you not be at your master's side? If you ask me, one cannot wash off one's sin with water . . .' He moved away from me and at that moment I dropped my waist rope and glanced at his shoes.

Both sandals clean. Perhaps they were too clean.

I came out of the lavatory in a state of excited agitation just as the brothers were filing out of the church. Lauds was over, soon it would be prime. I searched the sea of faces, but Andre was nowhere in sight. I went to his cell. Nothing. In fact I did not see him again until a little later that day when so many questions would be answered, and others raised, but I must hush my garrulous tongue lest I divulge too much too soon. I will continue instead by saying that having found myself alone, and feeling the comfort that only daylight brings, I resolved to find some sustenance, for the mind works best when the body is fed.

It was snowing again. The north wind sweeping through the deep gorges was as wild as the winds off the coast near Bayonne where I had lived as a young child. I remembered only turbulent seas, grey and frigidly cold, whipped up and churned by the icy currents from the north. I learnt to swim in those chilly waters. Now, as I neared the entrance to the cloisters, my ears aching, a gust nearly swept me off my feet, and I was greatly relieved to enter the relative shelter of the cloisters. I passed the scriptorium, observing the monks from below my cowl. Today, even the illuminators worked with gloves, pausing every now and then to slap their hands across their middle and stamp their feet to encourage the circulation. From the vicinity of the cookhouse delicious aromas hung in the air and the noise of industry filled me with cheer.

In the cookhouse proper, the assistant cooks were very busy. They stirred this pot, adding a herb to this cauldron, a pinch of salt to another pan. In the absence of their master, they tasted, slurped, and sniffed, and just to make sure, added more of everything. As I crossed the threshold of the vast hot room, I noticed that two brothers seemed engaged in a heated argument. The taller brother, of Italian origin, argued with the shorter one, whose accent I could tell was from the lands to the north, perhaps German. They argued as to how much rosemary should be in the sausage. The tall brother stated that in his country one could never have enough of this sainted herb, for the Virgin Mary herself had found it most pleasant when she sat on it on the way to Nazareth. The German brother stood stiffly, I believe using vulgar words in his native tongue, shouting that hyssop was also a holy herb, used in the Temple of Solomon, but one would rather die a thousands deaths in infernal hell than cook with it. Finally, when it seemed they would soon come to blows, they noticed my presence and invited me in.

The brothers asked me to taste the sausage, and this I found to be most delicious, much to the delight of the Italian monk, whose name I learned was Alianardo. He gave the other monk a smirk of self-satisfaction and showed me into the larder where he said I could eat whatever I desired. Perhaps I had learnt something of the diplomatic art from my master?

I entered the darkened room through a door to the right side of the great ovens and noticed only after a moment that above me smoked fish and curing sausages hung from hooks attached to the ceiling. As my eyes grew accustomed to the dimness, I saw that on shelves there were also stores of preserved fruit, olives, eggs, and rounds of cheese. Large urns of unknown substances that, in my relative ignorance, I guessed to be olive oil and vinegar, sat on the stone floor. Here some straw had been placed, no doubt to absorb unwanted moisture, but also affording a soft place on which to sit. I found a sheltered spot, amid baskets of beans, apples, and dried foods, and consumed – in concentrated gluttony – the generous plate brought me. There was melted cheese, olives, nuts, bread, throbbing sausages – whose juices ran down my chin – and smoked ham. Finally I ended it with a cup of warmed wine and, ipso facto, grew weary – as one is wont to do when one is satiated – and leant back on the pleasant, soft straw, using a bag of wheat for a pillow, the troubles of the monastery a million leagues away, the inquisitor with his wicked grin a point in a universe of points. I allowed my full stomach and the warmth from the fire that reached even into the larder, to lull me into a deep, contented sleep, in which I dreamt that I was flying into the arms of my beloved.

I must have been asleep a long time because when I awoke I could see that the light outside the larder had changed. Shadows stood where previously there had been light, and the kitchen, so lively with the activity of monks before I had succumbed to fatigue, now appeared to be very bare. It was then that I heard a strange voice whose owner was unseen to me. For a moment I was startled, but I heard only the sounds coming from the great fireplace, breaking the stillness with its crackling and spluttering. I sat up feeling dull and wondered drowsily how I had come to be here, as is usual in the case of daytime sleep. I slowly – and I must say shamefully – remembered first my gluttony, and then, in horror, my dream! It occurred to me that I may have missed the service of the dead, and not wanting to add this to my growing list of sins I hastily prepared to leave, when I heard the voice again.

My master would have been exceedingly proud of me, for I moved close to the door, remaining in the shadows so as not to be seen and there, crouched behind a barrel of ale, I listened. Lifting my head a little, I could only just see Rainiero Sacconi conducting a conversation with an unseen monk whose voice I at once recognised as belonging to Brother Setubar.

'So tell me, old man,' he said, 'why you have dragged me to the basest of places?'

'We are safest here. The walls of the abbey are the ears of the abbot, who is corrupt like all the others, but here in the cookhouse we are free to speak.'

I saw the inquisitor's eyes gleam in the firelight, 'Tell me everything!'

'I will tell you only what you need to know,' the old man said slowly with an authority that even the inquisitor could not deny. 'Firstly, you must swear that you will stop them, for theirs is an unnatural design. It is very close, and soon they must be prevented from using what they have been hiding –'

'Old man, you have brought me to this monastery on the pretext that you harbour Giacopo de la Chiusa, the murderer of Piero da Verona, now you must tell me where he is!'

'I told you there was a man here of great interest to you, but I did not name names. He was an accomplice to the murders, I know this . . .' There was a pause. 'Do not ask me how . . .'

Oh Lord . . . By the tone of his voice I knew that Setubar had to have learnt these things under the seal of confession, and he was divulging them! I crossed myself devoutly, feeling the presence of the devil close at hand.

'But this,' Setubar said, in his gruff voice, 'pales in significance in comparison with what I am about to tell you.'

'I want to know his name, if it is not Giacopo de la Chiusa then who? Manfredo, Thomaso? Do not tell me about heretical doctrines!' the inquisitor said. 'There is enough of this going on in all abbeys of Christendom to fill the entire libraries of hell! This does not interest me.'

The old man laughed a hard raucous laugh the nature of which degenerated into a hacking that shook his entire body. 'Heretical doctrines? More fool the pope whose ignorance is only bettered by his vice. If only that were all . . .' He sighed, gaining his breath. 'No heretical doctrine can compare with the heresy perpetrated by the monks of this abbey. This, inquisitor, is the source of the greatest heresy of all! Do you recall the siege at Montsegur? The four Cathars who escaped . . . I was one of them.'

'What say you?' the other man spat. 'No Cathars escaped, all died purified on the pyre!'

'You are ignorant!' The old man began to laugh, his shoulders heaving so violently that he had to lean on the wall for support. Presently after a burst of coughing he continued, 'And your ignorance will lead to your downfall! Do you believe that all those who offered their lives that day would have so willingly done so without first safeguarding the knowledge?'

'So you were a Perfect?' he asked as though the words were poison.

'I and three others . . . but they are now dead . . . we brought down from that great height what was vouchsafed to us . . . Something that would greatly interest you and perhaps mark your name in the annals of history for all time,' he smiled, nodding his head, 'but I shall not tell too much. You need not know the rest . . .'

'Do not waste my time, old man!' he said. 'Tell me the name, or I shall have you detained like the others.'

Setubar laughed once again. 'You may do as you will with this sinful body. I am prepared to tell you what I know because I long for death, unlike the others who desire to live too long. You must enter the tunnels and find it before it is too late...before it is consummated! There you will find the greatest heretical doctrine of all. Think of it! The world will resound with your name, you, the man who discovered the most important symbol of heresy in the known world! The pope will make you a saint! Every book will spell the name of Rainiero Sacconi. You will do what no other inquisitor has ever done. You will put a stop to heresy for all times to come . . . and if you do this I will also give you his name, so that you may avenge the terrible event at Barlassina, for this man may know where all the other assassins are hiding.'

At this point I felt a strange feathery sensation near my right ankle. I looked down to see a fat, hairy rat, perhaps the same rat that the cook chased away that morning in the kitchen four days ago, nibbling at some stray grain near my foot. I jumped a little, shooing the thing away, trying to be quiet, but there were others, furry little bodies scurrying to and fro, and in my shock, I must have made some noise because the inquisitor paused, leaning his head in my direction, narrowing his eyes slightly.

'Who is there?' He walked slowly toward the larder and I crouched like a ball behind the barrel of ale, thanking God for the first time that I was born small. Thankfully, just at that moment we heard a rumbling, like the roar of a great lion, and I must say that I believed it to be the voice of God, the voice that in revelations spoke like many waters, carried on the sound of great thunder. Later I was to learn that it was an avalanche, but for the moment, dear reader, it seemed as though God had chosen to spare me, for the inquisitor and Setubar left the kitchen hastily, and I was able to leave undetected, but not before taking an apple for my master.

I ran through the cloisters and out to the courtyard, realising that it was late morning and that I had slept a good hour or two. In the pale diffused light I saw that a large mound of snow had fallen from above, covering the graveyard. Some had also fallen over the church, but not enough to damage it.

Everywhere monks headed for a gathering barely discernible through the fog and snow. The abbot, the inquisitor, and my master were standing at the great gate where I saw riders on horses entering the compound. One man was slumped over on the neck of his horse, as though he had lost his senses. I noticed blood running down his leg, dripping on the fresh snow and making a deep red well there. Another rider, an older man whose stout form was richly adorned with a fur-lined cloak the colour of vermilion, at once jumped down from his horse crying out in Langued'oc. 'My son, my son . . .' He rushed over to a third rider, who appeared to be a woman, and in an agitated way helped her down from her horse. I could not see her face for it was obscured by the green velvet hood of her vestments, however, I knew that she must be beautiful, what other reason could she have to cover herself? Chaste eyes may look upon ugliness, as Brother Setubar intimated, but beauty . . .? My heart sank.

Once he had made sure that the lady was all right, the older man assisted the others to retrieve the insensible body of his son from the saddle.

I asked a monk standing nearby what had happened, and who these people were, but he did not know, so I walked the short distance to my master's side, and on seeing me, he grabbed me by the ear – not too harshly, but most embarrassingly – and said in a very loud whisper, 'By my sword, boy! Where have you been? I have been very worried!' To which I shrugged meekly, mustering a look I hoped would convey my deep contrition.

'Later!' he admonished, and left me to inspect the body of the man.

After a short, but decisive investigation, my master concluded that the young man had a broken leg. 'I will need help. I will need the assistance of the infirmarian.'

'He has been detained, and I will not allow it,' the inquisitor answered emphatically.

My master looked up calmly from his kneeling position at the young man's side. 'I shall also need the services of my colleague, Eisik.'

Hearing this the stout noble, with the broad bony face whose son lay prostrate on the snow, scowled. 'I will not allow a Jew to touch my son!'

'Perhaps you'd rather see your son dead, my lord?'

The man made a gesture of irritation, but said nothing, and walked over to the woman, embracing her in a fatherly way, his face paler than the snow.

'The bone here has been shattered.' My master pointed to the young man's left thigh, whose colour contrasted sickeningly with the gaping wound that exposed the two white protuberances of his femur. 'We must hurry . . .' he continued. 'Wrap him in the blankets, and take him to the infirmary . . . I think he may yet have life in him. You,' he pointed to a monk, 'find Eisik, and the blacksmith, and get me a file, one with the finest tooth you have, and two strong, straight lengths of wood, as long as a man's leg. We shall have to tidy those bones before we put them together.'

Two burly lay brothers wrapped the young man in thick woollen blankets, and carried him the long distance to the infirmary. Once inside, they laid his body on the table, where he was disrobed and once again covered. Andre ordered others to collect boiling water from the lavatory and to fill one-third of a bath in the infirmary with it, the other two-thirds with cold. It was at this point that the infirmarian, Brother Asa, entered the room, wearing a drained and weakened expression. Flanked by two guards, he looked shaken, but it was not until he came closer that we saw in his eyes that he had indeed suffered some measure of indignity.

'Ah, my colleague!' my master smiled, bringing him to the table. 'There was an avalanche, the boy was buried, and as you can see broke his leg.'

The boy's father, who was attempting to comfort the mysterious maiden, looked up. 'We are travelling to Prats de Mollo, we lost our way and we saw the monastery . . .' He paused, looking around him. His eyes were wide with images. 'The avalanche . . . all our retinue . . . our carriages . . . my son was trapped under the snow for a short time . . . at the foot of the abbey!'

I wondered if the pilgrims in their shelter had been buried too? But I did not linger too long on such thoughts, for at that moment Eisik entered the infirmary, looking grim, his face grey and his eyes wide with fear. My master smiled, and said he was preparing to treat the patient. In one glance Eisik became transformed. His shoulders squared and his eyes filled with purpose. It was as if the misfortunes of another made him forget his own. Perhaps this was why he had become a physician.

Asa listened to the man's chest 'His heart is slow, but it beats. He will die if he is not warmed.'

'Mon dieu! Hurry with that bath!' my master cried impatiently. With gravity he said to Asa, 'We shall have to fix his leg before we immerse him, otherwise he may bleed to death. Have you performed this procedure before?'

Asa shook his head. 'Not many times, but I know the formula.'

'Good,' my master said, and with the swiftness of one used to such things, he prepared the wound. Momentarily, the blacksmith entered holding in his thick calloused hands the file and the wood that my master had earlier requested. He took the file, and also a large knife of Arabic design which I knew to be his, and placed the two over the flames in the fire for a time. After allowing the articles to cool a little, he gave the file to Eisik and motioned for Asa to hold the leg. He paused before beginning. 'May the son of Apollo help us save this boy's leg.' He said this almost as a prayer, and I was instantly worried, for I could see the inquisitor's eyes narrow and his thin lips contort in a grimace that was too discomforting. Shortly after, my master began to cut away at the skin and muscle with the knife to reveal the two bones, and taking the file from Eisik, began to file away the broken edges, so that they were smooth where they met.

'Look at this thigh bone,' my master said, demonstrating the bone. 'Look how wonderfully it is constructed, the best craftsman could not make something so perfect. It is built with the minimum material, so that it is light and yet it is very strong.'

Those who had eagerly followed the party into the infirmary now took their leave, emptying the contents of their stomachs on the fresh snow outside.

The German cook called out rather loudly, 'Too much rosemary! For the love of Christ . . . too much!' as he ran out into the compound holding his stomach in his hands.

I began to feel unwell, remembering with distaste my earlier indiscretions. Somehow I managed to control these feelings by concentrating on the formidable skill of the two men.

Once the ends had been filed to my master's satisfaction he motioned for the infirmarian to straighten the leg and the young boy uttered a faint sound, like the breath that escapes the mouth of a dying man. My master, in turn, kept the two sides of the wound together as Eisik (who remained conspicuously silent) began with great precision to stitch the wound with what looked like string or fine rope given to him by Asa.

'Sheep's entrails, dried in the sun?' my master asked, obviously impressed.

Asa explained, as Eisik plunged the large needle deep into the man's thigh, making me wince with each insertion. 'Toughened with wax . . . better than string and kinder on the wound.'

Afterwards Asa retrieved a jar from the shelf to one side of his workbench from which he removed with his own hands a paste which he placed on the inside of a clean rag, doubling it, so that there was a layer of rag between the leg and the paste when he placed it deftly on the wound. I knew that it must be a poultice, for my mother had also used this curative method. He bound this firmly with a bandage of sorts, and said, 'A mixture of garlic, fenugreek, and calendula essence made into a fine paste. Placed not directly on the wound but betwixt two layers of cloth . . . Do you agree, my colleagues?' he asked amiably, some semblance of enthusiasm returning to his eyes.

'Perfected from the flesh of marigolds!' Eisik remarked, forgetting that all eyes were upon him.

'A fine mixture,' my master concurred, 'we have used a similar paste on wounds in the Holy Land, have we not, Eisik? Very fine for preventing fermentation of the skin.'

Asa's brown eyes sparkled, 'Yes . . . yes . . . I believe caused through the infiltration of imperceptible particles.'

However far and distant the changing aspects of that time appear to my frail mind, dear reader, one thing has remained; that little room, aglow with the fire of enthusiasm and industry, where three men, divided by race and philosophy, existed for the barest moment in total harmony and concord, in a universal and divine communion, mindless of past and future, living only in the present.

Then I noticed the maiden, she had made not a sound.

I would have expected that she would cry out, or leave as all the others. Instead, she stood motionless, her hood over her face, with only her father's arm for comfort. This intrigued me. Who indeed were these people?

Moments later Asa held the leg firmly in place while my master, with Eisik's help, used the two straight lengths of wood to splint it. 'He shall have a bad limp, if he lives . . .' He indicated that he was done by the wave of a hand, and several monks lifted the patient, still wrapped in blankets, carefully into the bath that had been prepared to my master's orders.

'You must immerse his head too, but not his leg,' Eisik hastily added.

They proceeded as instructed, allowing the man's head to sink below the surface, pulling him back up after a short space, but it was some moments before we could see colour return to his cheeks, and this was a sign that he should be taken out of the bath, dried, and placed in a bed in the empty dormitory.

The inquisitor had remained at the back of the group, watching with creased face, dark and impassive. Now he moved forward with a gesture of great condescension. 'If the three of you are done congratulating yourselves,' he said contemptuously, 'this cannot in any way delay our investigations, we will proceed as planned!'

My master turned to him, and they exchanged a look of mutual dislike.

Moments passed, the shadows changed and the two men held their stare. My master was the first to speak, 'As is your will, Rainiero.'

'Yes, as is *my* will,' said the other through his teeth.

Then the two walked away from each other and I breathed a sigh of gratitude that the heavens did not open up and strike them for their arrogance.

I told myself, 'How fragile is the human spirit . . .'

20

Capitulum

Before Sext

Snow continued to fall in a thick blanket, and one could see no sun, only a greyness surrounding the monastery like a silent enemy. I shivered a little as I followed Eisik and my master into the bleakness. Moments before we had emerged from the infirmary, leaving Asa (under guard) attending to the young man. And as we walked the compound, I told them firstly of my conversation with Setubar in the stables, and that he had mud on his shoes, second of my conversation with Anselmo, and third what I had overheard in the kitchen

'Excellent!' Andre exclaimed, happily.

'Oyhh!' Eisik glared at him. 'Now the poor child finds pleasure in your games . . . You use all of this to further your own vanity, Andre.'

'He has done well!' retorted my master in a good mood, 'and at the same time atoned for worrying me. So, it is as I suspected.'

'What did you suspect, master?' I asked, when it seemed he was not about to expand on his thoughts.

'That Rainiero has not come here to find heresy, but rather to use heresy as a pretext for finding something else, in this case, the murderers of the martyr. You see, now it all makes a little more sense . . . Only the killers of his beloved master, Piero, could have brought him here despite pressing matters that we know await him in Milan.'

'Who is this Piero?' I asked.

'The inquisitor's predecessor,' my master answered, 'murdered by a number of assassins. They ambushed him and his aide on a quiet country road and it is said that it was a violent and bloody mess. Two culprits were caught, but the others eluded the authorities. One of those who escaped was a certain Giacopo de la Chiusa. We are told he also tried to assassinate Rainiero, but that he did not succeed.'

'I see now why he is so anxious to find this man.'

'It does not look good to have the murderers of inquisitors go unpunished . . . however, in his seeking he has uncovered what the king and the grand master wanted kept from him.'

'The Gospel you have tucked away in your mantle?'

'It sounds like that might be part of it, and something else...he said Rainerio had to stop it before it was consummated...some form of initiation...perhaps...

'What could the gospel do, master, if they were found?

Andre pulled absently at his beard that, these days, looked a little greyer. 'It could undo the faith of many...I have not had time to read it, only in part...but believe me there is a reason it has been kept secret so long.'

Eisik muttered unintelligible things bitterly, and I was quiet for a moment thinking things through.

'So Setubar was the traitor,' I said.

'Our dear old brother has led the inquisitor here using the murderer of Piero da Verona as bait, knowing the inquisitor's obsession . . . hoping that he might stop whatever is happening in the catacombs. Something we know that all four brothers were party to, or at least knew of.'

'But how does this tie in with the murders?' I asked.

'Let us go through what we know once again . . . Now, at least one of them, Brother Samuel, was curious enough to try to enter the tunnels . . . though he had been duly warned not to go. Ezekiel, we know, was the only one with authority to visit the library, but that does not mean that he ever entered the Sanctum Sanctorum. We must also remember his sight was poor. Daniel, on the other hand, knew the orienting formulas through the chambers, because he may have frequented the tunnels, or because he was given the formulas for safekeeping without ever going there. He told Samuel the formulas.' He reflected. 'There was some red dirt in his room, and yet that may have been another's print we saw. I believe someone, very likely Setubar – who perhaps does not know the orienting formulas – may have been trying to draw this information from Daniel, but when he refused to disclose it, Setubar killed him, or perhaps he disclosed it and he was killed anyway . . .'

'But my sons, my sons!' Eisik threw in gloomily. 'All this does not explain why some enter the tunnels and live whilst others die.

'Yes, you are quite right. Yes, why is it that when Samuel entered the first chamber as we did he was overcome by something almost immediately or very shortly after, where others, we, for instance, were not?'

'Perhaps it works in this way, master, perhaps each brother knew one secret, Brother Daniel knew the orientation, Brother Ezekiel the library, Brother Samuel the organ, and Brother Setubar something else, and it is this something else that is perhaps the secret to staying alive in the tunnels,' I said, astounded at my own acumen.

'Christian!' He stopped with gaping mouth, 'You are a genius! I am truly sorry for all the times I have called you stupid! It is I who is the stupid one! Why did I not think of it? Perhaps

I am getting too old for these things. That's it! That's it! Each brother held one secret that together made up the mystery of the cunniculus – the tunnel . . . yes, it makes perfect sense.'

'But what poison kills so instantly?' asked Eisik.

'Pharaoh's serpent or as some call it, serpent de pharaon,' Andre answered casually, 'can be mixed with candle wax and as it burns it gives off a vapour that kills, but not so instantly, though if mixed with other compounds its effectiveness may be greatly accentuated so that in close confines it may lead to a sudden death.'

'But, master, we know that Brother Ezekiel did not die in the same way because we had dinner with him, and then we all headed immediately to the church. He was nowhere near the tunnels in all that time,' I pointed out.

'No, you are right, of course,' Andre said a little dejected, 'and yet we know that he did indeed enter the tunnels, because he had mud on his sandals.'

'Perhaps it is that he was there earlier, my sons . . . Ahh! We chase our tails, for nothing explains his death.'

'Because . . .' began my master, thinking as he spoke, 'he did not come in contact with the poisonous substance. In the same way that we did not come by it when we ventured there. But why not?' he asked loudly, losing his temper and pulling at his beard with vexation. 'What do all those who survive a sojourn in the tunnels do in common that enables them to escape death . . .? And why do some die instantly, while others die slowly . . . Perhaps there are two different poisons!'

I looked about the compound thoughtfully. We strolled under the vigilant eye of the inquisitor's men. Archers and soldiers stood guarding every entrance to and from the cloister buildings. Perched on the stone walls of the abbey they looked down on us, observing Eisik, like cats observe a fat bird.

'Alas, my friends,' Eisik said, almost in a whisper, looking about him with fear, 'the sounds of the trumpet awake Judah no more and I who am despised more than the despised must remain vigilant, for methinks those men await the roasting of my carcass.'

'And we, my friend,' answered Andre jubilantly, 'we shall be proud to keep you company.'

And my master was right, for even our own men had succumbed to the power of the inquisitor, and I did not fail to grasp the paradox of our situation, for the same walls that were indeed built to safeguard those inside from an outward devil, were the very enclosures used to imprison us by an inward one.

'Most importantly,' my master said finally, 'we must find brother Setubar before the inquisitor can ask him more questions, and this we must do now.' He pulled me in the direction of the aperture, telling an archer in a brusque way to step aside. He eyed Eisik suspiciously, but such was the respect and veneration shown to a knight of the Temple in those days that the man conceded to my master's request.

We searched the cloisters in vain. Brother Setubar could not be found, no one had seen him. This made my master exceedingly irritated. We did find Brother Sacar the master of music, however, on his way to the scriptorium. This afforded us an opportunity to question him, so when he said he was in search of a book, and asked us to follow him, that in a few moments he would give us his attention, we did so humbly.

There were monks at work in their carrels, as usual, but Brother Macabus could not be seen. My master brought this to my notice as we waited for Sacar to search through a large cupboard whose shelves were stocked with many psalters, hymnals and ordo missals.

'One must be vigilant, preceptor,' Brother Sacar brought down a book from the topmost shelf, 'to follow the rules of the liturgical year. Sometimes I confess that I am confounded and I need to consult my *Brevarium* as I am doing today,' he said, leafing through the enormous book that must have weighed a great deal, for my master had to help him hold it up. 'You see . . .' he continued, and we prepared ourselves for an involved discourse (for we were learning that it was his custom to expand on every subject, and fortunately my master tolerated this with a great deal of patience, for we shall see how illuminating and advantageous his words would prove to be), 'it is a crucial time. One must be extremely careful, for as you know the services do not follow in a similar way *per totum annum,* throughout the year, but with a multitude of variations, according to the *kalendar* that dictates our liturgical year. I, in my singular duty, have to choose not only the *proper* and *customary* hymns and psalms according to the *temporale* or yearly round of services, but also the *sanctorale,* or services for the saints that, as we have noted, number so many.' He paused in reflection. 'This season is always a little difficult because as we near Lent, there is not only the strict omission of the angelic hymns, but also variations on the usual responsories, antiphons, canticles, and versicles. We must also prepare in the forthcoming days for the Adorations, the Aspersions, Blessings, Consecrations, the Deposition and the *Improperia* . . . the processions, the washing of the altars, the *Mandatum* . . .' he lingered with a sigh of delight. 'I believe that Jews have similar rituals, though of course they are not concerned with weeping over the wounds of our Lord . . .' he trailed off, perhaps desiring to include Eisik in the discussion, but ending miserably, fearing he had occasioned an insult.

'Nevertheless,' Eisik said, 'your Christ was a Jew whose life was guided by Jewish tradition.'

'Oh yes,' Sacar blushed, 'you are quite right, one so easily forgets.'

'If our Lord were alive,' added my master, 'I am afraid such a program would afford him little time for sermons on the mount or for the healing of the sick.'

Sacar smiled. 'And yet we, his humble servants, can only remember his works in our *oratio Dei,* in the *cantus pastoralis.'*

'The shepherd's songs?'

'Why, the psalms, of course,' he admonished in good humour.

'Of course!' My master then cleared his throat by way of indicating that he was ready to discuss other things, and that the master of music should finish his work that he may do so.

Sacar nodded his understanding and gathered all the necessary information, writing out a little list of items down on a rough parchment. A moment later he closed the book carefully and with Andre's help, replaced it in its repository. And as we emerged from the scriptorium and walked in the direction of the church he turned his attention to us as promised.

'I am looking for Brother Setubar, perhaps you have seen him?' my master asked.

'No, he was missing from the services this morning, perhaps he is grieving as we all are for our dear departed brother . . . However, in light of recent events it is a little worrying.' His face then changed, it filled with torment, 'Oh, preceptor! What is happening to us?'

'It is unfortunate, brother . . .' my master said, and not waiting for a reply continued, 'I was unable to express my deepest sympathy before for your sad loss . . . Brother Samuel's death must have been very distressing.'

Sacar raised a hand in the air as if to stay my master's apology, 'I thank you, preceptor. I imagine him singing in the angelic choirs of heaven and this gives me peace.'

'Indeed, a great loss after so many years together?'

'The short years we knew one another were indeed precious ones,' he sighed, closing his eyes.

'So you have only come to the monastery recently?'

'Oh, no, I have been here since I was only a young man, no older than your scribe . . . ahh, those days were so –'

My master interrupted him by clearing his throat, 'So it was brother Samuel who had only been here for a short time?'

'Yes,' he answered, 'he and the others were from a monastery whose population was diminished and so forced to close its doors.'

'When you say the other brothers you mean Setubar, Ezekiel, and Brother Daniel?'

'Yes, that is correct.'

There was a pause, my master's eyebrows worked furiously. 'So around the year forty-four the four of them came here?'

'Yes, I suppose it was forty-four, does it interest you?'

'I am intrigued to know who the original founders of the abbey were.'

'Oh . . . well, we are told that nine brothers from many distant lands and four from France were called to this place, it is said, by a spiritual voice. Legend tells how they arrived here independently, and yet within days of each other, each calling out the other's name as if they had known one another all their lives.'

'Indeed. And did they live long?'

'I do not know,' he answered with a frown, 'I think they died shortly after the completion of the abbey. There is a grave with a headstone . . . one of our oldest . . . In any case by that time there were enough members to continue their work and an abbot was appointed.'

'And what was his name?'

'Nicholas of Aragon, a Spanish monk who lived many years in the Holy Land,' he turned his gaze to Eisik, 'the land of your forefathers! And yes, he was a wonderful translator. I did not know him, for he died before I came here.'

'I see . . . so are all the abbots translators then?'

'Oh, yes, it is a tradition. The next to succeed Abbot Nicholas was Abbot Otto of Troyes, and then of course Abbot Bendipur, who is himself a fine scholar and knows many languages including Aramaic and Greek, but more importantly Egyptian Coptic.'

The abbot knew Greek! So many thoughts were now

coursing through my mind.

'And so before Brother Bendipur became Abbot, he too worked in the scriptorium?'

'No . . . not the scriptorium, but the library,' he said almost in a whisper. 'Brother Ezekiel took the abbot's place as head translator when he was elected, and the secrets of the library were passed to him.'

'So the abbot was the librarian?'

'No.'

'How so?'

'The head translator is not always the librarian, and the librarian is not usually the head translator . . . you see, in most smaller monasteries it is usual for the master of music to look after the books and library, but as you see it is far too difficult in a larger one. So we have a librarian who looks after the day-to-day running of the scriptorium, but the library proper is the domain of the head translator. He and only he may enter its confines. You may find this strange, preceptor, but monks should not be allowed easy access to books, it distracts them from their work and meditation. Also, books are fragile and old and must be kept away from light and moisture, books that are handled constantly do not last. It is the acidic nature of sweat, so I am told, that causes deterioration. In any case, Abbot Bendipur was head translator, and when he became abbot, Brother Ezekiel. But Ezekiel was very old and his sight was weak, there was a need to find his replacement before now.'

'So Brother Ezekiel was grooming Anselmo for the position?'

'Who told you that, preceptor?' he asked, amazed.

'Brother Macabus mentioned that brother Ezekiel had taken Anselmo to the library on a few occasions. He did not seem too happy about it.'

'And one can see why.' He looked about him and moved closer. 'Anselmo is very young. None so young has ever been given such a privilege . . . and yet, preceptor, we must remember our vow of obedience, an obedience that is prompt and unquestioning. We must not follow our will, neither must we obey our own desires and pleasures, but follow the commands and directions of the abbot and his obedientiaries. If Anselmo was the abbot's choice, then Brother Macabus should have been happy that a fine translator could be found in the monastery and not procured elsewhere. In any case Brother Macabus is not a great translator, mediocre so I'm told, though I do not mean this in an unkind way. Anselmo was the better choice, but he proved too young and . . . petulant.'

'So Brother Ezekiel changed his mind about him?'

'Naturally, that is, when he went about boasting of the things he had seen in the library, what else could he do? It is also rumoured that Anselmo was not satisfied with the work that Brother Ezekiel was giving him, but that he wanted more, to see more, to do more . . . but this is monkish gossip.'

'Has Anselmo expressed to you his anger at being rejected?'

'To the contrary. He told me that it was a good lesson in humility and also in obedience.'

'And what of the other novice, the young Jerome?'

Brother Sacar's face darkened. 'He has disappeared . . . some say he sneaked away in the middle of the night, all for the better I say. He was a strange one.'

'How do you mean strange, brother?'

'There was something unnatural about him . . . a feminine quality . . . but he was good in the medicinal arts. A natural healer, the infirmarian told me once, though he also mentioned that the boy was a little too . . . enthusiastic.'

'Come now, brother, how can a physician be too enthusiastic?'

He lowered his voice to a whisper, 'All I can say is that Brother Asa had admonished his desire to know too much too soon on more than one occasion. There are certain things one must learn gradually, preceptor, as one's maturity dictates.'

'Did he say what these things were?'

'Not exactly, for I believe he did not know many things himself. Poor Brother Asa.' He sighed. 'In his master's eyes he would always be a student. I do not believe Setubar would part with many of his secrets and this led to a rift between them. In any case, it was not his belief that a physician should interfere with nature . . .'

'And Brother Asa was seeking to do so?'

'Oh no!' he cried aghast and his hand flew to his mouth, perhaps fearing that the devil might access an indiscreet portal with greater ease. 'I do not believe . . . I do not know.'

'I see . . .'

'But he is innocent of all these insinuations of sorcery. Of that I am sure.'

My master must have been satisfied because he changed the subject. 'So this is a monastery not only of fine music but also of translators?'

'Since the beginning,' smiled the master of music, suddenly relaxed.

'I thank you for your insightful observations. We must not keep you further, brother, I can see that you are busy.'

'I hope that I have been useful to you, though I am indeed limited in the affairs of gossip . . . You do not think that the Devil of jealousy is responsible for these terrible events do you, preceptor?' he asked a little anxiously.

'I do not know, Brother Sacar, but I am making it my aim to find out. One last thing, the organ, how does one operate it, is there a code perhaps?'

'Oh, yes,' he answered with reluctance, 'and I shall take that secret to my deathbed, preceptor, where I shall whisper it into the ear of my successor, as it was whispered into mine.'

'But surely if Brother Samuel died suddenly, as we have

heard from all accounts, how could he have told you?'

He was momentarily caught off guard. 'Yes, it is strange. He came to me the night before he died and told me, as if he knew his end was near . . .'

'This begs another question, do you have an oblate to replace you? Perhaps now that he is free of his obligations in the library . . . Anselmo?'

'Perhaps . . .' The other man fell silent.

'So you, too, will keep secrets from your acolyte, just as Setubar did with Asa, and Samuel with you?'

'Oh, it is only tradition,' he shrugged. 'What more can a good monk do than follow tradition?'

'I thank you again,' my master said with a bow, and the master of music left us for the church.

'Things are a little clearer, *inshallah*!' Andre said, carefully adding the precautionary exclamation (if God please) after the monk was out of earshot, the infidel in his nature momentarily surfacing like a hydra.

'How so, master?' Frankly, I found that hard to believe. There were further suspicions to confuse us and I was speculating on the abbot's motives, and even on those of Sacar!

'There is now little doubt this monastery has two functions; it operates on the surface as any monastery of its kind and below the surface as a centre for the translation of secret texts. Moreover, the four old brothers had only been here ten years and this date coincides with another event of interest.'

'The year of the siege at Montsegur,' Eisik added.

'It proves that Setubar was not lying to the inquisitor. The Cathar castle is some distance away, but not too far to discount its connection to this place. I am convinced that the old brothers were indeed the heretics of Montsegur, all four of them. Let us look at what we know. Firstly, the abbey was established the year before the fall of Jerusalem. Brother Sacar said nine of the founders were monks from distant lands, he did not say they were Cistercian monks. Four were from France. All the abbots had either lived in the Holy Land or knew the most important Eastern languages for translating. Each abbot was head translator before becoming abbot. We have seen one Templar grave in the cemetery, the first abbot of the monastery. Sacar told us this in his own way. There may be more unmarked ones that we have not seen.'

'Are you saying that the founding monks were Templars?' I asked.

'I told you, Andre! I could smell them,' Eisik waved a threatening finger at him, 'but you did not listen.'

'That may explain . . .' my master said absently, as though he had not heard Eisik, 'why the grand master was present at our meeting with the king and also why we have been sent here.

This is only an assumption, a hypothesis, and we must bear in mind what a dangerous thing it is to hypothesise because it may limit us to one idea when there may be others just as worthy of our attention.'

'Why would nine knights establish a Cistercian monastery so far from the Holy Land? Why not a preceptory?' I asked.

'Perhaps to carry out some arcane translations, with the sanction of St Bernard, away from ecclesiastic scrutiny, and that may explain why the abbots of this monastery have never attended a meeting of the general chapter. Perhaps our order in those days found the eternal gospel hidden in the bowels of Temple of Solomon . . .'

As we walked past the stables, my master said, 'Whatever it is the monks of this monastery are doing, we must above all stop the inquisitor from getting his vulturous claws on the original copy of the gospel.'

'But Netsamur!' Eisik exclaimed, his eyes fairly popping out of his bony skull. 'From what the boy says, Setubar may have already told him everything!'

'Yes, but I do not think Setubar knows the formulas of

orientation . . . unless he dragged them out of Daniel . . . We must see him and question him ourselves.' He looked around him reflectively. 'Where would the old man be? What time is it?'

'Almost sext, master,' I answered.

'We must also figure out what the strange numerical code on the organ means.' He looked a little distracted. 'The inner room . . . the sanctuary perhaps where a young boy brought here by the four brothers is sequestered . . . along with original sacred texts . . .'

'We had best sharpen our wits!' Eisik whispered harshly, afraid. 'Stop musing, Andre! The living are becoming rare in this monastery! Look around you, the corpses are piling up!'

'Yes, Eisik, that too worries me.'

'It seems to me you worry more about your puzzles,' he reproached, saying aloud what I had been thinking all along. However, I too had been seduced by the mystery and had forgotten that lives were in peril.

As we rounded the stables Eisik departed to his cell above the animals, shaking his head and mumbling dire omens under his breath, and we continued in the silence of our own misgivings. Upon nearing the blacksmith's workroom, however, our meditations were interrupted by a terrible sound. My master immediately left me alone for a moment at the entrance to the building while he inspected its source, and as I waited for his return, feeling a great deal of uneasiness under the stare of many eyes, I saw the bishop coming out of the cookhouse carrying something under his arm.

His haste and the folds of his habit hid whatever it was, and I could not see it, only that it was substantial. The friar, who was on his way to the service, almost bumped into him, as he rounded the church. There followed an angry exchange between them and the bishop continued through the aperture to the cloisters, while the friar looked on with malice. At that moment the Cistercian joined him, and they had a moment of conspiracy, each man looking around with suspicion, it seemed, before entering the church.

Also on the way to the holy office were the maiden and her father, making their way from the pilgrim hospice. Partially hidden as I was behind an old tree, I was able to observe her without being noticed. Her face, revealed by an imprudent wind that swept back her hood, was that of a young woman whose complexion was exquisitely fair, with noble features, and lofty demeanour. I saw the brilliance of her eyes, the perfect form of her teeth. With a casual air she tossed very slightly the sable tresses that, in little curls, fell upon her lovely shoulders . . . I was mute, as I should have been! Transfixed by her loveliness, I found my eyes riveted to the area of purest softness where her slender neck met the curvature of her shoulders. Here a large gold clasp brought together the folds of a crimson robe that hung loosely over a velvet gown of the same colour, and yet not concealing the form beneath . . . Thankfully, she soon entered the church, away from my sinful eyes. For a moment she had been the woman in my dream, the Goddess Natura, leaving the scent of jasmine in her step, and I felt myself blush violently.

I did not hear my master come up behind me, I only felt his hand as he slapped me on the back of the neck almost too sharply.

'The world would be sweet if there was no such thing as woman!' he said calmly.

'But, master, we would not have been born!' I answered a little annoyed, rubbing my stinging neck.

'Ah . . . but, Christian, we would not need to be born! We would all be in paradise. In any case, if not for the recent terrible incident with the mountain she would not have been given permission to stay. As it is she offers distraction for stupid squires and the sooner she leaves the better!'

'So what you are saying, master,' I retorted, feeling that Andre was sounding too much like Setubar, 'is that the beautiful should be shunned, but that is not what Plato teaches us.'

'No, you are quite right,' he agreed as we entered the hot oily room used by the blacksmith. 'He tells us that when one falls in love with the beauty in one individual (for how can one help but fall in love with such a diabolical deception), one then sees that this beauty is similar to that in all human beings, and that by loving the beauty of the body he comes to know the love of the mind that he soon realises is far superior to the other kind, and in this way he recognises the beauty of all forms of knowledge, *ergo*, attaining a love for beautiful words and thoughts that hopefully leads to apprehension of that one supreme form of all knowledge, God himself,' he ended.

'Yes that is it exactly!' I said triumphantly.

'Ahh, but, Christian, there is something you have not thought of.'

'Master?'

'Plato was not a monk and he liked to look at beautiful boys.'

'So,' I said presently, because I had been outwitted and because I did not want to know such things about Plato, 'what we heard . . .was that the sound of some animal being shoed or branded?'

'No . . . it was the cook,' he answered, and we climbed the stairs.

The cook was being kept in a small room that occupied a section of the building used by the blacksmiths. I sneezed immediately we entered the large space outside it, for there was heavy smoke coming from the furnaces and the smell of burning animal hair, tanning oil, and other irritating substances. We walked directly to a doorway guarded by two archers whose inscrutable expressions gave little insight into their persons, but rather made them look like those stone sculptures outside the church. My master ordered the two men to step aside in the name of the king. This caused a cloud of uncertainty to darken their brows, for my master's demeanour was such that it required a strict adherence to his command, and so reluctantly they obeyed his order, and let us pass.

Inside we found the cook, sitting on the floor of the large room that smelled very bad. His hands were tied behind his back at an awkward angle, and there was a rope on a kind of device hanging from the ceiling. Before us stood the inquisitor flanked by two more archers, his face red with anger.

'What say you, brother Templar, to this interruption!? We have grave matters to attend to here. If you will leave us . . .'

'I do not mean to interrupt you in your holy work, Rainiero, only that it has been brought to my attention that Brother Setubar remains missing since before the service. I need not mention what this may signal . . .'

The man frowned, a look of alarm crossed his face and then his eyes narrowed. 'Have you searched the abbey?'

'We have, but to no avail.'

'This will have to wait.' He ordered his two archers out of the room. 'We may have to add one more carcass to the rest!' he remarked, in order that all might hear his predictions and so pronounce him wise when they proved to be true. He paused before my master, measuring him with his eyes. 'I must go and order the captain of the guard to look for the old man, but the *inquisitio* will continue today even if all the monks of the monastery are found dead.'

With this he left the room, and we were alone with the cook.

The poor man's face was so disfigured that I found it difficult to recognise his former person. His left eye could not be seen, and his mouth I cannot describe. It will suffice to say that whatever teeth he had had were now gone and that his bruised and battered lips contorted into a hideous smile as he saw us.

My master untied his hands and helped him to stand. Later I was to learn that he had been hung by a rope from his wrists, tied as we saw, behind him. Then he would have been lowered abruptly a little at a time. The aim of such torture was to inflict the most terrible pain in the shortest time, because it did not take much to break both arms and occasion a terrible dislocation of the shoulders.

'*Por favor señor!*' he cried, tears running down the broken bones of his cheeks. '*Madre mía! Díos mío!* I have done nothing . . . nothing! Escape I must! No one is safe! Ohh, *miseria, miseria,* I have done nothing, you must believe me!'

Was it possible that this was the giant of a man that I had met that first day in the kitchen?

'If I am to believe you, you must tell me everything!' my master said.

The man looked up innocently, like a little child. 'It is my sin that in the kitchen of the popes' enemy I worked . . . that is true, but I have always been *un* good *católico* . . .! *Mi único error, señor ...*'

'Indeed, your only error is that you have been a heretic in league with heretics,' my master said sharply.

'What is heresy, *señor?* Is it heresy to do honest work? To think with your *cabeza* – your head? No . . . no!' he cried defiantly, shaking his head, and then broke into a sob, the great span of his chest moving rhythmically with his wide and now disfigured shoulders.

'Perhaps not,' my master conceded, 'but that still leaves us with the fact that you have not convinced me sufficiently of your innocence in the terrible matters of these last days.'

'*Por favor* . . .' He came closer and the stench of onion filled my nostrils. 'You must forgive me . . . I have not been totally *sincero* . . . is very difficult for me, *señor...*' he coughed, spitting.

'Tell me the truth, for Brother Setubar has told me of your secret.'

The man looked aghast. 'He told you?'

'He told me you were among those who murdered Piero

da Verona.'

There was a terrible silence.

'You are then not only a murderer,' my master continued harshly, 'but also a heretic and an enemy of the church, a man quite capable of killing again to stop his secret from being known.'

He straightened what he could of his back and answered defiantly, 'Is true, I murdered one filthy inquisitor . . . but never have I killed again. Penance I have done . . . but the others, they are free, Giacopo he is free . . . we were fighting a war, you must understand? You fight wars . . .'

'I have never brandished a sword against a Christian,' my master answered calmly, and so I knew him to be agitated.

'And you think you are better than me!' the cook said bitterly, 'I hear what they say about you, you are *un* infidel, you kill your own kind!'

'I am a Christian.'

'You think this makes you a saint because you wear a cross? How does it feel to kill your own blood? You are like me, you kill when it suits you!' For one moment he raised his chest, like a cock in those seconds before a crow, then he became disheartened, his shoulders drooped, perhaps he realised there was nothing to be gained by arguing with the one man who could help him. 'I have done penance, I have been absolved, I have come back to the bosom of the mother!'

'You lie too easily, cook, it will do no good to evade the truth. Come now, confess to me and I will see that you are judged fairly.'

The cook became hysterical, laughing and spitting and coughing, and for a moment I saw a hint of his former self in his eyes. 'Fairly! Too late, preceptor, for fairness, I am like *un cerdo* – a pig the day of the feast of St John. There is no hope for me. Now I am the one who is cooked, no?'

'Tell me, so that I might relieve your distress. If you are

honest with me I can save your life, for I have a letter sealed with the king's seal. I am to return with all those accused! Did you poison the old brothers?'

'I did not kill anyone!' he cried.

'Then how did you come by the substance?'

'What?' The man's face was suddenly inscrutable.

'The substance that induces your visions!'

'I saw *la Virgen! La Virgen!*'

'Tell me for I know you have abused some forbidden thing. Tell me or we shall soon see what the inquisitor thinks of it.'

The man blanched. *'Porel amor de díos!* I did not kill anyone . . . I only . . . the honey !

'Honey?'

The man looked about him, and lowered his voice to a loud boom, 'What Rodrigo is told, Rodrigo does, as penance . . .'

'What did you do? I lose my patience, come now!'

The great man trembled. *'Sí . . . sí . . .* before you came here, preceptor, I was told to take some *miel,* some honey, and put it in a pot, in this I put dry herbs given to me and I was to leave it aside for the old monks. Sometimes I dip raisins in it, sometimes it is poured into wine in the rooms of the old ones, to make it sweet. One day, *María Santísima,* I had a drink of it . . . *vos sabeís, yo también soy muy curioso* . . . I am curious like you, I wanted to know what makes it so special . . .'

'Go on.'

'She came . . . so dry was my mouth and I feel the heart, beating, and I fly to her . . . Ahh! But *he* found out, he was very angry *muy nervioso* – very nervous. Never do it, he told me . . . but I want to see *la Virgen,* no? I went to Brother Asa I told him I need some *hierbas* from the herbarium for the food. He let me in. I remember what the herbs look like and took a bunch to dry over the fire . . .'

I was suddenly struck, for now I knew two things. Firstly,

I remembered seeing the cook doing exactly as he said when I waited outside the blacksmith's workroom, the day my master was hit on the head. Secondly, I was beginning to see why I had been having the strange sensations! The dreams! It was the wine!

'Who asked you to prepare the honey, and who told you never to taste it?'

The man hesitated.

'Who told you, cook?'

'The old man, he told me it was for the old monks. He said if I ever opened my mouth he would tell the abbot my secret.'

'Setubar . . .' said my master pensively, 'The poison . . . on the raisins . . . and also in the wine . . . but Brother Samuel died quickly, only moments after entering the tunnels. The raisins, the wine, were poisoning the brothers slowly over a period of time in order to evade suspicion. Tell me about the tunnels!'

'Tunnels?'

'Answer me for I know that you are responsible for taking food to them!'

'How? Who?'

'I have seen you with my own eyes.'

'*Madre mía!*' The man was aghast, and so, too, was I.

'Tell me everything.'

'The secret! I have been sworn . . .'

'Tell me! You must tell me!' my master said a little roughly.

'The hidden manna!' the man exclaimed, falling to his knees. 'I was told one cannot know the secret and live.'

'But you are alive,' my master pointed out.

'I could not speak and the old man knew it . . . He said if ever I opened my mouth he would tell the abbot my secret. Do not ask me of the ghosts that are not ghosts, for ghosts do not eat! I did this as penance for sins, but if I tell you what I know, you will help me?'

'That depends on what you know.'

He thought for a moment, weighing things up. 'There are twelve,' he whispered finally, for he was in the grip of far too many fears to worry about one more. 'They are called the 'silent ones', I know there are twelve because I am told to take them twelve bowls of broth, and twelve measures of bread . . .'

'Should there not be thirteen?' I asked, 'including the boy?'

'You know of the boy?' The man trembled, visibly afraid. 'I . . . I . . . his name is not known, I have never seen him, others have, but only a few, only the old ones who bring him here . . . he was *solito,* alone, away from everyone, living in his own room only, close to the abbot since he came, years ago. They say that all those years the 'silent ones' have been 'teaching him', and so he visits the tunnels, the catacombs . . . this is well known, all know of it, but few speak.'

'Who are these 'silent ones'?'

'They are hermits . . . who knows?' He shrugged his shoulders and winced with pain. 'No one sees them, I leave food behind the drapes, I am told to leave *inmediatamente.'* He looked at me with his good eye and nodded his head. 'Because to see one of them is to lose the sight. That is why Ezekiel was going blind . . . they say also that they are *transparente,* that the bile and blood in their bodies is seen like through glass because they have seen no sun, others say that they are older than this monastery! That they never die! *Maria Santa!* The day you come something happens that is very suspicious . . . the abbot ordered absolute *silencio,* forbidding anyone to go out from his cell except for the *officio,* then the boy disappeared.'

'How do you know he disappeared if you have never seen him?'

'Because I always make him a special plate, never meat, only a little fish, the best from my kitchen . . . *ese día,* that day, the abbot told me, 'Rodrigo, do not make him any more food', saying that he was fasting. Everyone knows he is in the tunnel.'

'Fasting . . .' my master said, pulling feverishly on his beard, 'and what does everyone say he is doing there?'

'*María Santa!* He is learning the secret that no man can live who knows it. The secret of the hidden manna!' As he uttered these words he must have recalled that he would soon give credence to them and cried, 'Please you must help me! *Estoy muerto!* I am dead!'

'I will see . . . I will see,' my master said softly, 'where is the poisoned honey and wine kept?'

'In the larder, a clay pot with a crooked handle on the top shelf. The honey is also there in another. *María Santa!* You will help me? I tell you everything I know . . .'

'We shall try, but for now we must go . . . Come, Christian.' He pulled at my arm and we left the poor creature sobbing into his enormous, twisted hands.

'But, master . . .' I said as we braved a battering of hail. 'How did you know he had taken the same substance that poisoned the brothers?'

Once in the kitchen, now deserted, he answered me. 'Remember when we were in the tunnels I told you about witch's potion whose principal element is atropa belladonna?'

'Yes, it makes those who take it feel as though they were flying into the arms of Satan . . . I must tell you –'

'Do not interrupt my thoughts, boy! Now . . . the day in the kitchen, the herb drying above the fire was the first clue, when he then said that he flew into the arms of the Virgin . . . a natural conclusion.'

'But flying into the arms of the Virgin and into the arms of Satan are not the same thing, master.'

'Essentially they are, for if you will remember our discussion on the suggestive powers of magicians, you will know why the cook, under the power of such a drug, sees the Virgin, while a witch sees Satan.'

'So to understand it a little clearer, the drug only induces the vision that is sought by the organism using it.'

'To put it another way, the effect of the drug often corresponds to the disposition of its user.'

'And so I flew into the arms of a woman. I saw bees flying, and eagles . . . I somehow flew to the encampment outside,' I said miserably because this meant that my dreams were no more prophetic than a sneeze, forgetting how many times they had aided us in our investigations. I told him then of my suspicions about the wine that I had taken.

'That also explains your strange behaviour . . . Lucky for you, you must not have consumed enough to kill you.' Seeing that I was sufficiently contrite, he continued, 'Yes, the flying symptom is the physical one, the other effect has its origin in the mind . . . the wine. Brother Ezekiel drank a great deal of it the night that he died.'

'But that wine was meant for you, master.'

'Yes, perhaps someone was careless, as has happened with you.'

'May I ask you another question, master? How did you know that it was the cook who was involved in the murder of Piero?'

'I didn't.'

'So, he implicated himself because he thought you knew? But then how did you know that he supplied the food for the twelve monks of the catacombs?'

'It is quite simple,' he answered, 'even you would remember how that night we inspected the panel in the transept chapel, we were disturbed by a monk whom we later observed carrying something in his hands?'

'Yes!' I cried, astounded at my own stupidity. 'He went behind the drapes then left immediately, just as the cook said. But how did you know that it was food?'

'Think, boy! Think! Do you not remember our sojourn to the tunnels? When we observed that the twelve ghosts were indeed as human as you or I? I knew then, as you or any novice except stupid ones should know, that they must somehow have access to food.'

'But it could have been anyone.'

'The only people who have access to the kitchen between the hours of compline and matins are those who hold the keys, namely, Brother Macabus or Rodrigo the cook.'

'But from memory Brother Macabus said that the cook was to bring him the keys before the service of compline, and we saw him at the north transept chapel at about the eleventh hour, before the service of matins.'

'Precisely and this he does every night. How many times since our arrival have you seen the cook, or anyone for that matter, deliver Brother Macabus the keys before compline begins? There must be times when he keeps the keys. This morning, for instance, Brother Macabus could not open the aperture for us because he did not have them. Sometimes, in order to escape suspicion, the cook or – in this case someone else – simply does not lock the kitchen, as we saw that first night when we found we could not leave through the aperture, and as we passed the kitchen I remarked that it was odd to see only the outer cookhouse door locked, and not also the inner door.'

'Still, you had very little evidence, master, a few clues, nothing of substance, and yet when you spoke to the cook, you sounded so sure of everything.'

'Yes,' he reflected, 'this particular situation – unlike the situation with the brother librarian – called for a more forthright manner.'

'I see!' I said, suddenly enlightened. 'When one knows a great deal, one interrogates with prudence, pretending to know very little, so that the suspect will be unguarded and therefore make a slip of the tongue. On the other hand, when one knows very little, one pretends to know a great deal, thereby intimidating the subject into admitting things he would not have otherwise because he thinks that you already know everything!'

'Yes . . . that is it, more or less.'

I was elated at this splendid insight into human nature. 'Brother Setubar must be the killer! He killed all the brothers with the poisoned raisins and wine.'

'And yet we still have our poor brothers Jerome and Samuel whose deaths remain unexplained . . . I am not convinced on either point. We must not be tempted to draw conclusions until we are satisfied that we have gathered all the relevant information available to us . . . on the other hand, what we see with our eyes is very often more reliable than what we hear with our ears,' he said as we entered the larder, hurrying, for we could hear the service ending.

'Master?' I asked as we searched.

'Yes.'

'Do you think it odd that twelve men live underground? Surely they must come up sometime for air or confession? How must they survive?'

'Life is stubborn, Christian, the more a man punishes the flesh in order to ignore it the more attention he gives it, and the more he abhors life and longs for death the longer he seems to live. These hermits must sleep in underground cells, and may even have a chapel in which to pray. That is not as uncommon as it may appear at first.'

'I see. But who has been taking their food to the north transept while the cook has been detained?'

'That is a good question.'

We failed to find the poisoned substances, however, and this sent my master into a frustrated rage.

'By the curse of Saladin!' he swore under his breath. 'Someone has either removed it, or . . .' He paused for a moment, frowning. 'Of course!' He slapped me on the nape. 'Why did you not think of it? It stands to reason . . . he has already killed them all . . . that is, except himself!'

'Why should I have thought of it when you did not think of it either until just now?' I asked, a little hurt.

'You are right. Let us go to the infirmary. Asa, the dutiful student must know where his master Setubar is, if he is not already dead by his own hand.'

Outside, the inquisitor's men were still looking for Brother Setubar, the abbot, too, had sent monks in every direction. They called the old brother's name into the wet nothingness, but there was no answer.

We made our way to the infirmary in haste. My master ordered the guard to stand aside, and this he did almost by reflex, and we entered, closing the door behind us.

We found Asa tending to the young boy whose leg had been so badly broken. He was bending over the young man's face, looking into his eyes, checking his pulse. When he heard us enter, he turned around, a little startled. 'Preceptor.' In his hand a strange glass object, on the bed the velvet pouch that I had seen him replace hastily in the drawer the day that the cook had started the fire. 'I hear agitation outside,' he said, trying now to hide his implement, though he knew it was hopeless. We both had seen it.

'How is our patient?' My master walked over to the boy and checked his pupils.

The infirmarian shook his head. 'Unwell, he has a fever.'

'Help me to lift him a little then, Asa, I would like to listen to his chest.'

The man hesitated, looking at us like a hare cornered by two bloodthirsty hounds.

'What is wrong? Are your hands full? What do you have there?'

The other man narrowed his eyes and, with great hesitation, showed my master. 'It is a wonderful thing, preceptor. It measures the temperature of the corpus.'

My master looked at it in awe. A long cylindrical glass

whose base ballooned out a little and whose interior seemed to hold some substance.

'How does one read it?' my master asked, most intrigued.

'Well . . .' the other man became excited, 'one places this end,' he pointed to the rounded segment, 'in the patient's anus, or in his mouth. Inside the glass there is alcohol. When it is heated the gas expands and it travels up this chamber, indicating the extent of a patient's fever.'

'I am astounded! It is very clever. Did you devise it? Better still, what do you say is the normal and abnormal temperature?'

The man looked down shyly. 'I am not certain of its accuracy. I have simply marked incremental numbers along its side, and have come to know, after using it on both the healthy and the sick, where an unhealthy temperature differs from a healthy one . . . The glass maker and I have spent many hours perfecting it. You see the glass must not be too thick or it does not work efficiently. Also there is the added problem of the alcohol . . .'

'Why, it is a marvel! You are a credit to your calling,' he said with genuine admiration and warmth.

'I have been hiding it from Brother Setubar . . . he would think it a sinful tool of the Devil. He would rather see men die than rely on earthly things to effect a cure. In this way he is not so different from the inquisitor.' There was bitterness in his voice, but his mention of Setubar brought us back to the purpose of our visit.

'Brother Asa, we are looking for your master,' Andre said, in a grave tone, 'has he been here?'

'Here? No . . . Why, has something happened to him?'

'He is nowhere to be found and we fear for his life.'

The infirmarian looked down, but he did not seem upset. 'It is no secret . . . he did not like me, anyone will tell you, and yet I have always been, and shall remain, a good student. I must confess, however, that if he is dead, I will not mourn him,' he ended in bitterness.

'We believe that he has taken the poison with him that has killed so many. You have not seen him?'

'You are not suggesting that he was the murderer?'

'Was?'

'I mean, *is*, of course . . .' Asa corrected at once.

'I do not know . . .' my master eyed him penetratingly. 'What were you going to tell me about Samuel that day we were interrupted, something about his last words . . .?'

'Oh, yes, he said that he was flying. Those were his words . . . flying, just like Ezekiel . . .'

At that moment the bell tolled the commencement of the inquiry. Before anything else could be said two archers stormed in and took Asa away. My master called out to the larger of the two, ordering that he find Eisik and bring him to the infirmary. I thought he was about to perform an examination on the patient but instead he walked out of the dormitory and into the laboratory where Brother Daniel's body lay on the examination table, covered and still. I was not accustomed to death, even after so many years at my master's side a shiver still ran through me at the sight of a body covered by a sheet.

'If Asa had told us that little piece of information earlier we would have come by our conclusions sooner . . . No matter . . . we must find Setubar!' He walked to the door that led to the infirmary chapel. 'Anselmo intimated that there was some clue here . . .' It was bolted shut, but my master, in one of his moments of physical exuberance, managed to prise it open with an iron poker that he found by the fire.

Behind the door, steps led down to a dark rectangular chapel whose long and narrow nave drew the eye to a beautiful crucifix made from precious stones. There were no aisles, and no windows, only torches as we had elsewhere seen in these places, bracketed to the wall. Moments later my master discovered behind the altar that a little curtain obscured some small steps that led down once again, no doubt, to another tunnel.

'But I did not notice any dirt under Asa's shoes, master.'

'No, but by now he could have cleaned them. He knew that we would be looking for it.'

'Shall we go down?'

'What for, boy? What shall we find but more tunnels? No we are best to head for the chapter house, lest we incur suspicion, but now my dear Christian many things are clearer. This may explain why Asa was late to dinner that first night, perhaps he was in the tunnels looking for Jerome?'

'So Asa could have left the infirmary via this exit at any time. He could have killed Setubar and Daniel, even with guards at the door.'

'Yes, though Setubar may not be dead, Christian. Perhaps it is he who has been taking the food down to the brothers in the tunnels in the absence of the cook. Asa may have nothing to do with it and our dear Anselmo is putting two and two together and making three . . . then again perhaps he has everything to do with it. We must not be fooled, however, merely because we are sympathetic to him. Remember, never allow sympathies and antipathies to rule your reasoning.'

As we re-entered the infirmary once again we heard a muffled sound. It was the young man. We found him sitting up in his pallet, his black curls plastered to his skull and a bead of sweat framing his feverish lips. On seeing us his eyes widened and he said in the rough whisper of the infirm, 'He is here . . . I have seen him.'

My master moved to his side and placed the palm of his hand over his brow. 'You have a fever, my son, you must rest.'

The young man said something inaudible and my master knelt by his side, in order to hear him better, 'What did you say?'

'My name is Trencavel, we've come to get it. . .before it is too late, before the inquisitor finds it.' He grasped at my master's arm. '*You* must stop him! For I shall soon be dead . . . but before it I must have the *consolamentum!* You understand? Hurry!'

My master's darkened brow showed me that he knew something about what the boy had just intimated, but he said nothing.

He peeled back the sheets, and a sickly smell assailed our nostrils. My master nodded to himself.

We left the boy in Eisik's care, and as we stepped out into the cheerless afternoon Andre said, 'His leg is rotting . . . gangrene. The meat will soon be 'off the bones' as they say, though every precaution was taken. I am afraid his only hope now is cauterisation or amputation.'

The snow was wet, churned to mud by hail. My master ordered the guard standing outside to find the boy's father, for his death was imminent.

'But, master,' I said, 'we must do something!'

'But we cannot, dear boy.' He looked sad.

'Why not? In God's name!'

'Because he is a Cathar, he is a Trencavel.'

'A Trencavel?'

'The house of Trencavel was well known for its heresy during the Albigensian Crusade. He is ready for death, he has asked for the *consolamentum.*'

'But how do you –'

'*Consolamentum* is the last rite, given by a *perfect* or a pure one, to a believer before death. It is a ritual of purification. He is in effect asking to die.'

'But he may yet live!'

'You do not understand. To a Cathar death is a release from the bonds of the Devil. If he does not receive the *consolamentum* he believes he will die impure . . . His father must be a *perfect.*'

'What makes one *perfect?*'

'One who has taken the *consolamentum* and has lived a pure life, a very strict and austere life. You see the life of a *perfect* is so austere, Christian, so taxing on the mind and body, that few are able to live it. That is why most are given the *consolamentum* on their death bed, that way they can live life as they choose to and when the time comes they may go to God cleansed of sin . . . it is a matter of convenience,' he remarked.

'Not unlike our extreme unction, master.'

'No, not unlike it.'

'So they are heretics! Perhaps what you said about the Cathar Treasure is true, master! Can it be they came to find The Fifth Gospel?'

'Hush, Christian, do you want the world to hear? Our main concern now is saving our own carcasses. This whole thing may end up in the lap of our order with you and me as convenient pawns.'

My master looked pale, his eyes troubled, his shoulders weighed down with responsibilities. For the first time I realised how much he suffered because of his erudition. Knowledge, I now realised, did not afford much pleasure. It was a painful thing. For a wise man bears the great cross of honour, integrity, and principle. His every word is a certainty haunted by the possibility of error. I wondered how many nights he lay awake wondering, had his thoughts become deeds, would they have been good ones? Now I was more than ever in awe of him, as I looked up at his knitted brows, the unsettled movements of his dark green eyes, his beard whose tip was moulded to a point by the stroking of his hand. I wished that I knew him better. And yet, I wondered if he knew himself, as Plato has commanded us, or whether Eisik was right. Was he becoming hopelessly lost in the universe of his ideas? I shivered, hugging my cold tired self, and noting the apple I had taken for him in the repository of my habit, I handed it to him. He shook his head, he did not want it. My heart sank. I wished there were something noble or clever that I could say to help him. What could I say? I may not have been as erudite as he was, but I knew that as we prepared to set foot in the chapter house we were indeed preparing to enter into the mouth of the dragon.

21

Capitulum

After Nones

The tribunal occupied the dais as before, but this time archers were posted at every exit, and men at arms flanked the legation. This was now *inquisitio*.

We walked in late, under the stare of Rainiero who, at that moment, stood and drew his cowl back as a signal that the proceedings should begin. I thought I could almost see a smile of self-gratification. After all, he was about to perform a part that he not only enjoyed, but for which his temperament was eminently suited.

A psalm chosen by him commenced the affair, and I could hear his voice above all other voices, intoning with profound concentration the words, 'Blessed is the man who walketh not in the counsel of the ungodly, nor standeth in the way of sinners, nor sitteth in the seat of the scornful . . . therefore the ungodly shall not stand in the judgement, nor sinner in the congregation of the righteous. For the lord knoweth the way of the righteous; but the way of the ungodly shall perish!'

The solemn sound of so many masculine voices rising and falling in deep, prolonged notes would have been pleasing if it did not, at the same time, convey the singular sadness and resolution of men reconciled to their fate.

When there was silence once more, the man glanced his eye about the assembly, and after pronouncing the various opening formulas, ordered the archers to bring in the cook.

The giant entered the room flanked by two archers and though he seemed to have halved his size, the air vibrated around him. His vestments were covered in blood and excreta and his face showed his subjugation. He came to a halt before Rainiero, who shuffled some papers and straightened his habit. All expected him to begin. Yet, he remained silent. Long, anxious moments passed. The congregation held its breath. Still he made no move to start. Suddenly, unexpectedly, he turned his back on the congregation, raising his arms so that his body made the shape of a cross. For some time he remained as though lost in the contemplation of prayer. The cold air hung colder, the stillness became audible.

The cook looked as though he would soon collapse, when finally the inquisitor turned and with solemn tone ordered the interrogation of the cook to begin.

'These have been difficult days,' he paused, surveying the congregation of shaven heads and upturned faces. 'We have been witness to disturbing events that have seen the grievous loss of three lives, perhaps four, to the powers of darkness. Here in the house of God, we have heard the Devil. His voice communicated to us through his instruments, through his bloody deeds. Unfortunately we are not all strong. Not all of us are suitably constituted in mind and body to battle with demons. These are matters that threaten the quiescence of our souls, the very fibre of our beings, and so our beloved colleague the Bishop of Toulouse is found to be . . . feeling unwell. A condition that, although not a serious one, is such that will not allow him to accompany me in this odious task as inquisitor.' I thought I saw the slightest, almost imperceptible smile dawn over the faces of the Franciscan and the Cistercian.

My master whispered into my ear, 'What is this? He was present during lauds, and did not look any worse than usual.'

'I saw him leave the cookhouse, while I was waiting outside the blacksmith's, he was carrying something inside his vestments,' I whispered back.

'By God's bonnet!' Andre hissed, and seemed to be on the verge of further elucidating this when he was interrupted by the inquisitor.

'And so it is that we must appoint another to take his place,' his eyes fell on my master, 'as set out by the learned doctors of the church who, in their wisdom, saw the need for two minds to work together against the evil of Sathanus, whose minions are many. And so it is that I shall ask the Preceptor of Douzens, our esteemed and valiant Templar knight brother to take his place on the dais to perform this sad and gruesome task. So stand, dear brother, whose warlike achievements are well known, champion of the holy sepulchre. This day your God commands that you fight another battle, perhaps less fatiguing to the body, but infinitely more lamentable to the spirit.'

My master whispered in my ear, 'Remember the organ and the catacombs. If something should happen . . .' He looked pointedly at me. 'You can escape!' With firm voice and steady eye he stood and answered with remarkable calmness, 'I am deeply honoured, your grace, by your request, but I am not an expert on the finer points of theology as are those whose life is dedicated to this calling. And so, I fear that I am sorely qualified to a position that requires many years of serious devotion to canon law and scriptural interpretation. Perhaps this assembly should adjourn until a suitable candidate can be found.'

The inquisitor smiled a little. 'There is no need for adjournment, all I require from you, dear preceptor, as a *socius* in these awful, though necessary, matters, is that you hear the evidence with calmness of spirit. You may ask a question if you so wish, otherwise you might allow me to proceed as I have done so many times, relying on my experience as one would rely on the experience of an older and wiser brother. It is not necessary to be an expert in theological matters, it is enough to be a seeker after truth, for in the end, God will recognise his own.'

Having no other recourse, my master joined the assembly on the dais, and I was filled with dread.

'Now we begin . . . what is your name?' he asked the cook.

The cook raised his big head a little way from his chest and with a choked voice answered, 'Rodrigo Dominguez de Toledo, your grace.'

'Rodrigo Dominguez de Toledo, tell this assembly in your own words your history.'

He seemed confused, a terrible vagueness in his eyes. The archer standing on his left side poked him in the ribs and stunned him to his senses. '*Sí...sí* ... a young boy . . . I was in the care of Benedictines at the convent of St Miguel.' He paused vaguely and the inquisitor waved him on impatiently. 'In Gerona . . . I did not want to be a monk, instead, *un cocinero* . . . a cook.'

'Why did you not become a monk, as was the desire of your family?' the inquisitor inquired mildly.

'I . . .' He paused looking around, 'I was not . . .' He swayed a little, and an archer steadied him roughly.

'Come now, is it not,' the inquisitor smiled, 'because even as a young man you had a nature predisposed to the distortions of the Devil?'

'No!' the cook denied weakly, 'I wanted to see the world, I came to France to Toulouse, and worked at a monastery.'

'But it is not your time in Toulouse that interests this *inquisitio,* but your time in Italy when you conspired against the pope by serving the excommunicated serpent, Frederick! Tell me your history from the time you arrived in Italy.'

Slowly he returned from wherever he had been in his mind to answer thus, 'I came to know people . . . followers of a Cathar.'

'You see! A heretic! As I have said!' he exclaimed hotly. 'We see a man touched by the foul enemy whom we defy with every breath of our being!' he thundered. 'This history should be enough to convict you!'

The cook then straightened his back, and this made him appear doubled in size. The archers were immediately dwarfed and a look of discomfort settled on their faces. They did not know, however, that for this poor wretch, size was no longer a measure of strength. 'But the man was you, Rainiero Sacconi . . .!'

There was a loud stir in the audience. The inquisitor blanched and his face hardened into a hideous mask. 'What say you?'

'You were my leader . . . you Cathar!'

There was a pause. 'I do not know you.'

'No! You forget me because *mi nombre,* my name, was another . . .' He looked directly into the eyes of the inquisitor, whose face looked a little incredulous. 'Don't you remember me? Do you not remember your vows, your confessions?' He stopped, gasping for air.

'Stay your mouth you devil!' the inquisitor cried. 'See how the Devil binds a man! How the distortions of Beelzebub enter into the soul? Not only did this poor wretch commit numerous heresies that he freely confesses, allowing himself to be the accursed instrument of the evil emperor who seeks to destroy the church and to replace the pope in his own throne. But also following those other heinous enemies of the church, whose corruptions are too various for a holy man to utter from his lips. Now he seeks to bring the judge to judgement! The champion of truth he accuses! However, I know that the enemy tempts us to exalt our own deeds and worship our own qualities, and so I shall not be forced to do so to a confessed heretic whose debauchery and dissipation has, by his own admission, led him to a life of sin!'

The cook fell to his knees.

My master stood then and said, 'But you strayed from the narrow path, Rainiero, and you were forgiven! This man has confessed and performed penance.'

'Peace, brother!' the inquisitor exclaimed harshly. 'I have returned to the flock, while this man became a conspirer and a heretic! We see here before us the Devil incarnate, by whose hand three good men, perhaps four, have died!'

'But I see no evidence!' Andre answered assertively.

Sacconi ignored this and continued, 'Stand, you devil, instrument of Satan!'

The cook stood unaided, though with much effort.

'Did you conspire with the Devil to kill the three brothers?'

'No!' the cook said, almost in a whisper.

'As God is your judge if you do not answer the truth, I will condemn this entire monastery for having colluded with you to prevent the course of justice!'

The cook was stunned. He looked behind him at the anxious faces, and there followed a long pause in which one could see his whole body tremble under the weight of these matters then with a great measure of courage, summoned from the depths of some unknown corner of his soul he raised his square chin and said:

'No! I stand alone. It was I!'

My master, frowning, interjected, 'By what means, cook, did you kill these men?'

The cook glanced unwaveringly at my master. 'Satan told me, he whispered to me 'Rodrigo, kill the old brothers, use the evil herbs in the wine, which you will find in the *herbarium*. And when you have killed the old ones . . . kill them all!''

There was a loud murmur. Confusion reigned.

'Kill them all, God will know his own! *María Santísima, María Santa! Pecador de mí* . . . sinner that I am . . . *Mea culpa, mea cul-*

pa, mea maxima culpa!' He sobbed then, into his deformed hands.

'Peace! Peace!' yelled the inquisitor at him and at the congregation.

When the room had quietened and order was restored he continued, 'So we have it! By his own admission! Tell me, you wretched dog, did the infirmarian aid you in committing these ferocious crimes? Answer me in the name of God!'

The man looked up, suddenly confused, perhaps he had not anticipated that his confession might also implicate others. 'No . . . no!'

'You say this to protect the scoundrel, for how could an ignorant cook know which herb was poisonous and which was not?'

'I . . .' he looked around him.

'You see? I am right! Archers, bring forth the infirmarian!'

'No! I have told you, Satan told me which herbs to use.' He struggled to his feet.

'You lie!' the inquisitor growled, pointing his pale finger at the man, looking all around him. 'This is a convent of fiends, united through their worship of Belial! They protect each other like a nest of serpents. I do not believe you! Where there is one devil, it is certain there are others. Bring the infirmarian here!'

The infirmarian took his place beside the poor cook. His head was raised with a calm dignity.

'How say you to this charge?'

Asa squinted myopically. 'What charge, your grace?'

'The charge of colluding with this sorry scoundrel by means heretical or diabolical, to murder three brothers of your own order!'

'Which shall I answer to first, your grace, the charge of heresy, or the charge of murder?' he asked mildly.

'Do not double your tongue with me, you garrulous devil, it matters not which one you answer first, but that you do so without dissimulation!'

'I have neither colluded with this poor cook to murder nor to heresy.'

'But here I have a statement . . .' He produced a parchment, that he ceremoniously handed to my master and he to the other prelates, 'made by a woman whose child you cured of an incurable illness! Here she states that you gave the child some infernal substance, after which you further compounded your sin by pronouncing words in some hellish tongue over him as you made the sign of the cross!' There was a stir like a low hum in the room. Rainiero waited until there was silence before continuing, 'She said that you also ordered her to give the child some unlawful and magical pharmacopoeia! You call yourself a man of God!' He crossed himself.

'Your grace, what was the child's ailment?' the infirmarian asked, meekly.

'What difference is there in what ailment?' he scowled. 'Here it states that the child suffered from hellish seizures.'

'Ahh! That often accompanies many childhood ailments, especially if there is a fever . . . I would have given the mother a compound of sage leaves which is a very good medicament for many ailments. The convulsions would have abated naturally as the child's condition improved.'

'Rainiero,' my master interjected. 'The treatment prescribed is one that is not only well known, but is also used by many doctors.'

'Yes, we know of your enthusiasm for such things. We know, preceptor, that it was your own use of such questionable treatments that led to your expulsion from the University of Paris!'

My master blanched.

'You also treated a man with a substance whose origins were questionable.'

'A plant that when crushed aids the beating of the heart. No more, no less,' my master retorted. 'It saved his life.'

'I would expect an infidel to say as much but not a knight of Christ!' he said, turning on my master, and all in the room knew he was alluding to his Eastern blood, 'for infidels are not only renowned for their medical knowledge but also for knowledge of all things diabolical. You speak of an instant cure! Without the aid of prayer, without the anointing of oil! You see how the Devil may ensnare even the worthy to do his bidding. Even a man such as yourself – a man who has devoted his life to fighting the enemies of Christ –' he said this with a cold smile, 'is a perfect example of how persuasive the ways of darkness can be! How seemingly innocent and yet how abominable!'

Now I understood better my master's numerous sermons on prudence, and also the inquisitor's cunning in summoning him to the dais, for if my master was to contest the inquisitor's decision, he would be judged a protector of heretics, and his past would do little to help him.

'I heal in the name of our Lord, your grace!' cried Asa, diverting all attention back to him.

'Peace, necromancer! I wish to hear no more plausible arguments, I wish only to hear a confession to the crimes that have been committed in this abbey!'

'How am I to confess, your grace? I have committed no sin.'

'I see . . . and what of the strange words used over the child? What of those?'

The infirmarian looked in the abbot's direction, but remained silent.

'Answer me! What are these words you use to occasion your hellish cures? Perhaps an innocent peasant who has never heard a man command the chiefs of infernal legions would think such words strange! Perhaps an uncorrupted soul may never have heard the names of the fallen angels Armaros, Barakel, Azazel, Batraal, Ananel, Amazarak, Zazel!'

The room became alive with the cries of anguished

monks making the sign of the cross and reciting formulas against the evil eye.

'Are these the captains of hell whom you call on to aid you in your fiendish work?' he asked.

The infirmarian's eye was steady as he answered, 'No.'

'Please enlighten us . . .' He took in the entire congregation with his right arm, 'We are waiting.'

'We use words of comfort . . . holy words.'

'Holy words, I see . . .' he smiled malevolently. 'Holy words, but to whom are they deemed holy, to God or to the Devil!'

The infirmarian did not answer.

'Well then,' the inquisitor resumed, 'if you will not answer us, we shall have to accept this as a sign of your guilt.'

'How shall I continue, your grace, for if I say 'holy' you ask to whom? If I say 'good' you say this good is bad because I say it! It has always been my understanding that holy meant holy and not otherwise!'

'There are many heresies whose infernal doctrines are considered holy by their adherents! I only wish to know what these strange and magical words are,' he ended mildly.

The infirmarian changed weight from one foot to another uncomfortably, 'It is sacred, it cannot be openly discussed. I have taken an oath not to divulge it to anyone, on pain of death,' he said.

'So!' Rainiero smiled, satisfied. 'You are prepared to face death, rather than divulge your Catharan practices! You forget that I was once one of you. I know one gives the *consolamentum* just prior to death, this no doubt you gave the child, thinking it was going to die . . . but it lived! And alas you have been discovered. We need no further mention of these unlawful secrets for fear of staining our souls with their depravity, for it is enough that you will not divulge them. That is sufficient testament to your guilt!' he thundered. It was at that moment that my master interjected.

'Rainiero, I am ignorant in these matters and so I pray you will indulge me; I fail to see that there is much that associates the infirmarian, or indeed the cook, with the crimes of which they have been accused. There is no poison, no weapon, and as far as accusations are concerned, in many instances, as you know, they are falsely given. Heretics have been known to come forward and accuse pious men of heresy in order to confound the inquisition.'

The inquisitor turned his countenance in my master's direction, a benevolent, patient smile on his angular features. 'Firstly, brother Templar,' he said very slowly, 'we have heard that the cook has a history of heresy, we have heard that his soul became the seed bed of sin when he conspired with those whose intentions were to overthrow the church and the pope in favour of the emperor, by killing bishops and priests and defiling churches, and destroying the holy vessels! If this sin weren't enough, we then hear how he bathed this abbey with the blood of three men! This he freely confesses!'

On this point my master could not argue further and he sat down. Rainiero, satisfied that he had won, continued, 'Furthermore, it becomes obvious from his intimations that the infirmarian has aided him in this crime by supplying him with the poisoned herb! It is my belief that there is ample proof! Sorcerers often disguise themselves in the garb of physicians,' he glanced at my master significantly, 'because they can command the forces of evil without incurring suspicion! Because with their infernal cures they hope to secure the souls of their patients!'

'And yet, your grace,' Asa responded, 'we are told that a physician should be honoured for his works . . .'

'Only a heretic would be so well acquainted with Apocryphal writings!' he cried sharply, showing all how well he knew them, 'but should we honour sorcerers and whore-mongers, and murderers, and idolaters? Should we venerate whosoever loveth and maketh a lie? I say no! For I have further proof that you have been dabbling in the pot of Mammon!' He produced from the folds of his habit a small jar. 'You see what one finds when one searches the infirmary of an infidel? One finds jars on which strange Arabic, and therefore diabolical, letters have been inscribed.'

'This was given to the abbey many years ago by a brother who had just returned from the east, where he came upon this most wonderful cure for ulcerations,' Asa explained.

'The benefits of this infernal medicine are not my concern! It is better for a devout man to die than to be healed through the labours of the sons of mischief. And this!' He held up the strange instrument that Asa had used a short time ago on the young Trencavel to measure his fever. 'This is the tool of Satan.'

All faces were aghast. Many nodded their heads, perhaps because it was easier to believe the inquisitor and escape his justice than to remain loyal to a man who was already burnt flesh.

'It is becoming clear now that we are not dealing with a simple physician who works through orthodox prayer, using his simple hands to care for the infirm. NO! Answer me, oh, irreverent villain! Did you, or did you not, supply the herb by which three good men were killed at the hands of the cook?'

The man was silent. Oh dear reader, what a terrible silence it was! A sign of guilt?

'Perhaps . . .' Asa answered. 'There are many instances in which herbs and compounds of various kinds are used in a monastery . . . I could have given it to him unwittingly.

'Nothing done by the followers of Satan is done unwittingly, but willingly and gladly! Now answer me, do you or do you not conduct heretical practices on patients whose simple souls you seek to put to fiendish use?' he shouted, moving off the dais and onto the floor.

'I heal the sick when it is possible to do so, that is my job.'

'And you will tell us that your conduct has been authorised, nay, condoned by your abbot and master?'

Now Asa looked visibly unsure, oppressed by the weight of a thousand divergent thoughts.

'Answer me, by God!'

'I alone am responsible for the infirmary.'

'That is not what I asked you!'

He looked to the abbot, who, on his elevated seat, gave his monk a stern look.

'I am a physician!'

'Answer me!'

Asa was defiantly silent. The inquisitor's eyes narrowed and he moved around the infirmarian as does a cat, about to pounce on a mouse. 'If you do not answer me, I shall have to resort to measures which are odious and do no less than revolt the soul of the most hardened man. For the law is clear, God's justice must prevail, as it has since the beginning of time.' He raised one hand. 'Show this devil the instruments by which the truth shall be extracted and then take him to a place of confinement. Let his arms and legs be bound with irons. Let guilt ferment in his soul and for a time let him reflect on the evil that he has perpetrated. By degrees we shall see how long his lips remain sealed, for we will not be inspired by haste!'

'I invoke the bier right! *Jus feretri, jus cruentationis!* ' Asa cried and the congregation was startled, the abbot stood as did my master and the other members of the legation.

Rainiero gestured to his archers. 'Bring in the body and we shall see it if bleeds at the touch of the murderer!' and the men responded immediately.

There was confusion. I did not know what a 'bier right' was, or what it meant to 'bleed at the touch of the murderer' and I wished more than ever that I had my master at my side to enlighten me.

Moments later three men carried in the body of the dead Brother Daniel, blue and lifeless, his head now black with congealed blood. Around me monks were praying, holding up their crucifixes as the archers set the body down rather carelessly and stood aside. The inquisitor moved forward and began the prayer:

'Oh God, just judge, firm and patient, who art the author of peace and judgest truly, determine what is right, oh Lord, and make known Thy righteous judgement. We humbly beseech Thee that iniquity may not overcome justice, but that falsehood may be subjected to truth. Let this man come forth and touch the corpse, and if he be the murderer, oh Lord, let the corpse bleed from the nose or the mouth or any wound, so that Thy grace may detect diabolical and human fallacies, to confute the inventions and arguments of the enemy, and to overcome their multiform arts. May the guilty be justly condemned through Thine begotten Son, our Lord Jesus Christ who dwelleth with Thee. Amen.'

The inquisitor then gestured for Asa to come to the body. There was silence. 'Touch with two fingers the mouth, the navel and the wounds,' he said.

Asa stood over the dead bundle on the stone floor of the chapter house, perhaps saying a silent prayer. I could see him tremble a little as he leant forward and did as he had been commanded; firstly he touched the mouth, then the area of the navel and the man's disfigured head.

There was a pregnant pause and then a sudden gasp. I could see nothing, for monks had left their seats and were standing as a great agitation took hold of everyone. I heard voices crying out, 'It is true! It is true!' and again, 'The murderer!'

'Lo, behold! The cry of blood from the earth against the murderer!' the inquisitor exclaimed.

I did not see it, but I was to learn later that blood had oozed from the mouth of the carcass.

The judges and my master stepped down from the dais to have a better look. I could only see the tops of their heads.

'But the body has been moved,' I heard my master argue, 'when it should have been left out in the open air without movement for some hours, with breast and stomach bare to ensure a thorough coagulation of the blood!'

There was a loud murmur. I heard voices disputing whether the bleeding was occasioned by antipathy or sympathy, by the remains of the soul in the body, or by the wandering spirit of the dead man.

The inquisitor ordered quiet, saying, 'The causes are sometimes natural and sometimes supernatural. In this case it matters little, the blood is there, it is a sign that this man is lying in the name of the Devil!'

At about this time the cook began to laugh hysterically (having been aroused from his previous stupor by the great commotion). Incredulity filled the room, even the inquisitor was startled. I pushed my way to the front in order to see.

'You are the Devil!' the cook spat at the foot of the inquisitor, and his voice having acquired a semblance of its old strength roared and reverberated around us. 'I am glad that I have finally confessed my sins to God, for now I can savour death! But not this good, kind monk who has done nothing! I am the murderer, I am the heretic! I have denied the past for long years, and I soon will be cleansed and purified *en la flama* – the flames of the *Espirito Santo*. But you? If there is *justicia,* if there is fairness in this miserable world, may you suffer agonies as I have suffered in knowing you and having followed you into the arms of the Devil! You betrayed us because you loved power and you lay with the bishops and the pope and denied all that you taught us! Yes, is true, I wanted the end of Rome, the end of the pope! But this is not different from what you also had one time believed with all your heart . . . and yes! The emperor! I would give my life for him because he hated the church!'

'He was the antichrist! Guards, seize this man!'

The guards moved forward to take the cook, but he was strong, and with the power afforded him by anger, pushed them away as one would an annoying insect.

'No! I know what you came for . . . you came for me, not these poor monks . . .!'

The inquisitor smiled, and stayed his men with one hand.

'All of my life I lived hiding from the past like a rat, *como un ratón*. Used by Frederick, used by the Ghibellines . . .' He sighed deeply. 'A used man today is used no more! When I met you, Rainiero Sacconi, I was very young, and you used me also, used all of us and like an orange you spat us out when you were *convertido,* converted, changed, transformed into a whore who licks the hems of bishops' skirts by killing all of us that you knew from those days . . . *mi amor,* my love, *Teresa una mujer perfecta,* you burned her to death! But first, you tortured her little body until there was *nada,* no more life, bringing her naked with others to the crowds, and they spit on her, and poke at her. After the *humillación,* her body was tied to the pyre and lit like a torch, and her beautiful hair, gold like copper, turned black and melted on her little skull as she fell, because the ropes they break, and her little lungs choked on the smoke, and her heart exploded from the great heat. And I . . .' he cried like a child, 'I was in the crowds, like a coward, *cobarde!* I did not die with all of the ones that I once knew! *O qué miseria!* Wretched, wretched coward that I am! I did not save her! She was so brave that when she saw me, she smiled! She smiled because she was happy *qué había escapado* – the coward had escaped! And God forgive me I was glad also!' He covered his face with large twisted hands and wept.

'Tell me what I want to know.' Rainiero had the same look on his face that I recalled my master having in the library when he pursued the secret codices – ravenous.

'Yes, yes . . . it was I, with Stefano, Manfredo, and Carino, waiting for Piero to leave Como that Easter week. I followed him and the friar Domenico to Barlassina until we came on a lonely place. Carino opened Piero's head with one blow, but I saw that he breathed and put a dagger in his heart. That day I made up for letting her die! I avenged my sorrow! Again I ran away . . . Today

I am no more *cobarde!* I killed the old brothers before they could betray my secret . . . The infirmarian knew *nada!*'

'Enough! Enough! Peace! You instrument of evil! Nothing that he says can be trusted . . . and yet we have heard from his own lips his confession and although the infirmarian will not confess, his crimes are visible on the corpse of his victim. One can only hope that he does so before we commend his body to the earth and his soul to hell. Take them away.' He ordered the guards to remove the two men. The cook now exhausted and outwardly defeated, went willingly, though on his face there was the glow of an inner triumph.

There was silence. Rainiero waited, satiated.

'And so this interrogation would now be over,' he said finally, 'if not for one terrible addition . . .' He paused a moment, lifting his head, surveying the faces of those whose fear must have been legible. 'It is the task of the holy inquisition, not only to find heresy where it is evidenced, but also to recognise its supporters and heirs. For it is well known that the heretical depravity, like a foul seed, needs a suitable womb, an infernal bed into which it may be planted, nurtured and brought to incarnation. We know, firstly, that those who visit with heretics or live with them are their friends, since one cannot live, or visit, with a heretic, and be ignorant of his dissent. The three brothers who were killed, we have learnt today, were Cathars. The missing brother also shared in their lamentable dissent. We must therefore surmise that heresy has found a safe harbour, in the bosom of God's house! Within these venerable walls!'

Cold whispers circulated round the chapter house and were stilled by the raising of a hand. Satisfied, he continued, 'Further signs that alert us to the supporters of heresy are as follows: those who declare the unjust condemnation of heretics,' as he said this he glanced at my master, 'those who look away and allow heresy to bloom and take hold. Those who venerate, one, the bones of burnt heretics, and two, relics belonging to heretics, or books written by them! Therefore we cannot find otherwise! This abbey is guilty! Guilty on all accounts!' There was a commotion, the abbot stood and the archers, sensing panic, readied at the doors, 'For I know,' he continued, 'that below us in the hellish bowels of this monastery there are books hidden that have been deemed heretical by the church, whose infernal substance aims to bring about the downfall of Christendom! Therefore it is the finding of this tribunal that these crimes cannot, nay they should not, be attributed solely to the two men just taken away, though they may indeed be devils, for like a father who is responsible for the actions of his children, so too is an abbot responsible for the actions of his monks. In this case, responsible for the corruption of the souls placed in his care. I therefore pronounce, as rare and distressing as it is to utter these words, that the abbot is to be taken along with the other two to Paris, where together they shall be delivered to the secular authorities for purification by fire.'

There was great agitation. Monks stood, some cried out, 'No!', others made the sign of the cross, still others shook their heads in their hands, in lamentation.

'This monastery is to be closed,' Rainiero continued. 'Satan has lived here too long, too patiently, for it to be restored as a place of worship. Its displaced community of monks may find harbour in other institutions if any will take them. They will perform a penance by wearing yellow crosses on their clothing, so that all may know they have been tainted with heresy. Finally, all properties are to be turned over to the church and secular powers.'

Now there was a stunned silence, as the abbot was led off his dais and removed.

They found the bishop in the lavatory shortly after vespers, in one of the cubicles. It was a gruesome sight.

Because of his size he was still perched on the seat with

his great buttocks wedged tight against either wall, keeping him
from falling into the channel of water beneath. His face was
bloated and running down his chin the familiar substance, which
we now knew to be the thick honey content of the wine. His
obscene cross was gone.

'Just as I thought, our missing wine,' Andre said to me.
'The stupid wretch must have run out of it in his own room and
proceeded to the larder where he found the poisoned flask.' He
picked up the jug with the crooked handle and then he inspected
the man's shoes – no mud.

The inquisitor, seizing the moment, ordered an immediate
execution of the three men held responsible for the other crimes,
saying that the Devil would not cease his work until his instruments were purified by fire. At once he ordered the building of
three pyres inside the compound, saying that the service of compline would be carried out as usual in an effort to stay the hand of
the enemies of Christ, but that immediately after, the abbey would
be cleansed of evil.

In the confusion that ensued we crept away and I followed my master in the direction of the church. Outside the inquisitor's men were already making preparations for the terrible
event. Monks gathered around aimlessly, for there was little use
returning to any other work when the future of the monastery
lay in ruins. I frowned, pushing my head down further into my
cowl as we made our approach to the church.

'Will they not notice that we have gone, master?'

'Perhaps, but we cannot waste any more time. Soon there
will be three pyres burning two innocent men, and tomorrow
this place will be a carcass whose bones will have been picked
by the pope's greedy captains. We must get into the catacombs
soon!' he said.

'So who is responsible for these crimes? You said two
innocent men would die on the pyre, that means one is guilty.'

'A fine deduction,' he mocked me. 'Perhaps soon you will

see, Christian, why Aristotle was right when he said that evidence under torture is not trustworthy because under its compulsion men tell lies quite as often as they tell the truth. I fear there are a number of guilty persons. Perhaps in one way or another we are all guilty.'

'Who then, master?' I pressed. 'I know you know something.'

'One of them it is certain is a monk with small feet,' he answered as we entered the church. 'This morning after the discovery of Daniel's body, when you were sleeping off your gluttony in the larder, I visited his room again. Something bothered me, and I realised it was the size of the footprint on the floor. Before going there, however, I took the liberty of procuring a sandal that belonged to Daniel from the infirmary. I took it to his room and found that its size was inconsistent with the size of the print whose traces could still be seen – because blood that has congealed is not always easy to remove in haste. The print was not our departed brother's, but belonged rather to someone else, someone with very small feet. Do you remember how I said that the one who hit me on the head that morning also had small feet?'

'Yes . . . That means that we have finally found the evidence that we need to connect the author of our notes with the killer!'

'Yes, but only with Daniel's killer.'

'Then whoever it is must have killed Setubar, too?'

'That is what we are going to find out.'

'I thought we were going to the church?'

'Later. Anyone who saw us leave would naturally think so, and that is precisely what I intend them to think. We are really going elsewhere . . . to the infirmarian's cell.'

Once through the church we made our way up the night stairs and to the dormitorium. Andre led me to a room identical to all the others, and here he began searching about, inside a small desk, under the pallet, rummaging in the straw very carefully, until, after a moment, he exclaimed, 'Aha!' He had retrieved a short metal bar that he placed in the repository within the folds of his vestments.

'What is it, master?'

'The murder weapon,' he answered, and it was as plain as day Asa was the killer.

He looked at me with a satisfied look. 'It is as I suspected. Now we shall return to the church and await the service. We must not give the inquisitor reason to believe we know more than he thinks we know, must we?'

'If Asa is the killer, master, why did he demand to endure the ordeal?'

'Asa is a man of science, I believe he took a chance, he was doomed anyway and he knew it.'

'But master, come to think of it, Asa is not small.'

'No. See this note?' My master handed it to me. 'I found it in my room earlier.'

I read it, and found it was written in the same identifiable hand and blue ink.

Physician heal thyself – Basmallah.

'What is that word?'

'It is Arabic, a Koranic formula which translates to: in the name of God the compassionate, the merciful.'

'But what does it mean?'

'Numerically it is profoundly significant, Christian, for it connotes the seven planets and the twelve zodiacal signs. We are told that he who desires immunity against the nineteen henchmen of hell needs to recite the Basmallah.'

I gasped, trembling all over, 'Oh! He threatens your life, master, he knew you would understand it.'

'Hush now, Christian, soon all will be revealed.'

22

Capitulum

'And he dreamed, and behold a ladder set up on the earth,
and the top of it reached to heaven.'
GENESIS xxviii 12

hristian,' the man said, 'you have come finally. I have been waiting.' 'Who are you?' I asked, for he looked peculiar, like an Arab in his dress, and yet not like an Arab at all.

'My name is not important, only the words. Listen.' He looked about him at the nothingness. 'Listen to the key, for with it one can open the rings of knowledge.'

'The rings?'

Suddenly I heard it, like the duration of eternity, or a moment of liquid purity; pinnacles of resonance, columns of exuberance, the spinning vibrations of space that is *circumiectus* then *internus*. Oh, raised cusps of praise! Singing, sighing neptunian notes in aeolian and dorian scales of concordance. Miracle of being, oh majesty! Oh dissolving, diffusing, dispersing notes of joy, fear, pain, tears, wails! Limb-limbering, movement-inspiring, howling, weeping, laughing, telluric and celestial *vocalisms* and *melismas!* And as my heart was dazzled by the articulate eloquence of an origin indiscernible and unanimous, multifarious and exposed, I heard myself say in wonderment:

'What is this I hear?'

'The spinning of the rings of wisdom .'

'But I do not understand.'

'Do you think that bodies so great do not produce sound with their motion?' He pointed to the inky mantle pierced by light. 'Even bodies on the earth do so. You must remember that the stars and planets move about the universe at a tremendous speed and their sound is concordant.'

'But I have never heard it before.'

'You have heard it always, and so you do not hear it, for sound is only perceived when there is silence.'

'The pause!' I said.

'Yes,' he answered. 'The psalms reflect the tones whose rings are pure, the voice resonates forth and brings about creation. One day man will speak forth man. Even now his breath is filled with the promise of tomorrow.'

'And the key?'

'It has been hidden in the words . . . hear the words and the rings will sound.'

Then . . .

'Whosoever discovers the interpretation of these sayings will not taste death. Those who seek should not stop seeking until they find. When they find, they will be disturbed. When they are disturbed, they will marvel, and will reign over all. When you make two into one, and when you make the inner like the outer and the outer like the inner and the upper like the lower, and when you make male and female into a single one, so that the male will not be male nor the female be female, then you will enter the father's domain...Remember that is how a god became man, and a man became a god!

'Who are you?' I asked.

'I am the one who doubted. My eye were crossed but now I see!'

'Thomas Didymus?' I gasped.

'You have heard the message. Now listen to the rings.'

23

Capitulum

Shortly after the Service of Compline

hristian!' I heard once again, but this time it was not St Thomas, it was my master, and I knew that I had dreamt. 'Master, where am I, what time . . .?' I sat up rubbing my eyes.

'You slept through the service, dear boy . . . Anselmo was missing.'

'Anselmo?' I said in a foggy way. 'Oh! He must be dead!' I saw that the brothers were leaving in a single file through the north transept, led by the inquisitor and the prelates. 'Where are they going?' I asked, disorientated. 'To the pyres.' I blanched. 'Now?' My master sighed. He seemed infinitely tired. 'The prisoners await their fate outside.'

He helped me up, and soon we were tagging on the end of the line, following the solemn procession into the snowy cemetery grounds, where three stakes were erected atop a pile of faggots and straw. I realised that it must have snowed heavily while we were celebrating the holy service, for now the mud made by hail was covered with a soft powdery white that the wind (growing angrier with each moment) scattered about us like little phantoms. It was dark, but the area around the pyres was well lit by torches, for tonight all must bear witness to God's justice.

We waited in anxious silence. I admonished myself for being fooled by my affection for Asa and my dislike of Anselmo who, no doubt, either lay in a pool of blood or was poisoned. I recognised that my master had indeed been right when he had told me to deliberate without emotion.

Finally the prisoners were brought before the inquisitor and my heart sank as I watched Asa climb the ladder to the top of the pyre. Though I knew now that he must be guilty, I felt for him, his face so thin and gaunt, his eyes resolute. Were they the eyes of a killer? I asked myself. They did not seem so. And yet, if I had learnt anything these last terrible days, it was that the Devil was cunning indeed.

The wind whistled ever louder in our ears, and it began to snow as the abbot passed us, holding his head high. In his eyes, however, I noted that he was already dead. A little way off, as he was about to ascend the pyre, a loyal monk ran to him and sank to his knees embracing his paternity desperately, whimpering and crying out in his own vernacular something I did not understand.

The poor cook had to be half-carried to the pyre by two burly guards, tears making clear byways down his dirty face. He missed a step here and there as he ascended the ladder, nearly falling to the ground below at one point, but was helped by an archer, who had been designated the unenviable position of executioner. Later when the fire had consumed the bodies it would be his job to separate what was left of the carcasses, breaking up the bones, and throwing the viscera on a fresh fire of logs. I closed my eyes and said an *ave* that this nightmare might soon end, for surely I was dreaming!

Once they were all tied firmly to the stake, firstly at the ankles, below the knees, above the knees, at the groin, the waist, and under the arms, a heavy chain was secured about their necks. Their sentences were then read out by the inquisitor, who bellowed his strong voice over a gust, which made his habit flap around him like black and white flames.

'In the name of the Father and of the Son and of the Holy Ghost. Amen. We, Brother Rainiero Sacconi, of the Order of Dominican Friars, inquisitor appointed to investigate heresy in the Kingdom of France and Italy, being the representative of Apostolic Authority; we, Brother Andre – Preceptor of Douzens having special licence from the King of France; and we, Friar Bertrand de Narbonne of the Order of Friars Preachers emissary from the Priory of Pruille; and Father Bernard Fontaine of the Order of Cistercians at Citeaux, by divine authority of the pope have found and had it proved before us that you . . . *In nomine Domini amen . . .*'

I did not hear the rest, my mind became strangely numb, and it was only when the executioner covered the accused under faggots and straw up to their waists that I regained my senses in time to hear my master murmur.

'We must go.'

I looked at him with hot tears running down my cold face, 'But we have to help them!'

'They are dead men, Christian,' he said abruptly and I was filled with anger. Now I am wiser, and I know that my master could do nothing. He simply wished to spare me the terrible sight that no one but God could now prevent. But at that moment I must say that I thought him a coward, and further, a coward whose sole preoccupation was in solving his puzzle.

As we sank to the back of the crowd, I saw the young maiden Trencavel and her father. They did not look at us as we passed. I wondered if the boy was still alive and said a prayer for Eisik as we headed for the church and the executioner lit more faggots and threw them into the pyres.

Once inside, Andre ran to the organ, pulling at his beard nervously and mumbling.

'What are we doing master?'

'We are going to try and salvage something from out of

all this mess,' he said. 'What do these strange numerals mean, for the love of God . . . If they are a clue to diverting the water channel, how is it to be read? By Saladin . . .! Now, if you were to leave a coded message, titled *Cantus Pastoralis* ...'

We heard the screams, faint, pitiful, then there was silence and the smell of burning hair. I looked at my master and, for a moment, I believe I knew him not at all. He was a man taken utterly by his obsession, a man drunk with curiosity. Could he have forgotten his mission? Could he have forgotten that men were burning, that the monastery was condemned, and that our lives were in peril?

'Master,' I was out of breath, 'we have failed in our duty! We have failed the king, we have failed to save the Trencavel boy, we have failed our order and those who are missing or dying on the pyre though they are innocent! It is all in ruins, and yet here you stand reflecting, as if . . . as if you were deliberating a chess move, as if you had all the time in the world and not a care! I believe you are no better than the inquisitor! There, I have said it! Both of you are proud and stubborn and obsessed and I begin to see the line that distinguishes you only faintly,' I blurted out. 'One hates knowledge beyond mercy, beyond humanity, and the other loves it beyond compassion, beyond human reasoning. Knowledge is knowledge, master, but what happens to those who gain it if they have no heart? Why must you try to decipher that Godforsaken code now? We must find Eisik, we must . . . we must forget the code. Who cares about shepherd's songs, who cares also about the tunnels and the silent ones and codices and gospels? We should be praying for forgiveness!' Tears streamed down my face unheeded but my master did not notice, instead his face lit up like a candle.

'What did you say?'

'I said I do not care about shepherd's songs! I said that we should be praying, not preparing to go into tunnels. I do not want to go into the tunnels again, I want to leave this place! Since our arrival all I do is dream strange dreams about saints and psalms . . .'

'The psalms! Of course! *Aspectus illuminatus!* The songs of the shepherd . . . brilliant! Brilliant, my boy!' he grabbed me by the shoulders and shoved me toward the pulpit. 'Quickly, go to the great book of hours and when I read out the numerals you must look up the corresponding psalm and verse. Come, come, we don't have much time, the dog is at this moment falling on our scent.'

My master closed his eyes and attempted, I assumed, to tame the agitation that he felt. When he deemed himself calmer he read out the first numerals, namely, CL: IV, psalm one-hundred-and-fifty, verse four. I read it out, for I could not disobey him. 'Praise him with the timbrel and dance: praise him with stringed instruments and organs.'

My master nodded his head and rubbed his hands in anticipation. 'It is telling us that we are on the right path, namely, the organ.'

He stood, facing the great instrument, as he called out the next numerals, CIII: XIX, Psalm one-hundred-and-three, verse nineteen. It read, 'The lord hath prepared his throne . . .'

My master sat upon the stool in front of the keys as if he were being commanded.

CXLII: IV, Psalm one-hundred-and-forty-two, verse four, I looked on my right . . .' He did so.

CXLIII: VI, Psalm one-hundred-and-forty-three, verse six, 'I stretch forth my hands unto thee . . .' 'Aha! It is telling us that it is a musical note, a key,' Andre concluded. I was a little sceptical, but said nothing.

The next numerals were XC: XII, Psalm ninety, verse twelve, 'So teach us to number our days, that we may apply our hearts unto wisdom.'

'It is a number of notes, or perhaps one note in a numerical sequence.'

CXLIV: IX, Psalm one-hundred-and-forty-four, verse nine, 'I will sing a new song unto thee, O God: upon a psaltery and an instrument of ten strings will I sing praises unto thee.'

My master narrowed his eyes. 'The number ten.'

But it was the next – CVII: XXXIII, Psalm one-hundredand-seven, verse thirty-three – that showed me how little I knew, and once again bore witness to the extent of my master's vast wisdom and acumen. 'He turneth rivers into a wilderness, and the watersprings into dry ground.'

I looked at my master as I said this and my eyes must have been very wide because he smiled and said a little immodestly, 'Why so surprised? I am rarely wrong . . . Now we know that the organ is the lock, and the key is a number, or rather, a musical note . . . the number ten is the only number mentioned. Therefore we must surmise that ten notes to the right of the middle note of Ut, as we learnt in the library the other day.'

'In any case, how will we know if we are right?'

'If the organ works we will know that the water has been diverted. At least that is one hypothesis in a million.'

'But how do we know it is diverted from the channel in question?'

He fixed me with an icy stare and whispered so harshly that it echoed in the vastness of the church, 'Do not confound me with logic now, boy! We shall cross that stream when we come to it! Now, let me see...' He counted ten notes from Ut or as it is known middle C and pressed his index finger down on the note F or Fa, but nothing happened. He frowned, thinking for a moment. 'Daniel admonished us to 'Let the hymn baptise us with the nine resonances of water'. Perhaps it is not the tenth note from the middle Ut, by God's bonnet! But the ninth which when one includes Ut is actually the tenth!'

I was confused and angry with him, but some part of me was proud also.

However, just as my master was to press the ninth note

or rather the tenth including the middle Ut that was E or Mi, we heard someone behind us.

'I thought if I waited you would have worked out everything for me!' the inquisitor cried, flanked by two of his biggest men.

My master turned to him calmly, 'Rainiero, how fortunate, I was about to play the requiem.' He placed his hands on the keys as though he were about to depress the note.

'Stop!' the inquisitor cried.

'Why? What bothers you? Is it your conscience?'

'I have no time for folly . . . You know well enough what I am after. The old Cathar has disappeared without telling me the combination. I know that you are familiar with the access, and so together we shall go to the catacombs and you, who are most experienced, will guide the way.'

My master did not move, he said nothing.

'You must know that I mean to learn everything, even if I have to resort to distressing means, preceptor. Right at this moment my guards have seized your Jew. They await my orders. Should I tell you by what methods the inquisition extracts the truth from devils? I am sure you are acquainted with them, though your squire may not be.' He glanced at me with cold eyes.

'Leave the boy out of it!' cried Andre, getting up, his face red with anger, 'and furthermore, leave Eisik out of it as well. He has nothing to do with any of it!'

'No? Well I tend to disagree with you, preceptor. As I have told you, Jews are fomenters of dissent, known to dabble in necromancy and other unspeakable practices. It would take very little to convince the other members of the legation that he had some part to play in the murderous crimes.'

What was my master to do?

'All I seek from you, preceptor, is the truth.'

'Rainiero, you don't seek the truth, you seek your idea of what truth is and these are two different things.'

'My dear brother,' Rainiero seemed amused, 'there is only one truth!'

'And you think you extract it under torture? You are a fool, and an evil one at that!'

Outside, the earth rumbled in response, like the sound, John tells us, of the chariots of many horses running to battle, but the inquisitor smiled. 'In my experience, preceptor, there is pain in every truth, and therefore it is through pain that we come to know it. Like a child who is born into the world through the anguish of his mother – one instant of joy and a lifetime of sorrow – leading finally to the end, again, through pain. Do you see? You think of pain, and in it you observe only the detestable. I, on the other hand, can see only the holy.' His smile broadened, as though he were contemplating a truly wonderful idea. 'For pain, preceptor, is the purifying substance that denies nothing. Through it the mind becomes free because once it has tasted the greatest suffering, the body, whose sin is the seeking of pleasant things, is finally overcome. Pain is the gateway to God, the gateway to divine bliss, and celestial joy.'

These words reminded me of Brother Setubar, and I wondered if the inquisitor persecuted heretics so vehemently because he could never be free of his own heresy that, no matter how deeply hidden, managed to bubble to the surface like oil?

'No, you are wrong,' my master said bitterly, having lost his composure altogether, 'what you call bliss is only the absence of pain, which is a contrast to the most intense pain and nothing else. Just as someone who has never seen white might contrast grey with black. It is an illusion, and so, too, do you delude yourself. Never having known joy, you naturally suppose that pain is necessary and the absence of it blissful . . . but how can you ever be sure that what you hear from the mouths of those wretched and abused souls is the truth, and not merely a reflection of what they see in your eyes?'

'So says an infidel. Because that is what you are. Oh, yes,

you may wear a cross over your breast and a prayer on your lips, but I know that you are a man who whispers Allah in your sleep, a man not trusted by either Christian or infidel. Everything you have said and done these days has pointed to your dissent. Do not presume to know the mystery of torture and absolution, preceptor, it is vouchsafed only to a few.'

'A few who desire intensely to hear those things they are told, not because they are true, but simply because they want them to be true.' He gave me a look (his hand poised over the note). In it I discerned the message: 'When I depress it, run for the panel.'

'Do you know, preceptor, what anguish I have suffered? Tortured always on the one hand because I may have convicted an innocent man to die, and at the same time knowing that there are those whose deception has allowed them to evade the law, so that they may continue their destruction of the church!' Suddenly I saw the inquisitor's face take on a form almost human. I now sensed that he truly believed that what he did was right, and this filled me with further uncertainties. 'Can you for one moment comprehend such a dilemma? How can one ever know if he is avoiding the deceptions of the Devil, the misunderstandings to which he lures us? One no longer knows in these terrible times what distinguishes good from evil! So it is that we must let God choose for us. It is God, not as you would say, the Devil, who speaks through the mouths of those who are tortured because, in the throes of pain, that He too suffered for our sins, they see His shining light and cannot do otherwise than confess their own! You see? And so saying, I will remind you that one night with my guards will have your Jew begging to tell me everything, as God commands him, but I will not see him, not for three nights in which he will suffer countless agonies . . .'

Suddenly there was a deafening roar that shook the monastery church. It sent the book vibrating off the pulpit, and the inquisitor to the ground.

How am I to narrate the moments that followed? Things happen so quickly and yet so slowly.

As we heard the sound, my master – with unequalled presence of mind – depressed the note on the organ, but the inquisitor was upon him and they were struggling in the shadow of the pipes as a wall of snow hit the monastery from above, breaking through the rose window and flooding the church.

Almost instantly I could see nothing but white, an opaquely cold world filled with a light numbing. The white became grey, then black, and I no longer cared one way or the other . . . the struggle would soon be over. Images passed before my eyes. From out of the mist I saw Asa dressed like a goose, waving his glass instrument at the abbot who appeared in the shape of a monkey and did not look in his direction. The abbot was busy holding a phial of poisoned urine to the cook's lips who drank of it gladly saying that it was like the nectar of the gods, while Setubar sat back, laughing as though the end had come and so he could be merry, 'Levity in a nut is a sign of its emptiness!' he cried, after which he climbed atop the back of a devil but not before giving me raisins that were sweet like the breasts of the sainted mother who was the beloved of my dreams and who held in one hand a rose cross and in the other Eisik's severed head from whose mouth came these words, 'No good will come of it!' There were voices then, and thunderings, and lightnings and an earthquake, and I was an angel in the midst of heaven saying with a loud voice, woe, woe, woe to the inhabitors of the earth for they were wrenched down to the bottomless pit where arose smoke like the smoke of a great furnace and so a terrible pain assailed my chest. But I realised that it was not the Devil plunging his great white teeth into my lungs and tearing out my heart but my master who, having pulled me out of that dry, powdery sea, was hitting my back with much force. The vastness of the organ, with its pipes and keys, had preserved him and the inquisitor also.

'Keep sharp, boy!' he cried as I spat out so much snow.

'Don't go dying on me, by Saladin!'

He grabbed a lamp from the wall behind the organ, miraculously still lit, and seeing that the inquisitor was unconscious, pushed or rather pulled me down what was left of the north ambulatory and into the transept chapel. I saw the Virgin only faintly, for I was then shoved behind the curtain where both of us stopped to listen to the terrible silence. The pause. I knew instinctively that it was only a herald of the next beat.

Another roar shook everything. 'Quickly, the panel.' My master depressed the corresponding symbols releasing the lock and we were diving down into the bowels of the abbey once again.

The rest was a blur of images. We stumbled through the tunnels, in and out of antechambers, following our previous tortuous path, not caring to leave anything in the way of the doors, for there would be no turning back. I thought with sorrow of our dear friend Eisik, perhaps buried somewhere, I thought of the monks and the Trencavels and I prayed silently for them all. Above our heads a great stirring could be heard and here and there rocks had fallen, making our path hazardous, but we reached the second-last antechamber with little mishap. It was as we entered 'Philadelphia' and our lamp shone into its interior that we saw the figure of a monk sitting in an awkward way, his head to one side, obscured by his vestments. My master held the lamp to the monk's face and pulled back his cowl to reveal the identity of the poor wretch. It was Setubar.

His face now showed the familiar signs of the poison; dark honey was smeared everywhere. I concluded that he must have taken his own life.

He was not yet dead, however, for his eyes opened suddenly, causing me to gasp in surprise.

'So,' he coughed, 'you have found your way, very good. . . now you must stop them . . . go . . . . Stop them, Templar!' He managed to raise himself a little and grabbed my master's habit with his gnarled hands, letting some raisins fall to the floor.

'Your legs are broken,' Andre observed, bending over the man, and noticing the unnatural angle of his legs.

The old man winced. 'The devil is here! Stop them!'

'Tell me, Setubar!' my master said in a commanding voice that took the old man by surprise.

There was a pause in which Setubar took in a torturous breath and then, perhaps hoping my master would accomplish what he in his wretched state could not do, he told him everything.

'Nine . . .' He swallowed. 'Nine knights were initiated into the secret doctrine of St John the Apostle. Into the mystery of the children of the widow . . . vouchsafed by Ormus disciple of St Mark.'

'Heresy!' I cried, alarmed.

The old man laughed, poison escaping from his mouth, 'Yes, my beautiful one, heresy! Your master knows it, as do all those who become knights.'

I looked at Andre in disbelief, but he said nothing.

'Beneath the Dome of the Rock . . . your order found . . .' he paused for breath, 'the original Tables of the Law written by Moses. The Pentateuch, or the first five books of the Old Testament that had been buried when Jerusalem was threatened with invasion many years before. No one knows the treasures and also the abominations hidden here on this mountain.'

My master was silent, reflecting, as though the earth were not moving around us and about to descend over our heads.

The man fought for lucidity, grasping feebly at his legs. 'Why do you think you were required to spit on the cross and deny Jesus at your initiation into the order?' the old man said. 'So that you would know what to do if you were captured by the infidel? Bah! You are a fool . . . you are all fools! You spit on the cross because it is evil. It represents the earthly death, the imperfection of men! And you also deny Jesus because Jesus was mortal and so full of sin. Christ was the God, not Jesus! You and I are not so different, preceptor, are we? We are cousins, so to speak! Ahh but you are proud, it does not sit well on your proud neck that your order is heretical, but it is this pride in your own erudition that I hope will do my bidding . . .' He trailed off, breathing with great difficulty now. 'They will use him to bring about a great sin . . . death and becoming, they will raise him from the dead!' He was seized by a terrible spasm in his abdomen. 'Do it! Stop them . . . do this, not for me, I am dung, do it for yourself . . . Can you hear the bees, boy?' He stared at me for a moment and then rolled his eyes, filled with sin and hatred and bitterness, into his head.

Andre said a short prayer over his body and under his breath I heard him say, 'The poor misguided fool.'

'Master . . . is what he says true? Did you . . . did you . . .?' I crossed myself, almost in tears, not knowing what to believe.

'Come!' my master grabbed me by the arm hastily, 'there is not much time!' I could see that he was right, for we experienced another loud vibration that sent me reeling unsteadily off my feet, landing only a short distance from the body.

'Master –' I insisted as we toiled down the next tunnel avoiding the rubble that had fallen there. 'How could you have? To deny Christ! To deny the cross!'

'There is no shame in denial, Christian, because in denying what we previously held to be true, we learn to see the truth more clearly. We discern knowledge from opinion, but what the old man doesn't know is that such temptations are a test from the devils in one's own soul, overcome time and again through fast and prayer. Of course I did not spit on the cross. I wear the red cross. The living cross not the dead one.' That was all he would say as he tugged at my arm and pointed me in the direction of the next tunnel.

I wanted him to leave me alone. His hand was on my arm, the hand that had so many times soothed my brow and slapped my nape. The strong, earthy, heathen hands, so brown and strong, appeared to me now soiled, stained with sin. He had been deceiving me. He had deceived even himself for he was not the man I thought he was nor the man he presumed himself to be. I was angry, feeling like a fool for having believed in him, but with impending doom looming over my head, I forced myself to follow him and concentrated on staying alive.

Finally we arrived at the last antechamber, and as we entered the room and our lamp shone its light into the darkness, who should we find but Anselmo sitting in the dark, holding an unlit torch, a discarded lamp at his feet.

He gave us a dreadful look, but did not bother to stand.

'Anselmo, good evening,' my master said cheerfully. 'I thought I might find you here. Why have you not gone into the inner sanctum, then?' he asked. 'We depressed the note, there should be no water.'

'Ahh, but preceptor, the mechanism is not triggered off by depressing the note, but by lifting it! Anyway, the avalanche has damaged it, and as I cannot swim . . .' He shrugged his shoulders. 'As you can see I ran out of taper, but I knew you were coming and I have been waiting. You must have passed Setubar . . . is he dead yet?'

'Very . . . Your doing, I suppose.'

'Yes. How well you guess, preceptor.'

'Naturally. But tell me, how could you be sure that we knew our way here, and the combinations?'

He smiled. 'You are an intelligent man, preceptor. From the first day of our meeting I knew that you were a match for me, I knew that given time you would find out everything.'

'But all these deaths have been for nothing, all this anguish which you and Setubar have brought about together, one out of curiosity, and the other out of a mad belief, for now you will never see what you so dearly desire to see, leaving your friend Asa to die on the pyre.'

'I had suspected for some time that Asa was not interested

in the wondrous treasures of the catacombs, he was seduced by the idea of the immortal man . . . as if there could ever be such a thing, and so he died for his ideal.'

'And what of poor Jerome, the friend whom you infected with your lust for the new, with your desire for the unknown?'

'Jerome is a sad case, he had an unnatural affection for me, he came here of his own accord to find the codices . . . the ass! No doubt he expected a kiss for his labours . . .' Anselmo laughed and it echoed down many tunnels. 'I was not sorry to find he had indeed been kissed . . . by death. But tell me, have you worked it all out yet? It intrigues me.'

'More or less,' he smiled proudly, and I prayed for his immortal soul.

The boy nodded and my master continued. 'Firstly, I realised that the monastery was founded by Templars sent here by the Grand Master Gerard of Ridefort, after the fall of Jerusalem, have I guessed correctly?'

There was a nod.

'They came here in possession of the Tables of the Law, and other secret gospels, for Setubar had elucidated this for us, but we also because we saw translations in the library.'

'So you entered the library? Very clever . . . Ahhh . . . but perhaps you do not know that they were sent here after the loss of Jerusalem, when there was a difference of opinion between those who wanted to keep the order pure to follow the 'bloodline', and others who wanted to admit 'new blood'. Then there was the possession of the articles from the Temple of Solomon . . .'

'Ezekiel must have told you,' my master confirmed.

'Yes . . .'

'And so the grand master had the articles brought here by the twelve Templars . . . to hide them! By the sword of Saladin!'

The boy sat back with satisfaction. 'This is a monastery of Templars disguised as Cistercians with the sanction of St Bernard, and so you now see why each abbot is an accomplished translator . . . but none could translate the one precious item, the Tables of the Law.'

'But there *was* one who could,' my master said, 'namely a special child whose arrival had been foretold . . . only the one who was brought here by the four Cathar brothers was capable of reading the ancient texts. Before he could do this, however, he needed time to mature, but more importantly, he needed to undergo a special training, a kind of initiation into the mysteries in order to accomplish the task, the perfect work! Unfortunately the terrible war against the heretics by Gregory, and then by Innocent, made it difficult for the four Cathars to bring him here immediately, so they stayed at Montsegur waiting for an opportune moment. It did not help that they were caught up in the siege, which they luckily escaped with the help of Cathar nobles and other sympathisers. On their arrival here they found that the twelve initial founders had become hermits, and that there were others now who, during the course of time, had taken on the everyday running of the monastery. Let us say then that these four who had for so long kept this child safely guarded were now compelled to hand him over to the twelve, am I right? And were then to live out the rest of their lives without ever knowing what would become of him. Now these four wore the Cistercian habit, but they were Cathars and kept their *perfecti* status inviolate all these years. They integrated into the community well, and through time became important members of it until the brothers became curious about the boy whom they loved. When they heard his health was failing and that he was being taken to the catacombs regularly, they wanted to see him, but were denied this privilege. Brother Setubar had suspicions about whatever was happening and it became a great source of uneasiness. Somehow he found out about the great work, he disagreed with it and found a way of alerting the authorities. He sent a message to the Bishop of Toulouse, written by a left-handed person, outlining the numerous heretical tendencies that had taken hold in the monastery, alluding to the existence of a known murderer in their midst who he knew was sure to interest Rainiero Sacconi. This suited the bishop, for Rainiero was a fellow countryman and would do what was necessary to assure his interests in the monastery's wealth . . .'

'But Brother Setubar was not left-handed, preceptor,' Anselmo grinned.

'No, but you are,' my master answered, elated. 'He had you write the message, didn't he? Because his hands are gnarled with age, and also because if he were to send a message to Toulouse it would incur suspicion, you could say you were seeking some transaction pertaining to your duties in the scriptorium. Now, Brother Setubar knew that you were lusting after the position of head translator, so he told you he would talk Ezekiel into giving you the position if you helped him, am I right?'

'Remarkable, but how did you know that I was both left- and right-handed?'

'The handwriting in your translations was that of a right-handed man, and so at first I discounted you as the note writer, but when I heard you play the organ, you played your left and right hand with equal strength. Most right-handed organists play the left hand always a little softer, but this was not the only indication. That morning we met you in the church when you were with Sacar, you made the sign of the cross, and mistakenly used your left hand.'

'Did I? How careless of me, and how fortuitous for you. Tell me more . . .'

The earth shook above us, but my master went on as though he was immortal. 'Brother Setubar must have known that bringing the inquisitor here would mean the end for him and the other three Cathars. He was convinced that they would be discovered, so a week before our arrival, when word of the inquiry reached the abbey, he began to poison the raisins and wine with herbs provided by Asa, a potent mixture of substances, one of which is arsenic and the other atropa belladonna and so the delusions of flying.'

'If that filthy cook had not taken the herb for his own use, you may have never guessed.'

'Perhaps not.'

'If only Asa had listened to me.'

'He became suspicious of Setubar's need for the herbs, didn't he? He threatened to see the abbot, so you both swore him to secrecy and told him everything.'

'Yes, well in this case I am the fool, I loved Asa, he was so feminine, so . . .' he laughed wildly. 'You see, preceptor, how we are all drowning in a sea of sin? I should have known Asa would never understand, it was not in his character.'

'Then how did you stop him going to the abbot?'

'I told him that before he did I would confess our carnal sin to him.'

'So you had unnatural relations?'

'No, but the abbot would believe me, for who would lie in a confessional?'

'Diabolical!' my master exclaimed, and I thought I discerned the slightest hint of admiration in his voice.

'But I gave him the healing formulas that I found in the library and he was placated for a time.'

'And so the words he would not divulge, but what then caused the sudden death of Brother Samuel? He entered the tunnels before the poisoned raisins could kill him . . . Something else here was his undoing. Brother Ezekiel, too, had ventured here sometime before his death, but he did not perish as brother Samuel did. All I can think is that he must have known the ways of the tunnels, for he was the only one allowed in the library, so he knew that he must avoid something, or perhaps he had no need to avoid it for some reason that I have not as yet formulated. In any case, he died of the poison that first night. But, it was you who killed Daniel!'

Anselmo smiled broadly, 'Bravo!'

'The night he died you went to him and demanded that he tell you the ways of the tunnel. Daniel was the only one who held the secret combinations, he alone had been told on his arrival here many years before, and he refused to tell you anything. Moreover I believe he threatened to go to the abbot or perhaps to me . . . I don't know what he said exactly, but in the end you had to kill him, am I right?'

'More or less,' Anselmo nodded his head.

'Before you killed him you had been to the catacombs, you knew your way around a little because Brother Ezekiel had taken you to the library.

'No. Ezekiel knew nothing of the catacombs, he only knew how to access the library through the scriptorium. It was you who showed me. I followed you the night you entered through the panel. That is how I knew how to get this far.'

'Oh, so I have been mistaken . . . they were your footsteps we heard on our way back after we heard the great noise. The echoes made it sound as though you were coming our way, instead you were fleeing before us lest we see you, am I right?'

'Yes, the noise was the mechanism triggered from within the catacombs.'

Andre was thoughtful. 'You had no reason to kill Daniel. He could not tell you anything more than you already knew.'

'I had to kill him, preceptor.' Anselmo stood. 'It was the only logical thing to do, for you are a creature of logic. I knew that you suspected Setubar, but now also Asa, so that when you found the way through the infirmary chapel you thought that maybe he had slipped out through the tunnels and committed the crime after which he returned again through the secret passage. It was a simple way of throwing you further in both their directions. Ultimately, however, you expected that Daniel would be next. How could I disappoint you, preceptor?'

My master paused for a moment. 'You assume much. But you must not think me so clever . . .' my master retrieved the iron bar, covered in blood and, to my horror, hair also, 'for you thought that I would suspect Asa on such flimsy evidence.'

'He could have killed him. It would only take a moment to hide the bar in the straw in the pallet in his room and return unseen.'

'But why would he hide it under his own pallet when he could have left it in the catacombs? I may have been prepared to believe it, had I been less attentive. Something told me that all was not right.'

'But how did you guess it was me?'

'It was quite natural. You had dirt under your sandals after you left the tunnels that night, and so when you killed Daniel – I assume while we were in the library – the dirt became mixed with Daniel's blood and left a nice imprint of your sandal on the floor. You are an unusually small monk and therefore it was not difficult to connect you with the crime, and also the notes, for the day I discovered you in my room, and you so inconveniently hit me on the head, I only noticed (as I fell to the ground) your sandals. I did not know they were yours at the time, but the thing that stayed with me was their unusual size, that is, small. Asa, by contrast, was tall and so he had large, rather long feet. However, this was not the only clue on which I have based my calculations. Note this iron bar. The man who used this to kill Daniel was left-handed. You see the imprint of blood? The fingers clasping it point to the left and the thumb to the right, indicating that it was held in the left hand, and not the right, for in this case it should have been reversed with the thumb pointing to the left and the fingers facing right. You know there are no other left-handed monks in this abbey and not many with unusually small feet.'

'Very well surmised, but what about Setubar?'

'That one is a little obvious . . . After the others were dead there was nothing more he could do, but before he could kill himself . . .'

'Before the *endura,* that is to say, his suicide, he came to me in a fury . . .'

'Of course he was in a fury, you killed Daniel . . . after staining his hands with the blood of the others he needed another *perfect* to give him the *consolamentum,* he would need to be reconsoled, and now there was no one who could do it . . .'

'Of all things this pleased me the most,' Anselmo said sighing with satisfaction. 'When he came to me he said that he wanted the codices destroyed because he feared their secrets were being used to prolong life. This, he thought, was the end product of The Gospel of St Thomas...because it says in the first verse, 'Whosoever discovers the interpretation of these sayings shall not taste death', and as you know, the physical body of Setubar was most productive as food for worms.'

'But he did not know the orientation, you told him you would tell him if he came down with you. You then pushed him down some steps which broke his legs, and you left him to die.

'He told me that he wished the gospels would burn on the pyre along with the silent ones and the boy, because he said to prolong life was the greatest sin. He would have destroyed everything!'

'And so the reason why Asa turned on his master – his desire, as a man of medicine, was to discover the miraculous healing methods that you gave him a taste of.'

'He was a fool. There is no magical healing, only the gospels and the tables! Codices! Think what they could give the world!'

'You mean what they could give you?'

'There is nothing wrong with desiring knowledge.'

'Only if one kills in order to get it.'

'We are not so different, preceptor. Why are you here if not to see for yourself what I have longed to see? You understand me because you are not like the others, you are half-infidel and no one understands learning better than infidels, not even the Jews. But you are also a curious man, and curious men are of two kinds; there are those who justify their sinful desires by calling them noble, and those who accept the truth and can face their own imperfections.'

'What has led me here is not so dissimilar from your own curiosity, in that you are right, but I would not have killed for the pleasure.'

'And yet as a knight you killed men every day. Was your cause more noble than mine? Is it right that a dozen monks alone see the true intentions of God? Forcing humanity to continue to use false texts. Come, do not tell me that you do not burn to know the truth of it. I know that you who have studied Plato, Aristotle, Cicero – you more than anyone must recognise the value of the written word in all its awesome power because you know that it can transform the world!'

'Would it be transformed for the best, Anselmo?'

'I have heard you say that you are a seeker after truth. If that is so, and you have not deceived us, you must agree that a truth is still a truth, though it is unpleasant, though it may cause dissension. Christ did not come into this world to bring about peace! His coming brought only war! And so it is when one manifests an important truth, many do not accept it, some are too willing!'

'Tell me one thing, Anselmo. Why the notes? Was it to satisfy your pride, or to toy with us?'

'I suppose it was both, really, but mostly because I knew that if I aroused your curiosity you would find a way into the catacombs for me. You see how easily I have used you?'

'So you made those mistakes in Greek so I would suspect Macabus?'

'He is nothing but a worm . . . an insect!'

There was another rumble and the tunnels shook ominously.

'And yet, here we are,' my master said.

'Yes, and your taper is running out, preceptor, here, you had best light my torch . . .' He moved forward, a strange look on his face.

Suddenly my master was throwing the lamp to me, and I caught it just as it was about to hit the ground.

'Defender of the holy sepulchre! Now all is clear!' my master cried with excitement, 'I will not let you kill us all with your poisonous torch! The torches!' He hit his head with the palm of his hand quite hard and I almost felt the sting. 'I am a camel! An animal! The torches are coated with a poison, aren't they? Something akin to serpent de pharaon, or perhaps even more deadly. A salt powder that, when mixed with mutton and ignited, gives off a deadly fume! So deadly that, in an enclosed space, one dies almost immediately. That is why Jerome died holding something and why we found a spent lamp discarded on the floor. He must have run out of taper – just as you did – almost as soon as he entered the false chamber. Now here's the interesting part, before it could go out, he managed to light the torch, which hung on the bracket fixed to the wall. This explains why he did not have the time to search for a way out of the false room, he died instantly . . . The silent ones must have removed the torch from his hands so that none may know its secrets. Setubar knew, however, this was his one knowledge about the catacombs, and the one thing that he imparted to you. It also explains why Samuel died the moment he entered the first antechamber. He, too, must have lit a torch with the candle he took from beneath the statue of the Virgin! Ezekiel did not die in such a way, because his sight was failing him and he knew the way without it. You were right, Christian, when you said each brother knew one thing about the tunnels. Air, Water, Earth, Fire. Air is knowledge and the library, Water is the organ, Earth is the orientation in the tunnels and Fire is the poisonous torches. Not only did the cook provide the silent ones with food, but also with poison from Macabus' repository to which he held the keys on most nights, the poison they used to coat the torches . . .' my master ended proudly.

The youth smiled broadly and clapped his hands. 'Bravo, bravo!' He then moved forward aggressively, and I, with my own presence of mind, grasped the apple that I had kept all this time in my repository, and threw it as accurately as I could, hitting Anselmo on the head and moving him backwards. At that very moment it seemed as though the entire world above us gave way. The ceiling in the antechamber began to collapse, and a large section of it, followed by much rubble, came down squarely on Anselmo.

A rock hit my master's brow and left a deep graze. 'Through the door!' he shouted, shoving me through the aperture marked 'Aqua' and to the ledge before the roaring body of water now filled with debris.

'So we will either drown or be buried alive,' he said calmly. 'So many alternatives!'

'I can swim, master.'

'You can what?' He turned to me astounded.

'My mother taught me to swim, I can get you across.'

'Why did you not tell me from the first?'

'I was about to when we heard the terrible sound . . . and then it seemed a little futile, especially since you had so soon worked out the formula . . .' I trailed off lamely, not wishing to say that I had been afraid to mention my ability lest he made me do it.

'Never mind, how should we cross?'

'I shall gauge its depth,' I shouted, handing him the lamp.

'By all means, take your time!'

I sat on the ledge, my legs dangling into the freezing water, and immediately they were numb. The channel was the width of three men end to end and when my master shone the torch into it, it looked black. Saying a quick prayer, I plunged in and found that it was only waist-deep but with a very strong current that pulled one along furiously. I called out to my master, who followed me, holding the roll of parchments that had been hidden in his mantle above his head to keep them dry. Soon we were on the other side at the door to 'Laodicea', leaving pools of water where we stood, and shaking violently from the cold.

Moments later, we emerged through the door and I prayed silently: *'Te ergo quaesimus, tuis famulis subveni: quos pretioso sanguine redemisti. Et ne nos inducas in tentationem, sed libera nos a malo. Amen.'*

24

Capitulum

lmost immediately we were in a chapel, walking down a long central nave. It was only as we approached what we thought must be the choir and altar that we realised that in their place where the ambulatories customarily led to the arms of the two transepts, there was an elliptical chamber that could be reached only through four portals.

Timidly we entered through the portal marked 'Occidens', emerging within what we assumed must be the sanctum sanctorum of the holiest of holies.

A round table top made from smooth black rock occupied the centre of the room. Upon it lay a boy surrounded by twelve men dressed in grey or perhaps white, for it was very dark. The twelve men circled his form, not noticing our presence as we approached, for their eyes were closed in deep meditation.

The table supported fourteen columns cut from the same rock, seven on either side. Carved on the capitals I could barely make out intricate interwoven patterns, perhaps symbolic messages representing the seven planetary spheres: sun, moon, Mars, Mercury, Venus, Jupiter, Saturn, that we had seen elsewhere in the catacombs. On the walls behind the table, so that they appeared between the planetary columns, there were seven apocalyptic seals. These I could see clearly because they were lit by torches, and I wondered if the curious odour I could smell all around me was the strange poisonous gas, but I realised that it was, rather, an unusually sweet incense that seemed to be burning from an altar nearby.

Suddenly a light bloomed from within the circle of men, tongues, serpentine curls of cold flame danced at the centre, and through the form that became golden, I could see the boy transformed, in total splendour, washed in the clear brilliant light that illuminated the room. The brothers appeared to lose their original form, melting into this shining gold that was the boy, their mouths working in tender whispers. Approaching I saw that the boy was I, or he was me, or very like me, and I was overwhelmed, dropping to my knees, tears streaming unheeded down my cheeks.

It was as I knelt in this way, the world reeling around me like a turbulent ether, that I had a sudden powerful desire to be back in the warmth of the cloisters, to be back in the world of order, number, measure. But the ground seemed to fall away from me . . . what could I fasten onto? I felt as if I were hanging by the neck, suffocating with the world barely a hand's breadth away with no way of reaching it. Words reverberated like living things in the chapel. They surrounded me like candles burning without wicks. I saw the sun descend through the boy's head like a burning ball, and he became one with it. He became the sun and his body became the planets. Microcosm became macrocosm and a blackness engulfed me like a veil drawn over my senses. A soothing gentle darkness, poetic and beautiful, like night encroaching upon day, like the coolness of water over a flame. Then the abyss yawned and I fell into it . . .

25

Capitulum

The day has dawned a brilliant blue, and I sit once again upon my stool, witnessing the birth of the daystar, the intercourse of all plains; the above and the below, the *intus et foris scriptus*. And as I grasp my quill in my gnarled hands, and prepare to set down these last words, I am aware that I am a mere *corpus imperfectum* whose faculties can scarcely contemplate, let alone narrate the unknowable, indefinable glory of God.

Last night I had a dream. I dreamt that I was back at the abbey, listening with impudence to my master's discourses. In this dream I experienced the briefest momentary sun on my skin and the snow on my lips and the wind on my face. I stretched out my youthful arms and embraced the panorama of nature. I shouted out at the ancient and venerable mountains and heard their reply. I was young and foolish, frightened, and filled with wonder. When I awoke I was overtaken by a most profound sorrow and a terrible loneliness. For I realized I was back in the exile of my existence, long separated from my dear master, able to see but never touch the world beyond these stone walls. It was then that I asked God to take away my spirit. To take from my feverish lips this cup, this wisdom, whose contents have for so long held my mortal carcass from the abyss of death! But Alas, he did not hear me! And as it is in all such cases, this morning I am glad, for I can begin the sanctioned journey to the end.

I must warn those of you who have followed me thus far that, in the coming pages, my words may begin to sound like so many demented ravings from the pen of an old and tired monk. A monk, who has lived too long in exile, surrounded by crumbling walls and trivialities. But truth obliges me to tell even of the most fantastic things, for truth is indivisible.

I pray then, for strength to continue this, my strange and awesome path, to narrate to you, dear unknown reader, the complexity of that brief instant where the world is hushed and still and the secrets of the ancients are made manifest to its errant, but faithful servants – an instant of the purest freedom.

And if you are unable to see the serene light that bathes the soul with understanding I admonish that you proceed no further, for we are about to broach sacred and holy things.

Where to begin? Saint Michael protect me.

TEMPLE
OF
HIGHER WISDOM

'To him that overcometh will I give to eat of the hidden manna,
and will give him a white stone, and in the stone a new name
written, which no man knoweth saving he that receiveth it.'

REVELATION II 17

26

Capitulum

Out of the darkness I saw the boy again, only now he stood unnaturally tall, one hand extended in my direction. His body, translucent, almost vitreous, and his cheeks flushed with love.

'Come,' he said, and though I did not move we seemed to draw nearer, and we became, in a strange way, united, like two spirits within one soul. I became him and he became me. Terrified, I was hardly able to restrain myself from crying out.

'What strange thing is this?' I asked, but I was not heard. *Dominus illuminatio mea, et salus mea quem timebo?* I remember having heard these words before . . . Was it Brother Daniel who, in his confused state, had said them that afternoon in the north transept? That the Lord is the source of my light, and my safety, so whom shall I fear? In a blackness that has no shadows, but is indeed the darkness of the soul, I became afraid . . . I was now a being whose past was deserting him, and whose future was not yet written.

Naked as the day I was born, standing in the midst of nothingness, my soul transported beyond the world that I had heretofore known, I met the guardian.

Assaulting my numbness, the most terrible spectral being,

hideous beyond description, stood barring my way, guarding the first portal that was not physical, but spiritual. When he spoke I shuddered, wanting to look away, and yet I remained transfixed.

'Behold! You are me,' he said with authority, 'and I am that which you have made! I am the angel of death, but I represent a higher life that has no end. Enter my threshold and you will be released. Enter my threshold and you will finally see!'

Then the veil was drawn *and I, too, in Arcadia* experienced everything! It was as though my being were an eye, and an ear, for it was through majestic sounds resounding in the vastness of space, through colours whose essence pulsated and breathed light and air and water and fire, that I perceived. Through intuitions springing up from the fountain-head of inspiration I saw . . . and there was goodness and wisdom personified in every creature, in every being. With total clarity, and transparency, I observed the sun, not as a mere reflection, but as light itself, shining from within my own being that was indeed nothing, or perhaps something that I did not as yet recognise. This light shone into the surrounds, spread open like the pages of a great book. 'Have you sufficient oil in thine own lamp?' Could I illuminate the darkness with my own spirit light?

I felt a bliss, which none can know whose spirit has not escaped the mortal shackles of this physical nature and I no longer feared death whose face now seemed to be joyful and beauteous beyond description. I rather welcomed it, feeling myself die of tender piety. When I finally opened my being, like the petals of a rose opens to the first limpid rays, I beheld, with great reverence, the psalms whose garments were like that of a vital thought, spinning out wondrous imaginations. From within their incandescence the martyrs appeared as offspring of these holy words, their many faces upturned toward the One, whose superhuman form of Christ invaded the universe, His being resounding in sound throughout space like a mighty trumpet!

I then felt myself arrayed like a lyre, an instrument for

His music, each note a miracle of harmony and consonance. Upon me He played the seven tones of the stars, through the twelve tones of my own being!

Ex Deo nascimur
In Christo morimur
Per Spiritus Sanctum reviviscimus

Out of God we are born
We die in Christ
Through the Holy Spirit we are reborn.

A cup now descended from above, and from it emanated the most sublime and indescribable radiance.

'This is the Holy Grail that exists even now in spirit worlds as a gift to humanity that he, who is purified, may drink of the blood of the Christ and eat of the body, so that it may come to be one with him in spirit. Let he who hath been chosen come forth, and drink of the blood, for he drinketh of the knowledge of Christ and the knowledge of Christ is the knowledge of God and the Holy Spirit.

At that moment the boy tore away his spirit from mine like a breath that escapes one's lungs. His being went forth and knelt at the foot of the Christ who handed him the Grail, from which he drank.

The voice said again:

'Let thy temple be such that it may be a receptacle, purify thy body so that it may hold within it the spirit of the Christ, that is the blood of his love, and resideth in the Grail. Make it such that all men know this and feel this in their hearts and souls and spirits. Be ye a knight of the Golden Stone.'

After the youth had drunk from the cup, he turned his gaze to me and said these words:

'Let the Fisher-King come forward, so that he may know the grave and serious task before him, as guardian of the Grail!

Let him who hath been chosen see the wedding of man and God!'

I was given the golden chalice whose beauty bears no description, whose virtue has no equal, from whose womb springs the living water, the myrrh, the hill of frankincense, the bed, the litter, the crown, the palm and apple tree, the flower of Sharon, the sapphire, the turquoise, the wall, tower and rampart. From it springs all joy, all sorrow, all love, all chastity, all virtues combined in one single unutterable, ineffable, unmentionable, impossible word. The fruits of the garden, the honeycomb and the milk of the valley. The marriage of fire and water, of good that becomes saintly through having known evil. Of past, of present, of future, in which all are but one instant, within one singular moment. The sighing of planets as they whisper their secrets to the stars whose own wisdom could never be exceeded. All this I felt as I held the grail, the holy of holies, but I did not drink from it. I was not yet purified.

I fell upon my face, thanked God and praised His holy name, but I was beckoned to rise by the boy who was no longer a boy, but a man, and yet not a man, but an angel, and yet not an angel.

He said, 'Look! O, brother knight!'

. . . and I saw my life spread about me, like an immense spectacle of pictures. Before my eyes a world of visions appeared to pass at a considerable speed, so that I had to concentrate all my unworthy faculties, not to miss anything. It all appeared to me in a kind of backward motion. Firstly, my master, Eisik, the monastery, and then further and further, my father and mother, my earliest memories, and then I returned to the *uterus sanctus;* the dark womb, a germ, a speck, a root, a seed, the bud and the source of all . . . *Ecce homo!* I became the moon and all the planets, and the stars were my companions. I was at once inward, and outward. Diverse and singular. Had I not experienced this before?

Sound echoed now around me and I was caught in that which first moves and rules all nature in all natural things as the twelve Zodiacal gates opened up before, but I was barred from the higher worlds by the greater guardian who keeps the second portal.

'Behold!' He said, 'I stand before the portal of the higher regions! Follow the white path! Follow thine destiny! With self-less devotion and sacrifice you must now break the seven seals.'

I broke the first seal and the word, like a sword came from my mouth like a creative fire.

I broke the second seal and I was the bull, the eagle, the lion and the lamb!

I broke the third seal and the trumpets sounded, and I was the thunder of the horses and the calls of their riders.

I broke the fourth seal and the blue blood mingled with the red in my veins, and I was crowned with the sun.

I broke the fifth seal, and I was the child born from out of the loins of a woman who had conquered the Moon, but I was about to be seized by the seven-headed dragon when I broke the sixth seal.

I was saved by Michael, who held the key to the vanquishing of evil and was able to fetter the dragon and throw him into the abyss.

When I broke the seventh seal, the heavens opened up in the great expanse and I saw it all. I saw a Gospel, written in the clouds. Each moment captured in the minutest detail passed now before my eyes! I cannot say how long I remained in contemplation of it, except that I was started by the young man's voice, which spoke these words as if through thunder and lightning:

'What you have seen written upon the tables of the law is a heavenly script. It is written in the ether and is not the same as that which is written from the oral tradition, nor is a likeness of it found as a Greek translation of Hebrew documents of antiquity. It is only found in the cloud libraries of God!

'Who are you?' I asked.

'I am the incarnation of John the beloved of Christ Jesus. Before that I was Hiram Abiff, and before him Joshua. I have again been raised from the dead after three days and I too have seen it, all the wisdom of the world is contained in it in a Christened synthesis. Now my initiation is complete, never more will a man need to die before he can see into the *Imago Mundi*, for I have returned with the Gospel, the mystery of the Grail – the mystery of how, through Christ's sacrifice, men will one day know how to transform evil to become gods...such is the mystery hidden in your grandmaster's seal.' He added.

But I was thinking other things! The mystery of the Grail was indeed the mystery of eternal life, but not of the body, it was the secret of the immortality of the spirit, an immortality gained through knowing the Gospel of Christ! This was the dying and becoming, the initiation from the lowest to the highest!

'I must leave you now,' the boy said, 'but Ruach will live within you here below, as an eagle lives within and yet above, in the stirring of a prophetic wind.'

And the wind stirred around me and it became a great roar, which forced my eyes to open so that I realized I was back from the vision and in the chapel and that my master was lying prostrate at my side. I had no time to think on the marvels I had seen for the chapel began to collapse all around us and the walls were crumbling and rocks tumbled from above. I could no longer see the table nor the twelve who had encircled the boy lying upon it.

In the tumult that I likened to Armageddon, I concentrated on helping my master to his feet, and together we ran. But along the way he lost his gospel parchments, which scattered here and there in the debris. He made to go after them, but the world shook with such ferocity around us that we barely managed to escape the chamber before the entire roof collapsed.

Once in the central nave we ran through dust and rubble

to the aperture and I fumbled trying to open it, for my agitation made me clumsy and awkward.

'Hurry, the whole thing is coming down!' my master shouted near my ears, but I barely heard him over the great noise. Suddenly there was a violent movement, a cataclysm, a shattering. It was indeed the end of the world! An underground thunder then burst open the door, splintering it, as if it were only touchwood. For a moment I stood perched on the edge of the channel, not ready to die inside its cool depths.

'Jump in!' my master cried, 'It should carry us to the outside!'

'But master, you cannot swim!' Looking around I found a large piece of the door and handed it to him. 'Here, hold on to this!'

'Good boy! Pity it is as we are about to die that you start to think with your head.' He smiled, 'Go!'

An instant later I found myself being taken by the body of water, as it rushed with haste into an infinite darkness. It was so cold that I could no longer feel my limbs. The churning rose higher, threatening to overwhelm us, for it seemed to be gathering speed with every moment, and I assumed that we must be coursing down a steeper incline. Ahead of us rocks had fallen into the channels, and these we had to avoid by turning our bodies in this or that direction. More than once I nearly lost my talisman, but I held on tightly having faith in its protection. My master must have bumped his bad leg, for I heard him yell out, 'Damn the Count of Artois!' several times and I thanked God that he was all right. Around us the walls contracted with an awesome power and presently, somewhere in the darkness ahead, a light seemed to draw nearer. Finally it was upon us and I closed my eyes thinking that it must indeed be the great light of heaven. It was, however, the light of day, whose relative brilliance seemed a thousand times brighter than the sun. The mountain was expelling us from out of its loins and into a rocky stream.

Into its depths we plunged. I surfaced moments later, but I could not see my master, so I dived into the numbing coldness that stung my eyes and looked for him. There, lying among rocks and weeds and things that live in the watery element, was his form, easily discernible in its white mantle. Taking hold of his habit, I pulled, but he was heavy. I concluded that he must have hit his head and so I pulled again, but something was impeding me. I moved around in front of him, not looking up – lest I see his mouth open, his eyes in a deadly stare – and found that his waist rope had become caught beneath a stubborn rock. I released it and was able to pull him out into the air, dragging him to a nearby bank where I turned him on his front and gave his back a sharp slap. He coughed violently, and slowly came to his senses. I rolled over, dazed and weak.

I woke, shaking violently, but it was not the mountain this time, it was only me, racked with cold. I looked up and could see that the monastery was a long way above. We must have travelled a great distance in the watery darkness. I listened, for I thought that I could hear voices coming from a short way away and I saw the first survivors of the avalanche coming down the road we travelled some days before. My eyes moistened as I saw Eisik moving ahead of them, rushing to my side.

'Praise the God of our fathers!' he cried. 'You are saved.'

Suddenly there were blankets placed over my shoulders, and a beautiful voice saying, 'We must go. There is no time. Even now the inquisitor is looking for you. Quickly, we have some horses.'

'But my master!' I said, looking around dazed and saw that he was being helped to his feet by the girl's father.

'Your son, my lord, he cannot be moved,' Andre said.

'He and so many others are dead, preceptor, the abbey is now under a mountain of snow,' the man said with sadness. 'We must take you away.'

I looked up to the monastery. 'Asa and the others?'

'Carcasses, all of them,' the older man said.

'Where will I go? Master, do not leave me,' I whispered, sinking to the ground with exhaustion.

27

Capitulum

Draught of Forgetfulness

We travelled to the little city of Prats de Mollo, a retreat in times gone by for the kings of Aragon. Here we were kindly treated, given some hot broth, and the lord acquired more horses and provisions for our long and difficult journey.

It was as we thawed a little in the pale mid-morning sun, after having changed into laymen's clothes, that my master and I had a moment alone.

Eisik had, some moments before, said his tearful goodbyes and had left us to pray.

Now, my master was chewing some herbs. His eyes and the crease in his brow echoed the pain that my heart also felt, for how does one say goodbye?

I sat motionless, not wishing to utter the words that I knew must be said. Not wishing to turn my mind to Setubar's words in the tunnels. Instead I looked out at the mountains beyond the walls of the city and to what must be Spain. All was grey and milky white, silent, still, and peaceful, the river on one side and the endless range of mountains on the other.

Everything spoke to me of the duality of existence, a sign of our fragility in the presence of godly designs. I watched the swineherds and the shepherds moving their animals beyond the great gates, and I breathed the air, cold and moist, into my lungs. Were we not like those poor creatures, that, unguided, never proceed directly, but diverge here and there, always at the mercy of the mystery of the paradox, the contractions that rule the cosmos? Were we tended lovingly by the great shepherd, safeguarded from perils to attain that one ultimate goal to which our entire lives have been directed? To inevitably succumb to death? I had tasted death and it was not bitter, but neither was life whose brilliance spoke of that other and yet, in some ways, differently. I looked to my master. Perhaps my face had gained some wisdom, and lost some innocence, for he smiled and caught me in his embrace, patting me on the back with great affection.

He looked in the direction of the abbey, to the majesty of nature that was only a mirror of our Lord's countenance. 'An unjust king once asked a holy man what was more excellent than prayer. The holy man replied that it was for the king to remain asleep until midday, for in this one interval he would not afflict mankind.' He looked at me. 'What have we done, Christian? It is all lost...the Gospel is gone forever!' he sighed.

I was silent for a long time, thinking again a great many things, and then I spoke to him, for the first and last time, concerning these things.

'No, master,' I said, 'I believe all is not lost. You only say this because you grieve for those material things you fear were destroyed. But you must remember what you have always taught me; that nothing in this universe disappears. It is merely transformed, in the same way the alchemists make steam out of water and water out of steam . . .'

'It is a good argument, Christian, but what little consolation it gives me! I am torn between sadness that the only evidence of the gospel is gone, and relief that it did not survive to end up in some bastion of a library, the property of a few who long only to caress each page as if it were a woman's thigh. Perhaps war is less complicated? I long for some act of will, to leave all this thinking to someone else.'

'But master, the parchments were only outward signs from which shines an outward truth. Remember Plato's cave?'

'That is true, I have taught you well.' He smiled and there was a strange weariness in his eyes, 'but you must know, Christian, that a man of science can only ever hope to see phantoms, praying that they will lead him ultimately to the reality that lies behind them. I am afraid that I have devoted my life (and risked yours) to preserving the fire in order that I may see the shadow, indeed it has been wasted. Perhaps Setubar was right? Man should not thirst for something that he can never attain or scarcely formulate. It is the curse of my race that we thirst . . . The inquisitor was right, nothing can alter the colour of a man's blood.'

'And you have Christ in your blood, he is in your thinking, in your feeling, in your willing. I have seen it! I know now what you have been trying to tell me. Christ did not die. You were right, master, he lives in our hearts, in our blood. The black cross signifies nothing. Remember how you once told me that one must look for the antichrist in the eyes of a man? You were right there, too, for I saw him in the inquisitor, and I saw him in Setubar also. This is the stamp of the antichrist: ugliness and ignorance. I saw both in those men because they were blind, their vision was distorted and so it could not see a world that speaks to us of beauty, of divinity. Is it not by learning to read the book of nature with the eyes of faith that we come to recognise the drop of divinity that resides in our own souls though hidden, master? In the end is this not faith; to seek the light that takes us further, the light of Christ that brings that to which reason and knowledge alone can never raise itself? This is truth! I am certain of it, and you are a seeker of truth!'

He smiled a little. 'I am a seeker, yes, but I am also a slave to my seeking. I now know that one only frees oneself from that insane desire for truth when one is prepared to doubt in the existence of truth itself, for it is only to be found when you have discarded it! Only then are you truly free! I have always expounded just that! I have simply failed to take my own instruction, you see? It further illustrates how I have behaved stubbornly. My heart was eaten up. Perhaps I am indeed no better than Anselmo, no wiser than Setubar.'

'And yet, knowledge is a good thing, as you have always told me.'

'Yes, but knowledge is dependent on the piety of the one who has it, Christian, in this case it can be a blessing or a danger. I want you to remember something. Wisdom walks alone, but learnedness, learnedness can easily walk hand in hand with the greatest stupidity.'

'In all cases it is the beginning, is that not so? As you have always told me, knowledge is the seed of a faith that must follow. Because you were wise and good we proceeded in faith (for I surely would have given up) to see it, for ourselves, surely that is of far greater value than parchments!'

'To see what for ourselves?' he said with frown.

I realized at that moment, that my master had not seen anything at all! I did not know what to say to him.

He sighed. 'No. Eisik was right, Christian, never desire knowledge for its own sake. To desire it with such devotion is as dangerous, if not more so, as remaining ignorant, you see? It is only now that I begin to doubt, and that is a good thing, for as Augustine tells us, when a man doubts he knows that he is truly alive. Now you must go, Eisik and the others are waiting for you. It is safer if we are separated.'

We embraced for one last time. I held the small gem that had sustained me all these days, the tiger's eye, in the palm of my warm hand. This I gave him, placing it in his. He looked at it endearingly and smiled a little, and it was then that he turned and walked away. I was never to see him again.

28

Capitulum

Draught of Remembrance

Later, after I arrived in my present exile upon Gilgamesh (for Eisik had saved him from the avalanche and my master, in his selflessness, had given him to me as a parting gift), I heard that the inquisitor, Rainiero Sacconi, had escaped death and had travelled to Paris, where he could not convince Louis King of France to send men to scour the countryside for Templar heretics. His reputation, however, was done a great service in the apprehension of a conspirator to Piero's death, and he was to rise to the position of supreme inquisitor in Lombardy. Many years later, he approached Philip le Bel on the subject of the monastery and its secrets, but the king found a great resistance from Pope Boniface, who had set his own designs on obtaining the elusive treasures of the monastery. There ensued a terrible schism on the matter of jurisdiction that saw the king attempt to kidnap and kill Boniface. He did not succeed . . . but there are many ways to get a pope or two out of the way!

After a few years, how many I cannot say, I received word that my master had been relocated to a preceptory near Paris, and I was heartened to know that, under another name, he was teaching once more, having been granted permission to travel there several times a year to give discourses at the university. Even now I smile a little, warmed by memories.

At the university, he may have come to know Thomas Aquinas, who, I believe, occupied a teaching chair at about the same time. A man rumoured, so they tell me, to have caused quite a stir among the intellectuals with his aim to Christianise Aristotle. How strange . . . I seem to recall a dream . . .

And so Acre fell finally, and more and more of our brothers have fled to this place, though I have never seen them, for my cell window looks out onto the Mediterranean and I see nothing else save its monotonous blue. No one here knows my identity, except the grand master, and Eisik. The others think that I am a leper and so they do not burn with curiosity.

Yestereve the Grand Master, Jacques de Molay, came to see me, for I have, of late, become his confidant. He helped me to my palette and poured out his heart to me. He told me the Order is in peril. King and Pope are plotting to take the Order's treasures, both temporal and eternal. I told him something he must take with him to the end. At dawn I watched his galley leave for France from my little window and my heart sorely aches to think on it.

Soon what I have spent so many years setting down will find its way to the only man I can trust, a friend of my father's, Jean Joinville. I trust that he will vouchsafe it for the sake of the world.

I therefore bequeath to you in all humility: this gospel and my account of how I came by it. I know its pages will survive even as my poor sinner's corpse is eaten by worms and I hope you have read it carefully, turning each page with fondness, recognising that you have been the witness of my conscience, and the interpreter of my meditations.

Some men will find only the chronicles of a young monk here, whose life was transformed during several terrible, though wondrous days in a monastery now destroyed and unrecognisable. Others will see my journey to the Grail, to the Revelation of the Gospel and seek to emulate it. I have marked the way, though slow and perilous, to the cornerstone, now you must make your way to it. For if this little book stimulates the eye to see the world differently, if it invigorates the ear to hear the ineffable silence of the word, which it contains, then indeed it has rewarded its master.

Now there is little that can be said. After all, I have been here before, I am no stranger to death, and as you close these pages, you may deign to pray for me in the name of our Lord; for at last the twelve have spoken, the seven have resounded in the Temple of the Grail. That is all that I am permitted to tell you. As for all that remains? It is better hidden, *Sacramentum regis abscondere bonum est.*

Epilogue

ean de Joinville's servant left in the cover of darkness. As a solitary figure he incurred no suspicion and he set foot on Spanish soil in the early hours of Friday 13th of October 1307, as Philip le Bel's troops were moving in on all the preceptories of the Knights Templar in France. It was also the day Christian de St Armand flew into the arms of the Virgin . . . the Sophia..

...And she was indeed beautiful.

Glossary

Abbot – The superior Monk of the monastery

Ambulatory – The covered passage behind the altar. Linking, in this case, the north transept and its chapel with the south transept.

Apocrypha – Meaning to hide away – it is used to describe a group of important religious writings from antiquity that were not universally regarded as belonging to the authentic canon of scripture. They were found in the Septuagint, the Greek translation of the Hebrew scriptures. The Jews rejected the Septuagint and Saint Jerome, who translated the Bible into Latin, also came to reject writings found only in Greek and so left them out of his translation and called them the Apocrypha. Later there was controversy over the Apocrypha, with many believing that the books were important and genuine, while a minority believed them to be inspired by Gnostic thought. I have shown in my characters knowledge of the Apocrypha for it was well known among men of learning. However, at the same time, the characters are hesitant to quote from it, especially in a setting where there is suspicion of heresy.

Apostasy – Abandoning of the faith in a public way.

Aramaic – A north-western Semitic language related to Hebrew but somewhat different. By the first century CE, Aramaic was in general use in Palestine and targums or interpretations of the Hebrew Bible in Aramaic are known to have existed.

The books of Jeremiah, Ezra and Daniel were in Aramaic. Also there have been Aramaic texts found at Qumran in this language, these include parts of Enoch and a Targum of Job. Aramaic is known to have replaced Hebrew as the language of the people, and therefore it was the language of Jesus. I was therefore able to make two postulations, firstly, that a full version of the Bible written in this language existed at that time, alongside the Hebrew version, and secondly, that a translation of the Old Testament from Aramaic to Latin might be a desirable achievement for a learned monk wanting to distinguish himself.

Aristotle – Greek philosopher, pupil of Plato (c. 384–322 BC).

Benedictines – Monks who follow the rule of St Benedict of Nursia (c. 480–553 AD). They were renowned for their learning, their copying and their libraries and in time individual monasteries grew in wealth, playing a prominent role in secular life. The order was criticised by the younger, stricter orders, for its decadent use of ornate sculpture, gold and colourful adornment. Even so, Benedictines were chosen more often than monks from other orders for distinguished positions in the hierarchy of the church. They wore dark habits and were known as the Black Monks.

Bier right – A pagan tradition, the 'Ordeal', was sometimes adopted by judges to confirm the judgement of God. This particular ordeal had as its foundation the premise that at the approach of the murderer the corpse of the slain would bleed or give some other sign.

Cabbala – study of a secret esoteric philosophy preserved among the Jewish people dealing with the profound mysteries of God. It is the hidden thoughts of Israel upon doctrines of Jewish religion that in many cases are also Christian doctrines.

Canonical Hours – Time in the Middle Ages was measured by the ecclesiastical method of division into matins, lauds, prime, terce, nones, vespers and compline. Depending on the time of year and therefore the hours of sunrise and sunset, matins, the night vigil corresponded to the hours between 12 and 2 a.m., lauds was directly after it at sunrise, prime at 6 a.m., terce at 9 a.m., sext at noon, nones at 3 p.m., vespers before the evening meal and compline at sunset, before bed.

Cathars – Adherents of the heretical Cathar sect sometimes called Albigenses, after the city of Albi in Languedoc where their persecution began. This sect drew its inspiration from Manichean belief. The Manicheans were followers of the Persian Mani and believed in the duality of existence, i.e. good and evil, light and darkness. All material things were said to be intrinsically evil and created by an evil God. All flesh, all matter, was ultimately to be renounced and transcended in favour of the spirit where true divinity resided. Those who achieved this life of strict austerity were called 'Perfects' or 'Pure ones'. Others could become pure prior to death by taking the consolamentum– a sacrament. Cathars incorporated elements of Gnostic dualism, which flourished in Alexandria. Gnosis – meaning knowledge – was acquired first-hand without the need of an intermediary priesthood. It is not surprising that the church violently opposed this form of 'heresy'. Pope Innocent III ordered the persecution of the Cathars in 1208 and it became known as the Albigensian Crusade. Christian knights from all parts came to Languedoc and were ordered to kill men, women and children indiscriminately – for God would recognise his own in heaven. Many Templar houses became the only refuge for Cathar families. The siege of the Cathar fortress of Montsegur led to the well-known 'Massacre at Montsegur'.

Cell – The room wherein a monk slept and meditated.

Chapter House – In a monastery it is a hall where monks meet to read the chapters of their rule, to discuss transgressions and punishments or the day-to-day business of the monastery.

Cistercians – A monastic order, founded at Citeaux by the abbot of Molesme, though it was St Bernard who made the

order popular and seems to stand out in the minds of his con-
temporaries. The Cistercians followed a stricter version of the
Benedictine rule and shunned all excess. Their churches were
decorated simply and their habits were grey-white. They were
known as white monks.

Consolamentum – A Cathar sacrament given to a Credente, or Cathar believer. It signified the descent of the Holy
Ghost, and marked him as a Perfect – a perfect human being,
who had to live an austere life henceforth. Those Credente who
could not live the life of a Perfect, chose to receive the consolamentum for the first time on their deathbed. Taken in this way, it
was similar to the Catholic 'extreme unction'.

Copts – Christian descendants of the ancient Egyptians
who retained the patriarchal chair of Alexandria. The Coptic
church was founded by St Mark, a pupil of St Paul. The Coptic
language is derived from ancient native spoken Egyptian, however it is written by the use of the Greek alphabet, adding seven
vowel symbols from demotic to represent sounds not known in
Greek. The almost entirely religious Coptic literature contains
translations from Greek of the original writings of the Greek
fathers and founders of Eastern monasticism. The Copts are
known to have translated texts condemned by the church in the
early centuries. Texts throwing light on early Gnosticism and
Manicheism have been found. Examples include, the Pistis Sophia, the Bruce Codex, as well as apocryphal and apocalyptic
texts. The Gospel of Thomas, the Secret Gospel of Matthew,
and other secret gospels may have been preserved away from the
scrutiny of the church in this language, hidden below the ground
in Coptic monasteries.

Dominicans – An order of preaching friars founded by
Dominic Guzman in 1215, based on the rule of St Augustine
of Hippo. Dominic was noted for his vigorous fight against
the Cathar heresy and a large majority of inquisitors came from
this order of friars. They were sometimes called Domini Canes

(Hounds of the Lord). Known as the black friars, they wore a habit of black over white.

Franciscans – The Friars Minor were founded by St Francis of Assisi in 1209. They believed in austere poverty and were known for their preaching among the poor. Later the inquisition drew many of its inquisitors from this order. The splinter groups called the 'Spirituals' and the 'Fraticelli' suffered persecution by the church. They wore brown-grey habits of coarse wool and were known as grey monks.

Frederick II – Holy Roman Emperor, son of Frederick I Barbarossa, and grandson of Frederick II of Hohenstaufen, Duke of Swabia. Frederick struggled with the papacy for power and was excommunicated. He died in the year 1254.

Ghibellines – A political party in Italy who fought against papal authority. They were sometimes allied with heretical groups and known to support Frederick II in his wars with the pope.

Gilgamesh – Sumerian hero and king.

Gnostic – The word gnostic derives from the Greek word gnosis, which means knowledge or revelation. Gnostic beliefs were based upon the dualism of good and evil. This influenced Manicheism and Catharism.

Guedes – Craft or trade guilds.

Holy Inquisition – The name given to the ecclesiastical jurisdiction of the Roman Catholic Church responsible for dealing with the prosecution of heresy. Torture was authorised in 1252 by Pope Innocent IV, however an inquisitor could not draw blood; the maxim was to effect the greatest pain with a minimum of mess. Death by fire was a standard punishment usually conducted by a secular power. Other punishments included pilgrimage and the wearing of crosses stitched onto clothing, according to the severity of a crime.

Holy See – Denotes papal authority and jurisdiction.

Hospitaller – In a monastery he is the monk who provides for travellers and pilgrims.

Infirmarian – A physician.

Inquisitor – Church official given the responsibility of conducting an inquisition. Generally inquisitors came from either the Dominican or the Franciscan orders. Usually there were two at every inquisition.

Jean de Joinville – Born between 1224 and 1225, was a friend of King Louis and fought with him on crusade. He was commissioned by Philip le Bel to write a biography of his grandfather – the 'Life of St Louis' in his old age.

Knights Templar – The Poor Knights of the Temple of Solomon, also known as the Christian Militia, was an order founded to protect pilgrims on their way to the holy places in 1119. Monks of this order followed a strict rule, laid down by St Bernard, of chastity, poverty and obedience. The first order to engage in warfare, they became a well organised military force. They formed the advance guard to every attack and the rear guard of every retreat during the time of the Crusades. In time they became 'bankers', holding the titles and moneys of the wealthy nobility for safe keeping and lending money to those who aspired to join the Crusades and needed horses and arms. The order became prosperous and by the thirteenth century had numerous commanderies and smaller preceptories spread throughout Europe, and in the Holy Land. They answered only to the pope and paid no tax, and so it is not surprising that other monastic orders envied them, as did kings and nobles who owed them money. They wore white linen habits that bore a red cross.

Lay brother – One who, though not in holy orders, is bound by its vows, usually engaged in manual work.

Louis IX – King of France (1214–1270), later canonised.

Maimonides – Jewish philosopher, physician and master of rabbinic literature (1135–1204).

Montsegur – Refer to Cathars.

Monstrance – A chalice that contains the host (consecrated bread of the eucharist) given as a sacrament during mass.

Nave – The central part of a church or cathedral extending from the main entrance to the choir.

Obidientiaries – Senior monks in a monastery.

Outremer – Refers to overseas or those states established in the conquered territories of the Holy Land.

Palimpsest – A parchment on which the original writing has been removed and something else has been written. A practice adopted due to the shortage of material.

Perfect – Refer to Consolamentum

Plato – Greek Philosopher (c. 427–347 BC).

Preceptor – Among the Knights Templar a preceptory was a lesser house governed by a preceptor. The larger houses were called commanderies.

Psaltery – A book from which the psalms are read during liturgy.

Rere dorter – Latrines.

Sacristan – The monk in charge of the altar, sacred vessels and vestments for the celebration of the eucharist.

Saint Jerome – One of the great fathers of the Catholic church and known mainly for his translation of the Greek Bible to Latin (c. 340–420 AD).

Saladin – Ruler of Egypt and Syria.

Saracen – A loose term used to describe people of Eastern origin, i.e. Ayyubids; Fatimids; Mameluks; Muslims; Seljuk Turks.

Seven Churches – The book of Revelation written by St John was addressed to seven churches in the Roman province of Asia. They represented the entire church. Ephesus was founded by Paul (a centre of the Eastern church), Smyrna, Pergamum (this religious centre had a famous shrine to Zeus and a Temple of Augustus, hence Ezekiel's mention of the floor of the church being as cold as the crypts at Augustus, alluding to the worship of emperors), Thyatira, Sardis, Philadelphia and Laodicea.

Socius – The 'unofficial' term used to describe the less

senior of two inquisitors.

Thomas Aquinas – Dominican scholastic philosopher and theologian, who interpreted Aristotle's works and used them to explain Christian theology.

Tonsure – The shaving of the hair leaving a circle on top of the head, symbolising the crown of thorns.

Trencavel – Hereditary Counts of Beziers. This family was involved in the Cathar heresies of Languedoc.

Transept – The transverse arms of a church making the shape of a cross.

Waldensians – Followers of Peter Waldo of Lyons. They shunned wealth and criticised the church for its affluence and decadence. They believed that corrupt bishops and priests should not give the sacrament. They were condemned by the church and suffered persecution.